— ADVANCE PRAISE F

Connie Hampton Connally takes us into the ̶ ̶ ̶ ̶ ̶ ̶ ̶ ̶ nts and basement bomb shelters of Budapest with characters whose loss and grief seem profoundly real—and then shows how redemption is possible. *Fire Music* is alternately wrenching and beautiful, and you know from the first page that you're in the hands of a compelling writer.

—LAWRENCE W. CHEEK, author of *The Year of the Boat*

A sensitive, deeply touching story – masterfully written – about how love and music overpower and outlast oppression and despair. Highly recommended.

—DON PUGNETTI JR., author of *A Coat Dyed Black: A Novel of the Norwegian Resistance*

My heart has been seared by *Fire Music* and its touching characters who showed me the courage required to bring true rhythm and harmony to life. Light when you cannot see; notes that transcend language when you cannot understand.

—WENDY KENDALL, author of *Kat Out of the Bag* and columnist for *My Edmonds News*

Connally writes of the horrors of war through the lens of both the people living through it as well as their descendants who carry the pain of war's effects. A dual timeline takes the reader to the siege of Budapest in 1945 as well as sixty years later into the lives of the main characters' children and grandchildren, all linked through the power and comfort of music. Connally's descriptions on the page almost make the music—fire music—audible. This vivid, heartbreaking, and healing narrative is finely tuned, showing the power of the human spirit.

—IRIS GRAVILLE, author of *Hiking Naked: A Quaker Woman's Search for Balance*

What started in *The Songs We Hide* passionately continues in *Fire Music*. As the story deepens, the impact of the turmoil in Hungary is clear: the relationships, the secrets, and the heartache are evident as the story is woven through several generations. We're reminded that the experiences of those who went before us can shape how we see the world.

—ELIZABETH SZABÓ VOS, host of *Hungarian Living* podcast

When the yellowed sheet music shakes in the old violinist's hands, we know we are in the mature grace of a story worth telling. It's a story of violence and honor and love. It's a story of the fierceness of being in a world that has changed beyond what we had ever imagined.

—CYNTHIA BEACH, author of *The Surface of Water*

There was no way someone from a fearless country like America could understand the frailty of his own dismembered nation of Hungary, Antal Varga thought.
Well, this book will help you understand. It is uncanny how Connally, an American, has delved into the Hungarian psyche so deeply. *Fire Music* gives goosebumps to those of us whose families experienced that painful pre- and post-WWII and socialist era first hand. This lovely story with wonderfully relatable characters is an opportunity to learn how those tragic times affected entire nations and generations.

—KATALIN PEARMAN, Honorary Consul of Hungary for Washington and Idaho

Fire Music is an emotional, historical and musical gut-punch. Fluently speaking the language of love and connection, author Connie Hampton Connally brings to light both the suffering and hope of the Hungarian people.

—LISA BERGMAN, Classical KING Radio Host and Collaborative Pianist

Fire
Music

*To Lew +
Suzanne,
with best
wishes —
Connie H.
Connally*

CONNIE HAMPTON CONNALLY

coffeetownpress

Kenmore, WA

A Coffeetown Press book published by Epicenter Press

Epicenter Press
6524 NE 181st St.
Suite 2
Kenmore, WA 98028

For more information go to:
www.Camelpress.com
www.Coffeetownpress.com
www.Epicenterpress.com
www.conniehamptonconnally.com

This is a work of fiction. Names, characters, places, brands, media, and incidents are either the product of the author's imagination or are used fictitiously.

Cover design by Lance Kagey and Scott Book
Design by Melissa Vail Coffman

Fire Music
Copyright © 2024 by Connie Hampton Connally

Library of Congress Control Number: 2023945705

ISBN: 978-1-68492-159-1 (Trade Paper)
ISBN: 978-1-68492-160-7 (eBook)

In memory of Matt Pickard and Eliza Cerna,
two lights still shining.

VARGA FAMILY TREE

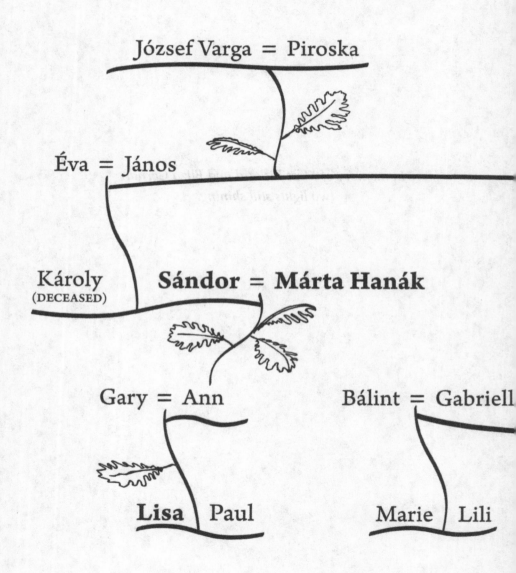

József Varga = Piroska

Éva = János

Károly
(DECEASED)

Sándor = Márta Hanák

Gary = Ann

Bálint = Gabriell

Lisa | Paul

Marie | Lili

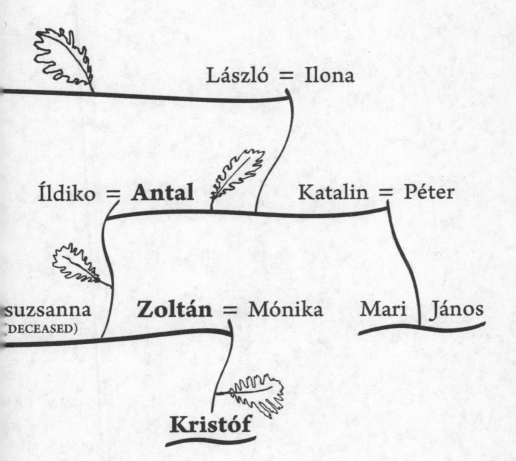

László = Ilona

Íldiko = **Antal**   Katalin = Péter

suzsanna   **Zoltán** = Mónika   Mari János
(DECEASED)

Kristóf

Acknowledgments

*F*IRE MUSIC HAS BEEN A LONG time in the making. It was 2006 when I first decided to write a teenage novel set during the siege of Budapest. I began the research, and with crazy optimism I spent a year plowing through a rough draft. My optimism evaporated, however, as I realized that I'd gotten neither the historical facts nor the fictional story-telling right. Acknowledging that this was no quick project, I started over.

The research grew exponentially. The novel went through countless revisions and became a story for adults rather than teens. The time span of the novel grew from eleven months in the first draft to sixty-one years in the final draft, involving a second story line and a second set of characters. Slowing things down even further, I ended up setting aside the work on the siege story while I wrote another novel (*The Songs We Hide*). All in all, eighteen years have gone by since I began that preliminary (and almost unrecognizable) draft of what would become *Fire Music*. Of necessity, I spent those eighteen years growing as I writer. The years also deepened my empathy toward people affected by war. I now realize that *Fire Music* could not have been written quickly—at least, not by me.

I'm grateful for the help I received along the way. Some of that help came from books. Foremost in my research was *The Siege of Budapest* by Krisztián Ungváry. Also important were *Hungary in World War II: Caught in the Cauldron* by Deborah S. Cornelius and *Hungary at War: Civilians and Soldiers in World War II* by Cecil D. Eby. I recommend these books to anyone wanting to understand how the war affected Hungary and its people.

Many friends and helpers came alongside me in the work on *Fire Music*. Márta Horváth answered my questions regarding Hungarian language and culture, and she checked the manuscript for accuracy in those matters. Drs. Gábor Győri and Bob Snyder helped me understand Hungarian health care and medical practices. Daniel Perrin and Svend Rønning helped with musical aspects of the story. Claire Gebben, Lois Brandt, Ushani Nanayakkara, Michele Genthon, Alisa Weis, and especially Roberta Gates and Ruth Tiger reviewed the manuscript and made excellent suggestions. Ruth, a close friend, gave me unfailing moral support throughout the work.

Thanks also to Jennifer McCord and Epicenter Press for their vision and commitment in editing, producing, and publishing *Fire Music*, and to Lance Kagey of Rotator Creative for the evocative cover design. In addition, I've received and treasured the encouragement of the Scriptoria Workshop, the Hungarian-American Association of Washington, and the caring people of Tacoma First Presbyterian Church.

Finally, I am grateful for the loving support of my family. My sons, their wives, and even their children have always honored the work I do as a writer. Above all I am indebted to my husband, Rory Connally. He has been my steady companion on *Fire Music*'s long and often unmarked path. His patience, confidence and love have not only kept me moving forward but have given me joy in the journey. No words of thanks go deep enough.

PART ONE

The Light Shines
in the Darkness

CHAPTER ONE

The American

August 17, 2006

ANTAL VARGA CROSSED THE MOSAIC FLOOR of the Budapest Opera House, heading for one of the side exits he'd used for more than fifty years. His left shoulder hurt, and he transferred his violin case to his right hand. He hadn't played the violin here today, only adjudicated an audition; but after the lootings and searches he'd lived through, he didn't let the instrument out of his sight for long.

Somewhere behind him a woman shouted: "Sir!"

It sounded like English. A tourist yelling in the opera house. Varga began to turn, but his neck cramped. Well, let her go on yelling; he was heading home.

"*Úr!*"

He paused. She was shouting in Hungarian now.

"Varga *úr!*"

Her pronunciation was off, but she was calling *him*. He pivoted his full body to avoid twisting his neck.

A blond woman who looked to be in her mid-thirties rushed toward him—jeans, wrinkled blue T-shirt, canvas bag swinging from her shoulder—probably American. He often saw Americans here. Amid the opera house's marble and gilding, they looked like street sweepers who had dashed in to use the toilets. But this one, somehow, knew his name.

The woman stopped directly in front of him. "Varga Antal?"

She had known to use the surname first. Unusual for a foreigner. "*Igen*," Varga said. *Yes.*

"Do—you—speak—English?"

"No."

The woman sighed as though in some great dilemma.

He offered German. "*Sprechen Sie Deutsch?*"

"No."

"*Russkij?*" he asked.

"No." She said it in Hungarian then. "*Nem.*"

He asked her in Hungarian what she needed, but she couldn't answer. They were accomplishing nothing here. He gestured toward the door, trying to remember enough English to leave gracefully. "Sorry, I go—"

"No!" She clutched his sleeve. "Please! *Kerem!*"

He pulled himself free and took a step back.

The foreigner pressed her hand to her chest. "Lisa. Denman." She riffled through her canvas bag, shook her head, and tried to say something in Hungarian, but he did not understand her. Then she stopped, righted her intonation: "*Varga Sándor.*"

Antal Varga's hand tightened on the violin case. "*Istenem,*" he rasped. *My God.* It had been sixty years since Sándor fled Hungary, twenty since he'd died. And how much time had passed without anyone's even saying his name?

The woman's impossible words rushed on, twenty English to one Hungarian. He gestured insistently toward the door. God in heaven, if she would just shut up and follow him several blocks, his grandson could interpret between them, at least for a few minutes.

Varga tried German again, shouting now: "*Komm!*"

It worked. She followed.

Leaving the building, he headed for Andrássy Avenue, which in some of the worst years had been called Stalin Avenue. The street roared with rush hour traffic—so many cars these days—and a crowd surged past from the Metro stop. Varga held his violin case in front of him and glanced at the woman. Something about her, maybe the strong cheekbones, looked familiar.

They crossed Andrássy and turned onto the busy sidewalk of Nagymező Street. The August glare of the sky was fading into evening. Varga, overwarm in the jacket he'd worn to the audition, felt a tightening in his chest and stopped. The woman seemed confused but waited with him until he was able to walk on. When they finally reached the outdoor tables of Három Páva where his grandson worked, Varga pointed the woman toward the bistro door, held it open for her, and followed her in.

Once inside, Varga lifted his hand, signaling the foreigner named Lisa to be patient as he did a visual sweep of the room. He spotted his grandson Kristóf taking an order at a far table, his dark hair neat and his white apron tied trimly around his middle. The customer, an attractive brunette, smiled up at Kristóf as she toyed with the corner of her menu. Varga stifled a sigh. This again.

The restaurant smelled of peppered gravy . . . Hungarian. Other places around here smelled Italian or French, but this one had recently found favor with the hotels and tourist guidebooks by raising goulash to elegance. The restaurant, painted in turquoise shades, was *hip*, if Varga recalled his grandson's English term for it. Lisa stood next to him looking around as though disoriented. Maybe it was the chalk menu she couldn't read. Maybe it was the Hungarians she couldn't talk to. Maybe she didn't understand *hip*. He wasn't sure he did, either.

An art nouveau mural near the bar showed three peacocks, for which the restaurant was named. He tipped his head toward it and gave her the Hungarian words: "*Három páva.*"

"*Páva?*" She hummed a slow, haunting line of notes which he immediately recognized: the opening of Kodály's choral piece *Fölszállott a Páva*.

He smiled approval. "Kodály."

"Yes, *igen!* Wait. Wait!" Lisa slid the bag off her shoulder, searched through it, pulled out a folded paper, and held it out to him.

He set the violin case on the floor and opened the sheet. It was an old page of music manuscript paper, yellowed and torn at the bottom, brittle in his hands. An untitled melody had been jotted in blue ink: treble clef, one sharp. He adjusted his glasses and read the first line.

The paper shook in his hand. He hurried through the second line, third, then the slurring tones in the fourth line. "*Jézus,*" he whispered.

He skipped to the bottom line where the trill would be. There it was. And the repeat symbol—yes. He turned it over, finding the three last, familiar lines. And under it all, in the time-smudged notation of his own teenage hand, his signature: *Varga Antal, 1945*. Yes, 1945, when his world was on fire.

He stared at Lisa, gripping the paper. "How did you get this?"

But of course she understood not a word he said.

Varga waved furiously, trying to catch his grandson's eye.

Kristóf finally saw him, stuffed his order pad into his apron pocket, and made his way over. He threw a baffled glance at Lisa. "*Jó estét*," he said to her, and turned to Varga with an eyebrow cocked.

"She speaks English," Varga hissed, "no Hungarian."

Kristóf greeted her in English. She answered and smiled briefly.

"I need you to interpret," Varga told him.

"I'm working."

"I know that. See if you could manage a break, would you?"

Kristóf looked at him, squinting a little. "God, Ópa, what's wrong?"

Varga refolded the paper and stuffed it in his breast pocket. "Hurry up! Go!"

"Yes, all right, go sit down outside, I'll see what I can do."

"Hurry."

At a metal table on the sidewalk, Varga sat with Lisa. He pushed the violin under his chair. A taxi, then a Citroen passed on Nagymező Street. From a circulating waiter Lisa ordered cola and Varga his usual Egri red wine, and they waited. Lisa smiled at him a little uncertainly and twisted her hair. Varga touched his breast pocket. That music: good God, how did she get it?

At last Kristóf sat down with them, water glass in hand, and began speaking to Lisa in English. Varga strained to listen but could deduce only that they were exchanging names and confirming that Lisa was, in fact, American. She gave Kristóf another hesitant smile.

Varga leaned close to him, speaking low. "Find out who she is. What's she doing here?"

Kristóf exchanged some words with her, then told Varga, "She says her grandfather was your cousin. Sándor."

Varga clutched his wine glass. "I never saw Sándor after 1945," he whispered. "Ask her if Sándor's wife is still living. Márta."

When Kristóf asked, Lisa shook her head as she answered.

Kristóf turned to him. "She says her grandmother died last November."

"No." Varga set down his glass. He rose to his feet, steadied himself with a hand on the table. "You'll excuse me a moment."

Kristóf stood up. "Ópa, are you all right?"

"Stay here. And watch my violin."

CHAPTER TWO

Second Fiddle

September 23, 1944

PEOPLE KEPT VANISHING.

Varga Antal, sixteen years old, sat in his music teacher's living room with the leftovers of a student quartet. The viola player had left Budapest. So had the former cello player, now replaced by a new, distracted cellist. Mr. Horváth, the teacher, was filling in on the second violin part that Antal used to play. The first violinist, Weisz Jenö, had disappeared on some Jewish work detail. Since then Mr. Horváth had put Antal on first, and that included leading rehearsal. This was strange new territory after second fiddle. Maybe it was an opportunity, but Antal didn't like the opportunity coming at Jenö's horrible expense.

Along the wall under the living room window leaned a blackout shade for the bombing raids at night. For now, the afternoon sun seeped through the window and lit the Haydn piece on Antal's music stand. The playing had come to a stop: the cellist, a girl named Márta, had lost her place.

"Measure twenty," Antal said, swallowing his impatience. The cello part wasn't that hard.

"Thanks." The girl adjusted the bobby pin that held back her light brown hair. "Could we slow down a touch?"

Antal had already slowed the tempo down. He glanced at Mr. Horváth, who mouthed, "It's your call." Antal counted off, slower, and they picked up again at measure twenty. Márta's tone was excellent when she relaxed, he had to admit. Her playing smoothed out over the rest of the rehearsal. If only this group could quit losing players, they could make some real music and perform it, if the auditoriums weren't bombed.

When rehearsal ended Antal asked Mr. Horváth if he'd heard from Jenö.

"No." The man pulled off his glasses and rubbed his temple as though it hurt. "And unfortunately, I don't expect I will."

"Probably not," Márta said.

Antal had suspected as much, with the armbands the Jews had to wear and the curfews and separation laws that had come down on them. Some German named Eichmann had mandated putting them on trains to God knew where.

"I need to tell you two," Mr. Horváth said, "we'll probably have to take a break before long." He laid his violin on his lap, the veins in his hands prominent. "Under the circumstances, my wife and I may leave the city for a while."

The cellist nodded. "With the Soviets coming," she agreed quietly, "and now the Romanians, too."

In silent dismay Antal pulled his sheet music off the stand. The national wreckage kept increasing. Just weeks before, Romania had capitulated to the Allies and joined Russia in their rampage across Hungary. How long Hungary could hold out was anybody's nervous guess.

"But we'll keep playing for at least the time being," Mr. Horváth continued. "Márta, I'm sure this is a trying time for your family. For now, just practice the first page of the Haydn."

"No, I'll try to do more."

"Good, then. Antal, we'll carry on with your private lessons for as long as we can. I'll see you this Thursday as usual. How are you doing with the Dvořák piece?"

Antal had had Dvořák's *Romanza in F Minor* for only two weeks, and the music wasn't easy. "Right now it's a mess," he said.

Márta laughed a little.

"A mess," Mr. Horváth repeated. "You always say that at first, then you work wonders. Keep going with the romanza, and let's assume you'll perform it."

"What kind of performance are we talking about?"

"I'm hoping you can solo with an orchestra. As for where and when, we'll have to see." He looked at Antal pointedly. "This is not beyond you," he said, as he often did.

Somewhere outside, a wagon rattled over the cobblestones and a man shouted orders in German. There were always German orders and Hungarian orders, and Hungarian swearing, and soon there would be Russian orders and swearing, and how on earth was a person supposed to perform Dvořák in the middle of—

"The romanza's a lovely piece," Márta said.

He turned to her, and perhaps for the first time really saw that the girl was beautiful: fine cheekbones, soft eyes, a depth in them that jarred him.

"The war's not all there is," she said.

"No."

He did not know what else to say, only knew she was right and he would learn the romanza.

It was Saturday, mid-afternoon. He caught the tram back across the Danube to the neighborhood where he'd always lived, a triangle between the opera house, the western train station, and the music academy. By long habit, instead of going straight home he veered off to Varga *Optika,* the family business. His cousin Sándor, one year older than him, lived in an apartment above the optical shop. They'd seen each other almost every day of their lives.

A bell jangled as Antal pushed open the shop door. This was where his father conducted eye exams and his grandfather fitted lenses, and where Uncle János, Sándor's father, used to work as well. When Uncle János died, his widow, Éva, filled in. Sometimes Sándor did, too.

At the front desk, Aunt Éva glanced up from her ledger book.

"*Csókolom,* Aunt Éva," Antal said. "Is Sándor around?"

She pointed toward the backroom doorway.

"Antal! Crazy cousin!" Sándor stepped out of the backroom, grinning. "Back from setting the musical world on fire, I see."

Sándor leaned against the wall beside photographs of his father, who had died of tuberculosis, and of Sándor's older brother, who had died on the eastern front. Sándor looked like them, sharing the family traits that

Antal and his father also had: strong brow, dark hair, broad through the shoulders. But Sándor had become the tallest Varga.

"Do you want to come over tonight?" Antal asked.

Sándor's brown eyes flicked toward his mother, and he gestured toward the front door. Leaving his violin in the shop, Antal followed him out onto the sidewalk corner. Over the years on this corner they had played marbles, learned to ride bicycles, and ducked out of earshot of their parents, as they were doing now. Antal lived a block and a half away on Dessewffy Street, where just last week an Allied bomb had grazed a building near his apartment house.

Antal watched in resentment as a German jeep passed. Nazi troops had arrived *en masse* last March in spite of the deal Hungary had cut with Germany. The one remaining grace of this awful arrangement with Hitler was that boys like him and Sándor were still in school instead of in the shot-up Hungarian army.

"Mr. Horváth plans to leave town," Antal told Sándor.

"Him and everybody else."

"So here I am. He assigns me this long Dvořák solo, and then goodbye."

"Do you want to play it?" Sándor asked.

Did he want to? That wasn't really the question. He had played since he was four, when his mother first positioned a quarter-size violin under his chin. He had wanted music then. Now it was a need, like needing sunlight, needing the feel of the wind, needing the war to stop.

"I'm going to play the Dvořák," Antal said and left it at that; Sándor played piano and would probably understand. "Want to come over?"

"I don't know," Sándor said. "My mother's having some bleak days."

It had been this way for almost two years, since Sándor's brother, Károly, died at Stalingrad. On bleak days Sándor and Aunt Éva stayed together. Antal had never met anyone as loyal to his mother as Sándor was, but maybe that was the way you were when your mother was all you had left.

"Bring her with you," Antal said.

"We'll see." Sándor pulled a cigarette from his pocket. "Guess who brought glasses in for repair today. Hanák, the columnist. Hanák Viktor."

"Hanák? I haven't seen his articles lately."

"Neither have I, not since the Nazis got here. I heard him talking with

Grandpapa." Sándor lit the cigarette, took a drag. "Sounds like his daughter plays cello with that group you're in. Hanák Márta."

Antal looked at Sándor in surprise. "That's the columnist's daughter?"

"Yes, and Grandpapa gave the man your family's telephone number."

"Why?"

"I don't know. Maybe Hanák asked for it. Not just to call about the glasses, but—I don't know, maybe in case something goes wrong."

Antal's neck tightened. Things were always going wrong. He could barely remember otherwise. Once the Russians arrived, things could go worse than wrong.

CHAPTER THREE

Translation

KRISTÓF PULLED THE VIOLIN CLOSER and sank into his chair. There went his grandfather back into the restaurant, white hair damp, necktie crooked and face flushed. What in hell was going on? The man had a heart attack eight years ago. Was there going to be a repeat?

"Gosh, I didn't mean to upset him," the foreigner said.

"He probably just went to the W.C."

Kristóf had an uneasy feeling of covering for his grandfather without knowing why. He couldn't do this for long. It was a Thursday night and the restaurant wasn't busy now, but that could change in five minutes. He glanced over his shoulder through the front window. In his section another waiter, his roommate Feri, was checking on that German brunette.

"Is your grandfather all right?" Lisa asked.

He nodded, though he was anything but sure.

Kristóf was twenty-nine, and as he took a fuller look at this Lisa, he guessed her to be a little older than himself. Her blond hair curled rather messily and she was a little thin, but even so she would be pretty if she didn't look so cataclysmically jet-lagged. As for her clothes, she could have weeded a garden in them. But here in the restaurant he'd grown used to American sloppiness. He usually liked Americans, and he would probably like this one if she weren't scaring the piss out of his grandfather.

"So, eh, tell me," he said. "In America, you are from where?"

"Tacoma, near Seattle."

With her left hand she reached for a paper serviette. On her inner wrist was a small tattoo, an unornamented cross. She wore no wedding ring. Kristóf watched as she drew a rough U.S. map on the serviette. She marked a star in the northwest corner and another one next to some scribblings that were probably America's big lakes.

Pointing at the northwest star, then the other, she said, "I live in Tacoma, near Seattle. And Chicago is where my grandparents lived. My mother is still there. She's a Varga."

"You are far from her."

"Yes."

Lisa said something in reply, but a lorry rattled by and he couldn't hear. She waved away cigarette smoke that drifted from the next table. Under tonight's strange circumstances, Kristóf would have liked a cigarette, but Americans always went so irate about the smoke.

"Why did you come here, to Hungary?" he asked her.

"I've always wanted to come. When my grandmother died, she left me a little money, and I could finally afford the trip."

"Did someone come here with you?"

"No."

At last Ópa returned to the table, having smoothed his hair and straightened himself as if for a concert. Turning to Lisa, Ópa pronounced carefully in English, "Welcome."

A relieved smile spread across her face as she thanked him. "*Köszönöm, Antal bácsi.*"

Somehow she had known to call him Uncle, the polite address for older men. Ópa sat down and pulled the violin next to his own chair again. Kristóf showed him the map Lisa had drawn and explained it.

"I can't believe this, that she's here," Ópa said. "What do I say, after sixty years?" He shook his head. "All right, to begin with, ask her how many children her grandparents had."

He asked, and Lisa's answer was, "Just one—my mother." Kristóf told Ópa this.

"Did the mother come?"

Kristóf explained that Lisa was here on her own. Ópa asserted that it wasn't safe for a young woman to travel alone. Kristóf didn't translate this for her. Lisa didn't look all that young to him, and anyway, some women traveled alone. He knew. As for her traveling without her mother, Kristóf certainly didn't blame her. Ópa then wanted to know whether Lisa was married, had children, so Kristóf asked.

"No," she said. "Not married." Lisa was silent a moment. "And no children."

American rock music poured from the club next door. Kristóf raised his voice: "How did you do this, find my grandfather?"

"I didn't have his address, and I didn't even know if he was still alive, but I knew he used to play violin at the opera house. So I went there and asked. Someone said he was hearing an audition, told me to wait, said to watch for a white-haired man with a violin. So I waited, and then there he was."

Kristóf told his grandfather this.

"For God's sake, Kristóf, ask her what she's doing with that music."

"What music?"

"She knows. Ask her."

More customers had arrived and Kristóf would have to get back to work, but here he was, trying to deal with sixty damned years in fifteen minutes. For whatever good it would do, he turned to Lisa and asked about the music. He didn't know all the English words she used as she tried to tell the story; but what she seemed to say, and what he told Ópa, was that the music was found among her grandparents' effects. Lisa worked as a school music teacher, and a few days ago on the plane she had begun reading through the music. Some pieces had lyrics and she couldn't read those, but she loved the melodies.

Ópa took a sip of wine, which he'd barely touched. "To think Sándor and Márta took that music to America. After all they lost. Why did she come looking for me?"

Kristóf asked her.

Lisa sipped her cola, her face pale in the half-light of the streetlamps.

"There's so much I don't know," she said. "My grandparents hardly ever spoke of their life here. Everything was always" —she placed her finger to her lips—"shh, shh, shh. But I know there was some little music group our grandparents had. My grandparents didn't talk about it, but my great aunt, my grandmother's sister, she said something about it once. And that music, I think the group was writing it and playing it while Budapest was under siege. How do people create something so beautiful in the middle of a war? I want to know that story."

Kristóf nodded. He could count on one hand the times Ópa had spoken of the war. Certain sounds and smells—fireworks, sulfur—could blacken the old man's mood in an instant, but he never explained.

"Ópa, she wants to know about your music group during the siege. As far as that goes, so do I. Why haven't I heard anything about it? Or about your cousin? Or this Márta?"

Ópa snorted. "And I suppose you tell me every detail of your life?"

"All right, all right." Kristóf took a swig from his water glass and turned back to Lisa. "You say your grandparents were very shh, shh. So is he."

"I see." Lisa shut her eyes in a sudden grimace as though in pain. She reached into her canvas bag. On the tabletop she laid another yellowed sheet of music, then a set of music pages held together with a large paper clip. She pulled off the clip and handed the pages across the table.

Ópa pulled them close. "Lord, that suite."

"Ah," Kristóf murmured in recognition: *that* suite. The note at the top read *Quintet in E-flat minor. Varga Antal, 1958.*

Wait, nineteen fifty-eight? Was that when Ópa wrote it? The suite wasn't performed until . . . when was it? It must have been 1990, part of saying good riddance to communism.

"Do you remember this music, Kristóf?" Ópa asked.

"How in God's wrath could I forget it?"

Kristóf was thirteen when the suite was performed at the music academy. He'd sat there in the front row between his father and grandmother, while on stage Ópa played his violin with four other musicians. Kristóf half-listened, toying with his program bulletin and wondering whether Budapest was winning their football match. The music hummed along, all lovely—until it snapped. The music twisted into dissonance, drove to a frantic crescendo. A snare drummer stepped gravely on stage, played a long roll, then slammed his stick down on the rim in a deafening crack. Kristóf dropped the bulletin. The musicians stood and left the stage. The lights went out. The audience sat in shock.

"Is that the end?" Kristóf had whispered to his grandmother.

"That's the end."

"Why?"

"Shh."

And everyone assumed that the final crack echoed the choke of a hangman's noose, but Ópa did not speak of it. That music came to be called the *Embers Suite*. It had never been performed since.

Lisa reached across the table and touched the suite music. "Today when I read through this," she said, "I saw that the themes in it seem to come from those shorter pieces from Grandma Márta's attic. Especially this piece." She pointed at the other sheet, which Kristóf now saw was titled "*Dal ellenségeinknek.*"

"What do the words mean?" Lisa asked.

"Song to our enemies."

"Hmm. Wow. Yeah, that theme comes at the end of the suite."

Ópa frowned, no doubt wanting a translation, but the evening had grown dark, and Kristóf checked his watch. "I can't stay much longer," he said to his grandfather. "Could you please tell her what's behind the music?"

"I would rather not discuss it. Not if her grandparents didn't tell her."

"But don't you think she deserves to know? She wants the story, not just the notes with the *ka-BUMM* at the end."

Ópa pulled back his shoulders. "This girl is American. Americans don't open their curtains one morning and find a war in their front garden. She doesn't know what she's asking for." He turned the pages of the suite one by one. At the last page he froze.

Now what? Kristóf peered at the music. There were the notations for the drum roll, the crack, and the silence. But beneath, in faded blue ink, words had been written. The handwriting was a woman's, if he had to guess.

Jaj, Antal, Sándor, miért kellett mindennek véget vetni?

"Good God," Kristóf said in Hungarian. "Who wrote that?"

Ópa touched the page, his hand trembling. "Ask her."

Kristóf asked, and she said, "It's my grandmother's writing. Márta's."

"And do you know what it says?"

"No."

Kristóf turned to his grandfather. "You're still not going to tell this woman anything?"

As if she understood, Lisa said, "If nothing else, I'd like to know why my grandfather left Hungary."

After Kristóf translated, Ópa shook his head. "If anyone was to tell her, it should have been Sándor and Márta." He looked at Lisa and continued in Hungarian. "I'm sorry. You're in my family. But if your grandparents didn't tell you about this, then neither can I. And besides, Kristóf has to work now." He touched Kristóf's arm. "Translate that. And then you will have to call a taxi for her. There is nothing more to be done."

"But she came all the way from America—"

"She could come here from the moon and I'd have to say the same thing. But ask her, please, if she is staying in a safe place."

Kristóf looked at Lisa, this tired cousin who'd descended from the American moon, sitting here with her T-shirt wrinkled and her face tightening, and he hated what he had to tell her. "My grandfather says no, he cannot tell you this if your grandparents did not."

"I see." Her disappointment plain, she reached for the music, but Ópa reached first and gathered the sheets.

"Go ahead," she said softly. "I made copies."

"Also," Kristóf said, "my grandfather asks, is the place safe, where you stay."

Lisa blinked. "Grandpa Sándor would have asked that, too."

Kristóf watched the slow manner in which she lifted her canvas bag, heard the strain in her voice as she thanked them for their time.

"Wait," Ópa said. He handed Lisa his card. His face had drained of color in the light of the street lamp, and he looked all of his seventy-eight years. He said to her, so quietly Kristóf barely heard him, "It is very good to see you."

"Do you want me to translate that for you?" Kristóf asked.

"Tell her I loved her grandparents."

Kristóf told her. She nodded wistfully. The poor woman. Kristóf flipped open his mobile phone and called a taxi. As he said goodbye, he pointed at Ópa's card in her hand. "In the case that you have a problem."

BACK INSIDE THE RESTAURANT, Kristóf put on his apron. The tables were filling with customers, and he had to work, and the fact of a strange new relative did not change that. He checked on the brunette German woman at the back table, who lingered over dinner and a novel. Seeing him, she smiled, her pretty lips spreading.

"You're back," she said in German.

"I'll be working until about eleven o'clock," he answered, as was his habit. Sometimes if he gave women this information, they reappeared at quitting time. He refilled her glass, bantering in German about the wine. "It's a smooth one. Easy to drink too much without knowing it."

She laughed a little. "Maybe that isn't so bad."

"No." He smiled. He would wait for eleven o'clock.

But all through the evening, as he served chicken *paprikás* and cold cherry soup, he kept hearing the questions Ópa wouldn't answer, kept remembering the American's disappointment, kept seeing his grandfather's troubled face, and his hand as it trembled over the music.

Chapter Four

For Safety's Sake

LISA CLIMBED OUT OF THE TAXI, walked through the iron-grated doors of her hotel, and headed across the warped floor to the elevator. In front of the *up* button a woman in red lipstick stood smoking. She wore four-inch heels, the kind Lisa herself had sworn off in her early twenties because they twisted her ankles and thrust out her rear end.

Lisa tried to reach for the button. "Excuse me. Uh—" She finally remembered the Hungarian word. "*Elnézészt.*"

The woman narrowed her eyes, blew smoke toward the ceiling, and shifted aside.

Lisa rode the clattering elevator upstairs. At her room door she pushed the key into the lock and jostled it. In the three days she'd been here, it had never opened on the first try.

She glanced around. At the next door over, a woman—this one in a pink blouse, plenty of cleavage—leaned against the jamb and watched her. Why? The woman frowned and said something Lisa could not understand.

"I don't speak Hungarian," Lisa said.

"*Átkozott orosz,*" the woman muttered.

Orosz? Lisa was fairly sure that meant Russian. What was going on?

At last the lock yielded. Lisa hurried into her brown room—brown curtains, brown duvet on the uneven bed, yellow-brown stain on the ceiling. A card on the scratched dresser stated in five languages that this was a non-smoking room, but it smelled of old cigarettes.

Her off-schedule body had not yet had a full night's sleep here, and tonight at the restaurant her cramps had kicked in. Lisa went to the bathroom sink and took some Midol. As she lifted the tablets to her mouth, she caught sight of her own left hand. For an instant, an eyeblink, it looked all wrong to her: where was her wedding ring?

Oh, yeah, it was back home, in the safe deposit box at the bank until she could stand to sell it. After eight years of marriage, these moments of confusion always threw her. At least she'd gotten things right today when she introduced herself to Antal Varga. She'd remembered to say Lisa Denman, not Lisa Fischer.

Sitting cross-legged on the bed, she reached into her tote bag for the card Antal Varga had given her, and she quietly practiced saying his name. Varga—say it *Vor-ga,* sort of. Lisa pictured him: angular brow, white hair, like her grandfather Sándor in his later years. And Kristóf, *Krish-tof.* Perfect jawline, beautiful eyes. Flashes of anger, flashes of kindness.

But what did it matter now, after they'd put her in a taxi? An ending line if there ever was one. And yet as the taxi drove off, every time Lisa looked back through the window, Varga was still on the curb, watching.

This afternoon she'd left most of the old music sheets on the bed here. She spread them out now and perused them again. Some were purely instrumental and written in musical notation. One was marked *gitár* and included only chord names and lyrics, line after line of cursive full of umlauts and dashes. Some songs had notation she could read and words she couldn't. One title contained the name *Pest,* the part of the city east of the Danube, where she was now.

She lifted another song. *Egy jó anya,* the title read. They were common words. She'd heard them. *Jó* meant good. *Anya* . . . she thought it meant mother. *Jó anya,* good mother.

A cramp struck, the worst of the evening, clenching this useless womb of hers. She took shallow breaths and, like acupuncture, pressed on her wrist just below her tattoo. The pain finally faded and she released the pressure. But she ran her thumb slowly over the tattoo, the inked cross she'd taken up after the last of her pregnancies gave her a tiny son. He lived five minutes.

She'd been a mother, a good mother, for five minutes.

HER BODY HAD NOT YET ADJUSTED to Budapest time, and when she went to bed that night she could not sleep. Next door a radio played rock music, the bass thudding over and over. Lisa pounded on the wall. Someone pounded back. A man laughed. The radio did not stop. Lisa phoned the front desk. No one answered. She pulled up the duvet over her ears and at some point drifted off, only to wake again. Through the thin wall came the sound of a bed rocking and creaking. Then, rhythmic moaning.

Oh, great. Lisa looked at the bedside clock. Quarter to midnight. She took more Midol, paced the floor, and returned to bed.

She woke again at 1:30 to more banging. Please, no.

At last the pounding stopped. Then, a woman's voice and a man's laugh.

Wait, this laugh was deeper, more explosive than the last one—a different man?

Lisa slammed her fist against the wall. "Shut up!" she yelled.

There was another laugh, the woman this time.

Lisa threw off the coverlet, strode into the bathroom and slammed the door. Downing a glass of water, she added things up: the cleavage lady, the ultra-high-heeled woman blowing smoke, the hoopla next door. It was clear what services were being offered. On previous nights, the room next door had been empty, but it certainly wasn't now, and the weekend was coming. She couldn't stick around. After four miscarriages and a divorce, listening to next-door sex was—no.

THE NEXT MORNING LISA TOOK SOME TYLENOL because she'd run out of Midol. She put the music carefully into her carry-on bag and crammed everything else into her suitcase. Opening her travel book, she looked up how to call a cab.

Then she went out to the sidewalk in front of the hotel's graffiti-stained face and waited, her bags at her feet and Antal Varga's card in her hand, for the taxi. This wasn't the kind of thing she did, ever, until now. If Varga didn't like her showing up on his doorstep, then let him please forgive her.

He had asked if her hotel was safe. Not for her, it wasn't. Yet because he'd asked, she could only believe that in some way *he* was safe. And for whatever it meant, he was family.

CHAPTER FIVE

Renegotiation

August 18, 2006

KRISTÓF'S MOBILE RANG. HE BLINKED AWAKE and rolled toward the night table, reaching across Meta, the German woman he'd brought home last night. She groaned.

He grabbed the phone. "*Hálló.*"

"Kristóf." It was his grandfather. "She's here. The American."

"What? At your apartment?"

"Yes. There is some problem, I don't know what, I can't understand her. Come over."

"Just hand her the phone. I'll talk to her from here."

"No, come. Please."

"But I'm not—" He broke off. With Ópa, it would help nothing to explain that he wasn't alone. "Oh, all right." He closed the phone and told Meta in German that his grandfather needed him.

"Now?"

"Yes. Get dressed. My roommate is sleeping in the living room."

It was the arrangement he had with Feri: whoever brought a woman home could have the bedroom, and the other one took the sofa. Meta dressed, and as Kristóf led her through the living room, Feri pulled up the blankets over his bare chest. Kristóf and Meta went down the building's back staircase and through the courtyard that served the apartments and Három Páva.

They walked on to Andrássy Avenue, and there he prepared to part ways with her. "Last night was lovely," he said, though it had actually been pretty perfunctory.

She shrugged. Her lips were not as pretty this morning, without her makeup, without her smile—definitely no smile. Well, maybe it didn't matter. He would never see her again.

KRISTÓF RAN THE REMAINING FEW BLOCKS to his grandfather's flat. He turned on Hajós Street and then onto the cobbled paving of Lázár Street behind the opera house, skirting the lorry that had pulled up to deliver stage props. At the building next to Ópa's apartment house, two Gypsy men and a woman sat with their small dog on a deeply recessed window ledge where they seemed to have taken up residence, at least in the daylight hours. Kristóf waved to them because Ópa usually did, and he punched the key code at the building entry. When the door clicked, he trotted through the open passageway and up the first flight of stairs to his grandfather's apartment.

The old man stepped out, unshaven, shirt wrinkled. "The guest of honor is inside," he said quietly, holding the door. "I have no idea what this is about."

The woman's suitcases stood just inside the front entry. She herself sat at the table near the small kitchen, this time in a black T-shirt. She glanced up at Kristóf with a strained smile. Her eyes were shadowed as though she hadn't slept well, but she had looked that way last night, too. "Thank you for coming," she said. "I'm sorry for the bother."

"This is not bother."

His grandfather had made coffee and set out three red Transylvanian mugs Kristóf hadn't seen in years. Back when Kristóf's grandmother was alive and healthy, this apartment had been bright: placemats on the table, flowers on the bookcase. Since her death thirteen years ago, things had washed out into the black and white of Ópa's newspapers, mail and sheet music.

The three of them sat down to coffee. Kristóf asked Lisa, "Something is wrong?"

"I had to leave my hotel, and I didn't know where else to come but here. I'll find another place if you could just tell me where to try. I only have a few more days here."

"In your hotel, what happened?"

Lisa tapped a finger on the cup handle and her eyes shifted away. "Prostitutes work there, I'm pretty sure." It seemed she blushed. "If that's what's going on, then that's their own unfortunate business, but I don't want to be there."

Ópa whispered, "What did she say?" Kristóf lifted his hand, shushing him.

"They bang around in the middle of the night," Lisa said. "They glare at me in the hall like I'm some kind of criminal. One of them called me a Russian. I don't know why."

He had heard about this—night women swooping in on tourist territory like pigeons in a public square. They hated foreign competition, people said. Throat tightening in embarrassment for his city, he told his grandfather.

Ópa sighed. "Tell her to stay here. As long as she wants. I'm damned sorry this happened to her."

Lisa thanked them over and over. Kristóf went into the one small bedroom, changed the sheets, and set out a towel for her. In the front room he pushed the grand piano back half a meter to make it easier for his grandfather to open the sofa bed for himself tonight. When he returned to the table, Lisa had set out a stack of music and was handing Ópa a black-and-white photo.

"Sándor *és* Márta," he said.

"A long time ago," Lisa explained. "At Lake Michigan."

Ópa studied the deckle-edged picture and at length passed it to Kristóf. It showed a young couple barefoot on a beach, the man with his trousers rolled up as though he'd been wading, the slim woman in a knee-length skirt with the breeze lifting her hair. Though the pose was casual, still the shot seemed serious, almost grave. The woman was beautiful.

Lisa then handed them a color photo of a couple in late middle age holding two small children. "Grandpa Sándor and Grandma Márta with my brother and me," she said, and set one more photo on the table, a head shot of a dark-haired woman probably in her fifties. "My mother. Ann. A psychologist."

"Ann," Ópa repeated. He lined up the three photos, his eyes moving between them, and asked, "Did Márta continue playing cello?"

Kristóf translated the question, and Lisa said no, not really, Grandma Márta was busy with her work, teaching German and French.

"But I play cello," Lisa said, and added that Grandpa Sándor had had his own business as a piano tuner.

Ópa scowled. "But surely that wasn't all he did. He played. He had to."

Kristóf turned to Lisa. "Didn't he play?"

"Well, yes," she said, "he played at home, and also in a bar."

When Kristóf told his grandfather this, the man sighed and shook his head. "In a bar. Sitting there playing old songs for hours, nobody listening, maybe they toss a few coins his way, and then he goes home smelling like a tavern." Ópa pitched his thumb toward the kitchen radio. "My cousin was writing better songs when he was eighteen than most of those radio idiots produce all their lives!"

"What did he say?" Lisa asked Kristóf. "What's he upset about?"

"Eh . . ." Kristóf drummed his fingers on the table. "He is not so happy of this, says your grandfather is better writing songs."

She seemed confused. "Grandpa was a good entertainer."

"Ópa," Kristóf said, "she says he was good at entertaining people."

Ópa waved his hand. "Oh, yes, that's Sándor, turning on the entertainment when he needs to. But in bars? Couldn't he have done better than that? For God's sake, isn't that why people go to America, so things will be better? Were Sándor and Márta even happy?"

"Ópa, do you expect me to ask her that? Honestly, if the answer is no, do you really think she'd say so?"

"I don't know. But I've spent sixty years wondering about this."

Feeling awkward, Kristóf asked her, "Were your grandparents happy?"

The refrigerator whirred. Outside, one of the Gypsies shouted. Lisa dropped her gaze. "I don't know if you'd call it happiness. Protectiveness, yes. Loyalty, certainly."

Kristóf translated. Ópa nodded, not seeming surprised, only thoughtful and maybe sad. "The way we got by," he said. He rose and turned on the CD player in the living room. If Ópa did things as usual, pretty soon he would ask Kristóf to identify the music. This time it was a familiar-sounding orchestral piece, romantic era, probably. He couldn't place it.

Nor could he stay much longer; he had to work the opening lunch shift today. But first he slipped out to the small front balcony for a smoke. It was a warm, clear morning. On the street below, workers had opened the large back doors of the opera house and were carrying in stage flats. Lisa joined him, standing against the railing.

"Thank you for your help," she said humbly. "I'm sorry about this."

"Don't worry."

Through the open balcony door, the CD music rose to a crescendo. Lisa listened a moment. "Grieg. Nice. Kristóf, before you go, could you tell your grandfather I'll cook dinner? I'm no chef, but I can make a decent stew. I'll buy the food, I just need to know how to use the stove. I'd like to do him a favor. I've thrown so much at the two of you, and I'm sorry about that."

She kept saying she was sorry. The woman had landed in a snake's nest, and if anyone needed to apologize, it wasn't she. Still, it was nice of her. Kristóf couldn't remember the last time a woman had apologized to him.

"I will tell him you want to cook," he said.

He spoke to Ópa about it on his way out. Ópa drew a breath, and Kristóf strongly guessed Ópa didn't want him to leave.

"You'll have fun," Kristóf told him. "An American dinner."

Ópa lifted a finger as though he'd just remembered something. He sorted through a stack of mail on the table and handed Kristóf a letter. "This is from your mother, for you. You still haven't given her your address, I see."

"No." He hadn't given her his email or phone number, either. It had been three years since he'd last seen her. She'd taken off for Germany fifteen years ago, and that was her own damned choice.

"Well, would you please write her back?" Ópa said. "Because when she can't reach you, she calls *me*."

"You don't have to talk to her."

"Forgive me, but I can't help sympathizing with someone who worries about you."

They had been through this before. Kristóf nodded toward the living room and the CD player. "Aren't you going to ask me who the composer is?"

"All right, who?"

"Grieg."

Ópa lifted his eyebrows. "Very good."

Kristóf smiled, winked, waved goodbye.

CHAPTER SIX

What Was Lost

After Kristóf left, Varga showed Lisa how the apartment lock worked. Steering her away from a neighbor who drank, he rode the lift downstairs with her, showed her the code buttons at the front entrance, and wrote down the numbers for her. As she headed out to buy groceries, he watched at the door until he could no longer see her. When she returned, he took extra care in showing her how to light the stove. This woman was the granddaughter of Sándor and Márta, and he didn't want to take chances with her safety.

He glanced at her from time to time as she cooked. At times she stopped to rub her abdomen or the small of her back. After she set the concoction simmering, she excused herself and went to the bedroom. During this lull, Varga picked up the telephone and rescheduled two violin lessons he would have taught this afternoon. A few minutes later, the phone rang again. It was Halmos István, a colleague from the music academy. Though they still called each other by their surnames, they'd been close friends since 1993, the year both their wives died.

"Shall we have a drink tomorrow night?" Halmos asked.

"I can't." Varga told him quietly about his houseguest and the shock and the music she'd brought. "There she was, with copies of that teenage music Sándor and I wrote."

"That's the music your suite is based on, isn't it?"

"Yes. She wanted to know what was behind it."

"Did you tell her?"

"No." Varga hadn't even told Halmos much about it. The only people who had known were his wife and his sister, and they were both gone.

"You know," Halmos said, "I've always wished you'd do more with that suite. Why don't you take another look at it?"

Varga rubbed his taut jaw. That suite had too much of the war in it. Too much of everything. It was like the old myth of the woman opening a box and hell flying out.

"I admit the suite is problematic," Varga said. "But, well, I don't know."

"Still . . ." Halmos sighed. "Well, call me when you have time for a drink."

THE NEXT DAY WAS SATURDAY, AND VARGA noted with relief that Lisa woke up cheerful. Now that she'd rested and pinned her blond hair into a bun, she looked pretty. It jarred him, her resemblance to Márta. The shape of her face, he supposed.

That morning he took her to see the music academy, and then she wanted to visit the nearby communist museum. He walked her to the *Terror Háza,* but God help him, he had no stomach for exploring the execution cellar, no wish to watch old newsreels of his country's misery. He waited inside the front entrance as she wandered through on her own. Overhead, a recirculating tape played a woman's voice reading off the names of the government's victims. When Lisa joined him again, sober-faced, he took her straight home.

In the afternoon she looked in her phrasebook and asked him where Sándor and Márta had each lived. Neither location was far, so they went out again. On Teréz Boulevard Varga showed her the smog-dulled apartments opposite the western train station. He said "Márta," but he couldn't tell her that though this was the place, Márta's home had actually burned down, bombed along with the train station during the war. Lisa took a picture.

He led her south half a kilometer to the corner where Sándor had once lived. Varga pointed. "Sándor." He spread his hands palms down. Leveled. She took a photo of the newer store and apartments that now stood here, recently painted beige, perhaps by a foreign owner.

They were only a block and a half from where Varga used to live on Dessewffy Street, so he walked Lisa that direction. He stopped in front of a plaster façade painted ochre now. But he remembered it as light gray, sooty in places, with a small angel statue over the front doorway. The angel lost a wing in the war. Varga pointed to a second-floor window with a tiny balcony and wrought-iron railing. Using German in hopes she'd understand, he said, "*Mein haus.*"

"Oh," she said softly, and lifted her camera.

He looked downward toward the grate-enclosed windows of the basement. In the worst of the siege of '45, that cramped, cold space was the home he shared with his family, with Sándor, with a Gypsy named Miklós, and forty scared neighbors. Feeling a pressure in his chest, Varga waited through several breaths, then touched Lisa's shoulder to turn her toward home.

Back at the apartment, she served strudel she'd bought that morning. As they ate, she pulled out her digital camera and showed him photos she'd snapped earlier in her visit. He instantly recognized the first one, which she probably had taken in the history museum. It was a comparison map, with the large outer perimeter showing Hungary's far-flung realm in the Austro-Hungarian Empire. Huge Hungary stretched south to the Adriatic and east into the Carpathians. But within this expanse on the map, another line showed Hungary's shrunken territory after the Treaty of Trianon in 1920. Austria-Hungary lost the Great War, the empire collapsed, and Hungary was amputated, with vast regions parceled out to Romania, Czechoslovakia, Austria, and Yugoslavia. Varga had no words to tell Lisa that this—*this*—was the foremost reason Hungary later threw in its lot with Hitler: to win back the lost lands.

He spread his hands in dismay.

Lisa went on to show him other photos of old communist statues, and buildings still riddled with bullet holes. Worst were the bronze shoe sculptures along the embankment, where in 1944 Jews were force-marched to the Danube and shot.

His left little finger hurt today. Varga rubbed the knuckle and looked at Lisa. There was no way someone from a fearless country like hers could understand the frailty of his own dismembered nation, no way she could know the desperation that had allied Hungary with Hitler. She could never fathom the terror of standing between Germany and Russia.

CHAPTER SEVEN

No Surrender

October 15, 1944

WORD HAD GONE OUT THAT HUNGARY'S regent, Horthy Miklós, was going to broadcast an announcement about the war. On this Sunday afternoon, Antal leaned against the unlit tile stove in the apartment living room while his grandfather twisted the radio dial. The family had gathered, with Antal's parents on the sofa and his sister, Katalin, on the piano bench. Sándor had come over and had pulled up a dining room chair. Antal hoped this wouldn't take long. He had to go to a quartet practice—well, trio practice—that Mr. Horváth had already rescheduled twice.

The radio static cleared. Melancholy music played. When it died out, Horthy in his familiar stilted cadence began to speak.

I am here informing the German Reich that we are concluding a preliminary armistice with our enemies and ceasing all hostilities against them . . .

Papa murmured, "Doing what Romania did," and Grandpapa crossed his arms.

Today it is obvious to any sober-minded person that the German Reich has lost the war.

Antal took a breath, waited.

With grief I am forced to state that the German Reich, on its part, broke the loyalty of an ally toward our country a long time ago. . . It has thrown formation after formation of the Hungarian armed forces into battle . . .

Sándor leaned forward on his chair, his right fist punching the left palm. His brother had been among those thrown at the Russians.

Under cover of the German occupation the Gestapo tackled the Jewish question in a manner incompatible with the dictates of humanity . . .

Antal swallowed, thinking of Weisz Jenö. He saw his mother close her eyes. Many of her voice students were Jews.

I appeal to every honest Hungarian to follow me on this path, beset by sacrifices, that will lead to Hungary's salvation.

The speech ended, and the mournful music began again. Grandpapa clicked off the radio. The mantel clock ticked. In his pockets Antal's hands clenched.

"A Russian occupation now," Mother groaned.

"Horthy surrendered us?" Katalin asked, absently twiddling a lock of her dark hair. "Will the Germans leave?"

"No," Sándor spat out.

Grandpapa lifted his hand, stopping Sándor. "Kati, we don't know. I have to admit, I—" He shook his head.

Antal went to the window and looked down into the street. A peasant family, one of the thousands fleeing the Russians, trudged along, pulling a cart heaped with stuffed burlap sacks, baskets, a kettle, a sewing machine. Behind him the telephone rang. Mother answered and called him to it.

Antal took the phone, heard a man's voice. "Antal. Hanák Viktor here. My daughter Márta is in your music group."

Antal stood up straighter. "Yes."

"I'd prefer that Márta not be walking around by herself today," Hanák said. "We live not far from you, as I understand. For rehearsal today, could you make the tram trip with her?"

"Yes."

The announcement, the surrender. Antal twisted the phone cord. It was not lost on him that this journalist, probably one of the best informed people in the country, was nervous.

THE TRIP TO MR. HORVÁTH'S HOUSE WAS UNEVENTFUL, the rehearsal itself fairly productive. Afterward, as Antal waited with Márta for the streetcar home, the autumn sun shone gloriously. A breeze set the trees vibrating yellow and orange as flame.

It was a perfect day, except that Márta's eyes kept darting around as though on sentry watch. On the way here they'd seen members of the fascist Arrow Cross militia walking about. They were losers, people said, stupid drunks. But they had guns.

The tram pulled up. Sitting on a wooden seat near the front, Antal and Márta left the old city of Buda and crossed the Danube into Pest. He looked sidelong at her. She was slim with hazel eyes and sand-colored hair in a braid—a simpler but prettier style than most girls had, he thought.

She pointed at his wristwatch, a gift Mr. Horváth had given him for winning a difficult competition. "Nice watch. When the Soviets get here, don't wear it in public."

"But Horthy surrendered, didn't he? The Soviets should turn around."

"We'll see."

A bell clanged. The tram stopped. A man brushed past them up the aisle, the door opened and shut, and the tram went on.

"I think you're doing a good job leading our group," Márta said. "Like today, when you had me crescendo on those three measures and then taper off. That was perfect."

It surprised him how much this praise meant, and he thanked her. "Your tone is excellent," he added in earnest.

The brakes squealed as the tram arrived at Márta's stop. They picked up their instruments and pressed to the front behind a black-haired woman. The door swung open and the woman stepped forward—then stumbled back against Antal.

Antal craned his neck to peer around the woman. Two fellows barely older than Antal shoved their way up the steps. They wore green shirts and armbands with red-and-white crossed arrow insignia. "Oh, God," Antal muttered.

"Here now," the conductor told the two. "Step down and let these people off first."

The taller of the two spluttered a laugh. "Not yet, uncle. We're going to look around."

One of the Arrow Cross greenshirts held a pistol, the other a truncheon. They were only an arm's length away and smelled of alcohol. Antal and Márta exchanged worried glances. The aging conductor, clearly jittery, moved through the aisle toward the back.

The driver stood up. "Put those weapons away," he said to the green-shirts. "Pay the fare and leave these people alone. Or I'll call the police."

"Maybe the police have a new boss," said the taller one.

"Get off the tram," the driver ordered. His chin shook.

The tall greenshirt shouted, "All of you people, sit down! You too, Mr. Driver!"

"Come on," Antal whispered to Márta, throat dry. They went back to the first aisle-facing seat. Antal sat between Márta on his right and her cello on his left. He slid his violin under the seat. The middle-aged black-haired woman sat down beside Márta, twisting her thin hands in her lap.

The tram remained stopped. Up front the greenshirt with the pistol kept watch near the driver. The other moved down the aisle with his truncheon, eyeing passengers, then forward again and stopped in front of Antal.

He was maybe eighteen or nineteen, badly shaven, with pale eyes and a cleft chin. Tapping the truncheon in his hand, he looked Antal over. "Deserter?"

"No." Antal glared at him. "I'm in school."

From the front the other greenshirt shouted, "Józsi, just leave him alone. He's a *boy*."

Márta leaned close to Antal. "Be careful," she whispered.

Truncheon in hand, Józsi looked at Márta with a lazy grin. "Pista," he called to his companion, "there's a nice little sweetheart here."

Antal summoned his voice. "Leave her alone."

Józsi sniggered and turned to the black-haired woman. "And *you*, Jew, where's your armband?"

"I—I'm not Jewish," the woman stammered.

"Boys." The driver stood up. "You really don't want to do this." He spoke carefully. "When this war is over you don't want to be remembered for harassing innocent people on a streetcar. Now leave that lady alone."

Antal looked at Pista, the greenshirt up front. For a moment Pista seemed to waver. Then he turned his gun, training it on the driver until the driver sat back down.

Józsi repeated to the black-haired woman, "I said, where's your armband?"

"Stop," the woman pleaded.

"She's not Jewish," Márta said to the greenshirt, a tremor in her words.

Antal's gaze flicked to Márta. What in God's name was he supposed to do? Her father wanted her safe. Over the knot in his throat, he told the greenshirt, "That woman isn't Jewish, and we didn't bother you, so leave us alone."

"That's right," the driver said.

Pista at the front shouted out, "She's a Jewish bitch, and the rest of you are Jew lovers."

Józsi grabbed the woman's arm and pulled her to her feet.

"Let go of me!" the woman yelled.

"Let go of her!" Márta repeated, panic edging into her voice.

The driver rushed over. Antal jumped up. As the driver reached toward the black-haired woman, Antal stood in front of Márta, spreading his arms, desperate for this to work—

The greenshirt lunged. The truncheon missed the driver and slammed down on Antal's left hand. Pain shot through his knuckles. Antal clutched his hand and barely knew what was happening, except that the black-haired woman was thrust aside, and she fell on the floor, and Józsi stamped away toward the front.

"Fuck the coward Horthy!" the greenshirt Pista yelled. "No surrender!"

BACK ON THE STREET, ANTAL SAW MÁRTA to her apartment building near the train station. They paused at her front door. Very gently she touched his left hand.

"Take care of it." Still shaken, she lifted her eyes to his. "Thank you."

"I don't know if I helped anything." He tried to smile. "But you're welcome."

"If I had to have a terrible adventure like this one, I'm glad it was with you. Goodbye, Antal."

He helped her through the door with her cello and she slipped inside, turning to look back at him.

AT HOME ANTAL SHOWED HIS HAND to his father. Papa, a physician, palpated the knuckles and immobilized the painful little finger by bandaging it to the ring finger. "Lay off violin for a while," he said.

Antal said nothing. He'd try to do right-hand drills with his bow.

"And for God's sake," Papa added, "stay away from Arrow Cross idiots."

Later that night, Sándor telephoned and told him the Germans had been driving tanks through the streets. The next day word spread that Horthy's son had been kidnapped. By the day after that, Horthy himself was gone. Szálasi Ferenc of the Arrow Cross was the new prime minister, Germany's chosen puppet. Antal listened to the news in confusion and disgust.

Mr. Horváth telephoned. He had heard from Márta's father about the episode on the tram. "How is your hand?" he asked Antal.

"It's just a sprain," Antal said.

"Sprains can be bad. We may need to hold off on your lessons."

"But you're leaving soon, aren't you? Could I please see you, even if all we do is talk about the romanza?"

"All right." Mr. Horváth laughed wearily. "No surrender. But wait at least a week, and I hope to God the dust settles."

"So do I."

Antal's hand throbbed as he hung up.

CHAPTER EIGHT

Fire Games

August 20, 2006

IT WAS SUNDAY, AND THIS WAS ST. ISTVÁN'S DAY. Lisa had read about it in her guidebook. If she had the story straight, István was the king who'd founded Hungary as a Catholic nation a thousand years ago, and in spite of the Mongols, the Turks, the Austrians, the Germans, and the Russians, Hungary was still a nation. That was perseverance.

She'd gone with Varga today to the high Mass of St. King István at the basilica. After they walked home, Varga's face looked flushed and damp. It was now evening. An hour ago, with gestures and her phrasebook, he'd given her to understand there would be dinner out tonight with Kristóf. What she hadn't understood was that Varga would stay home.

Now she sat at an outdoor table across from Kristóf, the river and the streaked sunset at his back. He was handsome, almost alarmingly so, with his brown eyes bold under dark brows, like some Spanish nobleman or a Brooks Brothers model. And here she sat in her wrinkled dress, without lipstick because she'd forgotten to pack it. Kristóf had made more headway with his dinner than she had with hers, and he was further along with his wine, too. She took a sip of her white, hoping she wasn't trying his patience.

"The wine is okay?" he asked.

"Yes, it's—it's nice."

He looked puzzled. "You don't drink wine, usually not?"

"I used to drink it more, but . . ."

What could she say, really? That she and Jake used to enjoy wine together, but that was done? Or that she'd not touched alcohol during four pregnancies that all became losses?

"I had a health condition for a while and couldn't have alcohol," she said. "It's over now, so I suppose I don't need to be so cautious." She lifted her glass and took another swallow.

"You are okay?" Kristóf asked. "After your condition?"

She said yes, although there was more to it. He gave her a time of quiet and let her eat. On the table a short candle glowed. After a little while, he asked if she liked Hungary.

"I do," she said, as the truth of this sank in—despite her awful hotel, despite the graffiti, despite trash heaps and worn-out proletariat apartments. "I love the river and the bridges, but especially the music. Everywhere I turn, something is named after Liszt, or Bartók, or Kodály, and I can stand in your grandfather's living room and hear opera singers practicing across the street. And even that guy over there." She gestured toward a Gypsy strolling by, playing the Beatles' "Michelle" on a violin.

"Don't look at him," Kristóf said. "Or he will play at our table, and then he doesn't leave until we give him money."

She averted her gaze, and the Gypsy wandered in the other direction.

"Speaking of music," she said, "I got your grandfather to play for me. I pointed at his violin and made a little begging sign." Lisa folded her hands as though in supplication. "He played the 'Meditation' from *Thaïs*. What a musician. I suppose he's very well respected."

Kristóf's hand dropped on the table top. "Not like he should be."

"No?"

He leaned toward her. "Years and years, he could play anything. Double stops, triple, making the bow bounce perfect. Every violin student knew it—you want good bow instruction, you go to Varga Antal, no one else. He was damned best violin player in this city, but the orchestra doesn't make him the concertmaster, they keep him in charge of second violins, they don't give him enough solos, and why? Because of this." Kristóf held up his left little finger.

She looked at his face, saw the hard set of his jaw. "What do you mean?"

"Always he has pain in that finger, all his life. The other players knew it. The conductor knew it. Never my grandfather lets this pain make him play wrong, but always others say he will. Jealous, I think. All the years until he retired and left from the orchestra. So."

Kristóf reached toward the inside pocket of his jacket as though for a cigarette, then shook his head and signaled the waiter. "Also, my grandfather was the better leader for the second violins than those other guys were, so the orchestra keeps him there."

Behind Kristóf, beyond the tables, a crowd had formed at the embankment. Dusk had fallen. Lisa put on her white sweater. The waiter removed their empty plates and brought coffee.

"Kristóf." She hoped she wasn't making a nuisance of herself. "I wonder if you could read a few lines for me and tell me what they say. It's only a little bit."

"Yes, sure."

She pulled a pen and small notebook out of her handbag, then the *Embers Suite*. She folded back the title page. "This is that quintet suite your grandfather wrote. This morning I looked at the way it's divided up, and—well, here, look." She handed it to him. "This first section, it's titled 'Moderato con moto,' but then there are those words in parentheses, and I think they're the same as one of those songs I brought."

"It says, 'Light shines in the darkness.'"

"Ah." She wrote it in her notebook. "And then if you could just flip through it to the other pieces, they all start with a little note like that."

Kristóf turned to the next piece. "This one, the words are German, '*Stille Nacht.*' That Christmas song." He hummed.

"'Silent Night.' Yeah, I saw strains of it in that section."

"Odd, he put Christmas music." Kristóf turned more pages, stopped at the next piece. "Okay, this one . . . eh, Pest, Duna . . ."

"Pest is this part of the city, isn't it?" she asked.

"Yes, and sometimes people say it to mean all the city. Duna—" He pointed behind him. "The river. Danube. These words mean, 'Pest, Along Duna.'"

Lisa wrote it down.

Kristóf turned more pages and stopped. "This says, 'A Good Mother.'"

Lisa had thought so. She nodded and wrote.

Kristóf pushed ahead in the music again. "Here. This one says 'romanza,' not Hungarian, I think it is Italian? Probably means romance?"

"A musical style. And there's one more piece."

He found the last one and pondered the words. "Song to—or for, maybe—enemies—enemies of us. Maybe say, 'Song to our enemies.'" Kristóf turned more pages and stopped on the last one. "No easy thing, singing to enemies."

Lisa peered at the score as Kristóf ran his finger under the frantic crescendo that had been notated, and the drum slam. She touched Grandma Márta's question scrawled underneath, and with a sense of opening a locked room, she asked, "What does this say?"

He seemed to hesitate. "Something like, 'Oh, Antal, Sándor, why did it all have to end like this?'"

Lisa traced her finger over the written words. Even in Kristóf's matter-of-fact tone, their plaintive sorrow had spoken.

"Must be, something went wrong like hell," Kristóf said.

"And I don't know what it was."

"No, it is as you said. Your grandparents, my grandfather, shh, shh, shh."

The candle flame dipped in the night breeze. She took another sip of wine. Kristóf asked her about a chart his grandfather had spoken of, and Lisa realized he meant the rough family tree she'd drawn with Varga on taped-together sheets of paper. She pulled it out of her bag and spread it open for Kristóf. He moved his chair closer and bent over it.

She pointed to the names Varga had written at the top, surname first in the Hungarian style: *Varga József és Piroska.* "Our great-great-grandparents," she said. In the next generation down, the chart branched to two brothers and their wives: on the left, *Varga János és Éva*; on the right, *Varga László és Ilona.* With her finger Lisa underscored Éva and János. "My great-grandparents. I didn't even know their names until today. Do you remember them at all?"

"No. They died before I was born."

Disappointed, Lisa moved her hand down another generation, where Varga had begun including surnames of the spouses: *Varga Antal és Brauer Ildikó. Varga Katalin és Benedek Péter.*

"Katalin was my aunt," Kristóf said. "Very good singer, died about two years ago. Ildikó was my grandmother. Ópa's wife. She died ..." He paused, looking off in the distance. "I was sixteen, I think. She played piano, she taught me."

Lisa nodded. In the apartment she had seen a framed photo of Varga and his wife probably in their fifties, she on the piano bench in the living room, he standing beside her with his violin, both of them laughing. Turning back to the chart, she saw Kristóf's name on a line by itself. She pointed at what was written directly above it: *Varga Zoltán és Koch Mónika.* "Your parents?"

"Yeah." Kristóf pulled a pen out of his jacket pocket and struck out the word és. "They are not together."

"My parents split up, too." She crossed out the *&* in *Ann Varga & Gary Denman,* then after Gary's name she wrote *Deceased 1981.* "He died, but they divorced before that."

"He died?"

"When I was seven. A car accident." She wasn't ready to say that he'd been drinking.

"This was hard, I guess."

Yes, it had been hard for a seven-year-old and her five-year-old brother, waiting for the dad who'd told them that even though he and Mom weren't together anymore, he'd come see them, and he didn't come; then he *couldn't* come. Lisa sipped her coffee and asked Kristóf if he had siblings. He didn't.

She showed Kristóf the name *Paul* on the chart. "I never see my brother. He lives in Africa. Works for USAID. I don't see my mother much, either. She lives nowhere close by, and, well." And, well, they'd rarely agreed on anything in years. "It's complicated."

"Ah. So you had to come to Hungary to find a family."

"Well. I don't know." Lisa crossed her arms against the breeze. "Do your parents live here?" she asked.

"No. My mother—" Kristóf jerked his thumb over his shoulder. "Gone to Germany. My father is in Pécs. Near Croatia. He works in a hospital— eh—*mikroszkóp*—well, a laboratory. I don't see him so often, it is not such a quick trip, and he has his complications also." Kristóf pointed emphatically at his father's name, then his mother's. "Still he is better than she is."

His sudden bitterness startled her. She waited for him to say more, but when he didn't, she asked, "Where'd you learn English?"

"University. Also I was in London three months, to learn it better, but still I do mistakes." He gave her a rueful smile. "But I swear very well in English, I'm sorry. My German, it is better, it is more. French, not so much."

"You've studied three languages?"

"Yeah. German was not hard. I heard it from my mother and her family. Also my Varga grandmother, her family was German."

"Is that why you call your grandfather Ópa? Isn't that German?"

"The word is not so unusual here. But my mother, she liked it that she was German, so I always called her Mutti. German for Mum. And I call my father Vati, also German. Probably not what he would choose, but he tried to make my mother happy." Kristóf shrugged. "For a while."

They turned back to the family tree. Lisa found her grandfather's name, Sándor. Knowing Kristóf couldn't tell her anything about him, she didn't ask. But she touched the name beside it, Károly, under which Antal Varga had written *meghalt 1943*.

"This was my Grandpa Sándor's brother," she said. "He died on the eastern front."

The humid wind blew. Kristóf weighted the diagram paper down with their saucers. Lisa pushed her hair out of her face, remembering what little her grandparents had said about Károly's death. "When the German troops retreated from Russia," she told Kristóf, "they used Hungarian soldiers as human shields. Have you heard of that?"

Candlelight shadows flickered across Kristóf's face as he nodded. "Yes."

"Has your grandfather told you about it?"

"My God, why would he want to talk of it?"

"But he wrote it on that chart," Lisa said. "He wrote, 'Károly.' And then, 'Died.'"

"To write 'died' is not the same as to write 'shot' or 'starved' or 'froze.'"

The chill of the wind ran through her and the candle's glow bent. Lisa moved the candle closer to illuminate some names farther down on the chart. Immediately beside the name of Zoltán, Kristóf's father, Varga had written *Zsuzsanna, 1956 július 17-1956 november 7*.

"Tell me about this," Lisa said. "Please."

"That child, that girl, she was my father's twin."

Varga had lost a baby, then. Lisa touched the date. "She died during the '56 uprising?"

"Yes, the baby was sick and the hospital was already full with people wounded, bleeding, and they ran out of medicine, and there was no help for the baby. I don't know, maybe the baby would die anyway, but this is what my grandmother told me. Ópa does not speak of it."

She understood. She so seldom spoke her own baby's name. Refolding the chart, she thought about Varga's loss. "Kristóf, when we get back to the apartment, could you translate between your grandfather and me, just a little more?"

"Yes, okay."

"Thank you." She looked toward the Danube embankment, where the crowd had grown. "Why are all those people standing over there?"

"Above the river, there will be fire games."

"Fire games?" She felt momentarily confused, then laughed. "You mean fireworks?"

He waved his hand. "Yeah, yeah, fireworks."

The sky was completely dark now. They pushed their chairs side by side facing the river. With deafening booms, great blossoms of red, white and green burned in the night sky.

The wind whipped up, tore at the tablecloth. It threw napkins and trash into the air and slapped grit at their faces. Rain dropped onto the table. Kristóf shouted for the waiter and paid the bill while Lisa ran under a tree, holding down the hem of her dress.

And now the rain pelted. Thunder ripped. The sky lit, pale and electric. The crowd at the embankment screamed and scattered. Kristóf grabbed Lisa's elbow and they dashed for better shelter, but the doorways and overhangs were already crammed with wet bodies. Lisa and Kristóf ran through the crowds and the drenching rain, jumping over flooded gutters, dodging fallen tree branches, past the basilica, past the opera house, until they arrived, panting and aching, at Varga's building. Kristóf punched the buzzer. The street door unlocked immediately and as they climbed the stairs, Varga came rushing to meet them, shouting at Kristóf and shooing them toward the apartment.

Lisa went into the bedroom and closed the door. She changed into dry clothes, combed her soaked hair, and sat down on the bed, putting off the next favor she had to ask. Finally, with a glance at the tattoo on her wrist, she collected herself and went out to the kitchen, where the two men stood talking in rapid Hungarian. They stopped and turned to her.

"I told him you want to talk to him," Kristóf said.

Lisa faced Varga, saw the blink behind his glasses. "Antal *bácsi*—um— when you drew the family tree for me, I was so sad about your baby that died in 1956. I know that was a long time ago, but maybe a sorrow like that never really goes away."

Kristóf translated, pausing every few words. Varga nodded slowly.

"I had a baby—" She anchored her trembling voice. "I had a baby who was born too soon and he died."

Kristóf looked at her soberly, then translated. Varga shook his head and murmured, "*Jaj.*" Lisa remembered it from her grandparents, a word for pain or worry or sorrow.

"That was almost a year ago," Lisa pressed on. "It's still hard. And I was wondering, could you show me where the Vargas are buried? I think I should go there and . . . I just think I should go."

Outside, the rain had stopped. Shouts drifted up from the street below. Kristóf translated haltingly. The men exchanged a few more sentences.

Kristóf told her, "He is not sure where are the graves of Sándor's family, but he knows where is Márta's little sister's grave."

Lisa nodded. Once long ago she'd heard about her grandmother's little sister. "We could go there, then."

Varga reached to her and closed her hand in both of his.

The next afternoon Lisa and Varga set out, waving to the Gypsies on the ledge next door, stepping over storm debris, and rode the Metro to Kerepesi Cemetery. She followed him to a row of crowded graves. Varga paced down the row and pointed at a low, plain marker. Lisa stepped close and read the weathered stone.

HANÁK
Livia Anna
~Anni~
1940-1945

Grandma Márta's sister, a five-year-old girl that might have looked like her. A child that might have looked just a little like Lisa's own Alexander, if he had lived. She steadied herself against the tremor rising in her. Varga set his hand on her shoulder, and she felt the sadness that weighted his touch.

Turning a finger toward him in the gesture they'd been using for "you" and "your," she asked where his child was, carefully pronouncing, "*Gyermek? Hol?*"

Varga led her back up the walk and over another stretch of lawn. He stopped between two flat markers, the larger one bearing his wife's name, the small one reading *Varga Zsuzsanna*. Lisa crossed herself and brushed away a tear. Beside her, Varga said two English words: "Yes, hard."

On the way home, they stopped into a grocery store, where Varga bought milk and eight poppy seed rolls. When they arrived at the apartment house, Varga sidestepped for a moment and gave some of the rolls to the Gypsies next door. Returning to her, he seemed to want to say something. With a shake of his head, he made a small gesture toward the Gypsies and could only repeat, "Hard."

CHAPTER NINE

The Fiddler in the Basement

October 27, 1944

OF COURSE IT HADN'T WORKED, Horthy's fumbling attempt at surrender. Germany cracked down. It dictated Hungary's military and put Arrow Cross stooges in charge of the government and the streets. The Soviet Army kept blasting across eastern Hungary, and Allied bombs pummeled the city at night. Antal slept in his clothes, throwing off the covers and running to the cellar when the air raid signal screamed. In the morning he woke tired and late. But what did it matter? School had closed.

He kept practicing violin. For about ten days he'd sworn off using his hurt finger, but he finally unbandaged it and put it back to work. Sometimes he wondered what he was practicing *for*. If the country got flattened, who would be listening to violin? But he tried to shut down these questions. He insisted to himself that practicing mattered. Music mattered. This was not a case of fiddling while Rome burned.

Two days after he unbandaged his hand, he was practicing scales before school when his sister stepped into the bedroom. She pulled the door shut. Almost fourteen, Katalin stood there in the school uniform she was outgrowing. Clothes, like everything else, were hard to replace.

"Antal. I went down to the cellar just now for firewood." Her words rushed. "There's some fellow behind the coal bins. Hiding, I think. When he saw me looking at him, he asked for something to eat. He's young, maybe eighteen or nineteen. And I think he's a Gypsy."

Antal lowered his violin. "Does anybody else know he's there?"

"I don't think so. Should I give him some food, do you think?"

Before the war landed here, he would have simply gone downstairs and given the poor fellow something to eat. But before the war, a Gypsy would never have turned up in their cellar. And weren't Gypsies being deported? Like Jews? You could get arrested for feeding Jews; could you get arrested for feeding Gypsies?

"He looks really hungry," Katalin said.

"Oh, Lord." Antal laid the violin and bow on his bunk. "Come on."

At least for the moment, his parents and grandfather were out of the apartment . . . good.

Antal put on his coat and took three rolls from the breadbasket in the kitchen. Any more than that, they couldn't really spare. He and Katalin hurried down the back stairs of the building, through the basement to the coal bins in back.

Behind the coal bins, a smelly black-haired stranger sat on an overturned bucket. A dim overhead bulb lit the stubble and dust on his face. He gripped a filthy blanket around his shoulders. Beneath it, an olive-green collar showed.

Antal stepped close and held out the rolls. The Gypsy grabbed them with a gasp, or maybe a sob.

"My name is Antal." He thought better of giving his surname. "And this is my sister." He stopped short of giving her name at all. "Who are you?"

The fellow's teeth tugged at a roll. Crumbs stuck to his mustache.

"What's your name?" Antal repeated.

The Gypsy mumbled.

"What?"

"Miklós."

"Where are you from?" Katalin asked.

He waved in the direction of the outside door. After a moment he held up the roll he was eating. "I kiss your hands."

"Why are you here?" Antal asked.

He didn't answer, so Antal said, "You can't just sit here in our basement and refuse to speak."

Miklós pointed a smudged finger at him. "I heard you play."

"You couldn't have," Antal said, confused. Then he remembered: during last night's air raid, he had brought his violin down here to hold it safe from the bombing. In the tedious wait for the all-clear signal, some of the residents had asked him to play. Miklós must have heard the music and peeked out.

"You play good," Miklós said.

"Thank you."

"But I play better."

Antal frowned. "You play?"

The Gypsy nodded emphatically. "I play fast. Fast is better. It makes more money."

So he was a violinist on the run—a *braggart* violinist on the run. Antal glanced at Katalin.

"What should we do?" she whispered.

He shook his head. Other residents would come down here before long. At least the custodian would, and he'd call the police.

"I don't think you're safe down here," Antal told Miklós.

"I'm not safe out there, either."

Of course he was right. Antal went to his family's storage compartment, found another bucket, and brought it to Miklós. God, this fellow needed a bath.

"Look," Antal said, "use this bucket instead of the loo in the courtyard, and empty it late at night. Or just leave it if you have to, and I'll empty it. If you hear anybody on the stairs, duck. And stay out of sight. About fifty people live in this building, and not all of them are as nice as my sister."

"We're sorry, Miklós," Katalin said, her dark eyes rounded in sympathy. "Everything is so awful."

Antal tugged at Katalin's elbow and led her out, just as Mr. Lukács, the big custodian, trotted down the stairs.

LATER THAT DAY ANTAL RETURNED TO THE COAL BINS. The Gypsy had disappeared. So had every trace of him except the piss in the bucket.

In bed that night Antal thought about Miklós. He was probably a deserter from the army. If the army caught him, they would shoot him. Antal could not sleep, thinking of a violin player being shot.

Chapter Ten

Re-entry

August 22, 2006

L ISA HAD TO CATCH A MORNING FLIGHT HOME. Kristóf came to the apartment while Varga was shaving, and Lisa took care of last details. She exchanged email addresses with Kristóf and handed him the bottle of red wine she'd bought as a thank-you gift for the two of them. While Varga phoned for an English-speaking taxi driver, Lisa stood drinking coffee with Kristóf on the front balcony. Opera house workers on the street below unloaded chairs from a truck.

"I'm leaving the music here for your grandfather," she told Kristóf. "I have other copies. The poor man, I think I gave him quite a shock when I came."

"Well, but a week from now, a month, rest of his life, he still will talk about when the American cousin came." Kristóf looked at her, squinting a little in the morning light. "Eh, Ópa asked me to tell you, we're sorry you had this sadness, your baby gone."

Next month it would be a year since the miscarriage—no, not just a miscarriage, but the death of a baby boy who'd grown in her for six months. Lisa drew a low breath, a trick she'd learned through singing, one she pulled out when she needed her voice not to shake.

"Thank you," she told Kristóf.

"Ópa hopes you will someday have another baby?"

"I'm not sure I can. And my husband left."

Kristóf frowned, his dark eyes inquiring. She hadn't intended the conversation to become so personal just minutes before she would leave, but in fact there was no other way to explain this whole last year of her life. She said, "He got someone else pregnant."

"While he was married with you?"

"Yes."

"What a bastard."

Lisa looked away. Bastard or not, she hadn't stopped loving him.

Varga joined them and stood next to Kristóf, the white-haired and dark-haired bookends of the family, the sky over them stark blue. He said something to Kristóf.

"Your taxi comes soon," Kristóf told her. "Also, he asks, will you miss Hungary?"

Lisa glanced at the opera house where she'd heard the singers practicing, and down the street where she'd run through the rain with Kristóf. She looked at Varga, with whom she'd shared food and music and whatever words they could manage. Wistfulness filled her as she told them, "Yes. I'll miss Hungary." She didn't have much to go home to.

They carried Lisa's bags to the curb and waited. The taxi arrived and the driver loaded her bags. Kristóf hugged Lisa awkwardly around the shoulders. Varga held her hand and said something in Hungarian.

"He says, please come back," Kristóf said.

"I wish I could."

It would probably be years before she could return. How many years did Varga have left? She squeezed his dry hand. "*Viszlát,*" she said, voice wavering. *Goodbye.*

HER TRIP HOME MEANT CHANGING PLANES in Paris and Chicago. While waiting at O'Hare, she decided she might as well call her mother, who lived in Oak Park. They usually talked once a month or so, whether or not they really wanted to. Lisa pulled out her cell phone, which hadn't functioned in Hungary. The phone rang four times before she heard her mother's rushed hello.

"Hi, Ann." Lisa had called her mother by her first name since middle school. "I'm at O'Hare. On my way home from Budapest."

"So you really did it. I didn't think you'd go without Jake."

"Well, I sure couldn't go *with* him—" She stopped. This was not the time.

Footage from a Cubs game glared from an overhead television. An intercom called for a passenger Singh. Lisa leaned forward on the seat, trying to ease her backache from the cramped flight.

"Ann. You won't believe this. I found Grandpa Sándor's cousin. And his grandson."

"*What?*"

She told her mother about the opera house and Varga's violin. She didn't tell her about slamming out of the hotel and then spending four nights in the old man's apartment.

"And these relatives speak English?" Ann asked.

"The grandson does."

"Thank God. Hungarian is impossible unless you hear it all the time. Which I didn't, growing up. My parents only spoke it to each other, only in private, like it was some big secret. I tell you—" Ann's voice cut out momentarily, came back in. "I didn't know you were flying through O'Hare. You should have arranged a stopover, spent a night or two with me."

Lisa grimaced. She glanced at the television news, which now showed a car on fire. "I have to get home for staff training."

"Same school, I assume? With the Catholics?"

"They're good people, Ann."

"I'll believe it when I quit hearing about pedophile priests. And when they pay you more. You need to find a different job, Lisa. You're not married anymore."

Oh, she knew. Lisa rubbed her back. "The plane's boarding now, Ann. Gotta go."

She could never sleep on planes. By the time her flight touched down in Seattle at nine p.m., Lisa had been awake for twenty-four hours. When her shuttle reached Tacoma, it had been almost twenty-six. She lugged her bags up the porch stairs to the entrance of the sub-divided house she'd moved into less than a month ago, then up another flight to her one-bedroom flat. Fishing her keys out of her purse, she let herself in and flipped on the light. Lisa looked around, blinking her gritty eyes in weary dismay. Unopened moving boxes cluttered the living room floor.

Unsorted mail covered the table. At the window a dry philodendron drooped.

Welcome home.

The next day she drove to St. Brendan's to prepare for the school year. The principal, Francie Russo, held the front door open as Lisa carried in a box of music. "Welcome back, Lisa!" she called. Francie had had her graying hair stylishly clipped and highlighted. It was a teacher pattern Lisa knew well: chic in September, frazzled by Christmas.

"There's a present for you in the music room," Francie said.

"Well, well! I can't wait."

Lisa walked down the hall, leaning in classroom doorways to call hello to the teachers setting up for the school year. She turned down the stairs to her basement-level music room and walked in the door. Carpeting!

Finally! Now the kindergarteners could sit cross-legged on the floor without their little rear-ends hurting. The third graders could do their circle dances, and if someone fell, no tears. The choir chairs wouldn't scrape. She'd hear the singers' voices, not their feet. Yes. Lisa kicked off her sandals and walked barefoot across the warm tan yarns.

She spent that day and the next attending meetings, pinning up charts in the music room, setting out xylophones and conga drums and choir chairs. She read through memos and reviewed her weekly class schedule. As with every year, she would teach the kindergartners through fifth graders twice a week, and she'd see the two middle school choirs daily. It was a frantic schedule. When she'd told Kristóf about it last week, he'd said she was riding five horses with one arse.

At the end of her second day of prep, she walked up the steep hill to Yakima Street, which ran behind the playground of St. Brendan's. At the crest she turned and looked back over the rooftops and trees, the streets sweeping down to Commencement Bay. The day was clear, the water churning strong blue, a freighter bearing through it. On the far side of the bay rose the hills of Vashon Island and northeast Tacoma, like the hills of Buda rising beyond the Danube. She lifted her phone and snapped a picture.

That night she wrote an email to Kristóf and attached the photo.

Wanted to let you two know I made it home okay. Here is a picture I took from the school where I teach. Please show Antal bácsi for me, and give him my thanks again for his hospitality.

I'm preparing for school next week, getting ready to ride five horses at once.

The time on her laptop said ten p.m. So it was seven a.m. in Budapest. On her last morning there, the sky over the opera house was vibrant. Was it like that again now? Was Varga making coffee? Would Kristóf stop by to see him? She felt an inner pang, as if homesick for a place that was not home.

SCHOOL BEGAN THE NEXT TUESDAY, and she had to re-introduce herself to the students. It was hardest with the eighth-grade choir, who'd known her longest.

"You're used to calling me Mrs. Fischer," she said. "I've had a name change. Please call me Ms. Denman now." She pointed to where she'd written it on the whiteboard.

They sat there in their uniforms, unusually quiet. Matt Hornsby raised his hand. "Why did you change your name?"

Jenna Ryan turned and glared at him. "Divorce, you dummy. Why do you think?"

"Jenna, that's enough," Lisa said.

A girl coughed. A boy said, "Whoa." Another girl said, "I thought Catholics weren't supposed to get divorced."

Matt's hand shot up again. "Yeah, is that okay? For Catholics to get divorced?"

Her husband wasn't a Catholic. He was a Lutheran who gave up, and this was too depressing to discuss with a roomful of thirteen-year-olds. "Class, we will not—"

"You guys!" Jenna blurted out. "Don't act like she's being a bad Catholic, because what if they fire her? Who wants that? Mrs. Fischer is a way better music teacher than at most schools. Have you heard about the music teacher over at St. Francis? She's—"

"Stop," Lisa ordered. She happened to know that the teacher at St. Francis was riding *nine* horses with one butt. "And I'm not Mrs. Fischer, I'm Ms. Denman. Now sit up straight for vocal warm-ups. And Matt, go spit out your gum."

Standing at the piano, striking keys for pitch, Lisa led them through scales. She checked their mouth position, listened to their tone. It was round and full. God bless them, they had remembered their technique.

"Right!" she yelled. "Good! Keep on going."

Keep going. It was what she'd been telling herself over and over.

THAT EVENING SHE SAT DOWN ON HER LIVING ROOM FLOOR with the eleven unopened boxes. The contents were leftovers, the things she hadn't urgently needed and Jake hadn't wanted. She and Jake had already divided up the furniture and the sale money from their old brick house. Neither of them had come away with much cash.

As she sorted through the boxes, she pushed things into three heaps: one for Goodwill, one for the dumpster, and one to keep. Towels, sheets, pans, candles, baskets, winter clothes, bric-a-brac, and a mind-numbing array of things she didn't have room for. The longer she worked, the more brutally she sorted.

Here was a box of books. She kept seven of them and shoved the rest aside. Except, wait, there was something else in the box, wrapped in a grocery bag. She reached for it, pulled back the wrapper. It was her wedding album.

She turned the pages of hopes now lost. There she was beside Wapato Lake, eight years ago at age twenty-four, slim bare shoulders, a white rose in her hair, face lit with pink lipstick and joy; and Jake in a gorgeous suit, twenty-six years old, smiling, slim, no glasses because he'd worn contacts back then, no stress lines across his forehead. It was hard, looking at the happily posed photos, but hardest were the candid shots that friends had taken after the wedding. In one, Jake spun her as they danced. In another, they kissed on the dock. A third was a view from the back as they crossed the parking lot, just married. She remembered that walk to the car. They climbed in and Jake said, "Let's take care of each other, Lise, because I want fifty years with you. Sixty."

Some divorced women questioned whether their husband had ever loved them. Lisa had never wondered. Jake had loved her. The unbearable question was when he had stopped.

Slowly she leafed back through the album and pulled out one photo: the two of them giving joyful high-fives to Jake's little niece. They were at their best then. Let this be what she'd keep and remember. She slipped the photo into an old journal. Then she took the album with its nearly full pages to the trash in the back alley.

But at the dumpster she bowed her head and crossed herself, because she was a Catholic and marriage was a sacrament, even marriage without a priest, without a Mass, even if everything fell apart. "Forgive me," she whispered, and dropped the album into the dumpster. Above, the half-moon shone yellow-white in the black sky.

Lisa went back inside and opened the one remaining carton, knowing what it contained. She pulled out the small metal box that had once held cough drops and now held a bit of ash. The note she'd taped to the top read "Alexander James Fischer, September 26, 2005." She and Jake had buried the urn with the ashes in Seattle beside Jake's grandmother, but this one small remainder she had saved. Lisa wrapped her hands around the box and closed her eyes. *Father, Son, and Holy Spirit.* She crossed herself once more, and afterward she carried the box to her bedroom closet and lifted it onto the high shelf.

That night Lisa sank into the bed she used to share with Jake and tossed her arm across his cold pillow. He was on the other side of town, asleep with a phys ed teacher who would give birth next month. Yes, he was gone. The months ahead, in all their emptiness, suddenly terrified her.

Keep on going.

The next morning during breakfast she checked her email. Kristóf had replied.

Hello Lisa,
Thank you for the photo of your city. I am a little jealous, I wish I see something so beautiful when I go to work. (Mostly I see traffic.)
Last night my grandfather and I drank the wine you gave us. It was good, and we clinked to you. Maybe you would like to know, my grandfather always is reading that music you brought. First he would not look at it, now he does not leave it alone. Write to us again.

She smiled a little. Two men toasting her: that hadn't happened in a long time. Lisa raised her coffee mug to them and again felt a twinge like homesickness, or whatever it was.

CHAPTER ELEVEN

Promises, Or Not

September 24, 2006

KRISTÓF WOKE ON A SATURDAY IN a tourist hotel, the sun glowing at the drapery edges. He watched with pleasure as the Spanish woman he'd slept with stepped out of the bathroom, long-legged, wrapped in a towel. She had come into Három Páva last night with a tour group and ordered schnitzel. That was how things started. Before bed she had taught him some Spanish words, but the only one he remembered now was *pierna*, leg. He wished she would drop that towel.

"Time to leave," she said in French, their common language. "I have to go downstairs for breakfast, then back on the bus."

"Stay here. Skip breakfast." He patted the bed.

She laughed. "Stop, stop."

He dressed reluctantly and walked downstairs with her. At the door to the breakfast room, they stopped.

"*Au revoir*, Inez," he said. "Thank you for last night."

She stepped away, looking back at him over her shoulder. "*Au revoir*, László."

"It's Kristóf!" he called after her. But she was gone.

She'd been his first Spaniard in a while. The women were usually Germans or Brits or, of course, Hungarians. He and his roommate Feri used to keep a bantering tally over beer of where their women came from, but the banter had dropped off now that Feri was stopping at two beers.

Kristóf walked home among the trees turning yellow and orange, leaving Váci Street and its restaurants, rental condos and shops meant for tourist money. About a month from now would be the fiftieth anniversary of Hungary's revolution against the Soviet Union. He had seen the city preparing for visitors, with workers tidying flower beds and yelling at people in Kossuth Square to get off the grass. Három Páva had sought extra kitchen help for that week.

When Kristóf stepped through the door of his apartment, he found Feri washing dishes, his newly spreading hair loss showing at the crown of his head. Kristóf joined him, wiping the dishes dry and stacking them in the tight cupboard.

"Where have you been?" Feri asked, in his pick-up-your-damned-clothes tone of voice.

"Hotel off Váci," Kristóf answered. As if it mattered. Since when did they keep track of each other?

Feri rinsed a shot glass. "I saw Juhász Zsófi yesterday at the market hall. Had a beer with her."

"Zsófi?" Kristóf hadn't seen her in at least a year and a half.

"Yes, her. Your old girlfriend."

"She wasn't really my girlfriend. We just—"

"Fucked around. What else is new?"

Kristóf threw the dish towel down on the counter and looked at Feri. "And we went places, and we did things together, and—"

"You took her places, you took her to bed, she fell in love with you, and you don't even call her your girlfriend?"

"She didn't fall in love with me."

"Yes, she did. She said so."

"Mother of God, how much beer did she drink?"

"Half a glass. Don't tell me you had no idea."

"I made her no promises."

"Well, she certainly sees that now."

Feri drained the dish water and stalked off to take a shower. Kristóf made some coffee for himself and sat down with it at the small table he and

Feri had bought at a flea market. What had gotten into his roommate? Feri was no saint, and God only knew neither was Zsófi.

Kristóf sipped the coffee, barely tasting it. He didn't like people acting as if he were some Don Juan, spoiling innocent women. They weren't innocent, and if they were, he left them alone. Just like he left married women alone. Always. He didn't pressure women, didn't make empty promises, and didn't skip the precautions. Things went fine. The women understood. Well, except Kovalchuk Blanka. That was harder, but that was quite a while ago. As for Zsófi, if she ever had any real feelings for him, it was news to him. She'd certainly never said so. Griping, yes; swearing, sometimes; but adoration? Hardly.

Kristóf flipped through the growing pile of mail on the table. He stopped when he came to an envelope with a German stamp. It was the letter from his mother, which his grandfather had handed to him on that rained-out night with Lisa. Kristóf picked it up and finally opened it.

Dear Kristóf,

I hope you'll take time off at Christmas this year and come visit. That's all I want for Christmas, my son with me. You haven't come to Stuttgart in four years. And I cannot come your direction. Our dog Elfi is getting old and I can't ask the neighbors to take care of her.

Klaus and I have made up the guest room very nice and you would be comfortable here. I wish you would come to Stuttgart to work and to live. You have no future at that restaurant. Germany has a better future than Hungary. Think about it, who is running the European Union?

There was more, something about how she was hoping for a promotion at her post office job. Kristóf skimmed the rest and dropped the letter, tired of this. If she had wanted him at age twenty-nine to answer her letters, then she should have answered the desperate pleas he wrote to her at age fourteen.

He grabbed his mobile phone and called Ópa. When his grandfather answered, music played in the background.

"This is Kristóf, and that's Beethoven's sixth."

"Very good."

"I had an email from Lisa yesterday," Kristóf said. "She has another question for you."

"Aren't we surprised."

"She asked about her grandfather, I can't remember his name."

"Sándor."

"Yes. Do you know when his mother died? And how?"

A pause. Beethoven played. "Autumn of '44." Beethoven again. "In a bombing raid."

"A bombing raid?"

"It wasn't good. It was after the Arrow Cross takeover. Night after night we ran to the basement because of the bombing. How much of this do you want to know?"

"All of it."

There was a longer gap. Ópa must have turned off the CD player, for Beethoven stopped.

"Well, then." Ópa's words came slowly. "So there we'd sit, cold and scared, with all this roaring and whizzing overhead, the floor shook, the air shook."

"Go on. I mean, what was it like?"

"Yes, all right, then one night there was this horrible whistling, very close, and then BANG, and the children started crying, and people were swearing and someone was saying the Hail Mary. I felt like a trapped animal and I wanted out of the cellar, but we had to wait and wait and wait for the all-clear signal."

Kristóf waited. "And then what happened?"

"Yes, and my father was very worried about Sándor and his mother and the optical shop, because the noise had come from that direction. So when the signal finally sounded, he ran out there, and I ran with him. It was middle of the night, but we could see, because half of Sándor's building was on fire. The other half was gone."

Kristóf sat with his lukewarm coffee and the letter from his mother, listening as Lisa's grandfather's world went up in smoke.

"And my father kept calling out for my aunt," Ópa said, "and I was yelling for Sándor and coughing from all the smoke and the sulphur. And then I heard Sándor screaming my name."

"My God, Ópa."

"Yes. Sándor wasn't injured, but his mother was dead. We had to lift a ceiling beam off her, and it took all night before we could get help from the police or the morgue. When we finally left, Sándor was so cold and in shock he could hardly stand up."

"Christ."

"So Sándor came and lived with us," Ópa said. "He moved into my bedroom, which I was already sharing with my grandfather, and Sándor and I made a promise we'd always look out for each other."

"Ah." Kristóf picked up his mother's letter, pitched it aside. How could anybody keep a promise for *always*? "That's hard, Ópa."

"But I tried."

THAT NIGHT AFTER WORK KRISTÓF WALKED to the neighborhood internet café. He logged into his email account, and after typing out *Hello Lisa,* he deliberated, wrote, deleted, and wrote again, telling her about the bomb, about her grandfather Sándor losing his mother and his home, and about his own grandfather's family taking Sándor in.

And they promised to keep each other safe always. I am sorry to tell you such sad things. Do you want that I keep asking my grandfather and telling you? Maybe this is too much.

Lisa's reply came the next day.

Thank you, Kristóf, for telling me, and please thank your grandfather, too. Yes, it's a hard story, but I would rather know than go on not knowing. I would rather understand. If it's not too much trouble, could you also ask him how my grandparents met?
Thanks again, Kristóf. You are kind.

Kristóf read her note twice and that last sentence twice more. Kind? She thought he was kind? Júhasz Zsófi wouldn't agree. Neither would his mother. He felt very tired, and he positioned the cursor to delete Lisa's message.

No, on second thought, keep it.

CHAPTER TWELVE

The Spanish Guitar

November 16, 1944

NOTHING STOPPED CHANGING. Antal's violin lessons ended. His father, now without his ophthalmic practice, went to work at the military hospital on Üllői Avenue. Sándor set up a cot every night in Antal's bedroom, orphaned and possessing nothing but the clothes he'd worn the night of the fire. Antal had opened his bureau and armoire and told Sándor to help himself, it was no big problem. The whole family had told Sándor for heaven's sake to make himself at home. Sándor thanked them, made the best of it, and seemed to hold himself together—until the Germans blew up the Margit Bridge and said it was an accident.

"That is an absolute, eternal lie," Sándor shouted, swiping away furious tears. "Have the Germans ever done anything by accident?" He threw out his hands. "No! They'll write up a master plan for every step of killing you and running your country into the ground, then they'll get it done and file the paperwork. Don't tell me they didn't intend to flatten the bridge."

That was early November. Now Sándor spent silent hours writing in a black notebook or staring out the window. For Antal this was the hardest change of all, seeing his once-effusive cousin so distant and morose. It was a godsend, then, when Antal's mother came home one afternoon from a music shop with a large object wrapped in her coat. She set it on the table. Antal and Katalin wandered over curiously. Sándor followed.

"Mr. Boros said it was too much trouble to sell," she said, "so you all can have it." She peeled back the coat.

"A guitar!" Katalin cried. She ran her hand over its scratched-up face and plucked the thickest string. Antal listened to its low vibration. Mother handed him an instructional book titled ¡Toca la Guitarra!

Sándor bent over the instrument. "Well, this is a lovely señorita." He carried the guitar to the piano bench. Antal and Katalin pulled up chairs and watched as Sándor spread his left hand deliberately on the neck. He strummed, and though the guitar was badly tuned, Antal recognized a D chord.

"You know how to play it?" Antal asked.

"Oh, a little."

The instruction book was written in Spanish. By looking at the pictures and guessing at the words, they found the note names of the strings and tuned them to the piano. Sándor formed a D chord again and hit the strings with his nails like a flamenco player. "Olé!"

Katalin tried out the chord, grinning, and passed the guitar to Antal. He positioned his fingers and strummed. The strings twanged. "Na, not olé."

Sándor laughed. Laughed. That hadn't happened since before the night of the bomb.

Antal adjusted his fingers and tried again. The guitar neck was so wide. Like a cello.

All right, then, he knew a cellist. He went to the telephone and dialed. "Márta. Varga Antal here. We're having a guitar party. I'll come get you."

SHE BROUGHT HER CELLO, TOO, AND he carried it as they left her building. The cold wind slapped them and tugged at Márta's scarf. Across the street at the train station, newly arrived German soldiers swarmed. Antal told Márta, admitting the truth, that this "party" was only his sister and his cousin and him.

"For me, it's a party," she said. "My sisters are squabbling, my father's always on the telephone, and I haven't gone anywhere in two weeks. So today's a party. How's your finger?"

"Better. Most of the time."

Arriving at his apartment, they found Katalin waiting for them. She introduced herself to Márta with delight, grasping her hand. "Oh, Márta, you'll like the guitar! It's fun, it's like in American cowboy movies."

Márta smiled. "Well, how can we resist that?"

"We aren't supposed to." It was Sándor voice. They turned, and he stepped forward, clutching the guitar neck. "Meet Señorita Guitar. She's quite the enchantress. And you must be Hanák Márta."

"This is my cousin Sándor," Antal told Márta.

"Ah. Hello, Sándor." Márta began unbuttoning her coat.

"I've read your father's newspaper columns," Sándor told her. "Most people would be afraid to say what he says."

Márta's hands went still on the buttons. "Being afraid is not the point."

"Absolutely, and that's why I'm glad your father told the truth. I just wish our fine news services hadn't cancelled his column."

"Yes. Well." Márta glanced uncertainly between Sándor and Antal. "Let's see how Señorita Guitar sings."

They gathered in the living room and Sándor handed Márta the guitar. Fascinated, she plucked its strings. Antal placed her strong, fine fingers for the D chord.

"Oh," she murmured, strumming it.

"Good job on that," Antal told her. "Better than me."

They passed the guitar from lap to lap, taking turns and trying out the chords diagrammed in the Spanish book. A contest evolved, and they voted on who played each chord best. Sándor usually won. Some chords he seemed to play almost without effort.

"It's not really fair," Katalin said happily. "Sándor's done it before. Who cares. Let's try something together. Maybe 'Erdő, Erdő, Erdő.'"

Sándor hummed the melody and tested different chords with it, then nodded to the group and said, "Let's try it in the key of G."

With Márta on cello, Antal on violin, and Sándor on guitar, they improvised on the old folksong of the forest, making mistakes and laughing. Antal waved the bow and shouted in rhythm, "Just-keep-go-ing," and Sándor shouting back, "This-is-cra-zy." Katalin tapped percussion on a sofa pillow.

The second time they played the song, Katalin began to sing. "Erdő,

erdő, erdő, marosszéki kerek erdő." Márta looked up, startled. Antal had seen this before, how the pure sheen of his sister's voice took people aback.

They continued through the song and repeated it. On the closing lines Antal lifted his bow off the strings and signaled Sándor to hold up. In Katalin's voice and the cello's undercurrent, the song became sunlight in the forest.

"My God," Sándor whispered. "It's beautiful." When the girls stopped, Sándor asked them to do the last part again.

"*Érted faj a szívem nagyon,*" Katalin sang of the heart aching.

The cello wove dark beauty around the ache. Antal listened to the girls, but his gaze flickered to Sándor, who sat with his eyes closed. With a choked gasp, Sándor suddenly stood up. He handed the guitar off to Katalin and rushed out of the room. In anxious confusion, Márta stopped playing.

"Sometimes," Katalin told her quietly, "everything just hits him."

When Antal walked Márta home, he told her what had happened to Sándor's family. "Some days we know to leave him alone. He goes in the bedroom, shuts the door, writes in this black notebook of his. Other days he seems all right, but then something happens—some memory or I don't know what—and all of a sudden, it's too much."

"That has to be hard on you," Márta said.

"Not half as hard as it is on him."

She slipped her mittened hand into the bend of his elbow, and as they walked he confided that he and Katalin had fed a Gypsy. "And I hate it, the way it's against the law to be humane."

Dusk was approaching when they entered her building and went through the interior corridor to her apartment. At her door, she pulled off her mittens and faced him, her eyes soft. "Antal, I really liked this. Let's do it again."

He held her hands between his. "We will."

THAT NIGHT HIS FATHER AND GRANDFATHER SUMMONED HIM and Sándor into the bedroom. Grandpapa shut the door. Papa told them that the Soviet army was drawing closer to the city and had begun arriving in some of the farther suburbs. Reports from the east were very bad, stories of Soviet soldiers looting and brutalizing and raping whole villages.

"This is not just Nazi propaganda," Grandpapa said. "It's real."

"Once the Soviets get here, Katalin will not go out by herself," Papa stated. "I'm counting on your help with this. Either go with her, or make her stay home."

Mouth dry, Antal promised his help. Sándor said he'd already thought about this and would do whatever he could.

"We understand each other, then," Papa said, and soon he left the room with Grandpapa.

Sándor turned to Antal. "I assume you'll also be looking out for Márta."

"Yes."

A silence stretched between them.

"Lovely girl," Sándor said.

Their eyes met, and then Sándor looked away.

CHAPTER THIRTEEN

Watchfulness

October 9, 2006

TWO WEEKS FROM NOW, ON OCTOBER 23, it would be the fiftieth anniversary of Hungary's uprising against the Soviet Union, and in four weeks it would be the fiftieth anniversary of the death of Varga's daughter Zsuzsanna. Whatever ceremonies the city was planning for the twenty-third, Varga was wary of the tumult and probably would not attend. Recently, right-wing demonstrators had gathered at the state television building to protest the left-wing prime minister, Gyurcsány Ferenc, who'd lied during his campaign. The lies were caught on tape and Varga had no doubt of the PM's guilt. However, he suspected that the right-wing favorite, Orbán Viktor, had done his share of truth-stretching and may even have stirred up this gang. Wherever the fault lay, the right-wingers' demonstration had ended up as a riot, and they'd been camping out in Kossuth Square since then.

So on the twenty-third, Varga would stay home. Both of his living children had spoken of coming to Budapest for the remembrances. He'd told his daughter Gabriella to please come some other time.

On a cold evening his son Zoltán telephoned. Varga sat down in the kitchen, rubbing his violin shoulder as they talked. He'd taken his beta blockers and was used to ignoring the shoulder ache if it wasn't too bad, but tonight it seemed worse and extended farther along his arm. Tonight Zoltán, like Gabriella, said that he wanted to come to town for the ceremonies.

"I can't recommend the show," Varga said. "Crowd, police, good Lord."

"I admit, mainly I want to see my son."

This invariably happened, the conversation turning to Kristóf. "All right, then come."

"How is he?" Zoltán asked. "Still messing around with foreign women, I suppose."

How the family had come to know about this, Varga couldn't remember. They just knew. "He doesn't give me the details," Varga said. "I don't want them."

"Neither do I. I just wish Krisz would grow up, find a better job, and find a woman who'll actually do him some good."

"From your lips to God's ears."

"Sometimes I wish I could do everything over," Zoltán said. "Things started off hard with Kristóf, and they never got any easier."

Varga shifted on his chair, trying to ease the pressure in his back. He seldom knew what to say when his son spoke this way. The truth was, things had started off hard in Zoltán's life, too. If Varga could go back and beat off the shadow that had overhung his son's early years, he would do it, many times over.

"I think we all wish for a second chance," Varga said.

"At what point will that stop? Kristóf's twenty-nine, and I still wish I could mend things."

"You've tried."

They had both tried.

"Good thing you're there," Zoltán said. "You seem to be the only person he listens to."

"You think he listens to me?"

"I hope so."

Soon they hung up, and Varga wandered into the living room, glancing at his wife's photo. She had loved Kristóf so. Varga still missed Ildikó, especially in the evenings, but he didn't speak to others of the lingering emptiness. There was no point. It wasn't a problem anyone could solve. He put on a Mussorgsky CD.

The phone rang again. This time it was Kristóf, asking if he could spend the night. Varga told him yes, and soon Kristóf appeared with his shaving kit, a carton of milk and a bottle of wine.

"Feri has a girl over," Kristóf said, by way of explaining his presence here. "And that's some Russian composer, I don't know which."

"Mussorgsky. And the understanding was that you would leave? It's your apartment as much as Feri's."

"It's awkward. He's with a girl I used to see. So. Here I am."

Varga massaged his violin shoulder and uncorked the wine. Kristóf went into the living room and began plunking around on the piano, playing a satirical old piece that Sándor wrote, which had arrived in that stack of Lisa's. "Jackboots," Sándor had called it. Varga couldn't remember what had inspired Sándor to write it, maybe a Nazi parade.

"Am I playing this right?" Kristóf called.

"More left hand on the downbeat. Heavy."

Varga filled a glass for Kristóf but only poured half a glass for himself; he was tired tonight. He carried the glasses into the front room, set one on the coffee table for Kristóf and sat down in his arm chair with the other. "And you pound the melody. *Molto staccato.*"

Kristóf pounded.

"We also had a Russian version of that march," Varga said. "Same thing, just drunker."

"That I can do."

Kristóf let his fingers land crosswise on the keys, jabbed his fist down and finally crashed both elbows onto the keyboard. Varga laughed.

"Before I forget," Kristóf said, "Lisa wanted me to ask you how her parents met."

Varga held his wine glass still. "I introduced them."

"I'll tell Lisa you were her grandparents' matchmaker."

"All I said was that I introduced them. Look, the wine is poured. Are we going to drink it or not?"

Kristóf came to the sofa and sat down, stretching a leg across the cushions. He lifted his wine glass toward Varga. "*Egészégünkre!*" As he drank, he talked about a sous-chef at Három Páva being fired for not showing up. Varga watched his grandson's face: the dark eyes like his mother's, the perfect jaw, the finest rendition of the Varga family's strong brow, the beauty that would erode with time and strain. He thought of his handsome son, Zoltán, whom life had not treated softly.

"Well, I'm glad you joined me tonight," Varga said, "not so happy to hear that your roommate threw you out."

"He didn't throw me out. But maybe the girl wanted to."

"And you say this was someone you used to see?"

"Oh, for a little while." Kristóf waved his hand. "When I split up with her, I didn't think it was any big deal. Now, according to Feri, she thinks I was a heartless dick."

"Were you?"

"Will Feri be a heartless dick when he splits up with her? Things don't last forever. What does the girl expect?"

"Obviously she expected more than she got." Zoltán's worries came back to Varga, worries that he himself shared. "Don't you ever get tired of this, running through women like groceries?"

Kristóf drained his glass. "Ópa, don't tell me you never had a little fun."

"I was married when I was twenty-three."

"But before then, you didn't—?" He shrugged.

Varga loosened his collar. His neck felt tense. "Think about it, Krisz. What good is all this bed-hopping doing you? You need a woman who knows you, who loves you."

"That's what my father thought he had, and look what happened."

"That's a topic for another night." Varga set aside his glass. "Have you ever protected a woman?"

"The women I know don't act like they want that."

"They might want it more than you think. Would you like more wine?"

"Please."

Varga pushed himself up from the chair. He picked up Kristóf's glass, carried it to the kitchen, placed it on the counter, lifted the wine bottle in his right hand and steadied the glass with his left—

His face flashed hot. Pain shot through his chest and back, ran down his arm, knifed open his fingers. The glass fell and shattered.

Then Kristóf's voice—"Ópa!"

Varga braced himself on the counter.

Kristóf came running. "Ópa! My God, what's wrong?"

"My arm," Varga rasped. "My chest—"

"Oh, Christ, no." Kristóf slung his arm around him. "Lean on me. Ópa! Fuck it, I said lean on me!"

Kristóf dragged him to a kitchen chair. Varga sank into it. He heard Kristóf pounding buttons on the telephone. And all went black.

Chapter Fourteen

Memo

October 9, 2006

LISA'S LUNCH BREAK WAS ENDING when she noticed an email from Kristóf on her classroom computer. She read it, her breath tightening:

Lisa,

Tonight my grandfather's heart wrecked up. I was with him when he fell down. I called the ambulance doctor and rode along. It was terrible, Ópa was white and silent and the bloody siren kept screaming.

He is in hospital now. I am waiting while they make some kind of surgery in him, and we are lucky that they had the gadget he needed because sometimes they don't. I type this to you on the old junk computer in the wait room. I called my father and he called my aunt, and they will come. I don't know when. The hospital workers keep asking questions to me, does he take medicines, who is his doctor, and I cannot answer. Always my grandfather has been strong. Never he says what to do if he is not.

I hope to God he will get well because this city would be nothing but shit without him. Pardon the way I say this. Sorry I go on and on, but I am nervous. Sorry I cannot tell you anything happy right now.

—Kristóf

P.S. I asked Ópa how your grandparents met. He said he introduced them, that is all he said.

Lisa heard sixth graders in the hallway and knew they'd arrive any moment. She wanted to tell Kristóf that people often survived heart attacks, but since her baby's death, she seldom spoke of beating the odds.

Kristóf, I am so sorry, she typed.

The first student strode through the door, his backpack slung over one shoulder.

She kept typing, faster now. *I'm at school—I'll write more later—*

Two girls walked into the classroom.

But I think that when your grandfather isn't strong, you will be.

CHAPTER FIFTEEN

Second Chances

October 10, 2006

Varga hadn't really been sleeping, just drowsing, so tired, under a light blanket. His arm felt sore. The air smelled of bleach or urine or antiseptic. Something beeped and someone moaned. Varga blinked. A curtain surrounded his bed, and where it gapped, he saw a nurse.

A nurse. Oh, God, no. This was a hospital.

Hearing footsteps, Varga turned his head. The curtain was pushed aside—more beds, more curtains behind it—and two men in hospital scrubs stepped in. Now what?

They stood over him in their green medical caps. The one on the left said, "Édesapa." Sweet father.

Relief flooded through him. "Zoli. Kristóf." He was not alone.

"Ópa, you scared us to death," Kristóf said.

Varga coughed to strengthen his voice. "Sorry, I'm not sure, what happened?"

Zoltán touched Varga's shoulder. "Last night you had a heart attack."

"Good Lord. Another one." How long had it been since the first one? Eight years? Overhead a light shone cold. "And this is not the afterlife."

"No." Kristóf laughed a little uneasily.

"What did they do, these doctors here?" Varga asked.

"There's an incision in your arm," Zoltán said. "You probably feel it."

"Yes." Varga shifted uncomfortably and waited for his son to go on. Since Zoltán worked in a hospital, Varga always counted on him to explain things the doctors did not.

"The doctors put in a stent through that incision," Zoltán said. "It's up near your heart, to open the blocked vein. There's been some damage to your left ventricle, but at least you probably won't feel so winded now."

Varga groaned.

"You had a close call last night, Apa," Zoltán went on. "It's a good thing Kristóf was with you. On your own, you might have died."

Varga tried to remember. He had dropped a glass. Then Kristóf came running.

These two looked so worried, with their wrinkled foreheads and unshaven chins. He tried to smile. "A hell of a night for you two, while I slept through it."

"I'm just glad you woke up," Kristóf said. "Listen, Ópa. We brought you some food—rolls, paté, juice, crackers. Also soap and toilet paper and all that. It's at the nurses' station, and don't let them tell you they don't have it. We'll bring more food tomorrow."

"And we're giving envelope money to the surgeon and the head nurse," Zoltán added pointedly, "and we're not going to let you be ignored."

Varga lay back on the lumpy pillow, trying not to listen to the moans beyond the curtain. "I want to go home," he said.

THE NEXT DAY AN ORDERLY WHEELED VARGA to a smaller room. A little later Varga's daughter Gabriella arrived from Geneva and brought a CD player. She hugged him and settled into a chair at his bedside. As Sibelius's second symphony played, she talked to him of her piano students and her family.

"Bálint will be soloing with the Orchestre de la Suisse Romande," she said of her husband. "Mozart's oboe concerto."

"Impressive. Congratulate him for me." Varga began to lift his arm, but the incision hurt. "And your girls?"

"They're fine, Apa. Marie will finish university in the spring. Lili's not far behind her."

"And still playing violin?"

"Oh, yes."

At fifty-three, Gabriella's gentle face was beginning to crease, and her hair, red-blond like her mother's, beginning to gray. Of the two children he'd raised, Gabriella had been the easier, the one who'd heeded warnings, the one who went to university, got married and became a parent all in the right order. Seeing her gave Varga peace. Sometime near the end of the Sibelius symphony, with Gabriella beside him, he slept.

THE FOLLOWING DAY, THE HOSPITAL PERMITTED Varga to leave. Gabriella rode home in the taxi with him and chatted with the driver about the upcoming 1956 remembrances. "I hear that on the Erzsébet Bridge they're hanging huge flags with the middle cut out," she said.

"Enormous," the driver agreed.

Varga kept quiet. The revolution: the flags with gaping holes where furious Hungarians had slashed out the communist star; the bullets, the screaming, the Soviet tanks. The streets became blackened with smoke and coagulated blood, a heinous replay of the siege of '45.

"Gabriella, stay away from the commemorations," he said, though he'd already told her. "There's too much frenzy going about."

"I know, Édesapa."

Gabriella said she'd stay with him that week. On her first day with him, she made phone calls to his violin students for him, explaining that he'd need to postpone lessons for a while. On her third afternoon there, since the hospital had told him to do no heavy lifting, he pointed out to her the large collection of handwritten music on the bottom bookshelf, and she carried it to the coffee table for him. He sat down on the sofa, and while Gabriella played Scarlatti on the piano, he began sorting through these pieces he'd composed over the decades. He gave each a cursory glance, occasionally more. Most were short studies for bowing technique or left-hand fingering. Many he'd marked with a student's name: "For Varkonyi István." "For Rónay Margit." With each piece, he had given the student a copy and kept one for himself. At this point there were a couple hundred. He sorted them into two piles: *Keep*, and *Throw Out*. He finished sorting an hour and a half later, the *Out* stack much the taller. It was a melancholy endeavor, for he was doing it to spare his children the trouble after he died—which might not be so far off.

His children might want the *Keep* stack as a kind of historical record, a family album. Varga leafed slowly through the sheets. There was an elegy he'd composed on the death of composer Kodály Zoltán, and a tribute to the dismantling of the Berlin Wall, with a nod to Gorbachev. He found a piano-and-violin duet he'd written for Gabriella and her daughter Lili. There were pieces he'd written on the deaths of his parents, on his wife's fortieth birthday, and for his sister Katalin's wedding in a farm village. Katalin was gone now after several bouts of pneumonia two years ago, and Varga's sadness over her death still came in sudden jabs. Her husband, Péter, was having a rough time of it. Péter had telephoned yesterday to wish him a quick recovery.

Varga shuffled through a few more pages. He stopped at one marked "For Zoltán and Mónika, 1976 October." It had been so difficult to write this waltz for his son's wedding. Zoltán was twenty and scared, his bride tired and pregnant. Things hadn't worked out. Varga set the waltz reluctantly on the *Out* pile. But he kept the next piece, written five months later: "On the birth of Varga Antal Kristóf, my first grandchild, 1977 March."

He turned to the next sheet and looked up. Gabriella had left the piano and was working in the kitchen. That was just as well. Varga laid his hand on the piece, a short capriccio, perhaps the most playful thing he'd ever written: "To Zsuzsanna, three months old, in celebration of her smiles, 1956."

His tiny second daughter, with her black hair and wide eyes, Zoltán's twin: almost from the beginning Varga could swear she knew him, looked for him from her crib, expected him. When he sang to her, she flung her arms for joy. Whenever she cried, she would quiet for no one but him. His wife was the first to notice that. "Antal, look how she insists on you," Ildi had said. "All she wants is her daddy."

He knew this daughter by touch, by sound. In November of '56 when the streets blasted and flared, it was he who noticed her hot cheeks, he who first heard the change in her cry, he who walked the floor with her in the hospital emergency room crammed with those who had been shot or shelled. Ildi ran from nurse to doctor to nurse, pleading, "Our baby is an emergency, too! Help her!" And it was he who held Zsuzsanna while Ildi in final despair dipped her fingers in a glass of water and placed them on the dying child's head: "Zsuzsanna, I baptize you . . ." Then his daughter was gone. Beyond the shaking windows, gunfire cracked.

These fifty years later, Varga rubbed his hurting incision. He laid Zsuzsanna's song back on the *Keep* stack. Some things you kept because you wanted to, others you kept because they would not let go.

LATER THAT DAY HALMOS STOPPED BY to visit. Gabriella served them lemonade at the table and then excused herself to buy groceries. Varga did his best to tell Halmos what had happened.

"So, a second heart attack," Halmos said. "Thank God Kristóf was here. And how long is Gabriella going to stay?"

"A few more days. After that—oh, I don't know. Kristóf will look in, I suppose."

Halmos frowned. "Is that enough?"

"I think so. I'm taking a break from teaching for a few weeks. God only knows what I'll do in this tedium."

Halmos ran a hand over his gray mustache. "I've said it before, but think about taking another look at the ending to your *Embers Suite*. I've revised the final measures on a few of my own pieces. There's something about rewriting the ending that changes the way you see the whole thing."

"I don't know that it's worth re-opening."

"It is, Varga," Halmos said, his face troubled.

That night Varga showed Gabriella the music he'd sorted and asked her to throw out the larger pile. She didn't want to, which he should have expected. Gabriella was sentimental.

"People in the family might want the smaller pile, though," Varga said.

"We *do* want it." Her gaze was steady, like her mother's. "And also that music that the cousin from America brought. You won't get rid of it, will you?"

He heard himself saying, "It doesn't belong to me."

"Then whose is it?"

"Sándor's."

"Who?"

Varga shook his head. *This damned medication.* "I mean, I think Kristóf wants it."

"So do I." She reached for his hand. "Zoli and I would feel better about things if someone were living here with you. What if you have another problem?"

"Gabriella, I'm seventy-eight. I'm already on my second chance. And I'm glad to have it, but do I really need a third and a fourth?"

She pressed her lips together and turned away.

WHEN GABRIELLA LEFT, KRISTÓF CAME TO spend the night. Varga carefully poured brandy for Kristóf and orange juice for himself. "Kristóf—" It was difficult to continue. "I'm not sure I ever properly thanked you for calling the ambulance that night."

"And did I thank you for *not dying*?"

His grandson's eyes looked scared. Varga had been able to tell Gabriella that his days would run out and enough would be enough. But he couldn't say it to Kristóf.

CHAPTER SIXTEEN

Sacrifices

October 20, 2006

"GOOD WORK TODAY, SECOND GRADERS!" Lisa gave a thumbs-up to the children sitting cross-legged on the music room carpet, some with xylophones in front of them, some holding hand drums. "Our time is up, so as I call your names, go put your instruments away and line up at the door. Nice and quiet. Noah, Bella, Danny, go ahead."

The school day had ended, and the children left with their classroom teacher. As Lisa put away the day's music, the principal appeared in the doorway. Lisa waved her in.

"I should tell you something," Francie said, "before you hear it through the grapevine."

Lisa stood still. This must be about Jake. He used to coach here, still had friends here.

"Jake's baby was born night before last," Francie told her. "A boy."

"Healthy?"

"Yes."

So Jake's new wife had managed it—a child, a living boy. Lisa reached for her purse. "I have to leave. An appointment."

IT HAD BEEN ALMOST A YEAR SINCE she'd been here in the OBGYN office for the postpartum check after Alexander's birth and death. Now she was back. Lisa sat up on the same examining table, naked except for a paper gown. Dr. McCartney had just finished probing. The stout doctor pulled off her latex gloves and reviewed the form Lisa had filled out. Lisa caught a glimpse of her own scribbled handwriting in answer to the question about pain during intercourse. "No sex now," she'd written. "Marriage ended."

Dr. McCartney set the form on a countertop. "I'm sorry about your divorce. It isn't uncommon. Loss of a child places a terrible strain on a marriage."

"I found that out."

"Listen, I have to bring this up. You've had four miscarriages, and your endometriosis isn't improving. It may be time to consider a hysterectomy."

How hopeless. Lisa pulled the paper gown closer across her torso. "I'm not ready."

"Then I think we should get you back on the pill. It will help you feel better."

Lisa stared into her paper-covered lap. The pill had been in and out of her life since she was fifteen. Now she'd be popping tablets out of the little cycle pack again as if she had a man. What could be lonelier at this point than taking the pill?

"All right," she told the doctor in defeat.

That night she wrote in her journal.

Horrible day. Dysfunctional body, back on the pill even though I'm alone. Meanwhile in Jake-ville, there's a new baby boy.

She wandered to her electronic keyboard, where the Varga music lay stacked on top. She might as well take another look at it. Using her headphones to keep things quiet for her neighbors, Lisa played through some of the songs. She repeated "*A fény ragyog a sötétségben*" five times, its tenderness seeping into her. Kristóf had said the title meant "The light shines in the darkness." The melody was beautiful, its message crucial. Maybe she could set the song in English and adapt the harmonies for her eighth-grade choir. Yes, she'd try it.

The next afternoon, a Saturday, she worked on the song at the piano in her classroom. She tried out ideas and experimented, caught up in the possibilities, not checking the clock. Finally she glanced out the window and saw darkness. Time had escaped her.

With the yellowed music in her tote bag, she dashed to her car and drove almost an hour to a Methodist church in Seattle. She'd heard that a Hungarian-American group was hosting a fiftieth anniversary remembrance there of the 1956 revolution. Arriving a little late, Lisa hurried to the darkened basement as people on folding chairs watched a black-and-white documentary. She slipped into the back row, whispering "Excuse me" to the elderly woman beside her.

On the flickering screen, demonstrators marched through gray Budapest streets. Citizens read out demands for free elections, evacuation of Soviet troops, freedom of the press, trials for hated leaders, and the list went on. Flags with huge holes in the middle fluttered from balconies and apartment windows.

Above a sea of faces in a crowded square, a bespectacled man stepped out warily onto a balcony. The crowd cheered.

The elderly woman tapped Lisa's arm. "That decent man is Imre Nagy. A leader with a brain and a heart. You will see what happens."

Shots blasted.

The film rolled on: guns in the hands of teenagers, factory workers, students, women; the wounded lying on sidewalks; Soviet tanks in the streets. Imre Nagy sent a frantic plea to the world—"Help Hungary!"—in the last moments of radio access. Hungarians wept and thousands fled the country. In the end, Imre Nagy was hanged.

The church hall lights came on, and a man with a microphone stood in front near a Hungarian flag. He announced that those who had memories of the revolution could share them. "But keep it short," he said. "There are about seventy of us here tonight."

The woman next to Lisa pushed herself up from her chair. "All I want to say," she shouted, "is, I had to leave because I was a student and they were rounding up students. I had to get out from Hungary or I would go to prison. That was how it was." She sat down.

Others of her age rose one by one. In their accented voices the people recalled the smell of blood and the wail of ambulances. A woman told of doing sentry watch from a university window. A man told of learning to shoot, and to kill, when he was fourteen. Five people described their desperate escape from Hungary at the end. One of them, choking up as she spoke, told of losing her little brother on the way out; he drowned in a swamp near the Austrian border.

Another woman rose and shouted, "And what did America do to help? Nothing! On Radio Free Europe, on Voice of America, they said, 'Good for you, Hungary! You're so brave!' But did help arrive? No."

An old man on a side aisle stood up shakily. "I was just a boy, but in my village near Yugoslavia I saw Russian soldiers rape our neighbor. Seven or eight men, one poor woman."

"Stop, András *bácsi*," a man near him said.

"They had her up on a wagon," András *bácsi* went on, "and they took turns holding her down—"

"András!" the woman next to Lisa shouted. "There are kids here!"

András sat down.

Lisa's neighbor leaned in. "I'm sure he saw that rape, but it was probably 1945. End of the war. Year of the rapes."

Lisa's jaw tensed. Her grandparents had left halfway through that year.

The testimonies went on. The topic seemed to have shifted to World War II. A man took the microphone and said he was a child in the Jewish ghetto during the war. "And most of my family members were killed, either at Auschwitz or in death marches. Say what you will about the Russians, but if they hadn't liberated Budapest, I'd be dead, too."

"They 'liberated' everything my family owned!" a woman shouted back.

A young woman waved her hand. "My uncle says Hungary was very anti-Semitic," she called out. "Is that true?"

"No!" bellowed a woman. "People all over Budapest hid Jews during the war."

The Jewish man who still held the microphone said resignedly, "And others turned us in." He handed off the microphone and sat down.

An embarrassed silence filled the room. A man with a fringe of white hair sat down at a spinet piano, and the people sang a slow anthem. Three scouts in green neckerchiefs retired the Hungarian flag. People began leaving their seats.

Lisa's neighbor turned to her again. "So who are you? Are you Hungarian?"

"My grandparents were Hungarian. My name is Lisa Denman. I'm a music teacher."

"Ah. Then you should meet Kálmán. Come with me. Are you hungry?"

"Well, yes, I didn't have dinner—"

The woman beckoned impatiently. She led Lisa to a table of finger foods, most of which looked no more Hungarian than the snack spreads at St. Brendan's.

"Eat," the woman said. "I'll be back."

Lisa filled a paper plate with cheese and crackers and sat down at a vacant table, feeling like a displaced person as conversations went on around her in Hungarian. Soon enough the woman returned with the piano player. "Here is Professor Barcza," the woman said, and left.

The man sat down with his snack plate. "Call me Kálmán. Well, I see you met Judit. In spite of that, I hope you've had a good evening. I understand you're a music teacher."

While Kálmán Barcza ate an Oreo, Lisa told him about her Hungarian grandfather who tuned pianos but also wrote songs, and her grandmother who played cello long ago. Lisa added, "Just two months ago in Budapest I met my grandfather's cousin, a professional violinist. I inherited some songs he wrote with my grandparents, back at the end of the war."

"They must have been very young," Kálmán said, his gaze roving the hall.

"Teenagers."

Maybe the man wasn't much interested, but she opened her bag anyway and handed "The Light Shines" to him. "Here's one of the songs. I want to adapt it for my choir students. I know the title means 'The light shines in the darkness,' but there are some other words I don't know."

He took a cursory look. "The rest means that the darkness did not, oh, what to say, did not extinguish it. Nice quote, maybe from the Bible." He began to hand the music back, then looked again, bent over it and studied. "Just a minute."

Kálmán went to the piano and played the melody, ignoring the people who turned to listen. He grabbed the music and strode back to her. "I heard this on Radio Budapest once."

"What?"

"Yes. Only once, when I was a kid. But I remember it because my sister was so taken with it, she kept trying to sing it. Did your relatives tell you this song was on the radio?"

"No." The more she found out, the more she realized how little she'd been told.

"Well, if you write a choral arrangement, tell me. Our group here has a little choir. We might want to use it, if you don't mind." He handed Lisa the music, then his business card, and looked at her earnestly. "This is very interesting."

When she got home late that night, an email had come in from Kristóf.

Hello Lisa,

My grandfather is better, I think. Today he is in bad humor because he does not like so much to rest. Also I try to cook for him like the hospital said, less lard, less salt, more leaves, and he is not used to it. He says he is Magyar and not a Frenchman or a sheep.

Thank you for your comment, that you think I will be strong if he is not. I don't know where you get this idea, but it is nice.

Sometimes on his piano I play that music you brought.

On Monday my father and I will go to the ceremonies about the anniversary of the 1956 revolution. My grandfather does not want to come, and probably this is best.

—*Kristóf*

P.S. I know I have English mistakes. You may correct me if you want to.

Too wound up to head for bed, Lisa wrote back. She said she'd never had any trouble understanding his English, but he could try using more contractions. She told him about the meeting tonight, about the film and the people's heartbreaking stories, and then about Kálmán Barcza saying he'd heard "The Light Shines" on the radio.

On the radio! What in the world?! Ask your grandfather about it. And please tell him I'm thinking of him. I'm glad that he's well enough to argue with you. That sounds like progress.

—*Lisa*

She hesitated.

P. S. Remember I told you that my ex-husband's new wife was pregnant? The baby was born this week. A boy.

Another hesitation.

Maybe it shouldn't have been hard news, but it was.

Chapter Seventeen

Injuries

October 22, 2006

THE DAY BEFORE THE BUDAPEST COMMEMORATIONS, Kristóf broke a year's silence and wrote back to his mother. He sent a paper letter. If he sent an email, she would turn around and flood his inbox.

Mutti,

My grandfather tells me that you keep writing to him and calling him, trying to reach me. Stop. He was in hospital recently with a heart attack.

Regarding visiting you at Christmas, I can't. The restaurant fills up with tourists, and the only person who gets days off is my boss. And anyway, Ópa will probably need help.

Later—
Kristóf

AFTER WORKING THE LUNCH SHIFT, KRISTÓF dropped the letter into a postal box and jumped on his bicycle. He spent the rest of the day pedaling in the Buda Hills. Heading home that night, all he wanted was a shower and, before too long, bed. But when he entered the apartment, there on the sofa in a short skirt sat Juhász Zsófi—his old girlfriend of sorts, who was now his roommate's girlfriend and showed up whenever she felt like it.

"What are you doing here?" he asked, not bothering to mask his irritation. "Did Feri give you a key?"

She frowned. "He let me in. And thank you for the lovely greeting."

Zsófi threw back her smooth dark hair, which he used to like to play with, and crossed her legs, exposing her thighs, which he also used to like. She was a pretty woman when she wasn't glaring at him. The television bantered on.

"You're staying, I assume," he said. "I was hoping to sleep in the bedroom for a change."

Zsófi rose and clicked off the television. "My God, Kristóf, every time I come over here, you make me feel about as welcome as a flea infestation. What's wrong with you?"

He strode into the kitchen and pitched his keys on the table.

"Come on," she called. "Feri doesn't throw a fit when you bring somebody home."

He grabbed a glass out of the cupboard and filled it at the sink.

She followed him into the kitchen. "What's going on? Is this something left over from the—what was it?—five or six weeks that we were together? It's not as if I left you for Feri. That was more than a year ago. And as far as that goes, it was you that quit, not me."

Kristóf drained his water glass. "See Feri all you want, that's your business and his, I don't care. But I'm damned if I liked finding out that you told Feri all about how I hurt your feelings and treated you like last week's trash. Because I didn't. We had a good time, we parted ways, and that was all."

"That's exactly it. 'We parted ways, and that was all.' That's the way you are. 'That's all.' 'Thanks, that was nice.' 'See you later. Oh, actually, I won't see you later.' So yes, my feelings were hurt! How could they not be?"

"How was I supposed to know you had any feelings for me? You never said that."

"Kristóf." She shook her head, open-mouthed. "If I had said 'I love you,' you would have walked straight out. You'd have run."

"You don't know that."

"But it's true."

"I don't know if it's true or not. No one's ever said it to me."

She dropped her hand onto the counter. "No one *can* say that to you. You don't let them."

He picked up his keys off the table. "Good night."

Outside, he pulled out his phone and called his grandfather. "Ópa. I'm coming over."

"Kristóf? Are you all right?"

"I thought I was, but nobody else seems to think so. Could I spend the night?"

"Zoltán's here. I mean, your father. The sofa's taken."

"The floor, then, if Vati's on the sofa."

"All right. See you soon."

Kristóf closed his phone. Vati was in town. Good. The last time he visited, they'd gowned up to check on Ópa in intensive care. Hopefully this visit would be less catastrophic.

Kristóf still reproached himself for the fury with which he used to lash out at Vati during those terrible months after Mutti left. Thank God he'd finally stopped biting the hand that was trying to feed him, finally caught on that only an asshole would tear down the tired man who'd been holding him up. Yes, there was this necessary thing called loyalty.

He slipped the phone into his pocket and left for Ópa's apartment.

THE NEXT AFTERNOON KRISTÓF AND HIS FATHER headed out on foot toward Parliament and Kossuth Square for the remembrance ceremonies. Ópa stayed home to watch them on television.

"I heard the police threw a bunch of protesters off the square this morning," Vati said, "so they wouldn't get in the way of all the foreign dignitaries. Somebody said there was also a big anti-Gyurcsány rally down at Déak Square."

"Those people have been protesting for weeks. They hate the prime minister."

He walked with his father toward Parliament. The crowds increased, jostling, bumping, stopping, and pushing. Down the street, people yelled.

And they yelled louder. Somewhere a police siren screamed, then another. A helicopter whirred overhead. Kristóf and his father were still blocks away from Parliament, and now they could barely move. Kristóf tried to push on, but the crowd in front did not give way.

"Quit pushing!" bellowed someone in front. "The police are blocking the street. Or the demonstrators—"

From the direction of Deák Square, a rhythmic chanting had begun: "Gyurcsány out! Gyurcsány out!" Kristóf stood on tiptoe. Marchers in the street carried huge letters that spelled out *SZABADSÁG*, freedom. Other demonstrators followed, one of them carrying an odd flag with green arrows—

Good God. The old Arrow Cross flag.

A bottle went flying. The crowd shoved. A girl behind him screamed. A man shouted that the fuckers were throwing paving stones, but Kristóf didn't know which fuckers. He took a step back but stumbled over a woman's feet. Somebody yelled something about rubber bullets.

"Can you see what's happening?" he shouted at his father.

"Those protesters are trying to duck behind their signs," Vati called back. "The police are shooting off water cannons."

"Oh, shit."

Kristóf felt his cell phone vibrate. It would be Ópa, no question. As he reached for his pocket, his father shouted, "Look out!" and yanked Kristóf's arm.

But something slammed Kristóf's head. Pain exploded. Kristóf grabbed his scalp and pulled his hand away full of broken glass and blood. His phone vibrated once more and stopped.

Vati tore off his coat and pressed it to Kristóf's head. "Get out of the way!" he roared at the people around them. Somehow the crowd parted, and Kristóf walked, gripping his father's coat to his skull. Blood ran down his neck.

"Can you keep on walking?" his father shouted over the ruckus.

Kristóf pushed through the crowd to the door of a building, sat down on the stoop, and laid his head on his knees. He closed his eyes as spots of light danced. Close by, a phone was ringing, maybe his father's.

There was a new round of screams, and bodies shoved in front of him. He raised his head, opened his eyes, squeezed them shut again. They stung like poison.

KRISTÓF LAY ON HIS RIGHT SIDE in the emergency room of St. Rókus

Hospital. Time had passed, but he wasn't sure how much. He'd got here by his father hoisting him to his feet, leading him away from the tear gas, and sitting him down on a less explosive corner. A taxi arrived. Ópa stepped out of it and helped him into the front seat.

Here in the ER, an intercom beeped. Kristóf touched the throbbing spot on the left side of his head where his hair had been shaved and his scalp stitched. A gray curtain was pulled back, and a nurse ushered in his father and grandfather.

"Krisz, I brought you a clean shirt," Ópa said.

They came alongside him and helped him change his shirt, helped him stand. He left the hospital walking on his own, but glad that they walked on his right and his left.

THE NEXT MORNING KRISTÓF'S FATHER CALLED HIM before he went home to Pécs. Kristóf hadn't been the only casualty, Vati said. Almost two hundred people had been injured. To add to the insanity, some war veteran had climbed into a Russian tank on display, fired it up, and drove it at the police, who pulled him out and beat him. At least, that's what people were saying.

Kristóf took some pain pills the hospital had given him. Guessing he could make it through the dinner shift, he combed his hair carefully, avoiding his wound. It was horribly ugly—a shaven oval with stitches running down the middle like some grotesque American football. Chagrined, he thought of his beautiful mother, who had never approved when he looked a mess.

He went to the restaurant a little early. Checking his email on the restaurant's computer, he found a message from Lisa. So her cheating husband was a father now. Damn. When Kristóf had more time, he would write back to Lisa. Some things were just plain fucked up, and one was that her baby died and so the man went and made one somewhere else.

Kristóf logged out, put on his apron and hoped the sick gash on his head wasn't glaringly visible. But as it turned out, the gash evoked some sympathy. As he handed a dinner menu to a pretty blond customer, she pointed to the injury and asked, "*Ach, was ist passiert?*"

"A souvenir of the 1956 anniversary," he told her in German.

"I was at the ceremonies, too. But not in the battle zone."

There was a sweet tenderness in her eyes. The restaurant was not busy, and he talked with her as he brought her dinner and later as he cleared her dishes. She was from Linz, she said. Her grandfather was Hungarian and had left in 1956.

"So I had to come," she added, "in recognition."

He nodded attentively. "Are you staying long?"

"I leave tomorrow."

She looked to be about his own age. Was she here by herself? He glanced at her hand: no ring, very good. Before the Linz woman left the restaurant, he told her his name. Hers was Petra.

"Thanks for coming in," he said. "I work until ten tonight. It would be nice to have you stop by again."

She did. At nine forty-five that night she came back and ordered vermouth. When his shift ended, he put away his apron, took another pain pill, and saw her out.

They walked along the river embankment. She asked him questions about the bridges and the castle across the water. He liked the warmth of her voice as she said that Budapest was beautiful. He put his arm around her and they stopped walking. For one moment her shoulders seemed to tense; but she drew nearer, and in the night breeze he kissed her. His hands delighted in her back, her side, her hip.

She was staying in a small tourist apartment near the basilica. They climbed the stairs to the flat and she unlocked the door. He knew the first moments inside could be awkward, so he was quiet and left the timing up to her. She took his hand, and soon they found themselves beside the bed. She was very still. Maybe hesitant.

Could it be she was unused to this? She was too pretty to be inexperienced. Wasn't she? Yet this shyness was endearing. He touched her neck and told her softly, "I'm glad you came here, glad I met you. I wish you weren't leaving so soon." It was all true.

"*Du bist schön,*" she whispered. *You're lovely.*

He helped her undress and lie down. As the night surrounded them, he kissed her over and over, caressed her, and held himself patient, waiting for her. Her body never eased. But in her tension she pulled him closer and closer, tightening around him until she clung in desperation. "*Ja,*" she moaned, and she was his.

Afterward, in the quiet, they lay with their backs together. He rubbed her hip. She took his hand, gripped it.

He heard a soft shudder of her breath, then another. Moments passed before he understood she was crying.

"Petra?"

Her fingers wrenched his.

"What's wrong?" he asked.

"We shouldn't have done this," she wept. "I shouldn't have done this. I love my husband. I love my little girl."

"You're *married?*"

"Yes."

"Oh, my God." He pushed back the covers and sat up, the night cold on his chest. She was married. And look what he'd done. Why hadn't he caught on that something was wrong? Now she was sobbing, and if her husband back in Linz ever found out what she'd done with a Hungarian waiter, the man would feel like a gutted fish.

"My God, Petra, why didn't you tell me? I would have left you alone."

"I shouldn't have done this." She turned her face into the pillow. "I thought I wanted to."

Kristóf rose and dressed. His pullover hit his wound. God, it hurt.

"I can't stay here," he told her.

"I know. I'm sorry."

"I am, too."

She sat up, crying and beautiful. If she were confessing any other trespass, he would have held her and told her it was all right; but she was another man's naked wife, and he made himself turn away.

"I can't stay," Kristóf repeated. "I have to leave." He tied his shoes. "Don't get up."

He let himself out and walked home on Andrássy Avenue. His wound hurt and he hated the night. He'd broken his one rule: no married women, not after what his mother had done to his father. It was no consolation telling himself he hadn't known the woman was married. He should have known. He should have asked. He should have stayed the hell away.

AFTER WORK THE NEXT EVENING, Kristóf went to the internet café to write back to Lisa. Another message from her had already come in.

Hi Kristóf,
I read the news about the rioting at the commemoration ceremonies, and I
thought of you and your grandfather. Are you two okay? Please let me know.
    Also, I've been playing our grandparents' song that in English is called
"The Light Shines in the Darkness." I'd like to adapt it for my choir (in
English). Could you ask your grandfather if he minds?

Kristóf rubbed his wound, avoiding the stitches. Lisa, so solicitous. He
wrote back.

Hello Lisa,
My grandfather was smart, he stayed away from the ceremonies. I went, and
I have a cut on my head but I'm okay.
    I don't know what to say about your husband and his new baby, but
this isn't right. I didn't have such a good week either, but I won't complain
because it is my own fault mostly.
    I'll ask Ópa about the music. I hope you make good progress with your
students. Tell me about it, I need good news.

                                                                    —Kristóf
P.S. Did you see how my note is full of contractions? I used your advice.

The next day before Kristóf left for work, Ópa telephoned. "How is
your head wound?" he asked.
    "Better. Itchy, but not so sore."
    "Good. Your mother called last night. She saw the news about the riot-
ing and asked about you. So I told her what happened. It would be nice if
you wrote and reassured her."
    "Oh." Kristóf shifted the phone to his other ear. "How are you feeling?"
    "Not bad. I taught today."
    "What, really?"
    "Two students came to my apartment. Next week I hope to go back to
the academy."
    "Well, for God's sake, use the lift."
    "Yes, I know," Ópa said curtly.
    "Ópa, I heard from Lisa. She wants to arrange 'A fény ragyog a sötétség-
ben' for her choir. Is that all right with you?"

"Choir."

"Yes," Kristóf said. "She teaches choir."

"A choral arrangement." Ópa sounded dubious. "Well, let her try it."

"It makes sense, Ópa. She's in a Catholic school. Wouldn't they like the light in the darkness thing? Good over evil and all?"

"I suppose so."

"Is something wrong?" Kristóf asked.

A sigh, and Ópa's voice weighed in heavy. "The winter we wrote it, the darkness stretched farther than the light."

CHAPTER EIGHTEEN

If the Light Shines

November 21, 1944

ANTAL STOOD AT THE WINDOW WITH SÁNDOR, watching the freezing drizzle outside. They wore their coats indoors now. Every broken chunk of coal was rationed, every scrap of firewood hard to come by.

"Even the sun is rationed," Antal grumbled.

"Hmmm." Sándor raised his hands, raised his eyebrows. In a great stentorian voice, he announced, "Antal! Imagine, if you will. A warm day—no, no, don't be such a skeptic! Just picture it! A warm day, and we are *not* having beans and caraway seed for lunch. Not at all. We've packed a picnic basket with bread, chicken, boiled eggs, and strawberries. Yes! And wine, too. We each bring a beautiful girl, and we catch the train, which is *not* full of stinking soldiers, and we go to Lake Balaton, and we eat and we swim and we kiss the girls, and no, we are *not* dreaming."

"I like your plan."

"The tricky part," Sándor said, "is that between now and then we have to *not die*." Sándor turned from the window and strode off, and the bedroom door hinges creaked.

Maybe Sándor was looking again through the photos of his family that Antal's mother had given him. Maybe he was reading, which he did all the time these days, whether he liked the books or not. Maybe he was crying.

Twice Antal had walked in on that, and Sándor was furious with embarrassment. At such times, the only person who could approach Sándor was Grandpapa.

The day after the speech at the window, Grandpapa took Sándor to see a priest. When Sándor came home, Antal sat with him on the lower bunk and asked about it. "I mean, did you talk to the priest, like confessing? Did it help?"

"He's a priest. So he said what you'd expect, told me to hold onto faith."

This sounded like grasping wind or clenching light. "I don't know how you do that," Antal said, "after what's happened."

Sándor stared toward the opposite wall. "I think when your whole family is suddenly—" he made a choking sound and a slitting gesture across his throat—"then all you have left is a soul. So I'm damned if I let go of mine. I mean it. Really damned."

He would say no more about it.

But later Grandpapa told Antal privately what he'd observed: Sándor seemed to handle things better on days when he made music. So Antal gave more thought to the music circle that had formed in their front room. Before this, he had brought the group together occasionally. Now Antal began picking up Márta for music practice whenever she could come.

On the walk they would see propaganda posters screaming, "Jewry and Soviets, the death of Hungary!" Márta would press her fingers into the crook of his elbow when they passed soldiers. Whether German officers, Hungarian infantry or Arrow Cross militia, Antal hated them eying her. When he and Márta reached his apartment, Katalin and Sándor were always expecting them. Katalin would greet Márta with a happy kiss on each cheek, as if they were picnicking instead of waiting out a war. Sándor might burst out singing "Lili Marleen" but substitute her name: "Li-li Már-taaaa!"

In the music sessions Sándor alternated between the piano and guitar. Antal set the tempo with his violin. He had taken to speeding crazily because it set Katalin laughing, then Márta; and if the girls started laughing, sometimes Sándor did. One day the girls began clapping in rhythm. Sándor leapt to his feet. He stomped and spun, holding the Spanish guitar as though it were a partner: "Dance, señorita, dance!" He bumped into the sofa and the guitar fell twanging to the floor. Sándor re-tuned it, saying the señorita's sense of pitch was little better than a drunk soldier's. This was the happiest Antal had seen him in weeks.

As December neared, the cold sharpened and the dark of evening pressed into late afternoon. Antal scheduled their sessions earlier so he could see Márta home before curfew. On one of these trips, as they entered her building, a child was jumping on the stairs with her doll.

"That's my sister," Márta said. "Anni! What are you doing out here?"

The girl looked to be about five years old. She ran to them, grinning and pointing at Antal. "I know who you are! The violin boyfriend!"

"Anni, go back to the apartment," Márta ordered.

Another girl, this one a young teen, ran down the stairs and grabbed Anni by the hand. She waved hurriedly at Márta and Antal as she marched Anni up the stairs.

"And that's my other sister, Sarolta," Márta told Antal. They climbed the stairs and headed down the hallway to her apartment. Outside her door they stood together, fingers entwined. He sensed she had something on her mind.

"My family may be moving," she said. "We live too close to the train station. Too close to a bomb target. We can't end up like Sándor."

"No. I hope you won't go far."

"I don't want to." She glanced up and down the hallway and dropped her voice. "Things have been so hard for my father."

Antal bent close to her. "With his work? More cancelations?"

"Yes, but we're almost used to that. He has other publishers, other places."

The man knew seven languages, Antal remembered.

"The worst part," Márta said, lowering her voice again, "is when he gets these telephone calls and somebody says, 'We're watching you,' and then—click—the line goes dead."

"*Jézus* Mária," Antal murmured.

Across the hall a door opened. They waited in silence until it closed again.

"Could I ask you for a favor?" she said.

"Anything."

"Our church's organist, he . . ." She seemed to choose her words carefully. "He isn't here. So this Sunday I'm going to play cello. It's not hard music, just hymns so people can sing, but I don't like playing alone. And I was wondering if you could you do it with me."

She said the place was the Reformed Church in Kálvin Square. She was Calvinist, then. He was Catholic, but he didn't often go to Mass, and he told her yes. If she asked him to play in every Calvinist church across Hungary, he could not say no.

"Antal," she whispered, "the organist. He was arrested for sheltering some Jewish friends. And we think it was somebody in the congregation that snitched on him. There's good and there's bad and everybody is so afraid. You don't have to come if you don't want to."

He drew her close, and for a moment that he wished would last hours, he held her. "I'll be there."

SUNDAY MORNING WAS SUNLESS, the Calvinist sanctuary dull. Two candles glowed on the communion table. Antal and Márta played two simple hymns while the congregation sang, and afterward they sat down in the front pew. Márta's father went to the lectern and began reading from the Bible. A tall man with thinning hair, he seemed to be one of the church's lay leaders. Antal's mind wandered until Mr. Hanák suddenly stopped; he then continued with slow, clear emphasis: "'The light shines in the darkness, and the darkness has not overcome it.'"

Mr. Hanák set his hands on the sides of the lectern and looked out over the congregation.

"Brothers and sisters!"

Startled, Antal waited. He didn't think this was part of the liturgy.

"The light shines in the darkness," Mr. Hanák said. "It will keep on shining. The darkness has not overcome it. It *will not* overcome the light. We must believe this. We must."

He closed the Bible and stepped down.

The pastor began to preach, but Antal barely heard him. The candles flickered in the dim church but did not go out. *The light shines in the darkness . . . the light shines . . . darkness has not overcome . . .*

The light had a melody. He heard it. Antal picked up a pen that had been left on the pew and turned over the slip of paper on which Márta had written the hymn titles. He lined a music staff and jotted the melody he heard. Beneath the notes he wrote, "The light shines in the darkness, and the darkness has not overcome it."

Márta glanced at him quizzically, and he passed her the paper. She read it, her finger moving under the notes. When she passed the paper back, she had added a lower harmony line.

"More," she whispered. "Keep going."

That evening Antal wrote variations on the melody. It grew to two pages long. The next day he went to Márta's apartment and showed it to her. She came back with him and they spread the music out for Katalin and Sándor. The group worked with it for three hours, playing it, singing it, adding a cello undercurrent and a piano accompaniment, creating an interlude for violin. They tested sections of it. Katalin would sing the main melody line, they decided. Sándor would sing with her on the closing measures.

"All right, let's do it all the way through," Sándor said. He set his hands into position on the piano. "No stops."

In the music, the longings and sorrows and hopes of this poor world found a voice and lifted. But Sándor could not sing, and at the end he could not play. He waved for the rest of them to keep going but pulled back from the keys. The cello finished alone. Sándor turned to Márta. "This is what your father read out in church?"

"That's right."

"And I hear he made sure everybody knew he meant it," Sándor said.

"Yes."

"'The darkness has not overcome.' Sándor pointed at the music, jabbed the words in vehemence. "*That* is the difference between giving up, or going on."

"I know, Sándor," Márta said with quiet conviction. "I know."

Uneasily Antal watched her face grow thoughtful, watched his cousin's eyes soften, as though Sándor and Márta had seen a deeper light, one that he himself could not see.

PART TWO

Stille Nacht

CHAPTER NINETEEN

For a Reason

November 28, 2006

SOME PEOPLE SAID EVERYTHING HAPPENED for a reason. Varga did not believe this. Girls were raped, boys stepped on land mines, dictators won elections, wives got cancer, cousins ran off to America, shot-up cities ran out of medicine, and babies died in their parents' arms. If these things served some great universal purpose, then it was a dreadful purpose indeed. No, Varga had resigned himself to things being senseless.

Still, it gave him pause, knowing that his heart had tried to quit and would probably have had its way if Kristóf hadn't shown up that night. There was also this: he had spent decades wishing for word from America, and if his heart had given up the ghost six months ago, he would never have met Lisa. Maybe the timing was luck, but it felt more like a sobering gift.

It was not quite December, and Varga had been feeling fairly well, back to teaching four students. He wished he could handle more, but still, this was an improvement. The thingamajig in his heart was doing its job. He decided to send Lisa a Christmas card, right away because mail to the U.S. was so slow. Standing before the display of cards at the drugstore, he settled on one with a violin on the front. The message was in Hungarian, of course. Kristóf would have to help him write a note in English.

As he headed for the cash register, he paused at a sign that read "*Mikulásnap, december 6.*" St. Nicholas Day would be next week. Varga lingered at a shelf displaying small toys, and chocolates wrapped to look like Father Christmas. Mikulás Day was a nice little tradition. As children, he and his sister had found candies and sometimes toys in their shoes on Mikulás Day. As a young father he'd filled his children's shoes with treats and presents, train cars for Zoltán and doll clothes for Gabriella.

And there was the winter of the siege when he was sixteen, when he and Hanák Márta had played music to scrounge chocolate for their sisters' shoes. It was the first time he received payment for performing, a hard beginning to his career. Well, all right. Varga walked on and joined the queue at the cash register to pay for Lisa's card.

KRISTÓF HAD BEEN STOPPING BY EVERY DAY since the heart attack, so when he came that afternoon, Varga asked him for help writing to Lisa. As they worked on it, Kristóf told him about her ex-husband fathering a child with someone else. Varga thought it was the height of unfairness, although he'd quit expecting fairness decades ago.

With Kristóf's coaching, Varga wrote to Lisa in English: "Lisa, for Christmas I wish you the joy you deserve. I am very glad that Kristof and I met you. Play good music and think of us. Kristof helps me write this, and he sends his greeting. Merry Christmas." There was more he might have said, and asked, if he could write to her without help.

"Kristóf," he began tentatively, "perhaps you could ask Lisa a few questions for me. I knew Sándor when he was young. What was he like when he was older? And Márta. And sometime, maybe, you can ask about their daughter. Lisa's mother."

Kristóf shrugged. "All right. You know what's crazy, Ópa? Lisa met someone who heard your light-shines song on the radio."

Varga frowned and barely nodded. Yes, he had played it on the radio, on one of the worst nights of his life.

"It's a good piece," Kristóf said. "What's behind it?"

"Is Lisa asking?"

"I'm asking."

"There isn't much to say. The idea for it came when I helped Márta play music at her church, and she wrote a cello accompaniment. Sándor wrote the piano part."

"Wait. This Márta. You've hardly told me anything about her. Did you know her well?"

Varga sealed the card into the envelope. "Pretty well."

"That day at the church, was Sándor there?"

"No."

"Was Katalin?"

"No. I was just playing music with Márta. I already told you that." Varga carried the envelope to the kitchen counter, pulled his address book out of a drawer, and addressed Lisa's card.

Kristóf followed him. "So you and Márta had a nice musical friendship."

"She was a nice girl."

"Ópa. Pardon me for being a little indelicate here, but I've seen pictures of her when she was young. She was beautiful, right? I assume you noticed that?"

Varga looked at him.

Kristóf crossed his arms. "Now, if it had been me in this story instead of you—yes, I know I'm not the pure soul that you are, but I can tell you I wouldn't have liked being the dutiful friend, the nice violin player, and then having my *cousin* gather the strawberries—"

"Kristóf, stop."

Varga turned his back, stamped the envelope, and said no more. The embers of that old story could still burn.

CHAPTER TWENTY

Dark December

December 3, 2006

Lisa had decided long ago that Tacoma's two ugliest months were December and January, and December had hit hard. Out her rain-spattered kitchen windows, the eaves and the fir trees dripped in the cold dark of evening as Lisa ate her Sunday dinner of canned minestrone and toast. December Sundays hadn't always been so awful. Jake used to cook *coq au vin* or beef stroganoff. The two of them would turn on light jazz during dinner, slow-dance afterward, and later still, make love. That was back before the miscarriages.

Lisa finished her soup and opened her plan book. All her classes were rehearsing for the school Christmas concert, and she wrote reminders:

4th grade: Clean up syncopation on "Virgin Mary Had a Baby Boy."

5th: "Good King Wenceslas" on xylos: PRACTICE STAYING TOGETHER.

8th grade choir: "Light Shines in Darkness": Firm up tenor and alto parts.

It pleased her that Varga's song was working. The choir liked it; she'd even heard two of the girls singing it in the lunchroom.

Kindergarten: Drill the lyrics to "Go Tell It On The Mountain."

She wrote herself an extra note to bring Hershey Kisses to put in the kindergartners' shoes on Wednesday, Mikulás Day.

As she later washed her few dishes, she thought about the upcoming Christmas, her first without Jake. She dreaded the emptiness. Two months ago she had emailed her brother in Africa to ask if by chance he was coming home this Christmas, but as usual Paul didn't reply. Maybe she should try to see her mother, her only family member on the continent.

How she missed her grandparents, especially in December. When she was a child, they had filled her shoes with treats every Mikulás Day. They took her to midnight Mass on Christmas Eve. As a child she wasn't used to church because her mother never took her, but on Christmas with Grandma and Grandpa she watched the candles glow and listened to the hush and fell asleep across her grandparents' laps. When she was in college, she stayed at their house over each Christmas break. They took her in—in fact, insisted on taking her in—when she confided that she didn't like encountering her mother's naked boyfriend when she got up at night to use the bathroom.

Well, the boyfriend was long gone. Lisa wiped down the kitchen counter and finally called her mother. When the voicemail clicked on, she said, "Ann, just wondering if you want to come out here. My concert's on the fifteenth. The choir's going to sing one of those songs from Grandpa and Grandma. You can stay through Christmas if you want. Let me know."

Ann called back a few minutes later. "Lisa, you can't just call me up in December and expect me to find money for a Christmas season plane ticket. Why don't you come here?"

"I can't afford it, either."

"Well, that's nothing new," Ann said briskly. "Look, I know you don't like me saying this, but you never have enough money. You aren't paid what you're worth, and you got a terrible divorce settlement."

Lisa paced to the kitchen window. The sky rained black.

"How have you been feeling?" Ann asked.

"Mostly better."

"Oh?" Ann's voice had brightened. "What changed?"

Lisa waded in carefully. "I'm on medication."

"The pill?"

"Yeah."

"Good, Lise. I'm glad you feel better. And you'll be prepared when you start dating again. You know what I mean."

Lisa shut her eyes. Yes, she knew what Ann meant.

"Too bad you can't come," Lisa said.

THAT NIGHT ANOTHER EMAIL FROM KRISTÓF ARRIVED.

Lisa, my grandfather asks, what do you remember about Márta and Sándor? And your mother? These are big questions, we understand if you don't have time to answer soon.

Yes, they were big questions, and not easy ones. Lisa didn't answer until after school the next day.

Kristóf, it would take a long time to write about it. Do you have access to Skype?

CHAPTER TWENTY-ONE

Mikulás Day

December 6, 1944

T HE COLD HAD MOVED INTO THE apartment and could not be driven out. Antal had given half his clothes to Sándor and this only made Antal colder. The family had no ration coupons for more clothing. But at least for now he wasn't outgrowing his clothes and shoes. His sister was outgrowing hers. Katalin's skirts were short, her sweaters tight. She could barely push her feet into her shoes, so she wobbled around in her mother's too-big pumps. Antal was walking down the back stairs with her when one of the pumps slipped.

She crashed down on her tailbone, grimacing, rocking, groaning. "Antal, I hate this! Nothing fits. Nothing's warm enough. And this is Mikulás Day! Remember the fun we used to have? It all seems like a dream now."

"I know," Antal said.

Katalin rubbed her lower back. "I miss what we used to have. I can say that to you, but I don't say it around Sándor."

"Neither do I." The whole family was conscious of how any self-pity would sound to Sándor. Antal reached to her and helped her stand. "Come on."

An hour later when the rest of the family had gone out, he called Márta. "Almost out of coal, almost out of clothes, almost out of food," he said. "I'm so sick of this."

"Me, too."

"If only I had one damned chocolate ration," he went on, although he usually tried not to swear around Márta. "I'd put chocolate in one of Katalin's outgrown shoes, I don't care if she's almost fourteen."

"We couldn't give my sisters anything this morning, either," Márta said.

Soon they hung up, but Márta called back later. "There's a drugstore down our street," she said, "and my parents are friends with the owner. He said if you and I come and play Christmas music, he'll save a chocolate bar for each of us."

"Without a ration card?"

"He's giving us the chocolate, not selling it."

"And we'd be playing in the store without Katalin and Sándor?"

She was silent a moment. "I hope you don't mind if it's just us."

He met her at the drugstore the next afternoon. She had brought a hymnal, and they set up a music stand near a magazine rack. Customers clustered and jostled at the pharmacy counter, some of them leaving without their prescriptions. An empty-handed young woman began to cry. A long queue had formed for whatever soap and razor blades hadn't yet run out. As Antal tuned his violin, he heard a man say the Russians had reached Ercsi. That was only thirty-five kilometers away.

"My father guesses the Russians will be here by Christmas," Márta told Antal quietly, worry unmistakable in her voice.

She sat down with her cello in a chair the proprietor had given her. They opened the hymnal and Antal led out on "*Mennyből az Angyal,*" the old carol about angels and shepherds. After two measures Márta began the lower harmony. Conversation in the queue hushed. On the second repetition, a few people softly sang along. "*Pásztorok! Pásztorok!*" Antal turned a page and took up "*Csendes Éj,*" the song about a quiet night and heavenly peace. Márta sang as she played its simple accompaniment. More customers joined in.

The front door swung open. With a blast of cold air, four German soldiers came in. Antal saw Márta's bow slip.

"Keep going," he whispered.

The soldiers did not patrol the shop nor queue up. They stood and listened, the closest only a meter from Márta. Antal eyed them between musical phrases. One soldier wore the insignia of a sergeant and was probably thirty-five or so. The others were younger, one of them just a thin blond teenager. Antal brought the song to an end. Most of the shoppers had quit singing anyway. What did these Germans want?

"*Noch einmal, bitte?*" the sergeant said. He wanted the song again. The man had asked politely, almost apologetically, as though sorry to trouble them.

Antal glanced at Márta and they took up the song yet again. As Márta played, she sang in German. "*Stille nacht, heilege nacht.*" She gestured for the soldiers to join in. Three of them did, singing in barely audible voices that went flat on the high notes. The young blond one did not sing. He stood dejectedly with his hands in his pockets, watching Márta. The Hungarian customers looked on in silence. At the end, the sergeant soberly thanked them in German and wished them a happy Christmas. He led his men out. The door closed.

"Poor bastards," one of the customers said. "They know they could be dead by New Year's."

"Well, good riddance," someone muttered.

Antal and Márta played through all the Christmas songs in the hymnal, repeating some as the customers and clerks made requests. When they'd finished and packed up, the proprietor's wife gave Márta two chocolate bars.

They headed out onto the street under a cold drizzle, passing three Arrow Cross greenshirts. Márta seemed subdued, maybe because of the greenshirts or the Germans in the store. Or was it something else? He remembered she had not wanted Katalin and Sándor to come today.

When they reached her building, she led him to the back courtyard. This surprised him, but she gave no explanation. They went to a corner behind the outer staircase and set down their instruments. No one was about. Márta said, "We're leaving the neighborhood tomorrow."

"Tomorrow." He hated that it had come to this. "Where will you go?"

"I can't tell you. I'm not supposed to tell anyone. We're trying to get out of the bombing path." Her eyes darted to the windows above. "And we need my father to be hard to find."

He grasped her hand. "*Jaj*, Márta, why?"

"I hope we can move back after this is all over."

She hadn't answered his question. "So you're leaving," he said, a frantic strain in his voice, "and you can't tell me where, and after the worst is over, how will I find you?"

Márta took another anxious look around. She pulled a pencil and a slip of paper out of her music satchel. After writing, she handed him a note with a woman's name and an address a kilometer and a half to the east. "This woman is my mother's best friend. She'll know where we're staying. Go to her after the Germans have left, and tell her your name." Márta looked down, her words slowing. "And that you're the violinist."

"*The* violinist?"

"My mother has told her there's a violinist from a trustworthy family." Márta raised her eyes to his. "A violinist that I care for."

"Márta." He touched her neck above her muffler, and when she smiled, he pulled her close. Her hair smelled softly of rain. He kissed her, first just a brush of the lips; then again, and the kiss lingered, filling him with her warmth.

"You have to come back," he whispered.

She clung to him as he kissed her once more, his own heat surging. It was then that his father's terrible words came back, and he feared for her.

"Don't let the Russians near you," he said. "Please. I wish I could be with you."

"So do I."

They stood in each other's arms against the cold and the dread, and he told her again that she must come back. After they could delay no longer, he walked her to her apartment door. He gave her the cello he'd been carrying, and she gave him the chocolate for Katalin, and he held her once more, long and hard. Then she turned the doorknob and let herself in, and when she said, "Goodbye, Antal," he knew by the shake in her voice that she was crying.

THAT NIGHT ANTAL AGAIN FILLED THE WATER JUGS in case the pipes broke in the bombing. After Katalin went to bed, Antal showed Sándor the chocolate bar, and they slipped it into one of Katalin's old, tight shoes. Sándor added a note.

Dear Katalin,
I'm looking for new shoes for you, but for now here's some chocolate.

Your friend,
Mikulás

Antal sat with Sándor awhile in the living room, talking about music and the war. If things were different, he might have told Sándor about kissing a girl for the first time. They didn't usually keep things from each other. But this time he said nothing. He hadn't known what sadness a first kiss could hold.

CHAPTER TWENTY-TWO

Protection

December 7, 2006

FOUR-THIRTY ON A THURSDAY AFTERNOON, Lisa sat at her kitchen table talking with Kristóf, his image flattened into two dimensions on the Skype screen. A bulletin board with a scheduling calendar hung on the wall behind him; he'd said he was in the restaurant's back room. In Budapest it was one-thirty in the morning, and Kristóf had the whisker stubble to show for it. He had just told her that his grandfather was teaching again, but only four students that he could instruct verbally, without demonstrating much with the bow.

"It's harder for him to play, then," Lisa said.

"Yeah. He doesn't say this, but yeah." Kristóf opened a notebook, picked up a pen. "Okay. Ópa asks what you remember about Sándor and Márta. And your mum."

"All right, well, Sándor and Márta lived in Chicago. I think they came to the U.S. with her family—"

"Do you know why he left Hungary?" Kristóf broke in.

"I'm not sure. Grandma Márta's father was a journalist, and I think there might have been some kind of political pressure on him, but I don't know why Grandpa Sándor came. Do you think your grandfather knows?"

"I think so," Kristóf said, "and he does not want to tell. And Sándor never came back to Hungary, and Ópa says he never wrote to him, neither."

"But how could he? Hungary was communist! Things could have been terrible for your grandfather if he received a letter from America."

"In the beginning, yes. But later nothing would happen. And still Sándor did not write."

They looked at each other, across the screen, across the world. They had inherited the same secrets. Lisa held up her hand. "What are we doing? Here we are, carrying on their old arguments. Forget that. You asked about Grandpa Sándor's life here. Well. My mother was their only child. And Grandpa tuned pianos for a living. He was my first piano teacher."

Lisa paused and thought while Kristóf made notes. Out her window the hard winter sun was fading.

"Let's see," she continued. "Well, Grandpa was Catholic. He didn't always go to Mass, but all his life he made donations to a Catholic orphanage. Grandma was a Calvinist and she didn't become a Catholic, but she attended Mass with him. They had my mom baptized into the Catholic Church. But when my mom grew up, she left."

Lisa could have said more, that Ann not only left the church but hated it for its stance on abortion, and she most decisively did not take Lisa and her brother to church. But Lisa always felt that her grandparents recognized something her mother didn't. When Lisa was twenty she took matters into her own hands and received baptism.

"When I joined the church as an adult," Lisa told him, "Ann said I was giving up my freedom."

Kristóf's brow wrinkled. "But you don't think so?"

"I have a different idea of freedom than she does. But about Grandpa Sándor." Lisa thought back over the years. "Whenever there was a death, it really affected him. I remember, he had a couple of friends that went through horrible losses. One man's wife died of pancreatic cancer, almost overnight. Another friend's son shot himself. My grandpa told them to call him night or day. And they did. Sometimes at, like, three in the morning. But really, the thing that was hardest for him, and for my grandma, was just . . . my mom."

Kristóf held his pen still. "Why?"

"That's the way Ann is. By the way, I guess I should tell you I call her by her name."

"Why?"

"It just happened. I first called my mom Ann when I was thirteen or so because I was mad at her. But she said if I wanted to call her Ann, she wasn't going to stop me. So it stuck."

Lisa crossed her arms against the apartment's chill. She didn't know how to explain to herself, let alone to Kristóf, all that had gone wrong between her and Ann; but when Lisa had the chance to leave, she took it. She headed for college in the Northwest because it was beautiful and far away, and she never looked back—except for missing her grandparents.

"From what I heard," she said to Kristóf, "Ann started giving my grandparents fits when she was a teenager. The kind of guys she dated, the drugs she tried, the way she argued with them nonstop, that kind of thing. Then when she got married, had kids, got divorced, things never got much easier between her and my grandparents."

On Skype Kristóf looked at her, his brown eyes serious. "What is her work?"

"She's a psychologist. She specializes in working with people who are at odds with their families. Gays coming out. People from Christian families becoming atheist. Things like that."

"I suppose," Kristóf said slowly, "people need what she does?"

"I guess so, but honestly, sometimes I think she's built her whole life around rebellion. And that's the thing between her and me. It's like I got along better with her when I was a teenage brat. I'm just not badass enough for her."

Kristóf cocked his head. "What?"

"I mean, I work in a Catholic school and I put up with low pay. In Ann's view, that's weak. But I like my job, and they can't afford to pay me more. And she wants me to take my husband back to court for more money. I don't want to."

Lisa's words came in torrents. It had been so long since anyone had listened.

"I don't want to go back to court," she said. "I'm sick of it, and anyway Jake needs money, too. He has a baby to feed, and he's not rich. The fact that he left me does not make it right for me to shake him down. I can't explain this very well, Kristóf, but what can I say? I'd like to tell you Sándor and Márta had a happy life, but my mother, oh, good heavens, she was always pushing them. I've never understood all this. One time she told me that Grandpa Sándor was really overprotective when she was growing up, wouldn't let her out of his sight, she felt so boxed in—"

"Lisa—my God—your poor grandfather! He lost his parents, his brother, his homeland. After everything so terrible happened, any man would be overprotective with his daughter, don't you think? I'm not a father, but I can imagine it."

"And so can I." Lisa felt her voice trembling, low and vehement. "And I thank God for my grandfather's overprotection, if that's what it was. Yes, he was moody. Yes, he had a temper. But he looked out for my brother and me. Like—" She broke off. "Maybe this is more than you wanted to listen to."

"No, I want to know."

"Okay." She picked up a napkin from the table. "When my mom left my dad, I was six and my brother was four. One night she woke us up and ordered us into the car. Drove away. I don't know why she did it like that. Maybe she went nuts." Lisa twisted the napkin. "We slept in the car for a week until Grandpa Sándor came and found us. Somebody recognized the car and told him, so he came. He grabbed Ann's car keys, yelled at her that he was taking Paul and me home to his house, to a *real* roof and *real* beds, said she could either come with us or not, but he'd call the police sooner than leave his grandchildren there to live in a car. So we all three lived with him and Grandma Márta for three years while Ann went to graduate school, and Ann didn't like the living arrangement, but Paul and I did. We felt safe."

Kristóf frowned. "What of your father? Didn't he help you?"

"No." It was so long ago; but as she spoke of it, she felt the wound anew. "After my parents split up, my dad said he'd come see Paul and me. But he didn't, and he didn't, and then, well, then he died, driving drunk. So he was gone."

On the screen Kristóf shook his head. "Shit. Lisa, this is bad, so bad, and of course your grandpapa would want to protect you, you had no father."

Lisa dropped her gaze, saw the torn napkin in her left hand with no wedding ring.

"There was one other incident I remember, him trying to protect me," she confessed, and maybe she was crazy. "But please don't tell your grandfather."

"I won't."

Lisa hesitated. "It was when my mother put me on birth control."

"Ah." Kristóf raised his eyebrows but did not look away. "Tell me."

"Okay." Her voice wavered. "I guess my mother thought she was doing the right thing. I was in with a crowd that was, you know, having sex. And me, too. I was fifteen."

"I was fourteen, first time," he said. She heard no cavalier pride in his voice, no nonchalance, only a quiet acknowledgment of the reality.

Lisa struggled with her own embarrassment but pushed on. "I don't know how Grandpa Sándor found out I was on the pill. But I heard them talking, him and my mother. She told him the pill was for my protection. He got really mad and said, 'A fifteen-year-old girl does not need that kind of protection. She needs to be protected from the shithead boy that's using her.'"

SHITHEAD BOY.

In Budapest, at two o'clock in the morning, Kristóf sat at the desk that passed for the Három Páva office. He looked at Lisa on Skype, a white refrigerator behind her and her blond hair held back in a big clip. She'd just said her grandfather thought she should be protected from a shithead boy.

Kristóf took a breath. "Probably your grandfather was right."

If he could voice it, maybe he would tell Lisa, with his eyes slanted away, that it was all too easy to be one of those shithead boys, and please understand that those boys had miseries of their own.

"These things are hard," was as much as he could say.

"But girls can be shitheads, too," Lisa said. "I was like that, dating a guy in college. He broke up with me because I was using him."

"You? Using someone? Lisa, how can I believe this?"

"No, but I did." Her eyes were full and earnest. "He loved me, and I didn't love him. But I kept calling him up because I needed him to drive me somewhere, needed a favor, needed a warm body. I hadn't faced it that I was using him, but I was, and when I finally saw it, I started crying, and I don't think I'd ever cried that hard in my life, not even when I was a kid and my dad died, not even when I teenager furious at my mom. I cried so hard I threw up. Because I'd been the shithead girl. It was like looking in the mirror and seeing a snake."

"But no," Kristóf protested. "You are no snake."

"But what if I'd let this go on and I became one? I felt so terrible I called my grandfather. And he picked up the phone, and my grandmother got on the other extension, and I poured it all out. Grandpa said, really gently, that they'd both been afraid I was getting hardened, and they were relieved I was upset about this."

Kristóf listened, perplexed but unexpectedly touched. "I think the boyfriend should have took you back," he said, "let you try again."

"No, it was better for him that he didn't." Lisa pushed a stray lock of hair back from her face and thought. "And as for me, I went for baptism and I learned to pray. If that hadn't happened, I don't know how I could have got through this past year."

"Damn, Lisa. All this what has happened in the year, this wasn't fair on you."

"I don't know how to think about the word 'fair.' But I hope this story made sense."

If she was calling herself a snake, that certainly made no sense. It was just her guilty feelings. But since seeing the tears of the married woman from Linz, and since hearing Zsófi's angry words—"Kristóf, if I'd told you I cared, you'd have run"—he understood guilty feelings more than he liked.

"I think I know," he said, and rubbed his eye.

"You're tired. I'd better let you get some sleep."

They said their goodbyes, and after her image disappeared and he had turned off the computer, he left the restaurant, locking the back door behind him. He skirted puddles in the rear courtyard, climbed the steps to his apartment and quietly let himself in. On the table stood a wine bottle with a note from Feri: *K—There's a little left. Help yourself.*

Kristóf poured the wine into a glass. At the table, he read back through the notes he'd taken for Ópa—Sándor teaching Lisa piano, Ann working as a psychologist, Lisa trusting Sándor and Márta more than anyone else. All this he could say to Ópa. But there was much more he couldn't.

Cold seeped in around the window beside him. He felt a strange sadness or nervousness or *something* about his conversation with Lisa. He was used to women's nakedness but not their secrets. Tonight Lisa had divulged stories more private than any woman had ever told him. Lisa trusted him, then? Maybe because they were some kind of cousins? Or because they were thousands of miles apart? Or maybe because of all the crap they had in common.

He sipped the wine, knowing the conversation had stirred up other things, too. It had been so long since he had mentioned to anyone, even obliquely, that night fifteen years ago when he'd torn up his boyhood. A drunk party, an older girl—good riddance, virginity—and a bicycle crash on the way home. He banged his head and bled like a slaughtered pig. That night was a sheer, utter loss. Still, it was nothing like the shock that had set it off. Earlier that day, a letter from his mother had arrived, postmarked Germany: *Dear Zoltán and Kristóf, I know this will be hard for you, but I am not coming back . . .*

CHAPTER TWENTY-THREE

Shattered Light

December 15, 2006

THIS WAS LISA'S THIRTEENTH CHRISTMAS CONCERT here at St. Brendan's, and she'd thought she was used to doing this. Even last year, three months horribly postpartum, the adrenaline had held her together. But last year, Jake was there. Tonight she hadn't counted on how bitter it would feel to put on her black concert dress again, the one Jake thought was sexy, and stand here leading the concert so close to his old spot in the front pew. Francie Russo sat there tonight instead.

Lisa faced the gathering of school families, parishioners, and school board members. "The last performance of the evening," she said into the microphone, "is by the eighth-grade choir. They'll sing a passage from St. John's gospel, which my relatives put to music. Then the choir will sing one verse of 'Silent Night.' After that, as we've done every year, please join in as we sing it again."

She signaled the pianist, who played the introduction Lisa had written in October. The students began to sing, some feebly, some entering late, but all gathering strength. *The light shines in the darkness, and the darkness has not overcome it.* Lisa sang with them under her breath, lifting her right hand, urging them: *Yes. Mean it. Yes. Tell us there's light.* The song spun into the church's white arches.

As the overhead lights dimmed, the accompaniment moved into a connective passage Lisa had written for this. The students filed to the altar candelabras, lifted lit candles and spread out in a shining circle around the pews. Lisa signaled the audience, and they sang. She joined them, singing of the night that was silent and holy. Yes, there was still such a thing as holiness.

As Lisa tidied the kitchen the next morning, a Saturday, the phone rang. "Your song at the party went great," Kálmán Barcza said.

Party? Oh, right. The Hungarian organization had had their Christmas party last night, with Kálmán's choir scheduled to sing "The Light Shines" in its original language. Kálmán had worked with her harmonies but kept the rhythm of the Hungarian lyrics.

"Everybody really liked the song," Kálmán said. "They asked that I tell you. Also, I looked at that suite by your Budapesti relative. Did you see, four pages are variations on '*Csendes Éj*'? You know, 'Silent Night'? But in the manuscript, it has the German name, '*Stille Nacht*.'"

"Yes, I saw that, but I don't know what's behind it."

"Well. So. How was your concert?"

"Good. I was proud of the kids."

"You should be proud of you, too. Well, I let you go now. Merry Christmas, Lisa."

"You, too, Kálmán."

She set the phone down and put the milk away. There was a fatherly kindness in Kálmán Barcza, something she barely remembered from her own father; that was too far back. But she missed her grandfather, and she thought of Kristóf's Skype call.

Later that morning she emailed her mother. Despite the tension of their last phone call, Lisa told her to watch for the Christmas gift she'd sent, said the concert had gone well, and added that she'd be having Christmas dinner with a few other teachers. Then she told Ann what she'd found out about the deaths of Grandpa Sándor's family.

So there he was, seventeen years old with no family left.

Lisa held up for a moment, recalling Kristóf's comment, then continued.

Ann, you've sometimes said that as a father he was overprotective of you, and it drove you crazy. But don't you think it's understandable, when you consider what happened to him? He lost his mother, his father and his brother. After all he'd been through, wouldn't it be natural to dread more losses? You were his only child. Wouldn't it be hard to let you out of his sight? It's something to think about.

Lisa sent the note and scrolled through her inbox. She found a message from Kristóf that she'd somehow missed, and she read it.

I saw Ópa a few days ago. I told him some of the things you said on Skype. Don't worry, Lisa, I talked carefully and didn't say private things. He was glad that Sándor and Márta helped you. Also I am glad of it.

I don't know the best way to say this, but I hope very much that you don't anymore think you are a shithead girl or a snake. I have known such people and they are not like you. You are better than them, better than most people I know, better than me. I don't like this, all that has happened to you. It is unjust, it is shit. If shit happens to me, okay, maybe I deserve it, but shit should not happen to you.

It's cold here and the days and nights are long at my work and I wish Ópa is stronger.

Did you do your concert yet? I'm sure it was good. Write to me again, your messages make things better here.

Lisa wrote him back.

Hi, Kristóf—
I received the nice Christmas card you and Antal bácsi sent me. Thank you. Please tell him my school concert went well, especially his light-in-the-darkness song. It was also sung by a Hungarian group in Seattle. People here like his music.

I was glad to get your email. This is my first Christmas without any family member, and it's too quiet in my apartment. I think of you spending Christmas with your kind grandfather, and I have to admit I envy both of you. I wish I were there.

Lisa stopped. The thing was, she truly did wish she were there. Talking with Kristóf on Skype, she wasn't sure he really understood her, but he wanted to. He actually wanted to.

She hesitated, then added,

With love,
Lisa

After lunch that day she set up a small Christmas tree next to the settee she no longer called a loveseat. Lisa wrapped a single string of lights around it. She decorated the branches with the ornaments that her students had given her—a shiny treble clef with a jingle bell in it, a heart that said "Best Teacher," an angel with a music book—and souvenirs she'd bought at Mt. Rainier and Yellowstone with Jake. She gave a prominent place to a goose egg shell ornament, delicately cut like lace, that she'd bought in Budapest.

Then there was the last one. Lisa picked up the wooden box that held the glass star for the top. No, not yet. With an inward pang she set it aside for later, and she plugged in the lights.

Nothing happened, nothing glowed, no light, only a nonfunctional cord on a puny tree. All right, then, she'd put on the top ornament. She reached for the wooden box again and carefully pulled off the lid.

There it was, the flawless cut-glass star Francie had given her last year. It bore the initials *AJF* in remembrance of tiny Alexander. The gift was beautiful and kind, and last winter beauty and kindness were the only gifts she could absorb.

But Jake had thrown out the sympathy cards and didn't want that star on the tree. "There are too many reminders," he said.

"Jake," she protested, "it's not as if we wouldn't remember anyway."

His face backlit by the damp sky at the window, eyes ringed by exhaustion, he said, "The sadness around here never lets up. Look, I wanted our baby, too, and it was the worst day of my life when he died. But could we please try to put this behind us? I can't go on reliving the worst day of my life over and over."

Yet Lisa had relived the day over and over no matter what she did; so last Christmas she tied the star on a low branch that didn't face Jake's recliner. Sometimes she bent to touch it, to caress the lettering, *AJF.*

Now her phone rang from the kitchen. Holding the glass star, she answered the phone.

"Yes, is this Mrs. Fischer?" a male voice asked.

Lisa stiffened. "No."

"I'm sorry to trouble you, but this is the number I have on file. This is Mitch at Sureco accounts receivable, and I'm actually looking for a Mr. Jacob Fischer—"

Lisa punched the off button, but she dropped the phone, grabbed for it, dropped the star. It crashed on the floor, breaking, throwing glass shards across the kitchen. She knelt, picked up the largest piece, and cut her finger. Blood ran onto her hand and over the shattered treasure. Blood dripped onto the floor in this kitchen where there was no Mr. Jacob Fischer, only mangled memories.

"God damn you, Jake!" she shouted into the emptiness.

She bandaged her finger and wiped blood off the floor. She swept up the shards. Since the Christmas tree lights didn't work, Lisa gathered all five candles and candleholders that she had in the apartment, clustered them in a circle on the coffee table, and lit them.

Plopping down on the settee, she stared at the flames. They dipped with the undulations of the forced-air heating. She sat for a long time watching the brightness bow and turn, bend and stretch, and a tired comfort slowly eased into her. For in this lonely year of grief, though the light had flickered and dimmed, it had not died.

Chapter Twenty-Four

Table Six

December 23, 2006

KRISTÓF HAD WORKED AT HÁROM PÁVA FOR TWO YEARS, twice as long as he'd intended. Before that he had taught Hungarian to ex-pats, but the language school had folded. He had a university education and knew four languages, and he needed a better job. So did everybody else. The country was full of underpaid doctors and overqualified waiters.

He had not had a day off in nearly three weeks. It was almost Christmas, and Americans and Brits crowded into Három Páva for strudel or hot spiced wine, laughing and tracking melted snow across the floor. He was tired, and this wasn't helped by Juhász Zsófi spending so many nights in the flat. Kristóf suspected Zsófi wanted him to move out so she could move in with Feri. On a Saturday morning when neither he nor Feri was working, Kristóf broached the subject over breakfast.

"Are you planning to marry Zsófi?" he asked. Why he had used the word *marry*, he didn't know, but there it was.

Feri sat in his wrinkled jersey, coffee cup in both hands. "How do you decide to call it permanent? I don't know. But I do care for her."

"All right," Kristóf said. "But are you hoping I'll move out? Because—"

"No." Feri shook his head. "I'm not ready. Stay here."

"It's damned embarrassing."

"I know. I'm sorry. But I hope you won't leave. Not yet."

Kristóf dropped his gaze and spread apricot preserve on his roll. The old arrangement wasn't working anymore, but who knew what would come next.

THAT EVENING WHEN KRISTÓF WENT TO WORK, Feri had already been there several hours. He said a good-looking woman had stopped by the restaurant looking for Kristóf. "I told her if she comes by about eleven tomorrow, you'll probably have time to talk to her before the lunch rush." Feri loaded bowls of soup onto a tray. "Good luck. She seemed nervous or something."

The next morning a little after eleven, Feri pulled him aside in the restaurant kitchen and said, "She's back. Table six. If you want to go talk to her, I'll cover your section. I took tea to her. That's all she wanted, that and a quiet table." Feri raised his eyebrows, and this seemed less a ribbing than a warning.

Kristóf took off his apron. Gripping a cup of coffee, he made for table six in the front corner. A woman with long brown hair sat with her back to him.

The woman turned. "*Szia*, Kristóf."

Only for half a second was he unsure. Kovalchuk Blanka. He and Blanka had met in London, two Hungarians trying to refine their English. When they later saw each other in Hungary, things ignited, and after several months they burned out. Or maybe broke, he wasn't sure. What he mainly remembered was that at the end, she cried.

He stepped toward her. "Blanka."

She gestured to the chair across from her.

He sat down with her. How long had it been? Five years? Six? "Well?" he began, taking in the strain on her face. "What's new? How are you?"

"Fine." She was older, less delicately slim, still pretty but all girlishness behind her. She had not yet smiled. "I'm married and I live in Kőbanya now."

It was a suburb to the south, not far. He tried to smile. "Married. Congratulations."

"And you?" she asked.

"Not married. So what are you doing here?" He pointed at the table, indicating *this place, looking for me.*

"I needed to talk to you and I heard you were working here."

He glanced around, hoping the rest of the staff would leave him be. "What is it?"

She set her purse on her lap and opened it, then snapped it shut. Moments passed.

"You didn't know about this," she said quietly, "but I have to tell you now. After our time together, I had a baby. There was never any question it was yours. I didn't sleep with anyone for a long time before you. Or after."

A wave of heat swept through him. He believed her. Blanka never took things lightly.

"Kristóf, you have a son."

Behind him, tourists joked in Italian. Across the room, Feri poured coffee. Somewhere outside, a car horn blared. And somewhere in Kőbanya a child existed because of him.

"My God," he murmured.

"He's five years old," Blanka said. "He started kindergarten a few months ago."

Five years old. Kindergarten. Kristóf coughed, trying to speak. "What is his name?"

"Mykhaylo. We call him Misha."

"Misha." Ukrainian, Blanka's family background. "Why didn't you tell me?"

"When I found out I was pregnant, I tried to. But you had left by then. When I called, you didn't answer. When I wrote and asked you to call me, you didn't. Then I stopped trying to reach you." Her gaze cut sideways, returned to him. "Because I found out your reputation. I knew you didn't want to marry me. You'd tell me to have an abortion—"

"You didn't know that."

"I pretty much did."

"You pretty much guessed. You pretty much assumed." His hands closed hard around his coffee cup. "So the boy was born five years ago, and in all that time you still wouldn't tell me?"

"I really didn't think you'd want to know."

"If I'm his father, why in God's name wouldn't I want to know?"

Her eyes flared. "If you're bedding every girl in Europe, why in God's name would you care? And why would I want you influencing my son?"

He stared at her, wanting to defend himself, wanting to tell her to quit calling him so fucking heartless, wanting to say that if anybody had treated anybody like shit, it was her, with her refusal to tell him about the child; but knowing—holy God, how could he miss it?—knowing that if he'd been any kind of man six years ago, he'd have answered the damned phone.

"I'm—" His voice caught. "God, Blanka, I'm sorry."

She lowered her eyes.

"All right," Kristóf said. "So why are you telling me now? Child support?"

"No. Like I told you, I'm married." Voice unsteady, she started over. "I'm married. Endre and I began living together when Misha was only about a year old, and for all Misha knows, Endre is his father. Endre wants to adopt him. You're the natural father. You'll need to have a paternity test, but you are. There will be some legal papers for you to sign. To relinquish rights and obligations, so that Endre can adopt him." She went on, humbly pleading. "Kristóf, I'm asking you to do this for Misha's own good. For his happiness. When you receive the papers, please sign off."

"Sign off?"

She nodded. "Please."

"Ten minutes ago I didn't even know I had a child."

"But we need this. Misha needs it."

"You're saying, 'Sign off, good-bye,' and I've never even met him?"

"Kristóf—"

"No. I'm not signing anything without meeting him."

"Please." Her voice choked up. "Endre and Misha and I are a family. You don't know what this means to us."

His mother flashed through his mind. "I know what it means for a parent to walk out like it doesn't matter, and I'm telling you, I have to meet him."

After last night's late shift, exhaustion slammed him now. It was all he could do to pull his pen out of his pocket and write his address and phone number on a paper serviette. He handed it to her.

"This isn't easy for either of us," Blanka acknowledged.

She opened her purse again, and after some shuffling she slid something across the table to him. It was her business card. But when he lifted it, underneath he found the photograph of a smiling, dark-haired boy with a strong brow and deep brown eyes. The child was so obviously a Varga that Kristóf could barely breathe.

"His school picture," Blanka said.

"Could I keep this? Please?"

She laid her hand over it.

"Surely you have other photos of him," Kristóf said. "You can part with this one."

"I didn't think you would want it."

"For God's sake, he's my son."

She blinked. Then she pushed the photo toward him, wiped her eyes, and stood up.

Kristóf stood, too. He managed to thank her as he put the photo into his chest pocket, managed to shake her hand, managed to keep his mouth shut when she said she and Endre and an attorney would be in touch with him. He managed to say good-bye, go back to work and get through the day. Sometimes, when he was sure others wouldn't see, he looked at the photo and slipped it back in his pocket. At one point Feri asked him what that woman had wanted, but Kristóf put him off. There was only person he could tell. During a break, he made a phone call.

"Ópa? Are you busy?"

Ópa laughed a little. "Well, yes, rather busy, because it's almost Christmas Eve, and your Aunt Gabriella and her family have arrived. And your aunt is fretting over the food." Ópa raised his voice as though teasing Gabriella. "Has she lived in the West so long that she thinks five bags of groceries aren't enough?"

"Oh." Kristóf rubbed his forehead. "I see—you're busy, then—all right."

"Krisz? Is something wrong?"

"Never mind, I'll see you for Christmas Eve tonight." Kristóf tried to banter. "So, will the five bags be enough?"

"You forget how many communist Christmases I lived through. And the Christmases of the war. Especially that last one."

CHAPTER TWENTY-FIVE

Fear Not

December 24, 1944

Antal STOOD IN THE NEGLECTED WALK SPACE behind an accounting office, holding a scrawny juniper bush steady while Sándor sawed its trunk. Katalin watched nearby. Shiny slivers looking like tin foil littered the pavement, dropped from Allied planes to throw off Axis radar. Artillery fire banged in the distance.

Antal held up the severed bush. "Tonight's Christmas tree."

"It needs tinsel," Katalin said. She paced around picking up anti-radar strips.

As the weak sun sank behind the roof tops, they turned toward home. Antal spotted a notice posted on a building wall, maybe by the desperate military or the Arrow Cross. He stopped to read it.

Anyone who hides Jews is to be shot.
Anyone who hoards merchandise, or sells at a higher price, is to be shot.
Every male sixteen years old or older must report for military service.
Anyone who fails to obey this general mobilization is to be shot.

"Sándor!" Antal beckoned furiously. "Katalin!"

"Oh, God," Katalin whispered as she read it.

Sándor pointed at the last two lines. "We're not reporting for duty." His voice quivered. "It's an empty threat."

"But I've heard that Arrow Cross greenshirts have been showing up in bomb shelters during air raids," Katalin said. "They're looking for deserters. Or maybe anybody they can grab."

An air raid siren blared. Antal gripped the trunk of the bush, and they ran home. As they entered the apartment house, their neighbors poured down the stairs toward the basement.

"I'd rather hide out in the apartment," Sándor said.

Antal headed for the stairs. "Me, too."

"Go," Katalin said. "I'll tell Mother."

Antal and Sándor ran up the stairs as people hurrying downward shouted, "Where are you going?" "Get out of the way!" "Antal, move that stupid bush!"

For the next two hours, Antal and Sándor huddled under the dining table while the floor shook and artillery whistled. Antal miserably pulled his coat around him. He thought of his father at the military hospital, dressing burns and pulling shrapnel out of soldiers' eyes, and of Márta, wherever she was, shivering between her sisters.

Finally the all-clear signal blasted. Antal and Sándor stood and stretched their trembling legs. Katalin, Mother and Grandpapa returned to the apartment. The Arrow Cross had not come by, they said, but a neighbor's nephew of military age had hid behind a coal bin.

"But come on, it's Christmas Eve," Mother said. "Let's put dinner on the table."

Very early this morning, before the market officially opened, Mother had managed to buy a small chicken and some misshapen potatoes. She'd had to roast them hours ago when it was safer to light the stove, and the food was cold now. Sándor and Katalin set the table. As Antal lit a few oil candles, Papa walked in.

He eyed the bush they'd left near the door. "What's *that* doing here?"

"It's a Christmas tree," Katalin said.

"Ah." Papa smiled wearily.

Over a subdued dinner, Grandpapa said the Soviets had surrounded the city. So far, telephone service was still functioning, and one of the women in the basement today had called friends at different points around the city's perimeter. All but one had seen Soviet soldiers.

"May this end quickly," Grandpapa said, "before even more is destroyed."

Antal hoped it would end before all food ran out. He looked down at his already empty plate. The cold chicken had been a rare luxury.

"A few neighbors are coming over tonight for Christmas carols," Mother said, "Magda and that peasant family that's staying with her, the Töröks."

In past years his family had shared Christmas schnapps with the Lutheran teacher from the ground floor, Magda *néni*—Aunt Magda, as they called her. A month ago a mother and two children from an eastern village had moved in with her after the Russians had razed their home. The woman's husband was away at war.

After dinner Antal and Sándor propped up the Christmas bush in the living room by setting books around its trunk. Magda *néni* and the Töröks arrived as they finished. Katalin let the two little girls help her drape the makeshift tinsel over the branches. The children bounced and chattered, fascinated.

Antal watched them work. Katalin had always loved the Christmas tree. When they were children she would wait excitedly with him in the bedroom on Christmas Eve while their parents set up the tree, lit the candles on it, and laid presents beneath. When all was ready, Antal would lead her by the hand to the living room. She gasped in joy over the glowing tree that, according to the stories, baby Jesus had brought.

The Török children clapped as Katalin twisted the last air raid strips into a messy star and set it atop the bush. Antal and Sándor fed the tile stove with a few more precious pieces of coal. Everyone pulled up chairs near the bush's shabby sparkle.

Mrs. Török handed Papa a small bottle of cherry *pálinka*. "Let's share this, and our Christmas tree might look brighter."

As Antal and the others clinked glasses of the warming brandy, the children touched the scratchy juniper as though in confusion. The younger girl asked, "Did Jézuska bring this?"

"No," Sándor told her. "I'm afraid Antal and Katalin and I dragged it in. Baby Jesus would have brought something much nicer. But did you know there's a song about that bush?"

The girl cocked her head. "Sing it."

Sándor trotted to the bedroom and returned with the Spanish guitar.

Strumming, he hummed "*O Tannenbaum.*" Antal laughed. The children gazed solemnly at Sándor as he sang in his clear baritone.

O Christmas bush, O Christmas bush, courageous is your bearing!
O Christmas bush, O Christmas bush, courageous is your bearing!
While planes were ripping through the air,
You grew in rubble without care.
O Christmas bush, O Christmas bush, courageous is your bearing!

The children began to smile.

O Christmas bush, O Christmas bush, so lovely and so gritty.
O Christmas bush, O Christmas bush, so lovely and so gritty.
Upon your scraggy branches' tips hang shining anti-radar strips.

Sándor strummed hard for dramatic effect.

O Christmas bush, O Christmas bush, you're just like our whole city!

Through the room rippled soft, sad laughter. Mother reached over and touched Sándor's shoulder. "Oh, Sanyi, it's so true."

Antal nodded. There was that notice that kept saying *is to be shot.*

"Well, let's sing," Sándor said.

Antal played carols on violin, sometimes stopping between verses to blow on his cold hands. The others sang, none of them strongly. Sándor's voice gave out completely on the song of the silent night, and he sat with his face in his hands. In the distance, artillery burned.

Magda *néni* read aloud from the Bible: "And the angel said to them, 'Fear not: for, behold, I bring you good tidings of great joy, which shall be to all people.'"

Antal's hand closed around the violin neck. With the city surrounded, and people to be shot, where was the angel?

Fear not.

CHAPTER TWENTY-SIX

Wishes

December 24, 2006

V ARGA'S APARTMENT HAD RARELY CONTAINED such jubilant noise. His daughter's whole family, his son, and his grandson all sang along with a *Messiah* CD: "WON-der-ful! COUN-sel-or!" Varga didn't know what these English words meant and could barely pronounce them, but he joined in. Why on earth not? "The Prince of Peace!" everyone sang in final exaltation.

Zoltán tapped him on the shoulder. As the others decorated the tree Gabriella had brought, Varga followed his son into the bedroom. Zoltán pushed the door closed. "How are you feeling?" he asked.

"Well enough. Gabriella already asked me."

"Any shortness of breath?"

"Not really."

Zoltán looked at him appraisingly. "Your color's all right. How's your strength?"

"I don't know." Varga sat down in his desk chair. "How strong is a seventy-eight-year-old supposed to be? I can't swim across the river, but I can walk to the grocery store."

"And you're taking your aspirin? Your beta blockers?"

"Yes." The beta blockers were his old friends. Even aside from the heart trouble, he'd sometimes used them before performances to calm his hands.

"I'm all right, Zoli," he said. "And how are you?"

"As a matter of fact, I have something to tell you." Zoltán's voice quieted. "I'm seeing someone. Her name is Erzsi. I guess you'd say we're getting fairly serious."

Varga sat forward, and as the family laughed in the other rooms, he plied Zoltán with questions about the woman. Zoltán had known her for a year, had met her at the hospital where he worked in the lab and she in the medical records office. Erzsi was divorced from a drinker and had raised a son and a daughter almost single-handedly. The younger one, the girl, had recently entered university.

"Erzsi's like me, she hasn't had the easiest time of it," Zoltán said. "So we're taking our time. She's a good woman, Apa."

This sounded hopeful. Zoltán obviously respected the woman. Varga nodded in tentative approval and asked, "Have you told Kristóf?"

"Not yet," Zoltán sighed. "You know how he is about women. I'm not ready to deal with his cynicism. So don't tell him. I'll talk to him when the right time comes."

A knock sounded on the bedroom door. "Come join us," Gabriella called. "We're going to play 'On Your Left.'"

Zoltán smiled. "Ah, yes, the yearly wishes."

The family gathered in the living room. Bálint, Gabriella's husband, carried in one more chair from the kitchen. Gabriella's daughters, Marie and Lili, clipped the last candles onto the tree, their long hair swishing with their movements. After these dozen years that the family had lived in Geneva, Varga still wanted to call his older granddaughter by her given name, Mária; but the girl used her French name now. It privately grieved Varga that his granddaughters knew more French than Hungarian.

Gabriella circulated with glasses of Bordeaux on a tray. She had to call Kristóf's name twice to offer him wine. He had seemed preoccupied this evening, and Varga wondered about that muddled phone call this afternoon.

They all sat down with their glasses, Varga between Kristóf and Lili. He hoped he'd have an uninterrupted moment to ask Lili about her music studies. She played violin very well, and it disappointed him that he'd never had the chance to teach her.

The wishing game began. Lili turned to Gabriella on her left. "Maman. I wish you a year when all your students practice. Every day. Without making excuses."

Gabriella laughed and lifted her glass. "The sun will rise in the west." She faced Zoltán on her left and wished him a raise in pay. Zoltán in turn wished Bálint a prestigious new job conducting an orchestra in Budapest, or Pécs, or Szeged, or Miskolc. He went on listing Hungarian towns, some barely larger than a village. "So that my sister and I will be in the same country again," Zoltán said.

"Yes," Varga agreed.

Bálint turned to Marie, thanked her for breaking up with her headache-inducing boyfriend, and hoped she'd meet the saintly hero her mother had been praying for. Gabriella rolled her eyes, and they laughed.

Marie shrugged. "Hmm. Well, speaking of romance . . ." She raised her glass to Kristóf. "To my cousin the heartbreaker: this year when someone falls in love with you, I wish for you to return the favor!"

More laughter, except from Kristóf. If anything, he looked chagrined.

"All right," Kristóf said to Marie, "when you meet your saintly hero, give his sister my phone number. We'll see if she's interested." He turned to Varga. "On we go. Ópa, my God. I wish you and your heart a strong year together. No more ambulance rides."

Everyone nodded and told Varga to take his medication.

"I do take it," he insisted. "And now, Lili."

She smiled at him expectantly.

"May your violin cooperate nicely with you," he said, "and when it doesn't, I wish you patience. And I wish you'd play for us tonight. My violin is at your disposal."

Marie and Kristóf carefully lit the tree candles as Lili played "*Jesu Bambino*," then "*Csendes Éj.*" Her touch was strong but gentle, the music tender and sure. The time would come, Varga knew, when his violin would belong to her.

Bálint turned out the lamps. The tree candles shone like haloed stars.

"It's magical," Gabriella murmured. She reached to Zoltán beside her and took his hand, just as she had done all those Christmases when they were children.

The Christmas of 1956 had been the hardest. Gabriella was three and Zoltán was five months old, and Zoltán's twin had been buried six weeks before. Heart empty, Varga had put up the tree and lit it for the sake of his living children. Gabriella stood tiptoe before the dazzling tree, and in Ildi's arms Zoltán stretched toward the glowing. Ildi held him tightly. Varga himself would have held Zsuzsanna, but she was gone.

Young Gabriella gazed at the tree, eyes radiant. "Jézuska brought it."

He and Ildi, despite tradition, had never told Gabriella that the tree and gifts came from Baby Jesus. Where she had heard this, he didn't know. He turned questioningly to Ildi, but she shrugged and her eyes teared up. She did not speak. Neither did he. He did not have it in him to set Gabriella straight. If she wanted to believe that this was, in some way, a miracle, let her. If she wanted to tell it to her little brother, let her do that, too. They all needed a miracle.

Over all these years he had never believed in miracles, but he had wished.

LATER THAT NIGHT GABRIELLA'S FAMILY AND ZOLTÁN went for a drive to see the city lights. Varga and Kristóf stayed behind. After the others had left, Varga handed Kristóf a package his mother had sent.

"I thought you might not want to open this in front of everybody else," Varga said.

"No." Leaning against the kitchen counter, Kristóf pulled off the paper and opened the box. He lifted out a blue pullover.

"Nice color," Varga said, "but it looks small."

Kristóf tugged it halfway down his chest, tore it off again. "Of course it's too small. She can't remember I'm not fourteen anymore." He dropped the pullover onto the counter. "Why does she keep doing this? Sending peace offerings I don't want?"

"Because she hasn't forgotten you, and you might as well quit trying to forget her."

Kristóf scowled and sat down at the table.

Varga joined him. "You called today."

Kristóf pursed his lips, reached inside his jacket, and handed Varga a photograph. It was a head shot of Kristóf in childhood, but why was he carrying it around?

"One of your old school pictures?" Varga asked. But the photo's color looked more recent, and the style of the clothes . . . wait. Varga peered closer. "Who is this?"

"My—" Kristóf cleared his throat— "my son."

Time hung tense, like a heart out of rhythm.

"Krisz," Varga said. "*Jaj.*"

"I found out this morning. I have to have a paternity test, but I don't have any doubt."

Varga studied the photo. The boy bore Kristóf's chin and eyes, and the brow of all the Varga males. "He's one of us."

"I know." Faint crow's feet showed around Kristóf's eyes. "His name is Mikhaylo. Misha."

Varga set the photo on the table but could not stop looking at it. "Who is his mother?"

"Kovalchuk Blanka. You never met her. What can I say, she and I had an affair. And now the boy is five years old."

"And you just now found out? Why didn't this woman tell you?"

"She tried to, when she was pregnant." Kristóf took a breath. "I didn't answer the phone."

Kristóf closed his eyes momentarily as though in pain. He explained that Blanka's husband wanted to adopt Misha, so Blanka asked Kristóf to sign away parental rights.

Varga sat upright. "Just like that?"

"Yes. I told Blanka to hell with that. Ópa, she assumed I wouldn't care." Kristóf slapped the table. "Well, here's a fucking surprise. I do—" His words broke. He pushed himself up from the table, strode across the kitchen. "Sooner or later that kid—no, sooner or later *Misha* is going to find out that this Endre is not his natural father. And he's going to ask, 'So who is?' And I don't want the answer to be, 'Oh, just some guy who didn't give a rat's dick.'"

Varga rose and stood beside his grandson. "How can I help? Shall I find an attorney?"

"I don't know. I can't think."

"Kristóf, your father would want to know."

"Not yet." Kristóf looked at him wearily. "I don't know what to do. All I know is that I'm going to tell Blanka to let me meet Misha. And when it happens, I want you there."

"Yes." Varga lifted his hand to Kristóf's shoulder, and the motion hurt his damned heart again, or maybe his soul. "Yes."

CHAPTER TWENTY-SEVEN

Damage

January 16, 2007

B Y THE MIDDLE OF JANUARY KRISTÓF had received the result of his paternity test. It was positive, as he'd known it would be. From Blanka's attorney he received forms for releasing parental rights and obligations to Kovalchuk Mikaylo. Kristóf stuffed the papers into his bureau and slammed the drawer.

He used to check on his grandfather by just phoning him, but Ópa had a habit of claiming to be fine whether or not he was. Now Kristóf went daily in person. Today he brought a book Lisa had recommended, *The Siege of Budapest* by an historian named Ungváry. As he walked through the slushy streets, he tried, not for the first time, to phone Blanka, and again left a message: "Blanka. Varga Kristóf here. Like I said before, I received those papers. So. When can I meet Misha?" He snapped the phone shut and dropped it into his pocket.

WHEN HE ARRIVED AT THE APARTMENT, Ópa did not come to the door, only shouted, "Kristóf! If that's you, use your key and come in."

Kristóf entered. An orchestral piece from some opera played on the CD player. "Is it Verdi?" he called. "And where are you?"

"In the bedroom. It's Puccini."

Kristóf found Ópa sitting on the half-made bed, a frown and a shine of sweat on his face.

"I didn't expect making a bed to give me heart flutters," Ópa said. "What's that book?"

"Something you might want to see. Lisa told me about it. Look, forget making the bed. Lie down."

Kristóf helped his grandfather stretch out. He pulled up the wooden chair from the small writing desk in the corner and sat beside him. "I should take you to the doctor."

Ópa shifted his hips. "How is Lisa?"

"Trying to learn Hungarian. Her mother sent her a language book and CDs for Christmas."

"Good. I have another question for her." Ópa closed his eyes. "Ask her when her mother was born. When Lisa and I made that family tree, she didn't put the date." He coughed. "Well, what's new?"

"I've tried to call Blanka to ask when we can meet Misha. She doesn't answer."

"Maybe she's nervous. Her husband, too."

"And I'm not nervous?"

"They may not know what to tell the boy."

"I don't know, either," Kristóf said, "but they should still return my calls."

"Could it be that Blanka is paying you back for when you didn't answer her calls? But never mind. We'll figure this out."

Ópa was still saying "we," thank God. Kristóf went to the linen closet for a face cloth. He dampened it at the bathroom sink, and when he brought it to the bedroom, Ópa was lying with the book propped open on his chest. "A book about the war," he said.

"Yes." Kristóf dabbed Ópa's forehead with the cloth. "A military history about the siege," he said. "But the last chapter tells about the civilians living through it. Or dying in it."

"Ah, yes. It used to be, this information was censored. The Soviets didn't want it out."

Kristóf looked on as Ópa turned pages in silence, pausing at the photographs: the Margit bridge crumpled into the Danube, a queue of war prisoners, a crashed glider plane sticking out of an apartment house, Jews lying dead on the river bank, soldiers' makeshift graves among the rubble heaps.

"I suppose you remember all that?" Kristóf asked.

"I'm afraid so."

"Did you have to live in a basement?"

"Yes, we moved in on Christmas. Everybody thought the fighting would be over in a few days, but Hitler didn't allow his army or ours to surrender."

Ópa turned more pages and stopped, his finger on a photograph of two men carving up a dead horse.

CHAPTER TWENTY-EIGHT

Survival

January 9, 1945

ANTAL, SÁNDOR AND THE REST OF the family had moved into the basement on Christmas Day, along with the other building residents who hadn't fled the city. Altogether, about forty-five people now lived down here, without plumbing, without electricity, and without heat except for what two stoves could provide with scant firewood. The battle that people had said would last a few days still pummeled the city these two weeks later.

Maybe it was more. Antal had lost track. Had there really been a time when he'd slept in a bed? Taken a shower? Flushed a toilet? Or had half a moment of privacy?

When low sun trickled into the basement through the few ground-level windows, Antal set the Dvořák romanza on his music stand and practiced. At first it had embarrassed him, people hearing his mistakes. But he soon realized that music mistakes weren't half as embarrassing as pissing in a bucket without a door to close. Besides, maybe nobody even heard the violin over the babies crying and artillery slamming like the end of the world.

At night he and Sándor slept under the stairs, crammed in with two men who had left the army. The big custodian, Mr. Lukács, had rigged up a wooden screen that they hid behind when the Arrow Cross came searching. The greenshirts had shown up three times, bellowing for deserters and Jews; but it had now been several days since they'd come.

"Maybe the Arrow Cross thugs are dead now," Mr. Lukács said. He yawned, crooked teeth showing, and rubbed the bridge of his nose. "Either that, or they're hiding, too."

Antal guessed it was both. The Soviets had arrived in Pest, and everyone in the basement worried about when they would reach this neighborhood. Nerves wound tight. Arguments broke out over what food belonged to whom, who had used too much water, who was pilfering cigarettes, whose child had started a fight. The dozen or so children here argued over the few toys, took each other's blankets, and teased each other out of sheer boredom.

Once when the children were at their angry worst, Sándor shouted out, "Once upon a time!"

The children instantly went silent and turned to him.

"Once upon a time, what happened?" asked a girl.

Sándor shrugged and told them the stone soup story. Then he told the one about the princess who wouldn't laugh. The next day it was "Looking-Glass Kate," and then "Once upon a time there was a fiddler named Antal," at which point the children went back to bickering.

It didn't help that most of the fathers had gone off to war, or somewhere. Antal had not seen his father nor heard from him since the day after Christmas when he'd left for the army hospital. Antal couldn't stand to dwell on this.

Somewhere in the thick of January Antal and Sándor were settling down for the night on their mats under the stairs when a furious pounding sounded through the outside door.

"No," Sándor groaned. "The Arrow Cross? The Russians?"

Antal lay still, listening. Maybe it was Papa. Please let it be Papa.

"Don't open the door," someone yelled.

"But it might be László!" Antal's mother shouted back. Antal heard feet run up the stairs, then Mother's voice again, calling, "Who's there?"

Antal could not hear the response, only heard his mother say, "Wait," heard her footsteps descend. He sat up. Someone slid the wooden screen aside. Into the dark, Mother's voice said, "Antal. He said you gave him bread once, says he plays violin. Kolompár Miklós."

It was the Gypsy. Good God, he was alive. Antal crawled out of the hiding space, climbed the stairs, and opened the door just enough to peer out. In the moon's haze he barely discerned ragged black hair and a stubbled face. Yes, it was Miklós. Antal pulled him in. Below, Grandpapa held a lantern. A crowd clustered at the bottom of the steps, staring.

"Everyone, this is Kolompár Miklós, a fine violinist," Antal said. Whether or not it was the truth, it might delay them calling Miklós a dirty Gypsy.

"I kiss your hands," Miklós mumbled, and Antal led him down. In the lantern light Antal introduced him to his family, knowing they were all disappointed the knock at the door hadn't been Papa. Miklós nodded to them, almost wincing in exhaustion. Somewhere farther back, a woman complained about a Gypsy in here. Mother brought him a bowl of beans and a spoon. He wolfed the food down, hands trembling.

That night the two deserters moved behind the coal bins, and Miklós crowded under the stairs with Antal and Sándor. He stank, but by now everyone stank. Though Antal asked him where he'd been and what had happened, Miklós said nothing and almost instantly fell asleep.

DAYS WENT BY. THE NOISE OUTSIDE CHANGED: upward whistles, then booms and shattering. An old man said it sounded like shelling. The Soviets must be within a few blocks. Papa still did not come home. Mother and Grandpapa kept saying that naturally Papa would be staying at the hospital because it was safer than walking home through the streets. Antal hoped they were right, but it sounded like wishful thinking and he couldn't shake off the cold fear.

He still had not been able to coax Miklós's story out of him. The residents watched Miklós warily. The children hung back from him, probably remembering old tales about Gypsies making off with naughty children, though some drew closer when he did tricks with string. Sometimes when Antal practiced violin, Miklós wandered over. He listened and watched almost hungrily, but when Antal held out the violin to him, he shook his head.

Still, the family had kept the plain old violin Antal used to play. Maybe if he handed that one to Miklós and left him alone, he'd play it. One morning during a lull in the shooting, Antal climbed the back stairs to the apartment and brought down both the old violin and the Spanish guitar. He handed Sándor the guitar, and the children gathered around curiously.

"A guitar," Sándor told them. "Her name is Carmen. She likes to sing, but she's not very good at it."

"It's a girl?" asked one of the children.

"Of course," Sándor said. "You can tell by the shape."

Two boys laughed behind their hands. Sándor let the children strum the guitar. Miklós sat nearby, watching. Antal gave him the old violin, but Miklós only set it aside, saying, "Not now."

That afternoon Antal and Sándor sat lethargically on a bench together when suddenly the air screeched. Creation pounded; the world crashed. Antal was thrown from the bench and slammed into a woman. A window shattered as a piece of paving flew through, hitting a man on the shoulder. Antal sat trembling on the floor while those around him wept into their hands or swore, asking for the hundredth time when this nightmare was going to end.

Mr. Lukács pulled a bench under the broken window. Wrapping his brown muffler over his nose and mouth against the cold and the sulphur, he stepped onto the bench and peered out. "I don't know what kind of explosive that was," he said, "but now there's a crater in the courtyard big enough to bury a horse in."

Some of the residents, Antal among them, crowded to the window to see. It was true. The air smelled of gunpowder; broken paving bricks lay strewn across the courtyard; and at the far end, smoke rose from a gaping hole. Antal hurried to his sleeping space to check on his violin. Frantically he pushed back the blankets he'd buried it under, and he opened the case. Oh, thank God. It was whole.

How he wanted to play it, to feel its good strings and wood in his hands and to hear its music—but what if another explosion tore it from him and crushed it? No, he left it in the case and re-wrapped it in blankets. He sat in the darkness under the stairs, picturing the Dvořák score, singing the music softly to himself, feeling the rhythm, imagining the violin neck and moving his fingers. It was all he could do.

JANUARY LENGTHENED. THIS CELLAR WAS A CAVE, a dungeon. Except for a few hours a day, Antal lived in near-darkness, broken only by the glow of the stoves or a rationed candle. Food supplies dwindled. A meal consisted of a single potato or a scattering of beans, at times just water thickened with a little flour and lard. Antal's hunger deepened. His stomach knotted easily and the smell of the toilet buckets made him gag.

They had been boiling snow for water, but no clean snow remained close at hand. The nearest well was at the Parliament building, more than half a kilometer away. None of the males dared to go; they could be forced into battle or shot as enemies. So when the errand could no longer be put off, Katalin and some of the women went out carrying jugs. Antal waited in silent dread until they returned, cold and trembling, three hours later.

"There was smoke in every direction," Katalin told Antal and Sándor as she tried to warm herself by the dim stove. "Tanks, broken-down jeeps. Sándor, down by your blown-up apartment, there's a war horse dying. Burnt mess everywhere. Dead bodies, and not just soldiers." Her voice grew thin with emotion. "I saw a woman dead in the snow, her neck all bloody, her little boy's dead body across her."

Antal and Sándor glanced at each other, appalled.

The evening sky rained gunfire. Dinner was a few spoonfuls of beans. Antal's grandfather fainted while awaiting his portion, and the family had to help him sit up and eat.

"This can't go on," Sándor said.

Far into the night Antal lay shivering. Water, food, light, warmth, he longed for them all, longed to walk in the sun, to touch Márta.

Jézus Mária, he was so hungry.

HE WOKE IN THE MORNING WITH KATALIN SHAKING HIM. "Antal," she said, "we can't find Sándor. He isn't here, not in the cellar, not in the courtyard, not in the apartment."

Antal's empty gut knotted. He looked at Sándor's mat. The pillow case was missing.

"Mr. Lukács isn't here, either," Katalin said. "His wife doesn't know where he is."

"Did they leave together?"

"No one knows."

Antal shoved away his blankets. Having slept in his clothes, he pulled on his coat and shoes and walked with Katalin out into the congestion of benches and trunks that they called the common area. His mother and grandfather asked him every question that Katalin had asked, and Mrs. Lukács did the same, her square face stricken and taut.

"I don't know where they are," Antal said.

In front of the building, something clattered, probably a weaponry wagon on the street. Men shouted, but not in Hungarian. A gun report cracked, echoed.

A woman at the food preparation table called out, "Has anybody seen the butcher knife?"

No one had. Antal waited through a blur of hungry dizziness. "Shouldn't we go look for Sándor?" he asked his mother and grandfather.

"We have to find Imre, too," Mrs. Lukács said.

"Antal, you're not going out there," Mother insisted; and Grandpapa said, "That's right."

People crowded close, asked who was missing, what had happened.

"I heard Imre get up," Klara Lukács told them, close to tears. "But I thought he was going over to the toilet bucket, and I fell back asleep. Antal, are you sure you don't know anything?"

"I'm sure."

He sat down on a bench, staring at the filthy brick floor. Katalin brought him gruel made from water, flour and caraway seeds. Miklós joined them, sitting at Antal's side.

"You better eat," Miklós said. "An empty belly only makes things worse."

The stuff tasted like wallpaper paste spilled in a bird feeder. Antal forced himself to swallow it. Terrible questions churned. If Sándor took the butcher knife, what did he intend to do with it? If he went out with Mr. Lukács, why? Where in hell were they?

He waited, paced, waited. About eleven o'clock the door rattled. He ran up the stairs and unbolted the latch. The door swung open. Antal's knees almost buckled in relief. Sándor stood there, face red with cold and hands clutching a pillow case.

"God damn it, Sándor," Antal shouted, "get in here!"

Below, the residents rushed to the stairs. Mrs. Lukács shoved through the crowd. "Sándor, where is my husband?"

Sándor's mouth opened. "Oh, my God," he whispered. "Mr. Lukács hasn't come back?"

"No," Antal said.

Klara Lukács ran up the stairs and stood facing Sándor. "Was he with you?"

"He came with me. But on the way home he ran ahead of me."

"And you let him? Tell me!" Mrs. Lukács demanded.

"I don't know where he is. I'm sorry. I thought—I hoped he had come home."

Gripping the pillow case, Sándor plodded down the stairs past Mrs. Lukács. Antal followed him. The family gathered in a back corner with Sándor and stood in a weary circle.

"I got us something to eat," Sándor told them. "Katalin said there was a dead horse out there, so I went and cut some meat. It's in here." He held up the bloody pillow case.

"Sanyi," Mother said, "you can't go out there in that cauldron!"

Sándor's face, pale with hunger and dirty, hadn't looked this bad since the night his mother died. "I know, Aunt Ilona," he said. "Going out isn't safe. Neither is starving."

Grandpapa said, "But you should have—"

"Could we just stop all this?" Antal broke in. "We've been hungry for three weeks, and Sándor did something about it. He's cold and tired. Could we just shut up and leave him alone?"

The arguing stopped. Mother said something about when all this was over, but Antal barely heard her. He didn't think this would ever be over.

By late afternoon, some of the women had boiled the meat into a thin, gamey soup. Antal and Sándor took their meager portions into the back corner. They lit one of the carefully rationed candles and ate with blankets over their legs.

"So what in the devil's name got into you?" Antal asked.

"I woke up before dawn, and right then it was quiet outside, no shooting, no strafing. And I remembered what Kati said about the dead horse, so I went out. And I *didn't* ask Mr. Lukács to come." Sándor spat the words. "He was in the courtyard trying to patch a rat hole. He asked what I was doing so I told him, and then he said he'd go with me, said I'd look less like an enemy if I had an old man with me."

"He's not that old."

"He's not young, either."

Sándor took a spoonful of the soup. "Antal, the streets look like a landslide hit. We got out there, had to wait around a corner while Germans ran past, then Hungarians, I don't know how long we waited." Sándor stared into his bowl as the candle flickered. "We weren't the first to get to the horse. Two other men were there with a saw, and the poor beast's rump was in shreds. We hacked away at the shoulder, but the knife wasn't enough, so I borrowed the saw, and I had to jump on the bone to break it. Finally we were done, but then we had to make it home."

"And what happened?" Antal pressed him; but the floor shook with the shelling outside, and some of Sándor's soup slopped out of his bowl.

"Damn," he muttered. "Coming back, we saw seven or eight Russians. Quilted jackets, fur hats. They were unloading ammunition in front of that tobacconist shop on the corner. So we turned, we circled the block, we wanted to get home from the other direction, but we couldn't. There were soldiers that way, too—"

Antal stopped him. "So the Russians are here. In the neighborhood."

Sándor nodded. "We waited in a recessed doorway, must have been half an hour at least, and then I don't know what got into Mr. Lukács, but he made a dash for it."

"Out there in the open?"

"Yes. And after he took off running, I heard a gunshot."

Antal swallowed the bile that came to his throat.

"I kept waiting," Sándor said, "until I had this gut instinct to run. And—oh, my God, Antal—as I ran I looked for his crumpled body, but I swear I didn't see it."

"Maybe some neighbors took him in." That was it. That had to be it.

Antal finished the soup, but his stomach and head hurt. "Sándor, you didn't ask me to go with you. We were going to look out for each other. Right? Wasn't that what we said when you moved in?"

"How could I ask you to go with me? You have parents. A sister. A beautiful girlfriend. If anybody was to risk it, it was me. The people who would miss me are gone."

"Shut up. We were crazy with worry. Don't think for one second that nobody cares."

From near the coal bins came the sound of a violin playing slow, listless Gypsy music.

"Miklós is finally playing that violin you lent him," Sándor said. "Sounds depressing."

Antal listened for a while. The violin was not tuned well, and Miklós was obviously tired, his hands no doubt cold and stiff. Even so . . .

"Not bad pressure on the bow," Antal said.

"That means something, coming from a perfectionist like you."

Antal closed his eyes. Perfectionist: that's what he was supposed to be. He'd been adjudicated too many times not to be. But yesterday on the Dvořák piece he'd sounded like a palsied cat, and had he even cared?

Outside, something whistled and banged.

Sándor rose and walked off. When he returned, he carried the guitar. "All right, Mr. Perfect Pitch," he said, "what key is Miklós playing in?"

"It's G."

Sándor strummed impassively in the key of G, a sluggish accompaniment to Miklós.

AFTER THE HORSE SOUP WAS GONE, they went back to rationing beans. How many days had it been? Someone today had said this was January sixteenth, but who knew?

Antal lay on his mat in the dark next to Sándor, kept awake by the gunning. What time was it? Eleven o'clock? One in the morning? The brink of eternity? Something rumbled close by.

Then the air split. Right outside the windows a shock of gunfire tore the night. Antal bolted upright, his pulse hammering. Sándor swore. Other residents shouted; children yelled; babies cried. More shots thundered and ricocheted. Soldiers screamed in German, then in some other language. Was it Russian?

A woman in the basement moaned out, "Oh, my Lord, they're in the courtyard."

Every nerve spinning, Antal waited through another volley of shots. Again. And more, until the shooting slowed, became sporadic. Then with last shouts and a clattering of boots, the noise moved off.

Mother of God, let this terror be over. Somewhere in this exploding world was his father. Somewhere was Márta.

THE NEXT MORNING ANTAL AND THE OTHER RESIDENTS lifted away the black-out boards from the windows and took turns peering out. After last night's barrage, shell casings lay on the shattered pavement of the courtyard. Bullets had sprayed holes across the lower apartments, and at the other side of the courtyard lay a dead German. Antal listened as the adults in the basement discussed this quietly. They didn't want the children scared by the corpse. It would have to be disposed of, maybe in the exploded bomb crater because the ground was too frozen to dig. They'd been emptying the shit and piss buckets in that hole, and none of them liked the indignity of laying the dead there, but no one had a better idea.

That afternoon and evening the din battered on without stopping. The sound seemed to come from close to the river. Blasts rocked the ground, jarred the bones, tortured the ears. Antal and the others sat together, coughing, covering their ears, clasping their empty stomachs. Some wept. Some prayed.

On his mat that night Antal lay awake hearing different shouts and screams, not furious soldiers this time, but women and men in what sounded like a great panicked mob.

"Sándor," Antal whispered across the darkness. "What's going on?"

"It sounds like people are trying to flee."

"Where can they go?"

"I don't know. Maybe across the river."

Tense and aching with cold, Antal gripped the blankets around himself. In the depth of the night the world convulsed in a horrendous explosion, then another, then a third. Antal's chest pounded with the crush of the shock waves.

Beside him Sándor groaned, "The bridges. No."

In the morning, the world seemed to have stilled. To the west, shots still burst, but distantly. Antal sat up. Sándor was already awake, and they put on their coats and shoes and crawled out from under the stairs. They found Magda *néni* feeding the fire in one of the stoves.

"Good morning, boys." She straightened up and tried to smile. "I suppose we can go outside today. A man from the apartments next door said the battle has moved across the river."

"The Soviets have taken Pest, then," Sándor said.

"Yes."

"Not Buda yet?" Antal asked.

"Not yet. But the western train station has burned, the man said. So have the big hotels and part of the Parliament building. The bridges are blown up." Her voice grew feeble, the wrinkles at her eyes deepening. "Our beautiful city," she said, and she began to cry.

Unused to comforting adults, Antal could only say, "Yes." But Sándor went to her and touched her shoulder.

A little later Antal ventured out into the courtyard with Sándor, blinking and coughing in the smoky daylight. Debris and spent bullets littered the broken pavement. Across the courtyard, face up in a pool of frozen blood, lay the German soldier they would put in the bomb hole.

Without speaking they approached the body. A dusting of snow had fallen over the bloodied uniform and into the hollow of the helmet, which had tumbled aside. Antal stopped several meters short.

But Sándor stepped close, then turned, his face contorted with horror. "Antal, he's so young. Younger than—" His voice choked off, but Antal knew Sándor's next word would have been his brother's name. Antal ran to him.

"I saw my father dead," Sándor said. "And I saw my mother dead. I never saw Károly dead. Just a telegram. Is this what it was like?" He gestured at the stiff soldier with the blue-white face, the staring eyes and gaping mouth. "Somebody shot Károly, and then did people say, 'Get rid of this carcass, dump it in the shit hole—'"

Sándor crumpled, kneeling in the snow. Antal bent next to him, his arm around Sándor's back. He had no words, only knew that they had to give this body a decent burial.

When they went back into the basement, people were wondering where Mrs. Lukács was. They said maybe she had gone out looking for Imre. About an hour later she returned, silent, her face ashen.

IN THE AFTERNOON ANTAL, SÁNDOR, GRANDPAPA and two other men went to the courtyard again. As echoes of gunfire drifted from across the river, they picked up ammunition pieces, shattered paving, and broken window glass. These they dropped into the bomb crater. Grandpapa beckoned the group to the German soldier. One of the men squatted and unclasped the dog tags.

"The name is Hoff," he said. "Dietrich."

After rolling the body in a sheet, the group hoisted it into the hole. They laid Hoff Dietrich on the detritus so that he rested on ammunition and glass instead of shit. They covered him with debris and as much frigid soil as they could break up. They had talked of having some simple ceremony, but not out here where they might be seen by the Russians.

They returned to the cellar near the stoves. Antal did the best he could to warm his stiff hands, and he brought out his violin. Others joined them. Miklós watched from the back and Mrs. Lukács from the stairs. Magda *néni* quoted something from the Bible about resurrection. Grandpapa led the Our Father prayer and others murmured along.

Antal lifted his violin. In case the Soviets were around, he didn't want the sound to carry past these walls, so he played softly the only German hymns he could think of, "*Schönster Herr Jesu,*" "*Ein Feste Burg Ist Unser Gott,*" and "*Stille Nacht,*" even though Christmas had passed. How long would it be before Hoff Dietrich's father or sister or girlfriend knew he was dead? Holy Christ, this was horrible.

Katalin and Sándor quietly sang Mozart's "*Ave Verum Corpus.*" Their voices sounded so tired that Antal added some violin arpeggios to keep them on key. He looked up. Above on the stairs, Mrs. Lukács wept, her shoulders quaking under her red shawl.

JUST BEFORE DUSK THERE WAS A POUNDING ON THE DOOR. Curses and mutterings about the Russians ran through the basement. A woman called out, "Don't anybody open it!"

But Mrs. Lukács bounded to the door and bellowed, "Who is it?"

A voice called back, "Open up! It's me, Varga László."

It was Papa, at last. Antal looked at his mother in unspeakable relief. She sighed, "Thank God."

Mrs. Lukács unbolted the door. Papa stepped down the stairs, unshaven, disheveled, snow on his dirty coat. Mother met him at the bottom and hugged him hard. Antal pressed forward with Katalin and Grandpapa.

"They let you leave?" Mother asked Papa.

"I walked away," he said. "There was no one left to shoot me. I'll go back in a few days, but at this point I can't face another dying soldier."

"László, what's it like out there?" a man asked.

"The fighting is still going on in Buda. Pest is torn to pieces. Romanian soldiers and Soviets all over the streets. Some look like Russians or Ukrainians, some like Kazakhs or Tatars." Papa took a rough breath. "And I think some of them are in our apartments."

A woman cried out, "No, not those animals!"

Antal, Sándor and Miklós gave their spot under the stairs to Katalin and Mother and two other women. In the corners and behind the coal bins, more women hid. The men did all they could to nail the basement door shut. That night Antal lay in front of his mother's and sister's hiding spot but could not sleep. If only he knew Márta was safe.

PART THREE

Pest, Along the Danube

CHAPTER TWENTY-NINE

To Understand

January 22, 2007

ON A DARK WINTER EVENING, LISA sat at her classroom desk with her phone to her ear. She'd been entering semester grades in her computer, but Kálmán Barcza had called.

"Everyone liked your relatives' song at our Christmas party," Kálmán said in his accented voice. "So I looked at more of your family's music. The Pesti song would be very nice for our March Fifteenth remembrance."

Lisa scanned her memory. March Fifteenth was some Hungarian holiday commemorating an uprising against Austria—which Hungary had lost, like they lost the October uprising against the Soviet Union, and two world wars, and big fights with the Turks. There was always some loss to remember. As for the song, she wasn't sure which he was talking about. "I'm sorry, what song do you mean?"

"The one about Pest. It's a sad look around the city at the end of the war. But in the song there's love for the city and the people, so the theme is right for March Fifteenth."

Now she understood. "Another choral arrangement, then?"

"Yes. Do you have time to write the arrangement? Or should I? Is this all right?"

Lisa looked down at her backlogged paperwork. "Could you do it?

Then send me your arrangement, and I'll add a cello part."

"Fine."

That night before she headed home, she checked her email. Kristóf had written.

Hi Lisa,

Thanks for telling me about that book, The Siege of Budapest. I bought it. My grandfather saw it, he turned the pages looking at the pictures. I think he was glad I am reading this book.

Sometimes he is more talkative, he tells me more about what happened. He said there was not enough food, almost none, and your grandfather Sándor went out during the fighting and cut up a dead horse for meat. After they moved into their apartment again, the whole family had a kilo and half of beans, that was all. So Ópa's mother found some Russians in the Oktagon, they had food in a lorry, and she gave them a gold earring for flour and lard and dry milk. Ópa said she came home very much horrified because right above them in the Oktagon there were four bodies hanging from lampposts. Arrow Cross, probably, being repaid. Ópa said also in Klauzál Square there was a big terrible pile of corpses, and the Jews went there to look for their relatives. The war wasn't even over yet, the armies were still fighting in Buda. I never understood before, what our grandparents endured. I told Ópa he was brave. He said he had no choice.

"Oh, Jesus," Lisa whispered.

Also, Ópa wants to know, when was your mother born?

I hope you are well, Lisa, and that 2007 will be better in your life than 2006 was.

—K

Replying to Kristóf, she said that her mother was born in 1949, and she told him about Kálmán wanting to use the Pest song. She mused on what they'd learned from the book.

I knew my grandparents had been through painful things, but they never said what. Your grandfather has started to open up more than mine ever *did. Maybe Antal bácsi needed to talk about it even though so much time has passed. For me, it hurts to think about my Grandpa Sándor chasing down horsemeat in the middle of a war. I wish I had known how much they suffered. Maybe I'm beginning to understand.*

After she sent her reply, she reread Kristóf's paragraph about the war. Horrific as it was, it meshed with everything else she was finding out. She saw that now. On her memo pad, she wrote "Send siege book to Ann," for she wanted her mother to understand, too.

CHAPTER THIRTY

The Rhythm of a Defeated City

January 20, 1945

AFTER BURYING HOFF DIETRICH, THE RESIDENTS STAYED in the basement two more days. Out the windows Antal sometimes saw rucksacks or rifles on the apartment walkways. He hadn't seen soldiers there, but others had. Then the rucksacks disappeared. When morning, night, and another morning passed without movement on the walkways, the residents cautiously concluded that the soldiers had moved on.

Antal and his family lugged their filthy bedding and clothes up the back stairs, along with the silverware and jewelry Mother had hidden in the cellar. They found the lock broken on the apartment door. Sándor pushed the useless knob and they entered.

The soldiers who had billeted here must have been shooting from the windows, with shots fired back from the street or the neighboring buildings. The apartment was a desolation of bullet-broken plaster, shattered glass, empty ammunition boxes, and blood spattered across the sofa and wallpaper. Sickened, Antal lifted the piano lid. He beckoned Sándor over. They found the strings covered with plaster dust. Three had snapped where a bullet had pierced the sound box. Sándor ran his fingers up and down the keys. The piano wailed in out-of-tune grief.

Antal and Sándor wandered through the apartment. They found shit piled in the clogged toilet and the bathtub, maggots in the kitchen sink, and blood-soaked bandages in their bedroom. What they and the rest of the family did not find was the kitchen clock, their fountain pens, most of the towels, and half of the pots and pans.

"Carried off in rucksacks," Sándor said.

Antal turned on the kitchen tap. Brown water spurted out, then nothing. "To think we wanted to come home," he said.

They spent the day cleaning. Everyone told Katalin not to go out because of the Russians. Toward evening Antal went to the basement to check on Miklós. On a bench in a back corner lay the blankets he'd used, but Miklós was not there. Where had he gone in this violent world? Antal heard guns across the river, and he remembered dead Hoff Dietrich, and Mr. Lukács, who had not returned.

THE NEXT DAY ANTAL WANTED TO SEE MÁRTA, but Papa forbade him to go by himself. Antal had promised Márta he wouldn't let anyone know where her family was, but now his only choices were to stay home or take his father along. He took his father.

They set out walking east toward the address Márta had given him. As they neared the bombed-out train station, Antal looked down the road to where Márta's apartment house had stood. Only one charred wall remained, and his heart knotted in dread. They trudged through the snow, skirting bloodied corpses, abandoned tanks, and snow-covered heaps of brick and rubble. Wrecked lampposts tilted at ghastly angles and torn streetcar cables hung useless. Antal looked back over his shoulder. Across the river in Buda, smoke roiled into the sky.

At last they arrived at the address, an apartment house with the windows boarded over. While his father waited in the foyer, Antal climbed the stairs, found the apartment, and knocked. Presently the door opened a slit and a woman with gray-streaked hair peered out.

"I come in peace," he said. "Are you Mrs. Messik?"

"Yes," she answered warily.

"I'm looking for Hanák Márta. My name is Varga Antal. I'm a friend. A violinist."

"Ah." She looked him over and opened the door. "Márta is here. For now. Come in."

Márta was here. Thank God.

Antal stepped into the cold apartment, taking in the piled suitcases and the stacks of blankets and clothes. In a corner sat Márta's cello and a case that probably contained a typewriter.

"Antal."

He turned. Márta hurried to him wearing her coat and a kerchief. Her face was smudged with something gray, especially under the eyes. She pulled off the kerchief, wiped her face without much improvement, and stuffed the kerchief into her coat pocket. "I hoped you'd come," she said. "But I was afraid for you to risk it."

"Is your family here?"

"Yes." She pointed toward the back of the apartment.

He touched a gray patch under her eye, and something like soot came off on his fingers. "What's this?"

"Katalin hasn't blacked her face yet?"

"Should she?"

"To look old." Her eyes flicked away. "Because of the Russians."

Apprehension rose in him. "You don't look old. You look like a pretty girl with a sooty face."

For this moment at least, they were alone in the room. He pulled her close and kissed her, and she felt thin and tired in his arms.

"I was afraid I'd never see you again," she said.

They sat on the sofa and she asked about his weeks in the basement. He told her about Miklós returning, and about burying the German, and about the terrible day Sándor went out for horsemeat, and about Mr. Lukács not coming back. He told her he was still trying to practice the Dvořák piece. At this she smiled and her eyes lit.

"You kept playing," she said. "You amaze me."

"It was the only thing that seemed normal." It cut him, seeing her face smeared gray like an orphan. "Are you well, Márta?"

"Well enough. But my sister got typhus."

Her voice struggled as she told him. Anni, the five-year-old, had taken ill two weeks ago when they were living in Mrs. Messik's basement. Anni cried, she shook, she was confused. A nurse checked her over with a flashlight and found lice in her hair and on her body. The Hanáks had to burn her clothes and her blankets. They bought gasoline from a Russian soldier and washed Anni's hair with it.

"Then we shaved her head to make sure," Márta said, "and now she looks like a skinny little slave."

"I hope she's getting better?"

"Not as fast as we wish."

"You won't catch it, will you?" he pleaded.

"I think if I was going to catch it, I'd have been sick by now."

He told her his father was downstairs and maybe he could examine Anni. She said, "Please, yes." When Antal brought Papa in, Márta's family had gathered in the living room. Mr. Hanák held Anni, nearly bald and wrapped in a blanket. Sarolta stood next to him, her shoulder-length hair uncombed. Mrs. Hanák, in heavy layers of winter clothing, clasped Papa's hand in grateful greeting. She was an attractive woman, somewhat younger than her husband. Márta looked like her, except Mrs. Hanák had darker hair and a fuller figure. Both she and Sarolta had smirched their faces as Márta had. Mr. Hanák laid Anni on the sofa. She was indeed thin, but she pushed up on one elbow and smiled at Antal. "There's Márti's boyfriend."

"Good morning, Anni," he said.

As Papa sat down with Anni, Antal and Márta went out into the dim corridor. She told him her family couldn't stay here long and would have to move again soon.

"Antal, I've missed you so much. I know it isn't safe out, but I'm really glad you came."

"I'll come again. Be careful." He touched her face. "Wear your charcoal makeup. I don't want you looking pretty around those bastards when they're drunk."

"If they're drunk, what difference does charcoal make? The Soviets don't care, they just want to shame us."

It was hard, hearing this new bitterness in her words. He began to take her in his arms, but the door opened a little and his father called him in. Márta went with him, following Papa to where Mr. Hanák stood waiting.

"There's something I want you to hear," Papa told Antal. He nodded to Márta's father.

"Soviet soldiers are pulling civilians into work projects," Mr. Hanák said. "That's not unusual and not necessarily dangerous. But it can be. Sometimes they don't let people go home."

Antal stared at him. "What?"

"It's true." Mr. Hanák explained that *malenki robot*, as the Soviets called work projects, might last for a day or two, or much longer and worse. The Soviets were looking for as many prisoners as they could find to work in their own camps, and if they were short on military prisoners, they'd take civilians and sometimes women. People could get put on lorries, then trains, and end up in Romania, even Siberia. The taking of civilians had already begun in Pest.

"That's right, Antal," Papa said, "and we'd better tell Sándor."

"It often happens at large intersections," Mr. Hanák said. "If you see soldiers stopping people, asking for identification—stay away."

"Yes." Antal's throat went dry. "Thank you."

He and Márta went back to the corridor for one more moment alone. They told each other again and again to be careful. He kissed her, held her close, promised to come back.

"I don't want you to go," she whispered, her arms tightening around him. Leaving her was almost more than he could bear.

AS THEY LEFT THE APARTMENT BUILDING, Papa said Anni would probably get well if she got enough rest and especially food. Antal fell silent. They walked toward home on side streets, detouring when they saw soldiers.

Pest lay in embers like the outskirts of hell. Smoke drifted on the wind from Buda. Crossing a street, Antal looked toward the river and saw the Széchenyi Bridge crushed into the river, its mighty chains dangling like string. He and his father plodded on, their tired footfall crunching the snow. It was the rhythm of a defeated city, a place where grand buildings crumbled and soldiers lay unburied and even the bridges mourned, a place without food or light, where men became prisoners and children got sick and beautiful girls made themselves ugly.

Over the rhythm of their paces, a lamenting strain of music began to form within him. Later, at dusk by candlelight, he wrote the music down. It was only the beginning. Maybe more would come. It would grow. Please let it grow, because so much had died this winter. Something had to grow, to live.

Late that night, Antal told Sándor about *malenki robot*, but Papa had already told him. With concern in his eyes, Sándor asked how Márta was.

Antal told him about the charcoal on her face.

"I hate this," Sándor said.

"Not as much as I hate it."

OVER THE NEXT SEVERAL DAYS ANTAL CHECKED the basement morning and night for Miklós. He hadn't returned. Not that they'd really been friends, but given what Mr. Hanák had said about *malenki robot*, Antal wished he knew where Miklós was.

The weather had warmed. One of the neighbors stopped by and said that some scouts had organized a clean-up project down the street where a building had collapsed. The wreckage had made the street impassable, and the scouts needed help clearing the mess. Antal and Sándor talked it over, wary of a work project; but since this one was organized by Hungarians, they took shovels and went out. The collapsed building was halfway between Antal's apartment and the burnt remains of Sándor's old home. Neither of them spoke of his horsemeat foray near here.

THE WORK PARTY CONSISTED OF LOCAL RESIDENTS, some of whom Antal recognized. He and Sándor joined in the work, stacking bricks, piling stones, lifting glass shards, shoveling broken plaster damp with snow. They cleared away horse droppings and shit from soldiers. After working four hours, Antal told Sándor he was cold and tired and ready to go home.

"Maybe not yet," Sándor said, glancing aside.

Antal followed his gaze. To one side a young Soviet officer in a khaki jacket and tall boots watched the work, smoking. What was he doing here? Had this neighborhood project become *malenki robot*?

"I don't want to stay," Antal told Sándor.

"Let's not leave until that Russian looks the other way."

They kept working. Antal's back and arms throbbed. Late in the day, he and Sándor lifted a broken door off the heap. From the rubble protruded a contorted leg in civilian trousers.

"Oh, no," Antal muttered.

Sándor shouted for assistance. Other workers gathered. A scout and a hefty woman helped dig the large man out. Antal swept plaster dust off him. The bloated face was chalky white, the hair gray.

And maybe they'd been watching for this all day, because Antal felt exhausted sadness but no real shock when Sándor, covering his nose and bending over the body, suddenly whispered, "My God, no. Antal, it's Mr. Lukács."

Antal stepped closer to the head, fighting off dizziness. Sándor was right. The features were distorted with death, but here was Mr. Lukács's high-bridged nose; these were his crooked teeth; this was his dirty brown muffler.

"It's our neighbor," Antal told the others.

"Yes," a woman said. "It's Lukács Imre."

People stared at the body or stared at the ground, and a child ran away. Antal felt Sándor grip his arm hard. "Are you all right?" Antal asked him.

"Damn it, how can anyone be all right?"

They had to take the body home to Mrs. Lukács. That was the way things worked, wasn't it? Antal looked over his shoulder. The Soviet officer had left. Antal helped Sándor and the scout hoist Mr. Lukács onto a wheelbarrow, one leg pointing stiffly off the front end, the other askew beside it. They wheeled the load home over the snowy cobbles as people moved aside. In their courtyard the three of them managed to lower the dead weight without dropping it. The scout took the wheelbarrow and left.

Sándor stood with his hand over his eyes. "I knew he was dead. But I wanted so badly to be wrong." He made the sign of the cross over the body, choking out, "Father, Son, and Holy Spirit." Antal steered him up the stairs.

At their apartment Sándor went straight to the bedroom and shut himself in. Antal told the rest of the family what had happened. "Somebody has to tell Mrs. Lukács," he said. "But please—I don't want to do it, and not Sándor, either. Please not Sándor."

After many questions, Mother and Grandpapa resigned themselves to the task and went downstairs to talk to her. Antal sat at the table with Katalin as two weak candles glowed. Day became night. On the street out front, soldiers laughed and shouted in Russian.

Mother and Grandpapa returned grim-faced. Mrs. Lukács had argued that it couldn't be her husband until they showed her the body; then she sobbed into her apron. Neighbors poured into the courtyard to offer condolences; "and she was beside herself," Grandpapa concluded.

"So we're going to bury him at Kerepesi Cemetery tomorrow," Mother said. "The neighbors said they'd help. Beforehand, there'll be a little memorial service here. Just short, out in the courtyard, with Katalin singing, and you on violin, Antal. And Miklós, if he comes back."

"Miklós?" Katalin asked. "Not Sándor?"

"She doesn't want guitar music," Mother said.

Antal slammed his palm on the table. "She just doesn't want Sándor. This whole time she's been acting like everything is his fault. If she's saying no about Sándor playing, then I don't want to play, either."

"And if Antal's not playing," Katalin said, "then I don't want to sing."

"Listen, you two," Grandpapa said, "give the poor woman some grace—"

He stopped as the floorboards creaked. Sándor had entered the room.

"It's just music," Sándor said. "I don't care. Keep the peace with the woman. But I don't want to be there."

In the end Antal decided to play at the gathering. He had liked Mr. Lukács even if he didn't like his wife. He told Katalin they might as well; they'd done it for a German soldier, so they could do it for a neighbor. But that night as he sorted through his violin music by the light of an oil candle, he pondered what he'd agreed to, and he wished he'd done things differently two years ago, and again three months ago.

If only he could amend this. He read through a violin solo transcription he'd written last winter of Shostakovich's second waltz. Before everyone went to bed, he took out his violin and asked the family to come into the living room. He set up his music stand and placed the Shostakovich piece on it. Katalin stood by with the oil candle so he could read the music.

"I think I'd better play this for you all," he said. "Especially for Sándor."

In the dim light Sándor looked at him quizzically.

Antal coughed, summoning words. "Two years ago, Sándor's brother died. We all remember, when we got word, we had a little memorial service for Károly at the parish church. And Grandpapa asked me to play. But I said no because I didn't think I could get through it. Then a few months ago Sándor's mother died." Antal glanced at Sándor, saw him bite his lip. "So we had a service at the church for Aunt Éva, and Grandpapa asked again to play. And I said no again."

He cleared his throat. "Well, a week ago I played violin to bury a

German soldier. Tomorrow I'm going to play to bury a neighbor. And it doesn't seem right, that I refused to do it for Károly and Aunt Éva. So."

Antal checked the tuning of his violin. "This is Shostakovich's second waltz. I remember once when it came on the radio, Károly jumped up and started dancing with Aunt Éva. So this piece is in memory of them both."

"I remember that," Sándor said softly.

Antal played, not too fast, emphasizing the jazz-influenced passages. His bow gave each downbeat and he left it to the rest of them to sense beats two and three. But Grandpapa began filling in, patting the beats on his thigh. Mother swayed a little with the music.

Sándor sat still, eyes downcast. Near the end he stood, pushed back the coffee table, and extended his hand to Mother. "Aunt Ilona?"

She rose. "Play it again," she told Antal. "A little slower."

He played and they waltzed, their movements flowing in sad rhythm. Antal heard his mother say, "I know it's hard, Sanyi." As the music ended, Sándor hugged her, held on.

THE NEXT DAY ANTAL PLAYED IN THE COURTYARD for Mr. Lukács's memorial. After the group had left for the cemetery, he packed up his violin and walked out the front entrance of the building, not following them, just exiting. He'd had too many weeks inside these walls.

A Soviet soldier stood beside the building door.

Antal's left hand stiffened around the violin case handle. This was the officer he'd seen yesterday. The man was in his mid-twenties perhaps, and over his jacket he wore a belt with the communist star at the buckle. He gave Antal a rather embarrassed half-smile, pointed at the violin case, and said something in Russian. Was the fellow ordering him to hand the violin over?

Antal took a step back. "Sorry, I don't understand," he said in Hungarian. The man looked at him blankly, so Antal tried German: "*Ich verstehe nicht.*"

The man's thick eyebrows rose and he pointed at the violin again. "*Das gefällt mir.*" His German was heavily accented but understandable: he liked the violin.

Antal lifted the violin case to his chest protectively. "*Das gefällt mir auch.*" *I like it, too.*

The officer said, "*Bitte, spiel?*" He followed with a few more German words, including *russisch*. The man was asking him to play something Russian.

Antal didn't want to stand here on the street, performing like an organ grinder; but if a Soviet officer told you to do something, did you have a choice?

He bent and opened the case. "Shostakovich," he said, and he blew on his hands and began the waltz he'd played last night for Sándor and Mother. He couldn't remember all of it and heard himself making mistakes, but he went on patching the melody together. Passersby on the street turned in surprise. The young officer smiled, and at the end, thanked him in Hungarian. "*Köszönöm.*"

Antal dared to put the violin away. The man spoke again, asking for his name.

"Varga. Antal," he answered with apprehension. Was this Russian going to ask for his identification now? Or tell him to do *malenki robot*?

But the soldier indicated himself with a gloved hand. "Kholodenko. *Leutnant.*" He gave a snappy nod, like a salute. "*Auf wiedersehen.*"

The officer left, boots thumping.

A Soviet lieutenant now had his name. It was innocent, Antal tried to tell himself. The man hadn't asked for his identification. He hadn't touched his pistol. He liked music. That was all this meant. Innocent.

CHAPTER THIRTY-ONE

Inspiration

February 1, 2007

FOR MORE THAN A DECADE NOW, VARGA HAD MET with his friend Halmos two or three times a month, for coffee or a glass of wine or to spread out sheets of music together. But Varga was aware of things changing. These days Halmos called him at least once a week and usually found some excuse to drive him somewhere or help with something. So today, a Thursday, they were here at the Central Market Hall with Halmos carrying Varga's shopping bag. A year ago Varga would not have permitted this, but the fact was that Halmos's heart had not gone on strike and his had.

Halmos suggested lunch and steered him toward the lift instead of the stairs. On the second floor they headed for the cafeteria that had originally served the market workers and now served the hundreds of shoppers and tourists that came through daily. While Halmos stood in line, Varga held their spot at a table. Nearby, a Gypsy fiddler in a black peasant vest played Monti's *Csárdás*. Back during the war, a Gypsy had told Varga the piece was good for show, a moneymaker.

Halmos joined him, placing their beer and plates of goose leg and dumplings on the red-checked tablecloth. Varga wasn't sure he could eat much. Lately that seemed to worry people.

Halmos lifted his glass and looked off toward the fiddler. "No comparison to you."

"Frankly, I'm not playing so well at this point," Varga confessed. "I have this stiffness in my hands, sometimes almost numbness. It's nothing new for me to have some trouble in my left"—he indicated the little finger—"but now it's harder in my right, too. Yesterday while I was playing, I dropped the bow. I tell you, it's infuriating."

"I can't play piano as fast I used to," Halmos sympathized.

Varga studied his friend, who was a few years younger—gray hair still thick, coloring still ruddy, his voice and his gaze still strong. Halmos could still teach. "In the fall," Varga said, "after I ended up in the hospital, I cut down my teaching schedule and only kept my four best students. Last week I called them up and told them I needed to stop."

"That had to be hard."

Varga nodded.

"It wasn't long ago," Halmos said, "you were teaching the top students in the city."

"It's pathetic, Halmos. My days are so restless. I looked around the apartment for easier music, and I started playing through that old assortment the American girl brought over. Pieces I wrote when I was seventeen. Mother of God, *seventeen*. And songs that my cousin wrote when he was eighteen. I always thought of that music as immature. I had to make it more complex when I put it into the *Embers Suite*." Varga set down his fork. "But when I went back to the originals, well, I don't know what to say except that I was touched. As if I wanted to tell our teenage selves, 'You'll survive. Keep playing.'"

"You always underrate your own music, Varga."

"Do I?"

"Yes. Ask anyone at the academy."

Varga shrugged.

"In your restless hours," Halmos went on, "why don't you write a new ending to *Embers*? I'm serious. It's a beautiful suite with a cacophonous ending."

Varga's head had begun to ache. He'd had reasons for the way he ended the suite. Maybe not good reasons, but reasons just the same.

KRISTÓF STOPPED BY IN THE LATE AFTERNOON with two heavy bags. "I bought you groceries," he said as he stepped into the apartment.

"I already have groceries. I went to the market with Halmos."

Kristóf huffed. "I'm supposed to do your shopping. Aunt Gabriella even sent me money for it." He set the bags on the kitchen counter. "All right, well, I have the night off, so I'm making you supper. *Rakott krumpli.*"

Varga sat at the table while Kristóf peeled and sliced potatoes and layered the slices in an oven dish with sausage and cottage cheese. As the mixture baked, Kristóf told him there was finally news. "We're going to meet Misha, you and I. Saturday morning." His smile seemed uneasy. "We'll ride the Children's Railway with him."

"Very good." They had certainly waited for this.

"Blanka and her husband will be there," Kristóf said.

"Yes, naturally."

"But Misha won't know who I am, and Blanka doesn't want him to. We're supposed to act like we're old friends, but Blanka's husband would probably rather see me hanged."

Kristóf's face sagged as though he hadn't slept well. He looked like Zoltán used to look after arguments with Kristóf's mother.

"Kristóf." Varga tried to sound soothing. "You've told Blanka we want to meet the boy. So we'll go and we'll meet him. For now, that's all we're doing. We're meeting a child. Misha will like you if he sees that you like him. That's how children are. Just go and be kind."

"Most people don't seem to think kindness comes naturally to me."

"Most people don't know. Most people haven't seen you cook for your grandfather on your day off. They haven't seen you sit with your grandfather in the hospital."

Kristóf regarded him with weary surprise. "Hardly anyone says that kind of thing to me. You and Lisa, that's all."

"Could it be that you're nicer to Lisa and me than you are to other people?"

"You and Lisa deserve it more. You're more decent. Even inspiring."

Varga shook his head. Inspiring? What?

Kristóf went to the cupboard and returned to the table with a packet of crackers. "A few days ago, when I was here and you were resting, I read through your *Embers Suite*. I can still sight-read, you know, after all that solfege you and Óma made me do. So why did you end the suite the way you did? All that noise and fury?"

"Halmos thinks I should change it."

Kristóf scowled. "The man's telling you to rewrite it?"

"No, he's *suggesting* that I change the *ending*."

"Don't do it if you don't want to."

"When I wrote the suite back in fifty-eight, we'd lost the war, lost our freedom, lost it again in the revolution." Varga tapped his fingers on the table, not mentioning the other losses. "Back then I couldn't imagine a good ending. So yes, the suite ends angrily. It's probably the only public anger I ever allowed myself."

"Ópa, Christ's sake, you don't even allow yourself private anger."

"What are you talking about?"

"Don't you know? When was the last time you yelled at any of us?"

"What's the point of that? The rest of you don't deserve—"

"That's rot. You even swear politely."

Varga leaned across the table. "Are you joking?"

"No!" Kristóf gestured wildly with a cracker. "I am *not* joking! You can be surrounded by absolute assholes and you're still Lord Dignity. If you ever lost control of yourself, we would all piss ourselves from shock."

Varga stood up. "And what, might I ask, is this little outburst all about?"

"I'm saying, if you don't want to rewrite the ending of that piece, then don't. The music you wrote is your business. Your anger is your business, too."

"Sometimes anger outlives its usefulness. I wish you'd understand that. Like your anger at your mother."

"This is not about my mother."

Except that a hell of a lot more was about his mother than Kristóf would ever admit. Varga took his medication and went to the living room. They said little else until the *rakott krumpli* finished baking and Kristóf called him back to the table. Kristóf spooned the potatoes onto both their plates and said, as though there had been no interruption, "You know what I saw in your suite? A line that looks like Mozart. *Ave Verum Corpus*."

"Yes, true."

"What's it doing there?"

Another time, Varga might have sidestepped. But after being told half an hour ago that he was *inspiring*, for God's sake, how could he refuse to answer? Maybe, somehow, this awful old story could do Kristóf some good.

He said, "It's from my memories of the war. My sister sang the *Ave* in a bomb shelter."

"Why?"

"We did a burial."

"Who died?"

"A German soldier. He was shot in our courtyard, so we buried him. I played some music, trying to make things less horrible, and Katalin and Sándor sang."

"Lisa's grandfather? Was her grandmother there, too? Márta?"

"No."

Varga looked at his watch. Seven o'clock. He was tired. A year ago, his body wouldn't have worn out so early.

"Ópa." Kristóf sat still, holding his knife and fork. "You wanted me to ask Lisa when her mother was born."

"Ah." Varga waited.

"She said nineteen forty-nine."

Kristóf was watching him. Varga said only, "Thank you."

Nineteen forty-nine. This was for the best. Yet it was strange, the twinge of disappointment he felt. He rose from the table and turned on a CD. Returning, he asked Kristóf, "Do you recognize it?"

Kristóf listened a minute. "Choral. Sounds like Kodály."

"It's his *Missa Brevis*. If you want to talk about inspiration, there it is. Kodály lived in the basement of the opera house during the '45 siege. Some of the singers performed this in the opera cloak room while Buda was on fire. When I turned seventeen."

"Good God."

"Indeed."

Chapter Thirty-Two

Resettlement

February 13, 1945

THE DAY AFTER ANTAL TURNED SEVENTEEN, he and Sándor tried to tune the piano. Antal sounded the tuning fork and struck the keys, and Sándor took a wrench to the pegs. An hour before, a neighbor had spread the news: the last of the Germans had broken out of their hiding place under Buda Castle, and the Soviets mowed them down.

Sándor yanked the wrench. "Yes, the Germans are dead, along with the Russians and Hungarians they shot, and that's to say nothing of the Jews."

Antal tapped a G key repeatedly as Sándor twisted the wrench. "Still flat," Antal said. "Up. Little more. That's it. Stop."

From the street below burst a ruckus of incomprehensible yelling, laughter, and a gunshot.

"What in God's wrath is going on down there?" Sándor asked.

Antal was vaguely aware that his father had gone out. Papa now burst through the door and shouted, "Ilona! Katalin! You're not setting foot outside this apartment!"

Antal and Sándor strode to the entryway. Within seconds the whole household had clustered around Papa.

"László, what's the matter?" Mother demanded.

"The Russians are celebrating the victory," Papa said. "The fall of Budapest. There was a Soviet lieutenant down there on the street, he spoke some German—"

"I think maybe I've met him," Antal said.

"He gave a warning," Papa went on. "The Soviet soldiers have been given three days of leave. The fellow says lock up and make the women stay inside."

Katalin clutched Antal's elbow.

"What is this?" Sándor asked. "Their officers tell them, 'Go ahead, boys, get blind drunk and sack the place and help yourselves to the women, but be back here in three days'?"

"I don't know what the soldiers are told," Papa said. "But that's what they do. Katalin, you're staying inside, do you hear me?"

"Yes, Katalin, stay inside," Antal shouted as he made for the door. "I have to tell Márta."

His father called after him, but Antal slammed out and ran—onto the street, down thoroughfares, across big intersections he would have avoided yesterday. It didn't matter now. This army was too drunk to send him to Siberia.

It was twilight. Soviet soldiers careened through the streets in their wagons, laughing and shooting into the air. Two jumped off and grabbed a woman by the wrists. Soldiers swarmed in and out of shops, carrying off bolts of cloth, glassware, whatever the besieged merchants hadn't already lost. Antal ran on, block after block, his side aching, until he reached Mrs. Messik's apartment house. He rushed into the building, passing two soldiers in a drunken stupor, and jumped the stairs two at a time. Heart heaving, he pounded on Mrs. Messik's door.

There was no answer.

Maybe they'd already been warned. Maybe they knew not to answer.

"It's all right!" he cried. "Varga Antal here!"

He waited, and still no one answered. "Stay locked up!" he shouted. "The Russians have gone crazy!"

As he dragged himself toward home, he passed a knot of armed soldiers surrounding two girls. He thought of Márta and Katalin, and he hated this. One of the girls looked his way and must have noticed his sorry expression. "We made a bargain with them," she said with resignation. "We needed dinner."

He plodded on, cold and tired, avoiding puddles of vomit and piss. These drunks had guns, and in this frenzy he couldn't find his girlfriend. He had never felt so helpless.

When he reached home, he hid his wristwatch and violin. For the three days of the soldiers' leave, Antal, Sándor and men in the apartment house took turns keeping watch. If they spotted soldiers, they clanged pans and ran along the corridors yelling, "Look out!" Women hid. People in the street-facing apartments leaned out their windows, shouting, "*Patrul, patrul!*" calling the Russian military police, who never came.

Twice, soldiers entered the building. Antal, Sándor and Grandpapa pushed the sofa and bookcases in front of the apartment door while Mother and Katalin scrambled under the beds. The soldiers shouted and tried the door but finally left. On the third day, when Papa came home from the hospital, he told them in grim tones what he'd seen: gunshot wounds, knife slashes, alcohol poisonings, and women torn by gang rape.

"We were lucky that lieutenant warned us," he said.

Antal wondered if it was Kholodenko, that man who'd liked the Shostakovich music.

THE NEXT MORNING ANTAL SET OUT AGAIN to try to see Márta, having told no one but Sándor of his plans. Detouring around debris, he kept to side streets. He carried a shovel because he'd heard you were safer if the Soviets thought you were already working. The streets were quieter today, the soldiers seeming subdued. Maybe they were hungover.

This time Mrs. Messik answered the door. She gave him a paper with an address and told him the Hanáks had moved. "Tear up this paper after you visit," she said, "and tell no one."

Márta's new shelter was on the *körönd*, a circular street that Andrássy Avenue ran through. The flat had its own stairs and its own front door with iron bars and broken windows. When Antal knocked, he was greeted first by an old man, then by Anni. Her hair had grown a little, sticking up like a bad crewcut. "There's a cat in this house," she told him importantly.

Márta came to the door. "Antal. Come in."

Today she wore no soot on her face, only weariness. She led him through a passageway into a study where a typewriter sat on a small desk by a window. Face down on the desk lay what he assumed were manuscript pages, one page sideways and face-up under the others. Antal saw a few lines of text. The words looked like English.

"Your father's work?" he asked.

"He's helping a friend write a book. A commentary, I guess."

"About what?"

"Just . . . recent history. Poland, I think."

Márta shut the door. Aside from the desk, the typewriter, and a large leather armchair, the room was blank—no paintings, no bric-a-brac, not even pens. They sat down in the armchair, Márta curling in next to him.

He traced his finger over her lips as desperate questions pressed in on him. "While the soldiers were running wild, I worried about you," he said. "I tried to see you at Mrs. Messik's, but no one answered."

He felt her shoulders tense. She said, "We thought it would be safer here."

"Is it?"

"I don't know whether it would have been better to stay there."

Her ambivalence unsettled him. "Were you hurt?"

"No . . ." Her eyes shifted away. "No."

"Really?"

"Yes."

"You seem so tired. Or something."

"It's been hard to sleep."

"What's wrong?"

"I'm sorry, Antal, I'm just—like you said, I'm tired. Please, could you do the talking? Tell me what you've been doing, what's happening?"

He told her about the clean-up project and Mr. Lukács. "We had a sort of memorial in the courtyard, but his wife wanted Sándor to have no part in it. She still blames him."

"So awful for Sándor." Winter light touched the shadows around her eyes. "And you—have you been safe?"

"So far, yes. An occupation officer warned us about the three-day rampage." Out in the passage, Anni's high voice called to the cat. He looked around the near-empty room. "Was this place looted?"

"Yes. Some of it happened before we arrived, some after. But at least my cello was hidden at Mrs. Messik's."

"Wait—this place was looted while you were here? Soldiers came in? You saw them?"

"One soldier. I heard him. He carried off what he could."

Antal lifted her chin. "But he left you alone?"

She was still, then nodded.

"Are you sure you're all right?" he asked.

"Yes."

He had to take her word for it. She had asked him to do the talking. He grasped for something that might cheer her. "I'm writing some music," he said. "It's not finished. The melody came to me when I walked home from visiting you at Mrs. Messik's. Everything was wrecked and your sister was sick, so it's a sad piece."

"Sad things can still be beautiful. I want to hear it."

"You will."

"I need something good," she said.

He kissed her, and she whispered, "You're good." Her embrace was warm but fatigued, and he wished he really knew she was safe.

That night on the apartment walkway he told Sándor there seemed to be some kind of threat, maybe something to do with Márta's father. Sándor leaned on the railing and looked down into the courtyard. "I'm not surprised," he said.

"What do you mean?"

"Her father wasn't only critical of Hitler. He's an expert on Russia and Ukraine, at least that's what I've heard, and he's criticized Stalin, too. And now Stalin's army is here."

Antal looked into the sky above the rooftops, the blackness unbroken by any city lights. If Márta's life had ever been safe, it wasn't now, and he had stepped into her threatened world.

THE NEXT AFTERNOON ANTAL SET UP HIS MUSIC STAND in the bedroom and spread the Dvořák romanza on it. It had now been five months since Mr. Horváth first assigned him the piece. Yes, he'd practiced over the winter, but with frigid hands and a numb mind. He reproached himself now for his own choppy tonelessness. *Smooth it out, you idiot. Come on, this is six-eight. Dancing, not goose-stepping.* If only Mr. Horváth were here.

Antal made himself work with the piece for three hours straight, singing it, tapping the rhythm, setting the metronome, repeating tough measures, focusing the bow pressure, stretching his left hand and especially the little finger, counting off the rests for the accompaniment. He took a break when Mother called him to dinner, then returned and spot-practiced the opening.

The door opened and Grandpapa peered in. "I thought you'd like to know, Miklós is here."

"Thank God." Miklós wasn't in Siberia on *malenki robot*. Antal grabbed his coat and ran to the basement. From inside the door he called, "Miklós?"

"Yes. Here."

Antal trotted toward a small glow in the back corner. Miklós sat on the pillow end of his bench bed there and gestured for Antal to sit down at the foot. He had placed an old stool beside the bed, and on it a jar of dirty oil with a lit wick. The loaner violin lay in its case next to the bench. Miklós, with the beginnings of a ragged beard, held a cigarette between his lips.

"We didn't know what had happened to you," Antal said.

"I went back to the Danube Bend. Home." Miklós lifted the cigarette, the smoke curling upward. "No one was there. My mother and father, gone. My sister, all my brothers, gone. Uncles, cousins, gone. The girl also."

"The girl?" Antal asked. "You mean your girlfriend?"

"Don't tell the others." Miklós's eyes fixed on the jar candle. "My father gave a horse to her father, and she was . . . my wife. She was pregnant when I left with the army."

"*Jaj*." The dark cold bore down, heavy as fear. "You lost a *wife*?"

"I hope not. I hope things are better than that. But bad fate happens, again and again, lose this, lose that, lose her, lose him, lose them. Just ask your cousin. He knows."

"My God, Miklós, how terrible."

"I was a fool to think they'd be there." Miklós shook his cigarette and the embers fell to the brick floor. "Your grandfather gave me a job. He said the custodian died, so now I'll clean around the building, carry water for the outdoor loo. Your grandfather says he'll ask people in the apartments to give me food. Or things I can trade for food. I don't know how long I'll stay."

Antal sighed. The work was certainly needed, but who knew if people would actually pay up. He watched Miklós's shadowed profile in the sorry light of the wick jar. "I suppose you know how to play Monti's *Csárdás*," he said.

"Oh, sure. I learned it years ago."

"I know it, too," Antal said, "but I want to play it faster." Not that he would care about playing it fast or slow if Miklós weren't so damned alone. "Maybe we can work on it."

Miklós dropped his cigarette stub and looked at him thoughtfully. "The little finger of the left hand is busy in that piece, and doesn't your finger hurt sometimes?"

"Yes," Antal admitted. "I hope that will change."

"But your right hand is iron, Varga. I've never seen anybody hold a long note the way you do. I could walk to Miskolc and back before your bow reaches the tip."

Antal laughed and went upstairs for his violin, more candles, and the music to the *csárdás*. They worked through it one phrase at a time, with Miklós taking it faster and faster, forcing him to keep up. Antal put up with the ache in his left little finger.

THE CITY'S PIPES HAD BROKEN DURING THE SIEGE, and now Antal wondered how he could ever have taken water for granted. Every drop the family cooked with, washed with, flushed with, or drank had to be lugged from a standpipe near the Parliament building. His family took turns with these trips, and now Miklós came, too. More than once Antal and the other males had turned back, nervous about *malenki robot*, if they saw Russian soldiers. Like every outing, the water treks had to be done in daylight, well before curfew and before the soldiers started drinking.

On a morning in late February Antal and Sándor used some of the hard-won water and tried, once again, to scrub blood stains off the sofa upholstery. Suddenly a girl's voice called from the street below: "Antal!" He ran out onto the balcony and leaned over the railing. Sándor followed. On the sidewalk, Márta in trousers and a cap grinned up at them.

"Antal! I tagged along with some neighbors," she shouted. "*Szia*, Sándor! I haven't seen you forever! Well? Is someone going to invite me in?"

They dashed down the stairs and Antal threw open the front door. Márta stepped in, pulling off her cap, shaking out her hair, even laughing. Antal picked her up and spun her.

Sándor kissed her on each cheek. "My cousin fretted like holy misery about you over the winter. But here you are, beautiful as ever. Come on in."

Katalin welcomed Márta into the apartment with a happy squeal. She made a weak linden tea and they all shared it at the table.

"Your hair looks so pretty, Márta," Katalin said.

"I washed it." Márta winked. "In liters and liters and liters of warm water."

"How?" Katalin asked, astounded.

"Sarolta and I washed our laundry at the thermal pools. Then we jumped in, clothes and all, and washed ourselves. I'm a new person."

"I want to be a new person, too," Sándor said.

"Maybe we should all go dunk in the Széchenyi pools," Antal agreed. For weeks they'd been bathing with nothing more than a cloth and a bowl of water. After Márta's sad exhaustion last week, what a relief it was to see her in higher spirits. Wistfully he thought of her splashing in the pool, her clothes clinging to her lithe body. He wished he'd been there.

After the tea, he and Márta sat together on the foyer stairs, a draft seeping in around the doors as they talked. She told him that Anni wasn't as sick, but not strong, either, and that their family would have to move again. "I don't know where," she said. "My father's going to Debrecen to help a writer who has cancer. The man's trying to finish a history book. The publisher will pay them both."

"How could any publisher in Hungary put out a book right now?"

"It's a British publisher."

Antal crossed his arms against the chill, dubious. The British were broke, too. Besides, when the Germans were in control, working for the British would have meant inviting a firing squad. He was quickly losing confidence that the Soviets would be any gentler.

"What do you think about this?" he asked.

"I'm not sure. My father really does have a writer friend in Debrecen who has cancer." She lowered her head, lowered her voice. "But if you're wondering if this is the story that my parents are giving while there's actually more going on—well, I've had the same question."

"And while your father's in Debrecen, where will the rest of you be?"

"I don't know. We can't keep staying with Mr. Sárosi." Her voice tightened. "I hate it there. And other people are living with Mrs. Messik now. I wish we had a place of our own."

He had heard that Mrs. Lukács was moving out to live with her daughter, and he told Márta about it. "Maybe your family could move into her apartment. It's here on the ground floor. Small."

Márta turned to him, agape. "I don't care how small it is, I want it!"

"Your parents should see my grandfather about it. He'll know who to talk to."

"Oh, Antal, that would be better than anything that's happened to me all winter."

He put his arms around her and wished. They'd had so many dashed hopes.

THE NEXT DAY MR. AND MRS. HANÁK CAME BY to speak with Antal's parents and grandfather. The day after that, Mrs. Lukács moved out. Mrs. Hanák came again, this time asking for Antal. As his family retreated to the back rooms, he sat down with her at the dining table, nervously aware that he'd hardly ever spoken with her.

"Thank you for being so good to Márta this winter," she said. "The girls and I will move in downstairs in a few days. My husband left this morning for Debrecen." She pushed back a strand of hair that had fallen out of her bun. "Antal, there are some things I need you to know. I could have asked Márta to tell you, but I don't want to risk things being miscommunicated."

Her voice was polite but dead earnest. "To begin with, I'm using a different name now. My legal name is Hanák Livia, but I'll be introducing myself here by my maiden name, Záborsky. You may call me Livia *néni* or Záborsky *néni,* but please, not Hanák. Do you understand?"

He didn't. "Will Márta also be called Záborsky?"

"I've told the girls not to give their surname unless they're asked. Then they're to use Záborsky."

"But what if they have to show identification?"

She nodded grimly. "My husband is trying to procure new papers for us. What I need you to remember is—" She closed her eyes a moment. "It's this. With people that don't already know us, we're keeping it quiet that we're Hanák Viktor's family. Viktor wants us to do this."

Antal rested his head in his palm, trying to take this in. "So is he hiding? Is that why he's in Debrecen?"

"Not exactly. It's complicated. But please don't use the name Hanák. And I'm not telling people he's a journalist."

"What are you telling them?"

"Just that he's a writer, specializing in history."

Everything Sándor had said, and everything Márta had half-said, now collided in his mind. "All right," was all he could say.

"We don't know how long this will have to go on," she said. "For this spring, the girls won't be going back to school. I'll teach them at home. But I can't cut them off from everyone, and I've told Márta she can see you and your family. But please be careful as you introduce any of us to others. I've already made the same request to your parents and your grandfather."

"I'll tell Katalin and Sándor," Antal said. God, how he hoped none of them would slip up. "So will Márta see her father at all?"

"Yes. But I'm not sure when. Travel is so difficult. The train routes are bombed out or commandeered by soldiers. At this point we can't go to Debrecen. Anni really isn't strong enough. If she doesn't get better soon, Viktor will have to come here, but we don't know what we're dealing with. This is all very hard on him."

"It's hard on Márta, too."

"I know. Oh, do I know." She pressed her hand to her lips. "I should be going. Antal, I know this is a heavy load for you, and I'm sorry." She reached across the table and touched his hand. "God bless you."

The Hanáks' moving day came. As Antal and Sándor left the apartment to help them, Mother handed Sándor a linen napkin with four eggs for the Hanáks. It was no small gift. Hungarian currency was inflating into sheer worthlessness, and Antal knew how his mother stood in endless queues to barter dishes or jewelry for scarce food.

Márta arrived with her sisters and mother. They pulled a cart laden with suitcases, bedding, a few books, Márta's cello, and, riding atop a blanket, Anni. The fire in their previous apartment had destroyed everything else that they had. Márta's mother unlocked the door to their new home, and Antal and Sándor entered with them.

Sándor introduced himself, pointedly addressing Márta's mother as Záborsky *néni*. He gave her the eggs. "From my aunt," he said. "Antal's mother."

"Oh," she breathed, a catch in her voice. "How kind."

Márta looked at her mother. "Oh, Anyu, it seems so long ago that we had eggs."

The Hanáks had bought from Mrs. Lukács what she didn't take with her: the sofa bed, an armoire, a small table, two kitchen chairs, mismatched dishes, and a few pans. Mrs. Hanák was especially glad to see a telephone, although service hadn't yet been reconnected. Antal and Sándor moved furniture to squeeze the family into the chilly studio apartment. Mrs. Hanák spread sheets on the fold-out sofa she would share with Anni. Behind the sofa Márta and Sarolta stashed sleeping mats they would unroll at night.

Anni climbed onto a kitchen chair with her doll. "I'm cold," she said.

Mrs. Hanák wrapped a blanket around her. "Márta, boil one of the eggs for Anni."

They needed firewood for the cook stove. Antal ran to his apartment to get some, and when he came back downstairs with it, Sándor was gone.

"He went to get more wood," Márta said. "To heat the apartment."

"Well, he didn't come upstairs for it." Antal glanced out the window at the basement door. If Sándor went to the basement, he'd be right back. But Sándor didn't come right back.

Antal helped Márta and Sarolta clean the dirty floors and windows. Maybe Sándor had gone into the streets to pick up wood among the rubble. People did that all the time. An hour later Sándor still had not returned. Magda *néni* came by and waved at Antal through the window he was washing. He introduced her to the family—the *Záborsky* family.

It was mid-afternoon when Antal left the Hanáks', and Sándor still had not come. He wasn't upstairs in their own apartment, either, and no one in the family had seen him. "We thought he was with you," Mother said, worry creasing her face.

It grew dark. They ate a supper of lentils and cottage cheese. Afterward Antal and Grandpapa went to ask the Hanáks, then Miklós, then other neighbors if they'd seen Sándor. They hadn't. At bedtime Sándor was still gone.

"Where *is* he?" Antal asked.

"Maybe—" Grandpapa shook his head, the kind of thing people did when all the possibilities were bad.

IT WAS ALMOST NOON THE NEXT DAY when Sándor returned. Antal yanked the door open and pulled him in. Sándor huddled cold and silent by the tile stove with Grandpapa. Katalin brought him a cup of hot water as Mother boiled one remaining egg for him.

"Did they put you on *malenki robot*?" Antal asked.

"Yes," Sándor muttered. "I reached down for a wood plank, and when I stood up, a soldier nudged me with his rifle butt. He marched me off with a dozen other men, and we pulled down half-burnt ceiling boards." Sándor winced, rubbed his eyes as though he'd hardly slept. "I'd still be out there if some poor bastard hadn't fallen off a ladder. Everybody looked his way, so I took off."

"Sándor, you shouldn't have gone out," Antal said, with twenty-four hours of fear straining his voice. "It's like when you went out for horsemeat—"

"Stop," Sándor ordered.

Chapter Thirty-Three

Misha

February 3, 2007

KRISTÓF PACED AROUND INSIDE THE SZÉCHENYI-HEGY station of the Children's Railway. He glanced over at Ópa on a bench, looked up at the old mosaic mural of happy scouts parading. When he was a boy he used to come here with Ópa and Óma, back before the transition, when this short rail line was a communist project and the scouts were Young Pioneers.

He'd been waiting for fifteen minutes. By the station clock, it was 10:05 a.m., and Blanka had said to be here at 10:00. He'd just bought five tickets—four adults, one child—from the girl at the counter, who wore a dark blue suit and looked to be about twelve. Slipping his hand into his pocket, Kristóf fingered the tickets and the toy train engine Ópa had helped him choose. Something for Misha. He walked over to Ópa on a nearby bench. Ópa held a cane because it had snowed, and his doctor had told him he absolutely must not fall.

"When are they going to get here?" Kristóf fumed.

"Patience."

Five minutes later, as Kristóf was wondering if Blanka would stand him up, the station door opened. A chap with early-thinning hair and a mechanic's jacket held the door, and Blanka walked in, her long legs in tall boots. At Kristóf's side, Ópa rose.

"Misha," Blanka called back through the doorway. "Come on."

The boy hurried in. He pulled off a striped cap, tossing his dark hair askew. Kristóf caught his breath. This was his son. He pushed down an impulse to rush to the boy.

"My God, Kristóf," Ópa whispered. "He's just like you. Like Zoltán."

Blanka took the child in hand and looked up. "*Szia*, Kristóf. Sorry we're a little late."

"No, no, it's all right," he stammered. He tried to smile, but the fact was that his history with Blanka had consisted only of the recent arguing and the long-ago affair. And here was a man standing with her, eying him, placing a firm hand on Misha's shoulder. Blanka introduced the man as Lengyel Endre. This Endre nodded, shook Kristóf's hand and said a grave hello.

Ópa transferred his cane to his left hand and offered his right to Blanka, then Endre. "Varga Antal," he said. "I am Kristóf's grandfather."

Kristóf clasped hands with Blanka, trying not to think about the nights that had begun with a touch of her hand. Endre's serious expression did not change.

Kristóf turned to his son and found the boy looking up at him. "And you're Misha," he said with a touch of wonder. Misha blinked and nodded.

Blanka bent close to the boy. Kristóf could only guess that she and Endre had discussed this moment, planned it, maybe even rehearsed it. "Kristóf is an old friend of mine," she told Misha. "He and his grandfather wanted to meet you. You can call them Kristóf *bácsi* and Antal *bácsi*. We're going to ride the train with them."

"But I'll sit with you and Apuka?" he asked her.

"Near us. Near them."

Kristóf wasn't prepared for how it stung, hearing Misha call Endre his daddy.

Ópa nudged him. "Give him the toy train," he said quietly.

Misha watched as Kristóf pulled out the engine and handed it to him. The boy ran the wheels on his hand.

"What do you say, Misha?" Endre reminded him.

"Thank you."

Kristóf handed Blanka the tickets as Misha chugged the toy along a bench. Blanka and Endre said he shouldn't have bought their tickets and Kristóf said no, no again and watched his son playing.

He sidled over to Ópa. "I want to talk to him, but I don't know what to say."

"We'll try solfege."

Kristóf scowled in confusion. *Do-re-mi-fa-sol* in a railway station?

With a chuff and a rattle, the train pulled up on the narrow-gauge track outside. Kristóf followed his grandfather to the platform and into the red-and-white train car, watching to be sure Ópa managed the steps safely. They sat down on a wooden seat across the aisle from Blanka and Endre. Misha plopped down next to his mother, gripping the train toy. The conductor, an adolescent boy in trousers too long for him, circulated among the few passengers, checking tickets. Outside the window, a girl worker in a blue cap stood on the platform and saluted. The train wheezed to a start, heading off through the snow-dusted trees of the Buda Hills.

Misha began walking up and down the aisle. Kristóf called his name, but he walked past. Was this the way the whole visit would go, with Misha oblivious?

Kristóf leaned close to his grandfather. "What were you saying about solfege?"

"Just a minute." Ópa reached into his pocket and pulled out a cellophane bag of colored gumdrop bears. "Misha, come here."

The boy approached curiously.

"Did you know these are singing bears?" Ópa asked him.

Misha pulled a crooked smile. "No, they're not."

"Yes, they are," Kristóf said, remembering his grandparents' old game. "You have to sing if you want to eat them."

Ópa lined up eight colored bears on his coat sleeve. "Kristóf *bácsi*," he asked, though his eyes were on Misha, "which one would you like?"

"Let's see." Kristóf pursed his lips and looked at the boy. "Which one is best?"

"The red one," Misha said.

"Red. Hmm. That one's *fa*. Right, Antal *bácsi*?"

Ópa made a show of shrugging. "Try it and see."

Kristóf sang *do, re, mi, fa,* on each note pointing at a candy in turn. "Well, look at that. The red one's *fa*, just like I said. So now I get to eat it." He turned to Misha. "Or should I give it to you?"

Misha grinned. "Me!"

Kristóf handed him the candy. Ópa set a new candy bear in the place of *fa*. Then, pointing at the bears as though counting them, he sang through the scale three times, demonstrating.

"Which one this time?" Ópa asked Misha.

"Yellow."

"And what note is that?"

Misha sang the ascending notes, *da-da-da-da-da*, while pointing at the candy bears. "I can't remember what that one's called," Misha said. "But it sounds like . . ." He hummed *sol*, perfectly pitched.

Ópa raised his eyebrows and nodded. Kristóf saw Blanka and Endre watching as he handed the yellow bear to Misha. "It's *sol*," he said. "Very good."

"Do another one," Misha said.

They played the solfege game the rest of the train route. Soon Misha had learned the note names and was quizzing Kristóf and Ópa. "What's the orange one?" or "Where's *ti*?" Kristóf hummed notes without naming them and had Misha find them. The boy almost always succeeded. Soon the candies had all been eaten and Ópa was setting out coins instead.

The train came to a final stop at Hűvösvölgy, the end of the line. They stepped off onto the platform, and Misha pointed to the station diner. "Can we have a treat?" he asked Blanka.

She shook her head. "You had candy on the train. That's enough."

Kristóf was seized with dread that this might be the last he saw of Misha. "Couldn't I buy him a glass of milk?" he asked Blanka. "Or something?"

Endre laughed uneasily. "He won't be content with milk."

Blanka beckoned Kristóf aside. "You wanted to meet him. Now you have."

"I like him."

"He's a nice boy, a happy child. Endre is one of the main reasons for that. Kristóf, I hope we can finish this now."

Nearby, people assembled for the next train. A child in her father's arms dropped her dolly and wailed until her mother picked it up.

"I'm not ready to say I'm finished," Kristóf told Blanka.

"Misha has a good life. Don't disrupt it. Please," she implored him, voice on edge. "We need you to sign those forms."

"I'm not ready to do that."

"Then what's it going to take?"

He gaped. If he didn't know Blanka better—and when it came down to it, maybe he *didn't* know her better—those words would sound like a bribe offer. "For God's sake," he hissed.

Misha had been standing with Endre and Ópa, and now the boy ran to his mother. "Anyuka! The old uncle says he has a violin, and he knows how to play it, and he has a piano, and he plays that, too, and so does Kristóf *bácsi*. We can go to their house, and I can try it. The piano. Even the violin. That's what the old uncle told Apuka. Can we go? Please?"

Kristóf glanced at his grandfather for confirmation. Ópa gave a slight nod.

"Of course you're all invited," Kristóf said, as a troubled look shot between Blanka and Endre.

"The thing is, Misha has some musical aptitude," Ópa said to both of them, in the professional tone Kristóf had heard him use countless times with students. "You'll forgive me, I hope, if I was testing him, but it's true that Misha has a ready ear. And excellent pitch. He would do well with music lessons. You're free to do as you like, but that is what I would recommend. I'm inviting you to my home so he can see how a violin feels in his hands. And the piano, too. Certainly. Of course it's up to you. Naturally, Kristóf and I would enjoy more time with him."

"That's right," Kristóf said.

"We should go there," Misha told his mother, pulling on her arm. "These uncles are fun."

"Misha, enough," Endre said. "Your mother is tired."

"What about next Saturday?" Kristóf asked.

Misha gazed up at him. "I want to come," he repeated.

Kristóf looked into the boy's brown eyes, aching over the years he had not known Misha existed. He touched Misha's shoulder. "I hope you can come. We'll make hot chocolate."

Blanka grasped Misha's hand. "Excuse us a minute," she said to Kristóf. She led Misha a few meters off to talk with Endre. Kristóf stood in tense silence while the boy pleaded with his parents—yes, parents. He tried to tell himself that this standoffish Endre, with his high forehead and mechanic's jacket, was not Misha's father, only a step-father; but what was a father, or a step? Endre was the man that Misha would go home with, the man who loved Misha's mother and put food on Misha's plate.

"Uncles!" Misha suddenly shouted. "We can come!"

"I guess we'll see you next Saturday," Endre said to Kristóf as though he had lost an argument. As they made arrangements, Kristóf sensed Endre's strain like his own.

"Thanks," Kristóf said.

"Right."

It was the best that either of them could do.

IT MADE KRISTÓF NERVOUS, HIS GRANDFATHER on the snow with a cane. He called a taxi and saw Ópa home. Back in the apartment Kristóf made coffee and sat with him awhile since he didn't have to be at work until five. Both of them kept saying Misha was smart and probably talented and looked like a Varga. Very much like one.

"He's wonderful," Ópa said, sounding as perplexed and astonished and wistful as Kristóf felt; and he asked, not for the first time, if Kristóf wanted to talk with an attorney.

The dilemma weighed on him like a fear he couldn't name. "I don't know what to do."

WHEN HE LEFT HIS GRANDFATHER'S FLAT, he took a long walk along the Pest embankment of the Danube. Ice crusted the surface in places. He hunched his shoulders as new snow swirled down, and he remembered Misha looking out the train window at the snow and calling that other man his father. Not until today had Kristóf envied a married man. He couldn't escape it: if he had married Blanka, even if he had so much as answered her calls and stood by her in her pregnancy, if he had just been braver, Misha would know him, trust him.

He wished Lisa were here. Her words would be kind. Probably not easy, but kind.

He left the cold river and walked to the internet café.

Dear Lisa,

You will be happy to know that my grandfather is thinking about changing the ending to that suite he wrote. Also I have to tell you something. A month ago I found out I have a son, five years old. His mother and her husband want me to sign papers to give him up. Today I met him. I don't know what to say except that he is a Varga, he is my son, and this is very hard. I didn't know I would love him.

Every time I tell you something, it seems you understand, and that is why I tell you this. Please write to me when you can, it doesn't matter if it's a long note or short.

—Kristóf

CHAPTER THIRTY-FOUR

The Bomb Shelter Quintet

March 8, 1945

THE WAR HAD LEFT BUDAPEST LIKE A MURDERER LEAVING the scene of a crime. The fighting had moved west to the towns near Austria. Antal's family and neighbors blamed that insane bastard Hitler for keeping this war going when he should have surrendered long ago, and they blamed the Soviets, too, for the current drunken rampage. News circulated of soldiers killing wine merchants to get at their stock.

"And yet I've seen people wearing red arm bands," Antal said to Sándor as they tuned the piano again, for it had slipped. "And red star badges."

"Well, they've smelled the shift in the wind."

Antal struck the tuning fork and knew Sándor was right. Márta had said pretty much the same thing. The Arrow Cross government had collapsed, and a provisional government had been set up in the east in Debrecen, which the Soviets had occupied since last fall. Márta said the main Hungarian leaders had been trained in Moscow. Everyone was saying that when peace terms were finally drawn up, the Allies would insist on Hungary's having free elections. But Márta said, because her father said, the communists would find some way around it.

Sándor played a D major chord on the piano to test it. The middle F sharp note didn't sing: it clunked. The strings of E, F and F sharp were still broken.

"This thing is like a typewriter without vowels," Sándor complained. "But there may be hope. A few days ago, I talked to Mr. Boros."

Antal knew both the man and his music shop well; Mr. Boros had been a family friend for years.

"The shop has three pianos," Sándor said, "all out of tune after the bombing. I told him about tuning this piano, and he asked me to tune the ones in his shop. Says he'll order replacement strings for us. If there are any available. And for the work he'll pay me with lighter flints."

Flints seemed to be the currency of the week. "Good," Antal said.

An hour or so later Sándor left with the tuning fork and a wrench. While he was gone, Antal stood at the brightest window for light and practiced the Dvořák romanza for two hours. After that, he opened his music manuscript book and made a few changes to "Miklós's Fiddle," a Gypsy-style violin solo he'd written after practicing with Miklós. Then he experimented with the piece that had come to him amid the wreckage and the cold, which at some point he'd started calling "Song to Our Enemies." It was becoming a set of variations on a theme. Today he heard a new variation—lower register, inverted melody. He wrote this down. What perplexed him was how to end the piece. So far it was such a gentle thing, as though their enemies had merely raised a few sad questions. He played through it again, hummed it, backtracked, tried out end lines, tried adding dissonance. No matter what he did, it wasn't strong enough. If he could just talk to Mr. Horváth—but he couldn't. On the incomplete manuscript he wrote, *Ask Márta.*

THE NEXT MORNING ANTAL WANDERED OUT OF THE BEDROOM and found Sándor sitting at the piano with his journal and the guitar. Sándor wrote, strummed, and reached over the top of the guitar to tap on the piano keys. Stepping closer, Antal peered at the open journal and saw words with chords jotted in. "A song?" he asked.

"It's not done." Sándor waved his hand dismissively. "Maybe it's not even any good."

Antal left him alone and began assembling whatever he could find of his textbooks, because school would start in some form tomorrow. The government had decided that students who returned would get credit for the whole year, despite the months lost. Antal felt relieved to go back.

Math proofs, irritable teachers, his seatmate Palocs Jakob bumming pencils: maybe something would feel normal now.

But as it turned out, an entire wing of the school had been destroyed in the bombing. On their first day back, Antal and Sándor stood against a cold wall in the lunchroom. The headmaster, roaring to make himself heard, announced which teachers had left the city or died. He began calling roll. At the gaps when no one answered, other students shouted information if they had it: "Bodnár left to live with his uncle." "Fekete won't be back in school until fall." "Kemeny's apartment was vacated and nobody knows where the family is." "Palocs is dead. Shot in the crossfire."

Antal sucked in his breath. Palocs dead? How many times had he lent Palocs pencils? Laughed with him? Repeated the teacher's instructions to him because Palocs never listened?

Antal sat through classes in a corner of the lunch room, dazed and barely hearing what was said. Palocs was part of *life*, not—oh, God, not this. Somehow Antal got through the school day. He went home and told Márta that his disorganized seatmate was dead. She put her arm around his back, absorbing the shock with him.

After a long time she asked to hear the piece he'd been writing, and he brought his violin to her apartment. While Mrs. Hanák coached Sarolta through a German lesson and Anni through phonics, Antal played "Song to Our Enemies" for Márta. Again the notes mourned the downed bridges, the convulsed streets, the smoky sky, and the dead boys, like Palocs. Márta listened. When he reached the end of what he'd written, he said, "I don't know how to end it," and he waited on edge for her response.

"I don't know, either. But it's beautiful." With her finger she tapped the title. "'Song to Our Enemies.' Why did you name it that?"

"It's just what came to me, I guess."

"Is the piece too lovely to be a message to enemies?" she asked.

"I don't know." By now he couldn't think of the song by any other name.

"We should get our music group together," she said. "Miklós could come, too."

"I don't think he'd come. Our place is too *gadje*, or whatever he calls it. Too strange, not Gypsy enough."

"Then let's go to the basement. Where he is."

That evening they pulled up benches near Miklós's set-up and opened their instruments. By candlelight Antal leafed through the music they'd played—Christmas pieces now out of season, German hymns they'd used for burying Hoff Dietrich. The only piece in their stack that Miklós knew was "*Erdő, Erdő, Erdő,*" so they played through it several times, Miklós finally joining in when they sped it up to his liking.

After the fourth round, Sándor said, "I guess that wasn't too bad, considering the last three months. Is anybody practicing much? I mean, anybody besides Antal?"

The others said no.

"None of you?" Antal asked. "Come on."

"Well, I wrote something," Sándor said. "Just a ridiculous little ditty."

"Let's hear it," Antal said.

Sándor shrugged. Katalin held a candle close while he picked up his journal from the bench and set it open on his knees. "Inspired by recent experiences." He strummed and began to sing, reading from the journal.

> *Boy, you better look out, better stay off the street,*
> *'Cause if you have two hands and two functioning feet,*
> *Then you're a wanted man and you'll certainly get caught:*
> *You'll find yourself slaving at malenki robot.*
> *Oh, oh, oh, oh, oh, malenki robot.*

Miklós sniggered. Katalin giggled. Márta smiled. Antal listened uneasily. The memory of Sándor's disappearance was still too fresh. Sándor continued.

> *I told Uncle László I'd walk down to the store.*
> *Well, he grabbed my collar and he bolted the door.*
> *"No you don't!" he shouted. "Stay away from there"*

—Sándor shook his finger, scolding in rhythm—

> *Or you'll end up in a parade to God-knows-where!"*
> *Oh, oh, oh, oh, oh, malenki robot.*

Katalin joined in on the *oh, oh, oh*. Antal smiled, picturing his father. Sándor had the finger-shaking down cold. The song went on.

Antal and I, when we have to go out,
We plan extra hours going alternate routes,
Keeping out of trouble, but it's harder than we thought:
On every damned corner there's malenki robot!
Oh, oh, oh, oh, oh, malenki robot.

Katalin jumped up. She pulled Miklós to his feet and the two stamped, marched, saluted, and stumbled against each other, laughing.

Oh, I cross the streets with caution and I wait 'til danger's gone.
I look where I'm headed and I keep my radar on.
But malenki robot seems to follow me around,
And—wait, who's that soldier with the furious frown?

Sándor pointed at Antal, then Katalin and Miklós pointed at him, too. Antal gave them a furious frown. Sándor kept singing.

Something's gone wrong. Here I am on a train.
Long ago we passed through the Hungarian plain.
We keep on heading eastward for malenki robot.
And I would jump off now, but I'd probably get shot.
Ooooooooh—
Uncle, I tried to be careful, but it all has come to naught.
I'm off to purgatory on malenki robot!

Sándor ended the song with a crashing strum as Katalin and Miklós laughed. Márta clapped but seemed no more certain about this than Antal felt.

"It would be easier for me to laugh," Antal told Sándor, "if you hadn't actually been prodded with a rifle butt."

"I know, but that's why I wrote the song. I can go crazy being scared, or I can laugh."

"Laughing," Miklós said. "Cheaper than getting drunk."

Sándor nodded.

"Antal's writing a beautiful piece," Márta told the group. "It's called 'Song to Our Enemies.'"

"It isn't finished," Antal said.

"Play it," Katalin urged him.

Márta held the music and Antal played it, conscious of his own mistakes. After Sándor's vaudeville, the music felt heavy, and Antal told himself—as Mr. Horváth had told him so many times—*don't apologize*. When the music ran out, he set the violin on his lap and said simply, "That's it."

"My God, Antal," Sándor said, "if that's what you do for your enemies, what do you do for friends? Serve a banquet, too?"

Katalin said, "It's gorgeous."

"Yes, it is," said a voice from the stairs.

They turned. Magda *néni* stepped down carrying half a loaf of bread, a jar of yogurt, and a spoon. She handed them to Miklós.

"Thank you, I'm starved," Miklós said, tearing into the bread. "You and the Varga grandfather are the only ones paying me lately."

"Oh, dear," Magda *néni* said. "Well, may I listen for a little while?"

Antal said, "We're not really—"

"Of course you may," Katalin broke in. "Let's do 'The Light Shines,' all right, Antal?"

They were pitifully out of practice. But they played and sang "The Light Shines" while Miklós ate.

"It's wonderful," Magda said at the end. "You know, people are sad and afraid, and they need some music. *This* music. I wish you'd give us a little concert. We could do it down here."

"How soon?" Antal asked. "We haven't prepared."

Sándor set his guitar aside. "Antal, people heard you practice down here all winter. That wasn't perfect, and this doesn't have to be, either. What the hell, why not?"

"And anyway, Antal," Márta said, "you always sound better than you think."

Magda gestured toward Miklós. "And when I invite people, I'll tell them to bring food for our custodian."

"Then the sooner, the better," Katalin said.

Antal turned to Magda *néni*. "I guess we will."

Miklós's gaze circled the group. "Thank you," he sighed.

At the end of the evening Antal walked Márta back to her ground-floor apartment. Lanterns in a few windows broke the darkness. The winter's iciness had passed, and she wore a short jacket. They lingered outside her door and he held her at the waist, his fingers delighting in the warm contours under her jacket hem.

"Sándor was impressed with your piece," she said. "Sometimes I have the feeling he envies you."

"Who wouldn't, when I'm with a beautiful girl?"

He kissed her, felt her closeness deep and good. Her fingers caressed his throat. To his surprise, she gently unfastened the top button on his shirt, uncovered a sliver of his chest, and kissed it, a small gesture, scarcely more than a touch, but oh, how her tenderness gripped him.

"Every time I'm with you," he whispered, "it's harder to leave."

MAGDA *NÉNI* SCHEDULED THE BASEMENT CONCERT for the last Sunday in March, barely more than two weeks away. The group only had two pieces well prepared and not much time to rehearse. Antal hoped some of the group members could do solos that wouldn't take much practice. He began asking them. Katalin said she could sing the Bach-Gounod *Ave Maria*, and she'd talk to Márta about a cello accompaniment for it.

"Good," Antal said. He assembled a bowl of boiled potatoes and a dekagram of cheese and took the food downstairs to Miklós. "At this concert," Antal said, "could you play the Monti *csárdás*?"

Miklós bit into the cheese and nodded.

"And what about the 'Rákóczi March'?" Antal asked. The march was so blaringly Hungarian that Austria had once outlawed it. If any music was likely to get the residents cheering, that was it. "Do you know it?"

"Do I know the march? Yes." Miklós waved his hand as though shooing away a fly. "Have I played it? Yes. About five hundred times. Am I bored with it? Yes."

"But do people like it? Yes. And will it rouse them to pitch in for your keep? If that doesn't do it, I don't know what will."

Miklós reached into the rucksack he kept next to the bed and pulled out a fork. "Hmm."

"I'll back you up," Antal said. "Let's go through it a few times, I'll write down an accompaniment."

"Suit yourself. But I don't know why you like music written down, Varga. You play from this"—Miklós tapped his own skull—"instead of from here." He touched his heart.

"As a matter of fact," Antal shot back, "I play from the heart, *and* the head, and even the gut when I have to. And if you don't want me to accompany you, then all right, I'll skip it."

"No, don't skip it." Miklós stabbed a potato with the fork. "I don't want to play the fucking march on my own."

Miklós, Rákóczi, check.

Márta had told Antal she'd once played in a Bach cello-violin duet. She thought she could play it for the concert if they could find the music— her own copy had burned in the apartment fire—and if he took the violin part. They would work it out, he told her. Antal bought the music from Mr. Boros's shop, and he and Márta practiced the piece whenever they could. Her tone, as always, was rich, but she tripped up on the more difficult passages. Sometimes, so did he. He had hoped she could help him work out an ending to "Song to Our Enemies," but they only had time for the Bach duet, or occasionally for fine-tuning Márta's accompaniment to Katalin's song.

Then there was Sándor. One afternoon as they sat at the dining table with their schoolwork, Sándor said he might as well do the *malenki robot* song for the concert. Antal closed his history book and considered. The threat of *malenki robot* was diminishing, people said, with fewer men shipped off. And since the concert would be in the basement, they'd only be telling the bitter joke among neighbors, not occupation soldiers.

"Do you want the rest of us to play it with you?" Antal asked. "Or sing?"

"Oh, maybe Kati could do the 'oh, oh, oh' parts." He thought. "Just a minute." Sándor pulled his journal out from under his physics book. "There's this other song I'm working on, and maybe I'll do it for the concert if I can finish the words." He leafed through the journal until he reached a page half-filled with musical notation and some lyrics. Sándor seemed to hesitate but finally handed it to Antal. "See what you think."

Antal read the melody, humming it. "Tempo?" he asked. "Maybe *andante*?"

"I think so."

"It's a good melody so far. Is this all of it?"

"It's the first verse and the bridge," Sándor said. "I'm trying to write more verses."

Antal then read the words Sándor had scrawled under the first few lines of notation.

Pest, along the Danube, below the rising hills,
North of Csepel's factories, upriver from the mills,
Pest where I first breathed, and where I learned, and where I grew,
Home of all I've ever known, I love you still.

Sándor said, "I know the first verse doesn't say much—"

"But it's starting to."

"Really? You think so?" Sándor asked, apprehension in his voice.

"Yes."

"What if you wrote a violin part for it?"

There wasn't much time. But as Antal read the words and music again, the city's grief welled up in him, just as it had on that walk through the ashen, bloody snow. He told Sándor he would try, and Sándor tore out the page for him. Over the next week Antal experimented with violin interludes and harmonies. Twice he asked Sándor if he'd finished writing the words, because in a song wasn't the music supposed to lift up the meaning? But Sándor wasn't finished. If anything, he seemed nervous about showing what he had.

One evening after practicing scales, Antal played his own "Song to Our Enemies," again frustrated by having no good ending to it. Then he picked up Sándor's song again and heard, as though for the first time, the sympathy between his melody and Sándor's. He went to the living room, where Sándor was making another try at the lyrics.

"If I play my piece in the key of G instead of F," Antal said, "it would flow naturally into your song."

Sándor looked up. "That's perfect for my piece, but wouldn't it—I don't know—minimize yours?"

Antal looked off toward the shattered window and the scorched city beyond it. Things in this world were not only minimized but destroyed. "For now, let's not worry about it."

"Thanks," Sándor said humbly. "Very much."

ON THE SUNDAY AFTERNOON OF THE CONCERT, Antal and the rest of the group set up in the basement near the courtyard windows, the only spot with enough light. The neighbors crowded in, sitting on the stairs or benches, bringing their own chairs, holding children on their laps or standing against the walls. Antal's parents and grandfather sat in front with Márta's mother and sisters. Mr. Boros from the music shop sat with them, his thin dark hair combed across his high forehead. Antal looked around. Almost all the people in the building had come—except, conspicuously, two women who'd been friends with Mrs. Lukács. Antal pushed down an irritated guess they were boycotting Sándor.

Magda *néni* stood up and addressed the crowd. "Well, we're back in our favorite place, aren't we?"

Chuckles and groans ran through the audience.

"But we *are* with our favorite musicians. Ladies and gentlemen and children and whatever mice and ants may be in here, please welcome the Bomb Shelter Quintet."

Antal whispered to Sándor, "Since when is that our name?"

"That's what I told her. As a joke."

The audience applauded. Antal signaled Miklós, who stepped forward in a fedora he'd been given as pay. Together they broke into the "Rakóczi March." The audience, recognizing it, applauded wildly. The children jumped to their feet. Katalin lined them up and led them in a march around the chairs. Even Anni in her scrub-brush haircut stomped and grinned with the others. By the end, everyone cheered.

"You see?" Antal told Miklós. "You play that, and everybody loves you."

Miklós smirked and went on to the *csárdás*. The children whooped and twirled, Anni in the middle of them. Marta shot Antal a smile.

"*Hurrá,* Miklós!" Sándor shouted at the end. Miklós moved aside and Sándor sat down on a stool with his guitar. "All right! Who's having a good time?"

Hands shot up.

"And who had a good time last winter?"

All hands dropped. A man swore.

"Well," Sándor said, "we're not done cursing yet. Because here's a song about . . ." He strummed with a flourish and gestured to Katalin.

"Oh, oh, oh, oh, oh," she sang, "*malenki robot*."

People broke into confused titters.

"Good God," a man shouted, "that's not a song, it's the daily news."

Sándor and Katalin sang as people nodded or laughed or, with Sándor's encouragement, swore. On the ohs, Katalin lifted her hands and the audience joined in. As Sándor strummed the last chord, Katalin called out gaily, "So watch your step out there. And in case you couldn't tell, Sándor wrote that song."

Sándor rolled his eyes and pulled a face. The people laughed and applauded.

The next piece was the Bach duet. Márta sat down to play. Antal knew she was nervous, and he let her set the tempo. Soon she was leading. He had prepared himself to smooth the music if she faltered; but her rhythm was flawless, her tone pure and at ease. He watched her as she pulled the long last note, her hair drawn softly back into a bun, her eyes unusually peaceful.

"Beautiful," he whispered.

Márta then accompanied Katalin as she sang the *Ave Maria*. When their piece ended, Antal soloed on the Shostakovich waltz. A few couples carved out space in back to dance. Children swayed on their parents' laps.

"Thank you," Antal told the audience when he'd finished. "And now my grandfather would like to say something."

Grandpapa rose. "As you all know, Kolompár Miklós works as our custodian, and Magda has asked us all to bring him food or something he can barter. At the end today, those things can be given to Magda or to Miklós himself."

Nearby, Miklós stared at the floor. Magda held up a large bag.

"Now, here's some good news," Grandpapa continued. "The neighborhood water pipes have been repaired, and tomorrow our water will be turned back on. Please—*please*—boil the water before you drink it. The filtration system isn't working yet. But at least we won't have to haul the water—"

"Will the toilets flush?" a man shouted.

"Yes."

Cheers erupted. Antal roared with them. Miklós threw his fedora into the air, set it back on his head, and broke into playing a *verbunkos* piece, an old military recruiting dance. Anni slid off her mother's lap and spun in front of Miklós. Other children joined in the antics, jumping and colliding. Márta laughed, grasped Anni's hand and twirled with her.

"Sarolta!" Anni called out. "Anyuka! Come on!"

Antal watched Márta's family spinning in a circle of joy. "Thank God for Miklós," he said to Sándor.

After the last screech of Miklós's bow, the quintet began "*Erdő, Erdő, Erdő.*" The audience sang along, the dim basement ringing. When it ended, Sándor repositioned his stool. A tremor of nerves ran through Antal as he set his piece and Sándor's Pest song on the music stand. He stretched his hands and touched the bow to the string.

With the opening note of "Song to Our Enemies," the sorrowing cold bore in. His left little finger stiffened. *No.* He played on, demanding strength in his hands, and felt the little finger obey. The notes sang out, remembering. Antal looked away from the music, closed his eyes, kept playing, followed an inner guidance as notes reached, climbed, swept on, insisted. *Fire.* He pulled hard on the bow.

The music peaked. Antal gentled it, softened it, slowed it down. *Heart.* Catching Sándor's eye, he nodded. Sándor began plucking arpeggios on the guitar, cleared his throat, and without looking at the audience, he sang.

> *Pest, along the Danube, below the rising hills,*
> *North of Csepel's factories, upriver from the mills,*
> *Pest where I first breathed, and where I learned, and where I grew,*
> *Home of all I've ever known, I love you still.*

Sándor's voice strained. Antal listened anxiously. These were all the song's lyrics he'd ever heard. When they'd practiced together, Sándor had only hummed, saying he hadn't finished the lyrics. Now what? Antal entered on the accompaniment he'd written and glanced out over the audience. The adults shushed their children. Sándor went on.

> *Pest, the place of heroes, of musicians and of priests,*
> *Ravaged, starved and ransacked from the west and from the east,*
> *O city full of enemies, O city full of friends,*
> *Home of all I've ever known, I wish you peace.*

People pressed their hands to their lips or closed their eyes. Antal glanced at Márta. She stood watching Sándor almost expectantly.

Pest, you've bled into the river, and you've shouted to the skies,
And your proud, stubborn people have horror in their eyes.
O city still determined to strengthen what remains,
May you heal, may you stand, may you arise.

Antal played the arching notes that led into the song's bridge, and Sándor sang out in a passionate crescendo:

Weep, rain of heaven! Flow, Danube, flow!
Cleanse the blood from our streets and grant us peace.
Dona nobis pacem, dona nobis pacem, grant us peace.

In the front row, Grandpapa murmured, "Oh, our God, yes."

Pest, my mother city, may God spare you further pain.
May it never—no, no, never—be this way for you again.
O city of my people, live on! Live on still!
Pest, I love you, and I always will.
Pest, I love you, and I always will.

Sándor's voice wobbled and gave out on the last words. He played a final arpeggio pattern as Antal held the last violin note. Men stared into their laps. Women wiped their eyes, one openly weeping. Antal's mother sat with her face in her hands. At length someone applauded, and others followed.

Sándor lifted his eyes. "Thank you," he told the audience. "I had a hard time writing it because of what we've gone through. I couldn't have done it without help. Antal wrote the excellent violin part."

In the front row, Mr. Boros nodded. "Stunning."

"Another person helped me with the words," Sándor added, "and that was Márta."

Antal turned quizzically to her. She mouthed the word *yes*. As the audience applauded once more, she bowed slightly in acknowledgment.

The group went on to perform "The Light Shines" and ended the concert with everyone singing "*Himnusz*," the sad national anthem. Afterward people gathered around the group. They filled Magda *néni*'s bag with food, cigarettes, and barter items for Miklós. A few people handed the donations directly to him. Several neighbors surrounded Sándor and Antal.

"That song about Pest," a woman said. "My Lord, it had me in tears."

"It could be the city's theme song at this point," her husband agreed.

"And to think you wrote it," another woman said to Sándor. "What talent."

Mr. Boros stepped up to Antal and touched his arm, turning him aside. "That song was good, yes. But let me tell you, your violin prelude to it was simply superb."

Others said Katalin's voice was astonishing, or Miklós was quite the Gypsy fiddler, or the cellist and her music were lovely, or as always Antal was impressive, or heavens but wasn't that Sándor an entertainer?

Antal tried to listen, tried to reply, but the words blurred. Sándor and Márta had written a song together, and neither of them had told him.

THAT NIGHT HE SAT ON THE FOYER STAIRS WITH MÁRTA, a blanket across their laps and a kerosene lantern beside them, turned down low. She rested her head on his shoulder. "A good day," she said. "Miklós gets to eat. And it was unbelievable seeing Anni frisking around."

"She must be getting better."

"I hope so. She's had so many weak days." Márta looked up the stairs, checking for anyone who might overhear. "And Anni keeps asking when our father is going to come back."

"When *is* he coming back?"

"My mother won't say." Márta shook her head. "You played really beautifully today."

"So did you."

"Not like you, though. You're exceptional."

He gripped her hand. For months he had been playing into the silent dark, forcing his hands to continue when his mind was numb and his heart cold, composing in confusion, following paths that became lost or circled endlessly or stopped.

"Didn't Mr. Horváth say you were one of the best violinists in the city?" she asked.

"Not counting the professionals. And Weisz Jenö."

They fell silent, neither of them saying that Jenö might very well be dead.

"Are you still practicing the romanza?" Márta asked.

"Yes, but it needs accompaniment. The orchestra's part."

"But isn't there a duet version with piano? Sándor said Mr. Boros is a good pianist, maybe he could do it. I want people to hear you. You have the talent to play in great places."

"I used to dream of big stages with the whole city listening, but now the city is in pieces."

The lantern shed a haggard pallor on Márta's face. Márta glanced up the stairs again. "Maybe you need to dream about stages somewhere else. Really. It might be better to leave."

He looked away, unable to fathom it.

"I didn't know you helped Sándor with his song," he said.

"Yesterday afternoon he came and asked me. So we worked on it."

"Sándor didn't say a word to me about it."

"Was he supposed to?" Márta asked.

"Why shouldn't he? He's my cousin and we live in the same house—the same bedroom, for God's sake. And you didn't tell me, either."

"That was only yesterday, and then I didn't see you until the concert today." She reached under his open jacket and put her arms around him. "I don't know why this is bothering you."

"Why do you think? Because you're beautiful and sweet and he's lonely as all hell."

"Antal, don't be this way. Sándor is a friend. Only a friend. But *you* . . ."

She pulled back and looked at him, her lips parted as though searching for words. "I love you. Haven't you seen that?"

Antal pulled her into his arms and clung. Yes, he'd seen it in her face, heard it in her voice, felt it in her touch. He loved her, too. He understood that now. When Pest fell, he'd trudged through war-blasted streets to see if she was alive. When he got word of the three-day leave, he ran between drunk soldiers to warn her, and when he couldn't find her, he went back and searched again. When she spoke of her father hiding, it tore him up, because some faceless enemy had struck too close to her. When she was scared, her fear cut through him.

"And I love you," he whispered. "And I want you safe and I can't stand it that something could happen to you and I could lose you."

"Shh, no."

She kissed him, and her body against him was warm, and the kiss grew fierce, and her warmth became fire within him.

PART FOUR

A Good Mother

CHAPTER THIRTY-FIVE

Alexander

February 3, 2007

LISA STOOD IN LINE AT TARGET WITH SOCKS, tampons and a microwave dinner in her cart. Ahead of her, a woman paid for diapers. Her small child, sitting in the cart seat, clutched a plastic dinosaur . . . and dropped it.

"Uh-oh," Lisa said to the boy.

"Ah-oh!" he repeated.

Lisa smiled, picked up the toy, and gave it back to him. He grinned and dropped it again. "Ah-oh!"

"Another uh-oh." Lisa bent for the toy and handed it to him.

The mother turned around, receipt in hand. "Thank you," she said to Lisa. "Nicky, don't throw your dinosaur."

"How old is he?" Lisa asked.

"Thirteen months. Nicky, time to go. Say bye-bye."

"Bye-bye!" Nicky waved as his mother wheeled him away.

Lisa paid for her purchases and rushed out to her car. It was almost evening, almost dark. She sank into the driver's seat. Clutching the steering wheel, she laid her head on her hands and closed her eyes. *Thirteen months*. If her son had lived, full-term and healthy, he'd be thirteen months now, saying uh-oh and bye-bye, dropping toys and grinning. Why couldn't Alexander have lived? The question swept her up like a tide of sorrow whenever she saw young children or pregnant women, whenever she prayed. Why had joy grown in her only to die?

Alone, she stuck her key in the ignition and drove home through the darkening streets.

ALEXANDER HAD LASTED LONGER IN THE WOMB than the other ones had. Her first had died at six weeks gestation, the second at nine weeks, the third at eight. Jake saw her heartbreak over each loss, and after the third he said maybe they should stop trying. She pleaded for one more chance.

That fourth one pushed past the first trimester. The doctor said this was hopeful. Lisa outgrew her jeans, wore sweats. Her nausea began to subside. At four months, her fear began to subside. She bought two pairs of maternity pants.

Four and a half months: the baby was a boy. There it was—there *he* was—on the ultrasound screen, sucking his thumb!

She felt him tumbling in her. Five months: Lisa put Jake's hand on her belly; he gasped in amazement and she laughed with joy. Already she knew the baby's name was Alexander, the English form of Sándor. His middle name would be James, the English form of Jacob. Five and a half months, and Alexander kept growing. When Lisa was alone, she would touch her abdomen, his warm enclosure, and whisper to him. Six months and—

Three a.m. Lisa bolted awake, every nerve screaming. Something was very wrong. She sat up, felt wetness pooling under her.

"Jake!"

"Lisa—" He rolled over. "Oh, Lise. Oh, my God." He grabbed his phone and called 911.

At St. Joseph's Hospital, panting through the pain, Lisa begged the doctor, the nurse and God to save the baby. But on the fetal monitor Alexander's heartbeat became small, low blips. Someone called Father Doyle. He arrived just as the child slid out, pale and bloody. The priest touched water onto the doll-like head: *Alexander James, I baptize you in the name of the Father, and of the Son, and of the Holy Spirit.*

For the five minutes that her son lived outside the womb, Lisa stroked him, kissed him, told him she loved him. For an anguished hour afterward, she held him close, her shattered heart pulsing the blood and heat and life Alexander needed but could not receive. When all warmth and spirit had ebbed from the tiny body, she relinquished her son and sobbed on Jake's chest.

AFTER THE TRIP TO TARGET, LISA ATE HER MICROWAVED TERIYAKI and checked her email in hopes that Kristóf had written. Yes. She opened and read his note. Kristóf was a father, being asked to give the child up. He said he hadn't known he would love the boy.

"Oh," she whispered.

She thought about Kristóf all evening and wrote back to him late that night.

I don't know your story, Kristóf, but I can see how this has affected you. I think I understand. My son Alexander died five minutes after he was born. That was more than a year ago, and I am not the same person. I'm not a childless woman; I'm a mother with an empty spot inside.

And I think of you, meeting a beautiful child that is part of you. He'll always be part of you, even if you never see him again. Which sounds heart-breaking, and I hope the outcome will be happier than that. I don't know what to tell you except that you did the right thing by meeting him. And loving him. Sadness is hard, but I think regrets are worse.

Kristóf replied the next day.

Thank you, Lisa. I'm sad about your baby. I will tell you more about Misha when I can.

Lisa wrote back.

My heart is with you in this, Kristóf.
On somewhat the same topic, could I ask for your help? Kálmán Barcza, the Hungarian musician in Seattle, wants to do a choral performance of my grandfather's song "Egy Jó Anya" for Mother's Day. I know the title means "a good mother," but could you tell me what the song lyrics mean? (Just the gist is enough.) I think the song is in that stack I gave your grandfather.

Thanks. I've been thinking of you.

Two days later Kristóf answered.

Szia, Lisa—
It's good you said just give you the gist (I looked up "gist") of your grandfa-
ther's song, because I can't translate poetry word by word.
    In the first stanza your grandfather tells about his own mother, the beat
of her heart, the touching of her hand. It says a good woman's love doesn't
die, it goes on in her children. I think the next part is about Mary the Virgin,
and hope, and light. It says a good woman's love comes from God's heart, I
think this is the sentiment. (Sorry, I don't know much about religion.) Then
it says Hungary is like a wounded mother, but the Hungarian people will go
on. Something like that. Does this help you?

She read back over the words about the good mother's touch, her beating heart, her wounds. Lisa's eyes filled. Her son had lived under her heart
for six months. With everything in her, she had wanted to be his good
mother.
    Three days passed before she wrote back to Kristóf.

Thank you for explaining the song to me. I have to admit, I put off answering.
Anything to do with motherhood is hard for me. I guess I'm still raw.

    The next day she saw Kristóf's reply:

Ópa says the song was hard for Sándor to sing. He was raw, too.

Chapter Thirty-Six

A Good Mother

March 26, 1945

Sándor had use of the bedroom desk tonight. After a supper of bread and oil, Antal sat at the dining table to read his literature assignment, poetry by Ady Endre. He was distracted by his mother coaching Katalin through a voice lesson at the piano. It was some song from *La Bohème*, and Katalin strained on a high note.

"Breath support underneath," Mother reminded her. "One more time through the whole song."

Antal closed his literature book and listened to them singing in unison, then laughing in unison over Katalin's shaky last note. Katalin left the room. Mother walked over and set her hand on Antal's shoulder.

"Sándor told me Mr. Boros wants you all to do a concert at his shop," she said.

"It'll be a tight squeeze in there," Antal said, "but I think we'll tell him yes."

"Good." She pushed back her bobbed hair. "Antal, at your concert in the basement, I thought you did a really nice job of bringing out everyone's best."

"Well, I didn't really—"

"Yes, you did." She kissed him on the top of his head and went back to the piano.

It was then that Antal noticed Sándor across the room with his black notebook. Had he been watching them? His face looked stricken, as though something in him had been jarred. Sándor pushed past him to the door and out into the night.

Antal followed him. Sándor sat on the walkway leaning against the apartment wall, long legs stretched in front of him. He lit a cigarette. Antal sat down with him. The black notebook lay at Sándor's other side.

"Are you all right?" Antal asked.

Sándor shrugged and took a long drag on the cigarette. "Yesterday was my mother's birthday," he said. "I made a ragged little wreath out of a spruce branch and took it down there." He pointed his thumb toward the corner where his mother had died. "Today the wreath was gone. Like she is."

No one in the family had remembered about Aunt Éva's birthday. Antal sat in silent guilt.

"You're lucky to have your mother," Sándor said. "Having no mother is like having no home."

Sándor seldom stated the loss so baldly. He flicked his lighter, not for another cigarette but for illumination, and passed it to Antal, then searched the pages of his notebook. Antal held the lighter, stinging with helplessness. He had shared his room with Sándor, shared his clothes, shared his food, shared his music, tried to share his scant happiness, and in some way, if it were even possible, he'd shared his mother, too.

"Sándor, you *do* have a home. It's here with us."

"I know. Your family has done everything they can—"

"Don't say 'your family.' Say 'my family.'"

"I have something to show you." Sándor handed him the open notebook. "I wrote this after Mass last Sunday. A song. I have a melody in mind for part of it but not all."

Antal held the lighter close. As he read, he sensed Sándor waiting anxiously, his knee bouncing.

A kind, good woman was with me at the start.
I found my first shelter in her warmth.
The first song I ever heard was the beating of her heart.
The touch of her hand was my true north.

Antal nodded. Aunt Éva.

And I believe, yes, I believe
That the love of a good mother never dies.
It pulses in the lifeblood of her daughters and her sons.
The love of a good mother carries on.

"Oh, Sándor," Antal said.

A young, good woman brought divinity to earth,
A gift of hope while we were in despair.
She brought to us a miracle. Light was given birth.
Redemption came in swaddling clothes and prayer.
And I believe, yes, I believe
That the grace of a good woman lives on.
It pulses from the heart of God and offers mercy wide.
The gift of a good woman never ends.

Antal glanced at Sándor. He had turned his face away.

Like a wounded mother is the country I call home,
But mothers don't forsake their wounded sons.
She will stand up, though she's injured, and she'll bid her children come.
Our lineage will live, we'll carry on.
And I know—oh, yes, I know—
That the life of a good mother flows in us all.
The gift of a good woman carries on.
The love of a good woman carries on.

"This is important," Antal said. He barely knew how to speak of his cousin's great loss. "People need to hear this."

Sándor crushed out his cigarette on the walkway floor.

"What's the melody?" Antal asked.

"I only have this part." Sándor pointed at a repetition of *And I believe, yes, I believe.* "I don't want to sing it right now. I feel too shitty."

But as Antal reread the lyrics, Sándor began to hum. Later, after Sándor had gone to bed, Antal wrote down what Sándor had hummed. The next morning he rose early and quietly worked out a violin line, possibly for a descant, possibly an interlude. It was up to Sándor.

BEFORE DUSK THAT EVENING, ANTAL WANDERED down the street a block and a half to the corner that had once been the second center of his own life. It had been the very heart of Sándor's. Here had stood the optical shop that was the livelihood of both their families, and above it, Sándor's home. Now this corner was ash and rubble, the place where Sándor's mother had died. Near here Sándor had carved flesh from a dead horse, and Mr. Lukács's body had lain under a pile of broken plaster.

"Antal."

He looked around in the fading light. Sándor joined him, the wind lifting his dark hair.

"I still come here pretty often," Sándor said, "even though nothing's left."

Antal nodded. They stood in remembered sorrow, together in the wind.

CHAPTER THIRTY-SEVEN

The Bad Mother

February 7, 2007

KRISTÓF WALKED PAST ST. ISTVÁN'S BASILICA, his collar turned up against the cold. Soon he would face his mother at Café Kör. She was in town for a wedding, or so she'd said. Yesterday while Kristóf was visiting Ópa, she'd called. Ópa had beckoned him to the phone, whispered to him that his mother wanted to see him, told him to be humane and say yes.

Pigeons scattered in front of Kristóf as he crossed St. István's Square. He'd not spoken to his mother in three years. She'd been gone for fifteen.

It had happened in 1991, after the rusty Iron Curtain ended up on the scrap heap. People said what an astounding chain of events it was—the borders opening, people carrying off the Berlin wall in their pockets, cars flooding from East Germany, through Czechoslovakia, Hungary, Austria and finally into West Germany. In 1991 Kristóf was fourteen, not old enough to be astounded, not old enough to resent the communists like his grandparents did; but when his mother went to Germany for the fourth and fifth time, he was old enough to think it strange she was visiting Aunt Trina *again*. He was definitely old enough to notice his father's resentment. Then a letter arrived from Stuttgart. *I've found my heart here*, she wrote.

The heart's name was Klaus Meier. Kristóf and his father became a two-person family. Kristóf occasionally traveled to Stuttgart; but he didn't like the train ride, didn't like leaving home, and had no fondness for Klaus Meier, either. He hated hearing his mother *explain* why she had left Zoltán, dumping shit on the one parent who had stood by Kristóf. No thanks, Mutti.

HE PULLED OPEN THE DOOR OF CAFÉ KÖR and immediately spotted his mother at a small table near the bar. Her long hair was blacker than it used to be, her figure thicker under a fuchsia-colored sweater. He made his way to her. Standing up, she flashed a taut smile and caught him in an embrace. She had changed her perfume: the scent was no longer flowery but something sharper, and he felt he was hugging a stranger.

"Kristóf," she murmured.

"*Szia*, Mónika."

"Can't you still call me Mutti?"

Kristóf hadn't planned on calling her by name. He hadn't planned anything. He gestured at the table, and they sat down. The restaurant was fairly small but popular and routinely crowded. Waiters rushed by. Dishes clattered and conversations buzzed. Kristóf looked across the table at his mother. When he was growing up, she had been beautiful. Everyone remarked on it. Now she was forty-nine and covering time's damage: thick makeup, stark pink lipstick. It made him unexpectedly sad.

"Well," he said, "shall we order?"

"Why don't you order, please." There was no mistaking her nervousness. "I'll just have what you have."

So he asked for veal stew for them both, because it would already be cooked and would be quick. He ordered Riesling for her but no wine for himself, stretching the truth in telling her that he would need to go to work before long. She nodded, but he knew she was disappointed.

"How is your grandfather?" she asked after her wine had arrived. "I heard about his heart attack. I hope he's well."

"I'm not sure he is."

She waited. He didn't elaborate.

"And how is your father?" she asked.

"At Christmas he was fine."

The light at the front windows was a haze of gray. She lifted her wine glass. "Kristóf, how are you? Please tell me."

How was he? He couldn't tell her how he'd lain awake last night thinking of the boy that was his son.

"How is work?" she prompted. "You're still at Három Páva?"

"Yes. And you're still at the post office?"

"Yes."

There was a crash as something at the bar was dropped.

"Are you playing piano at all?" she asked.

"Sometimes at Ópa's house."

"I remember how nicely you used to play. Such a talented family. Your grandmother and your aunt on piano, your grandfather with his violin. You with your piano. And your father—"

"He didn't play."

"No, but Zoltán understood music. He could talk about it. He could sing. He could hear something on the radio and it was almost like he could take it apart and put it back together. And I didn't fit. I didn't belong."

"No, that's not true," he argued.

Except that it was. At Varga family gatherings when the music began, she would usually wander to a back bedroom and read a romance novel.

The waiter set plates of stew before them. Kristóf had known his mother would bring up Stuttgart, and as they ate, she did. "You should come live with Klaus and me."

"I'm staying here."

"But you'd have more opportunities there. You don't want to be a waiter all your life, do you? You speak German so well."

"I'm not German, and I never will be."

"No, of course not, but—"

"This is my home."

"Please. Listen. Here, your father is two or three hours away by train." She looked at him, her brown eyes rounded and earnest. "I'm sorry to bring this up, but when your grandfather is gone, who will you have here?"

"My grandfather is not gone." Kristóf leaned closer, speaking over the room noise and over his anger. "When he goes, I'll deal with it then. But I'm not discussing it now."

They ate without speaking until his mother pushed her half-eaten meal aside and said, "Kristóf. There's something I need to say. Please don't cut me off."

"All right."

"I've had time—too much time—to think things over, and I see how much I missed by not being with you."

Oh, God. He set down his fork and knife.

"When I left Pest—"

"When you left Pest, you left my father and me."

She lifted her hand. "Stop. Just listen. Please. When I left, I didn't want it to be the end between me and you."

Her voice had dropped to a low, confessional tone. Kristóf could hardly hear her. She must have known that, for she pulled her chair around the corner of the table and sat close to him. "When I left, I thought you would come see me more often. I thought I could come see you. I didn't know you would be so resistant."

Kristóf wished he had a cigarette.

"Also," she said humbly, "you have a way of choosing loyalties. You chose your father. This is obvious to me now, but I didn't foresee it at the time. And I made a terrible mistake." She dropped her gaze. "Please forgive me."

The waiter removed their dishes. A customer left, and cold air blasted through the door. Kristóf hunched his shoulders. Forgive her?

"I don't know how," he said. "I'm not fourteen anymore."

She put her hand to her face. "What do you mean?"

"I knew how to be your son then, but I don't know now."

"Can't we try?"

"I don't know."

She sniffled, pulled a tissue out of her purse, and turned her face away. Mutti—or maybe it was Mónika now—was crying, and the sight unleashed angry memories of her playing the tears card with his father. If all else failed, cry.

"I'm not the only one whose life you screwed up," he said. "You walked out on Vati, too. So if you want to ask somebody for forgiveness, ask him."

She dabbed her eyes and nodded. Perhaps it was her silence that made him back off. Kristóf reached over and patted her hand, trying for gentleness, because God damn it but he was supposed to be doing the humane thing. He paid the bill while his mother wiped her tears. Then he told her he had to go to work, and he opened his cell phone and called a taxi for her.

He waited with her on the curb. She did not speak to him until the taxi arrived. When he opened the back door for her, she turned and looked him hard in the eye.

"I still love you, Kristóf," she said, defiance flaring. "Maybe you don't believe me, but it's true. And I am not calling this the end." She climbed in, shut the door, and waved once.

Kristóf watched the taxi drive off. He lit a cigarette, though his hands shook and the wind blew and it took several tries before the flame caught. She loved him, she'd said.

He stopped by the internet café.

Szia Lisa,
Today I had lunch with my mother, first time we have talked since three years.

Kristóf flexed his cold fingers.

When I was fourteen she went to a lover in Germany and made everything like shit for my father and me. So today in Café Kör, exactly there, my mother was so full of tears, and she said, 'Will you forgive me?' and what in the burning hell does she expect? After what she did, fifteen years gone, how can she think this makes everything right? You are Catholic and you are the better person than me, but I know also you don't get on with your mother so well. If your mother did this, what would you do?

AFTER WORK THAT NIGHT, ALONE IN HIS APARTMENT, Kristóf listened to a phone message from his father: "Got a strange email from your mother this evening. Call me back, all right?" Kristóf called him immediately.

"So," Vati said, "Fifteen years after the fact, she's suddenly asking me to forgive her. Do you know anything about this?"

Kristóf sat down on his bed and told him about the lunch with her. "She asked me the same thing. Would I forgive her. What was I supposed to say? 'There, there, all you did was completely fuck up our lives, but it's no problem.' Actually, there's a big problem, so I told her to ask *you* for forgiveness. But I didn't think she'd do it."

"Well, she did."

A television droned next door, the sound coming through the thin wall.

"What are you going to say to her?" Kristóf asked. "I mean, are you going to . . . forgive her?" The word felt foreign in his mouth.

"Krisz, this is hardly relevant on my account. When she left, I wasn't surprised she wanted out of the marriage. But what really upset me was that she would leave *you*. So when I got this letter from her yesterday, I wanted to tell her, 'To hell with asking me for forgiveness, go talk to Kristóf.' But apparently she already did."

"So she apologized to both of us. Now what do we do?"

The pause was long, the apartment chilly.

"I've pretty much given up being angry at her," Vati said, "but I'm more worried about you. For your own sake, I wish you'd let the anger go. If that's forgiveness, then so be it."

"But then she'll keep calling. She'll keep telling me to come to Stuttgart."

"You don't have to get on the next train for Stuttgart, just quit blaming her. You asked me what I'm going to tell her, and I guess I'll say I'm all right. As for what you should say, that's up to you. You have to admit, for her to apologize like that must have been damned hard."

Kristóf shifted on the bed and lay back. "And you think this is easy for me?"

"None of us have had an easy time of it. It's horrible what she did, walking out like that. But I know I was no fountain of kindness, either. Christ, I was silent. The poor woman probably thought I hated her."

Yes, Kristóf remembered his father's silence and bleak moods, and Vati had finally seen a doctor about the problem after Mutti left. But somehow, even in the worst, Kristóf had known that his father cared for him and didn't hate Mutti. Didn't hate anybody, except maybe himself.

"But you felt shitty, too," Kristóf objected, "and no matter how shitty you felt, you didn't leave. She did."

"I know. But people can get pushed until they fall. Maybe that's what happened to her."

"You didn't push her!"

"But listen, she really isn't in a position of hurting me anymore." Music of a commercial drifted from next door. "Kristóf, it's time I told you, there's a woman I've been seeing."

"What, really?"

"Yes. Her name is Lendvai Erzsébet. Erzsi."

So his father had a woman. Of course there was no reason he shouldn't, no reason at all. But Vati had always seemed so solitary, even while he was married.

"She's a good person," Vati was saying. "I waited a long time for someone like her. Erzsi and I have taken things slowly. I didn't tell you sooner because, well, you know, sometimes things don't work out."

It was like Vati to assume things wouldn't work out. Kristóf said, "I ought to meet her."

"In fact, you can. Erzsi and I want to come this Saturday to see you and Ópa. But he said to talk to you first, said there might be a conflict?"

Saturday. Misha. Kristóf got up and paced across the room, gathering the words. "I have to tell you something, too. There's a boy named Misha coming to visit Ópa and me that day. He's five years old. And his mother will be there, and her husband. Misha calls the man his apuka." Kristóf leaned against the armoire, blurted out, "But the real apuka is me."

"What did you say?"

"Yes." Kristóf shut his eyes. "I'm the boy's father."

A long silence on the other end. "You're sure?"

"Yes."

"Kristóf. My God."

"Yes. I didn't know until Christmas."

It had to be said. Kristóf told him about the affair with Blanka, and about her showing up at the restaurant, breaking the news and begging him to sign off. He told his father about meeting Misha on the Children's Railway and playing the jelly bear game, and that Misha looked like a Varga, no question, and he was smart, and lively.

"And Blanka and Endre just want me to sign the papers and get out of the way," he said. "It's not that easy. I'm not just the damned sperm donor."

"No. No, not at all."

Kristóf walked back across the room and sat down on the bed again.

"Kristóf, do you want to be the boy's father?"

"I don't know how to be his father." He coughed and tried to go on. "I don't want to demand custody, because wouldn't it rip up his life? I don't want him to be miserable. But I can't stand to sign him away and lose him. So here I am, stuck, and Blanka doesn't like it that I'm keeping her waiting."

"But what does she expect, if she took five years to tell you about your son?"

Kristóf sighed "She tried to call when she was pregnant, and I didn't answer."

"You didn't answer? You'd been having sex with her, and you didn't answer?"

"We'd broken up. I thought we were finished." It sounded so lame to him now. "Blanka, she just—I don't know, she tried to hang on to me, and—"

"And you weren't having it."

"No." Damn all this. "If you're going to tell me I was an asshole, I already know that."

"I wasn't going to say that, but I hope you've changed." A stretch of quiet. "And what does your grandfather say?"

"He wants to help. If I can figure out what kind of help I need."

"Good. I'll help, too." Vati's voice softened. "Your son. My grandson. I want to meet him, Krisz."

"Then come to Ópa's on Saturday. If Blanka isn't happy about it, too bad." The weariness of the long day hit him. "I was afraid to tell you," he confessed.

"Well, don't forget, I had to do the same thing once, telling my own father I got a girl pregnant."

Kristóf had always known he was born only five months after his parents' wedding, but no one had ever told him the story. "How did Ópa react?" he asked.

"He listened really quietly. Then he said he knew how easy it was to get carried away with a girl, but this was very serious." Vati's tone was serious, too. "And then he asked me if I loved Mónika, and I said yes. Because I did. So he asked if I wanted to marry her, and I said yes again, and that was true, too. And he said that he and your grandmother would help, and they did. As you know."

"Ópa's still helping out. Even now, when he's sick."

Vati said he knew, and they talked about Ópa's health. Then Vati asked him how he was going to reply to his mother, and Kristóf said he didn't know. They ended the call agreeing that in a week or two Kristóf would move in with Ópa.

Yes, a week or two. Kristóf hoped this would ease things for Ópa; it certainly wouldn't ease things for himself. It would be harder to come and go, harder to smoke. And then there was sex, which he hadn't had since October, with the Linzer woman—the married one, for God's sake.

Things had changed.

CHAPTER THIRTY-EIGHT

The War's Postlude

March 31, 1945

SCHOOL HAD NEVER SEEMED SO USELESS. Who wanted to study German after months of hearing German soldiers swear? Why read history when Sándor said the new regime would just revise it anyway? Antal opened his textbooks nightly but couldn't recall a time he'd cared less.

It surprised him, though, how Sándor dedicated himself. Sándor still intended to go to university next fall. He studied long hours, and after that, Antal would see him writing in that black notebook. Sometimes he would slam it shut with some bitter outburst: "I don't want to be here ten years from now." Or "This country is exchanging one set of assholes for another." Some nights it was more than Antal could stand.

Márta wasn't attending school at all. She stayed home, reading chemistry without a lab to practice it in, reading Shakespeare's *Julius Caesar* in English. Antal knew she missed her friends and her classes. Her family wasn't attending church, either, for the first time in Márta's life: they avoided those who might ask about her father. He would try to come home Easter weekend, Márta had said, but the family still wouldn't go to church. "But don't tell anyone he's coming," she said, "not even Sándor."

ANTAL WENT TO MÁRTA'S APARTMENT ON THE SATURDAY afternoon before Easter, and her father was there. Shirt wrinkled, thin hair untrimmed, eyes tired behind his glasses, he sat at the table with Anni on his lap. Anni, still thin, leaned contentedly against her father's chest. Antal joined them at the table while Márta made tea from dried chamomile. Her mother and Sarolta had stepped out.

Anni picked up a tan egg and a pencil from the table. Three more eggs lay in a bowl, two of them covered with childish pencil markings. She said, "Antal, my apuka came home and brought eggs. Apuka said if I ate two, I could make Easter eggs out of the others. So I ate two." She smiled as though pleased with herself. "Now I'm making Easter eggs. With a pencil, because we don't have any paint. Apuka, I'm going to make an egg for Antal. With a violin on it."

"Good girl, Anni," Mr. Hanák said.

She set her pencil to the eggshell and began to draw. "See, Antal?"

"*Szép*," Antal said. *Lovely.* He smiled at her but didn't want to take food that she herself needed. Márta had said that Anni still dragged through too many days.

"Draw that egg for me," Antal told Anni, "and tomorrow, eat it for me." She scrunched up her face and kept drawing.

"Antal," Mr. Hanák said, "Márta told me you've been composing."

"Well, yes, I'm not Mozart, but—"

Mr. Hanák lifted his hand. "But you're good at it, I hear."

"I told him that," Márta said as she set cups of tea on the table and sat down. As they drank tea, she coached Anni's artwork, and a crude but accurate rendering of a violin emerged: two *f* holes, four strings, four tuning pegs. Anni drew a circle at the top of the egg with two dot eyes in it and a crescent mouth. "That's Antal," she said.

"Ah," he said. "I didn't know I was so handsome."

Mr. Hanák smiled at him. Antal felt he should talk to Mr. Hanák, but he wasn't sure what the man would want to say in front of Anni.

"Is it going well for you?" he ventured.

"The work is necessary. The distance is hard. I wish the family could be with me."

"I don't want to go to Debrecen, Apa," Márta said. "I want to stay here. Right here. In this apartment."

"We'll discuss it later," Mr. Hanák said.

Mrs. Hanák and Sarolta soon returned, and Márta asked her parents if she could go for a walk with Antal. A disheartening amount of discussion ensued, but after handing out warnings her parents finally allowed her to leave.

It was almost April now, the trees budding and the sun warmer. Antal and Márta headed east on side streets, steering away from markets and crowds. At every corner they checked left and right for knots of soldiers or *malenki robot* projects. Not nearly as many Hungarians were being taken for forced labor now; still, Antal had made a habit of changing direction whenever instinct told him to. As they walked, Márta talked about her father's train ride home. He'd sat on coal in a boxcar going to Eger, then bribed a Russian soldier with his best pipe so that he could stand squeezed in the aisle of a train into Pest.

"Apa is so worn out, and concerned for my mother—" Márta stopped. "He's worried about Anni."

They had come to a battered storefront where three women on the sidewalk divided a rare dekagram of sugar. Márta lowered her voice as they skirted the women. "Apa hears things in Debrecen. So much fighting between parties, and the communists keep getting what they want."

They walked block after decimated block until they entered City Park. Spring showed: grass sprouted on the pitted lawn and dandelions bloomed. Farther off, boys shouted and played football, but right here the park was quiet.

"It's nice," Márta said. "I wonder why more people aren't here."

He smiled. "Maybe I got lucky. Or maybe I told the whole city to leave us alone."

He spread his jacket at the base of an elm and they sat down together. She pulled off her jacket and rested against him in her light pullover. He kissed her long and slow, gently at first; but she pressed close and her answering kiss deepened into sweet torment. He caressed her throat and her shoulder under her sweater. She laid her hand over his, maybe stopping him from straying further, maybe stopping him from letting go.

"Antal." She drew back. "My mother talked to me about us."

Apprehension pricked him. "Oh?"

"She said feelings could wash over me and I'd want more than I could handle. I didn't tell her I already know."

He sighed. The Hanáks were dedicated Reformed Church believers and he could guess what their standards were. But sometimes all he wanted in this torn world was to be alone with Márta behind closed doors.

"It'd be so hard if we ever had to part ways," she said.

"I don't want to part ways," he answered. His soul would hemorrhage.

The light shifted with a passing cloud. Márta laid her hand on his knee. "Maybe I worry too much."

"Please don't." But he worried, too.

EASTER MORNING ANTAL STOOD BEHIND SÁNDOR in the church aisle, awaiting the Eucharist. He had not attended Mass since St. István's Day last August. The church was drafty, the colored glass windows broken from the siege. Antal gazed ahead at the dark wood crucifix behind the choir. When he was a child, it had scared him to look at the almost-naked Jesus, bloodied and dying; the child he used to be had never seen a dead body. But by now he'd not only seen dead bodies, he'd lifted one out of the rubble and buried another one in a bomb hole.

In front of him in the communion queue, Sándor took a step forward—Sándor, who in spite of his losses and bitterness still insisted that God was good, still believed that death didn't have the final say. Márta believed that, too. How did they manage it?

And how was Márta doing this morning? Yesterday he heard her sadness as she told him her family would stay home, read the Easter story in the Bible, maybe pray, maybe sing a little bit. At some point, when her father was less likely to be watched, he would leave again. Márta's mother would cry. Maybe she could hide the tears from Anni, possibly even Sarolta, but Márta would know.

Antal raised his eyes to the crucifix again, and deep within, he lifted the words *please, please*. In front of him Sándor received the Eucharist, crossed himself and turned out of the way. Antal stepped forward and the priest placed the wafer on his tongue.

"The body of Christ, broken for you," the priest said.

Antal didn't want any more bodies broken.

IT WAS A WEEK LATER THAT THE QUINTET GATHERED in the basement again. They said they would rehearse. But as Antal lifted his violin from the case, Katalin began talking. A girl in her school had gone to visit relatives in the country, she said, but the relatives were gone. So were all the animals except a hungry dog. The house was an empty shell: no furniture, no pictures on the walls, no food in the pantry. Even the floorboards had been stripped away.

"The Russians did it," Katalin said. "They didn't leave a thing. They were locusts!"

"Oh, yes," Márta murmured.

Miklós grunted. "I wonder what happened to the women. No, I don't wonder."

Antal set his violin back in the case and looked over at the girls. Katalin nodded soberly and said she hoped those women got away soon enough. Márta stared into her lap.

Sándor turned a tuning peg on his guitar. "A fellow in my history class said there was a gang rape outside his building a couple weeks ago. I guess it was really bad." He plucked a string to test it. "Nine or ten soldiers on one woman. They cut her with a broken bottle."

Katalin covered her mouth with her hand. Márta looked at Sándor, tight-lipped.

Antal said, "Sándor, that's enough—"

"Damn," Miklós said to Sándor. "Did the woman even live through that?"

"I don't know, but—"

"Stop!" Márta stood up, glaring at Sándor. "Do you have to drag this up? Do you think we want to hear it? As if we haven't already had enough?" She ran for the stairs.

"Márta!" Sándor called.

Antal ran after her, catching up. Behind him he heard the guitar twang and thud on the bench. Sándor's footsteps pounded across the floor. Antal turned and shouted, "Leave her alone, would you?" He shoved open the door and pulled Márta out into the night.

She took off across the courtyard. He ran after her through the building foyer and out onto the battered sidewalk in front. It was past curfew, the street dark but for a few candles in apartment windows. Márta leaned against the post of a dead streetlamp and wept into her hands.

"Márta, what's wrong?"

She shook her head.

He tried to tell her they couldn't stay here, it was after curfew, the police would come, but she kept crying.

"What is it, Márta? What's the matter?"

"I don't want to listen to news like that, and I don't want my mother to hear it, either."

Antal touched her shoulder, bewildered. Márta was hardly naïve, her mother even less so. Stories like what Sándor had told were so commonplace, so unavoidable, no one was shocked anymore. Unless . . .

God Almighty. "Did something happen?" he asked.

She lifted her head and looked back to their apartment building.

"Márta, tell me. Were you—"

"No," she whispered, "but my mother was."

"Oh, my God."

He held her, feeling her tears hot on his neck, here where the light didn't shine. She wiped her face with her hand and told him in choked phrases what had happened. It was while they were staying with old Mr. Sárosi after the siege. Some soldiers were making a drunken ruckus in front of the house. Her father told the family to stay inside. Knowing Russian, he went out and talked the soldiers into leaving. But inside, the girls and their mother heard boot steps. A soldier had got in, maybe through a passage in the basement.

"And Anyu locked Sarolta and Anni and me into an armoire," Márta said. "She told us to make no sound, no matter what. But then she didn't have time to hide."

Márta swallowed and waited through several rough breaths. "So the soldier found her, and he—you know. And I heard it happen, and there was nothing I could do but crouch in that horrible armoire with my hand over Anni's mouth."

Antal gripped her fingers, his heart burning with anger.

"Then Apa came running in," she said, "and the soldier ran out, and Anyu was crying, and by then Anni and Sarolta were both screaming. And when Apa let us out of the armoire, we saw Anyu's dress torn and her lip bleeding, and it's so terrible, Antal. Apa can't forgive himself. Anyu has told him they both did what they had to, they kept us girls safe, and when he had to go to Debrecen, she told him yes, go, above all keep himself safe. But he has no peace."

Antal clutched Márta and stroked her hair.

Behind them the front door of their building clattered. They turned, jumped apart as it opened. Márta's mother stood in the doorway.

"Márta!" she shouted. "Get in here! Antal, you too!"

He told Márta quietly, "I have to see you tomorrow."

At the door, Mrs. Hanák grabbed Márta's hand and led her away. Antal went upstairs to his apartment. Sándor was waiting for him on the walkway.

"What's the matter?" Sándor blurted out. "Is Márta all right?"

"She's managing, no thanks to you and Miklós."

"I'll apologize to her."

"No." Antal pushed past him. "Just leave her alone."

THE NEXT AFTERNOON MÁRTA MET HIM IN THE COURTYARD. She pushed her hair behind her ear, unbearably beautiful, and said that Sándor had apologized.

"I told him to leave you alone," Antal said.

"But he was nice. He said that when he saw how upset I was, he felt terrible."

Antal glanced around. They were alone. "You didn't tell him about your mother, did you?"

"What? Absolutely not."

Antal could hardly account for how this relieved him, to be the only one who knew her secrets.

CHAPTER THIRTY-NINE

Bread and Ibuprofen

February 8, 2007

Lisa had just arrived home from school. She sorted the day's mail at the kitchen counter: a pizza coupon, a letter hawking insurance, and here was something from OmniHealth. Oh, please, not again. She opened the envelope and looked in dismay at yet another lab bill. Why did the cost for delivering a dead child never end?

Lisa dropped the bill on the counter and cut a slice of French bread. She ate it without butter because she'd run out. She was always running out of things. For all of Jake's failings, at least he had kept up with the grocery shopping.

Her laptop lay on the table. She carried a glass of water and some ibuprofen to the table, sat down, and opened her email inbox to reread Kristóf's note about his mother.

She said, "Will you forgive me?" and what in the burning hell does she expect? . . . You are Catholic and you are the better person than me . . . what would you do?

Lisa typed, *Honestly, Kristóf, I can't imagine my mother using the word "forgive."* Then she reached for her glass of water and swallowed the ibuprofen. Obviously Kristóf deserved more of an answer, but as she sat there with the glass, she could think of nothing helpful, nothing at all, because she'd received horrid mail, and because the sixth graders were extra-mouthy today and the first graders couldn't pay attention to save their lives, and she was exhausted, and yes, of course she was irritated with her mother, but her mother was nothing compared to Kristóf's mother and nothing compared to Jake. She continued typing to Kristóf.

You're right that I'm Catholic but I'm not so sure about the "better person" part. Could we Skype in a few days and talk about this? Also, I've been thinking a lot about you and Misha, and I want to know more.

Lisa sent the note, and with the movement of her hand, she glimpsed the little cross tattoo on her wrist. She pulled out the folder that contained her grandparents' music. "A Good Mother" lay face-up before her.

She'd told Kálmán Barcza he was welcome to the song for Mother's Day, but she couldn't help him with it. The decision still stood, and she didn't want to discuss it further with Kálmán. But she thought about her grandfather, writing this song in the year his mother died.

Lisa played through Grandpa Sándor's song on her keyboard. It was a simple but compelling melody, with a descant that had been marked *hegedű*. By now she knew that meant *violin*. Antal Varga must have written that part. If Kristóf were here, she would point that out to him in the music. Well, maybe she'd say something about it to him on Skype. She just wished he were here.

CHAPTER FORTY

Those We Try to Keep

February 10, 2007

WHEN THE WOMAN NAMED LENDVAI ERZSI ARRIVED at the apartment with Zoltán, the first thing Varga noticed was her hair: chin-length, auburn fading to brown. It reminded him of Ildi, his wife, and so he was inclined to like this Erzsi. Next to catch his attention were her hands, moving with warm ease first as she greeted him and Kristóf, then as she poured coffee. Most soothing, though, was her alto voice quietly telling Zoltán, "Good, then," when Misha's family pressed the buzzer.

Kristóf opened the door, and Misha bounded through it. "Kristóf *bácsi! Szia,* Antal *bácsi!* Where's the piano?"

Blanka stepped in. "Misha, calm down."

The adults gathered in a knot near the door. The handshaking was rather cool, Varga observed, until Zoltán grasped Misha's hand with dumbfounded wonder. "I am—eh—Kristóf *bácsi*'s father. You can call me Zoltán *bácsi.*"

"So many uncles," Misha said.

Erzsi smiled at him. "And friends."

They crowded into the living room and Varga surveyed the awkward mix from his armchair. He made small talk with the group, trying to ease the strain. Blanka and Endre sat straight-faced on the sofa holding cups of coffee. Blanka had barely tasted hers. Zoltán and Erzsi leaned against a bookcase, their eyes on Misha as Kristóf raised the lid on the piano and showed him the inner strings. Kristóf and Misha sat down on the bench together. Kristóf touched the keys of the C scale and sang its notes.

"Let's have you try it now," he said to Misha. "Give me your right hand— yes, that one—and we'll curl your fingers like this—that's right—and we'll put your thumb on this key here, and now you press down. Not hard."

Middle C sounded.

"Yes." Kristóf sang *do* with Misha. "Now this finger on the next key."

Varga glanced at Misha's parents. Blanka lifted her cup but lowered it again without drinking. Erzsi stepped over to her and spoke quietly, pointing at the cup. After a short exchange, Erzsi took the cup into the kitchen and returned with a glass of water for Blanka.

Misha pressed D, sang *re*, and went on to E. Varga nodded approval as Kristóf lifted the boy's wrist, correcting the position. "Pet the keys," Kristóf said. "Like they're your favorite cat." Ildi used to say things like that when she first taught Kristóf.

Nearby, Zoltán raised his mobile phone and took a picture. Endre shifted on the sofa and Blanka gripped her water glass.

Misha curled his fingers on the keys. "Nice kitty, nice kitty."

"Oh, but sometimes cats are naughty," Kristóf said. He pointed out two keys. "Play G, G, G, A, G."

Varga smiled to himself and heard Zoltán chuckle. Misha played the notes in order and grinned at Kristóf. "It's the naughty cat song."

"Right! Play that twice while Zoltán *bácsi* sings it. Then we'll finish the piano part." Kristóf turned to his father. "Ready, Zoltán *bácsi*?"

"Ready."

Kristóf helped Misha touch the keys as Zoltán sang: "Naughty kitty cat, you are very fat, you have butter on your whiskers, naughty kitty cat."

Erzsi laughed, and finally Blanka smiled a little. Kristóf taught Misha the rest of the song one phrase at a time, and soon Misha played the whole thing on his own.

"He learns quickly," Varga observed aloud.

Endre reached for Blanka's hand. "Yes. Our son is smart."

"Certainly," Kristóf said. Varga thought he sounded curt.

Kristóf showed Misha how to play the French song about the Avignon

Bridge, then the happy birthday song. "You know, a few days ago was Antal *bácsi*'s birthday," he told Misha, and winked at Varga.

"You should have a party for him," Misha said.

"We're going to. Zoltán *bácsi* and Erzsi *néni* brought a cake."

"Can I have some?"

"Misha," Blanka broke in. "You can't just invite yourself—"

"It's all right," Varga said. "You're all invited to stay."

"Thanks, but we can't," Endre said. "Could you please show Misha the violin now?"

Varga exchanged glances with Kristóf, who raised his eyebrows, clearly as irritated by the hurry as he himself was. But Varga fetched the instrument. He let Misha touch its glossy contours and pluck the strings. Varga lined up Misha's right-hand fingers along the handle of the bow and positioned the violin at his collar bone.

"Let's see if it will sing for you." Varga helped Misha pull the bow across the highest string. "Now try pushing it the other way. Careful." The boy smiled and did as he'd been instructed. Kristóf applauded. There was a flash as Zoltán took another picture.

"Good start," Varga told Misha. "Your bow movement was nice and even."

Varga saw pained pride in Kristóf's eyes and Zoltán's. He felt it, too. Misha belonged to them. If they couldn't keep him, if their hands had to let go, still their blood and hearts would hold on.

Blanka and Endre rose from the sofa. "Misha, say thank you to Antal *bácsi* and Kristóf *bácsi*," Blanka said. "We have to go soon."

"But I don't want to go yet."

Endre leaned close to him. "Don't argue. Your mother's tired."

"But she's always tired."

"Misha, stop," Blanka warned.

"Blanka," Kristóf protested, "we were just getting started. He was having fun."

Endre set his hand on the boy's shoulder. "Misha, what do you say to the uncles?"

"Thank you," Misha said, all disappointment, "and I wish I didn't have to go home."

Kristóf tried to smile. "So do we."

Blanka turned to Erzsi. "Our coats, please?"

As Erzsi left the room with Misha and his parents, Zoltán hurried over to Varga and Kristóf. "Good Lord," he whispered. "Goodbye so soon? This isn't for good, is it?"

"Not if I have anything to say about it," Kristóf said. He strode with Zoltán to the front door, where the others had gathered. Varga's chest tightened. He waited, then trailed behind.

Misha chattered as Endre bundled him into his coat. "I like the piano best, Kristóf *bácsi*.

Because it's big and has all those things to push. We should play it some more."

Blanka draped her muffler around her throat. "Misha, you can't just tell other people what to do—"

"He's not ordering me around," Kristóf insisted. "He wants to play piano."

Endre took Misha by the hand, nodded briefly to Kristóf, and turned at Varga. "Thank you very much."

"Misha, time to go," Blanka said. "Come on."

Misha scowled.

Varga said goodbye, trying to be cheerful about it, and Zoltán and Erzsi did the same. Kristóf stepped close to Blanka, though, and Varga saw him mouth, "I need to talk to you."

Looks and gestures flew between Endre and Blanka. Endre left with Misha, and Varga could hear them retreating toward the lift. Kristóf followed Blanka out the door, not bothering to put on his coat. Outside the apartment, Kristóf's voice rose and strained, then Blanka's, but Varga could not make out what they said. He wandered to the kitchen and waited with Zoltán and Erzsi. After ten minutes the door opened and slammed. Kristóf walked into the kitchen.

"Well?" Zoltán asked.

Kristóf snorted. "So Blanka says, 'All right, you met Misha, you played music with him, that's enough, we're done with this, now would you please just sign the papers.' Of course, all this would be easier for them if I would just drop dead."

"What a hard spot you're in," Erzsi murmured.

"She hid him from me for five, almost six years, and now?" Kristóf lifted his hand in exasperation. "I said, 'Imagine this, Blanka, I *like* Misha.

He is my *son*. S-O-N. In some way that neither of us understand, I love him.' She stared at me like she was terrified."

Varga thought she probably was.

"'Sign, sign, sign,' she and Endre keep saying," Kristóf fumed. "I don't know what the goddamned rush is."

Zoltán shook his head.

"I think I know," Erzsi said. "I think Blanka's pregnant. From certain angles, she looked like it. Tired, didn't fasten her coat, didn't want coffee. I can see why she'd rush the adoption. She wants Misha to be as much Endre's child as the new baby will be. That's how I would feel, if it were me."

Varga thought about it. "You may be right."

"I don't want to be a shithead about this," Kristóf said. "Endre's probably a good father for Misha. Better than I could be at this point, I know that. But I don't want to put my name on some paper and then never see him again."

"He looks exactly like Kristóf," Zoltán said. "Misha's his. He's ours. How the hell do we just give him up?"

"I don't know, I can't imagine," was all Varga could say; because all his life, he'd only let go of people when they were torn from him.

KRISTÓF LEFT FOR WORK AFTER LUNCH and birthday cake. Zoltán and Erzsi caught the train home after dinner. With the apartment empty that evening, Varga took his aspirin and beta blockers and sat down with the music of his old *Embers Suite*. He was tired in a way that he didn't want to tell Gabriella and Zoltán and Kristóf about. They'd all worry and tell him to see his doctor, which would be of no use. A man could only ask so much of his worn-out heart. He didn't know how long he had left. The family had talked of coming together for Easter, and that seemed a safe bet.

Varga perused the pages of the suite. He had decided to revise it, maybe for Lisa, maybe somewhat for Halmos, maybe for Kristóf, maybe even for Misha. He would have to do this soon while he had the strength. There were other things he wanted, too, like seeing Zoltán married to Erzsi, and seeing Kristóf come to terms with his mother and with his son, for whatever that would mean. Varga glanced toward the bookcase at his wife's photo. If only Ildi could have met Misha.

There was one other thing he'd have to do before all this was over, something he'd promised Ildi, then set aside, then almost forgotten. As she had urged him in her last months, he would see a priest, take the Eucharist. Ildi hadn't called this an act of faith, which he wasn't sure he could manage. She'd called it an act of hope.

CHAPTER FORTY-ONE

In Public

May 1, 1945

THE RUSSIANS HAD LAID SIEGE TO BERLIN and were showing no mercy. Antal often heard about it from Márta, because she and her mother listened to the BBC whenever they could. On the first day of May Márta told him in the courtyard that Hitler was dead. "Germany's saying he died defending the fatherland," she said, "but he probably killed himself. His mistress is dead, too."

It should have been good news, or at least satisfying news, but Antal felt nothing. Numbly he went to his apartment and told Sándor and Katalin. Sándor said, "At last." Katalin burst into tears. "That horrible, horrible man."

Later Antal saw Miklós on the back stairs and told him. Miklós spat. "Hitler, Goebbels, all of them. I fuck their dead relatives."

THAT EVENING THE QUINTET MET IN THE BASEMENT. Electricity had come back on in the city, and they gathered under one of the hanging bulbs and practiced for the music shop concert a few days away. After rehearsal they lingered and talked about the turn of events.

Miklós slouched on his bench. "They should have shot Hitler a long time ago, sent him to the devil."

"You make it sound so easy," Márta told him.

"It should have been."

"Well, it wasn't," Katalin said.

"No," Sándor snapped. "And it still isn't. Now we have Stalin."

Miklós shrugged. "Any enemy of Hitler is a friend of mine."

"Oh, Stalin's a great friend for sure," Sándor said. "Just ask his joyful comrades in the Siberian gulag."

Márta nodded.

"I don't want to think about all that," Miklós said. "I have problems enough already." He stood up and pulled off his outer garment, a German army tunic he'd turned inside-out. On the shirt collar underneath he'd pinned a red star badge. Those things seemed to be in circulation lately. So were red arm bands.

"Where did you get that badge?" Antal asked.

Miklós waved in the general direction of southeast. "The parade."

"There was a parade?" Katalin asked.

Márta sighed. "Of course there was a parade. This is May Day and the Soviet Army's here."

"Yes, good old proletariat May Day," Sándor said. "Power to the people and so on."

"Power," Miklós echoed. "Might not be so bad, after having *none* all my life."

Antal waved his hands, cutting off their banter. He hadn't known there was a parade today. And why was it that Márta and Sándor always seemed to know things he didn't? "So you went to this parade?" he asked Miklós.

"I didn't try to go, I was just there, and I got pulled in. They made me carry a sign with somebody's picture on it. What's-his-name, Lenin."

"Oh, wonderful," Sándor muttered.

The electrical bulb shone its weak light, and from the street drifted the off-key noise of drunken Russians singing.

BERLIN WAS IN SHAMBLES, HITLER WAS DEAD, and the world waited for Germany's surrender. During the music shop concert, Antal was still waiting for it. The quintet had played through half the program, and Antal had seen from the beginning that this was an attentive, enthusiastic audience. Even so, the people kept doing as he himself did: glancing toward the street as though expecting some sign of the war's end. Maybe a newsboy would come running.

The day was warm, and Mr. Boros had removed the plywood from the broken front window. Listeners had squeezed into the twenty seats he'd set up, and more stood against the back wall of the shop, Antal's family among them. Márta's family wasn't here, and until an hour before the performance, Márta hadn't known whether she herself could come. She now sat playing cello behind the rest of the group, much of the time with her music stand hiding her face.

Antal and Miklós finished romping through Monti's *Csárdás*, pulled the last note, and bowed. The audience whistled. Antal took off his jacket. "I hope you don't mind," he told them. "We're working up a sweat."

A bald man in front laughed and said, "Go ahead." Antal had no idea who this man was, but he'd been writing on a steno pad and had brought in what looked like a camera case.

Antal, Márta, and Miklós stepped to the side. Sándor and Katalin stood in front of the piano and faced the audience. The group had chosen Sándor to introduce the songs because people said he was entertaining.

"So, friends," he announced, although the audience was half strangers, "in the first part of this concert I played Carmen, the Spanish beauty there." He pointed at the guitar he'd set aside. "Which was given us by our excellent host here, Boros György. I like piano better, but over the winter Carmen substituted, because at least we could take her into the bomb shelter."

Audience members nodded and smiled.

"And after we came back to our apartment," Sándor went on, "we discovered that the crossfire had taken out three indispensable notes on our piano, so once again Carmen came to our rescue. But now—ta-daaaa!" Sándor gestured toward the music store piano. "I have the great privilege of playing this post-war rarity, a piano with eighty-eight fully functional notes."

The audience chuckled.

Sándor sat down on the piano bench. "So here's a little tribute to this year's spring sport: dodging *malenki robot*." He rolled his eyes ironically, played a boogie-woogie bass run, and he and Katalin began to sing. "Oh, oh, oh, oh, oh, *malenki robot*."

"Sing it with us!" he said, and Katalin lifted her hands to the audience. "Oh, oh, oh, oh, oh."

Sándor kept singing, the audience joining in on every *oh* and *malenki robot*. "Keeping out of trouble, but it's harder than we thought, on every damned corner there's *malenki robot*."

The shop door clattered and swung open. The audience turned, froze. Sándor pulled his hands off the keys. Márta backed up, turned her face downward. In walked Lieutenant Kholodenko.

Antal gripped the neck of his violin, stepped forward, and forced a smile. "That was fun. But enough. Now for Shostakovich."

He had planned to play it later, but he pulled it from the back of his music stack and set it on the stand. Breathing deeply to calm himself, he raised the instrument and began to play. After half a page he glanced up. The audience listened quietly. Lieutenant Kholodenko leaned against the back wall. Others back there had shifted, giving him wide berth. Antal's left hand tensed as he carried the piece through. At the end, he bowed.

"'The Light Shines,'" he whispered to the rest of the group.

Márta went to the chair where she'd been playing cello and pulled farther back. Antal positioned himself in front of her. The sooner the lieutenant left, the better. But when "The Light Shines" ended, the man remained planted.

It was time for the last piece, "Song to Our Enemies" merging into "Pest, Along the Danube." Antal began to play. From within the music's grieving intervals, the January shadows fell—the cold, the hunger, the gunfire, the charcoal on Márta's cheeks, charred homes and broken bridges and drowned Jews, and the blood-soaked pillow case Sándor had carried.

Antal turned to him. Sándor played his guitar arpeggios and started singing.

Pest, along the Danube . . . home of all I've ever known . . . ragged, starved and ransacked . . . I wish you peace.

Antal played a violin interlude. In the audience a woman rocked as though keening.

Pest, you've bled into the river, and you've shouted to the skies,
And your proud, stubborn people have horror in their eyes . . .

A man bowed his head. A woman gripped her handkerchief. The man in front wrote in his steno notebook.

> *Pest, my mother city, may God spare you further pain.*
> *May it never—no, no, never!—be this way for you again.*
> *O city of my people, live on! Live on still!*
> *Pest, I love you, and I always will.*
> *Pest, I love you, and I always will.*

Antal played the last violin notes as Sándor's guitar faded. Several people in the audience cried softly. Lieutenant Kholodenko stared at the floor. After a silence the audience clapped, not loudly, but for a long time. Mr. Boros came forward and thanked both the quintet and the audience. The quintet bowed, and Márta turned quickly away.

Antal then found himself surrounded. People told him it was a marvelous concert, such an accomplishment, especially now, and he was so talented, and everyone sounded beautiful, and oh, that *last song*.

"Thank you," Antal repeated, "thank you." The other group members had also been swarmed, but he couldn't see Márta. Where was she?

A boy who looked about thirteen came up to him. "That was really good," he said, his voice in that awkwardness between child and man.

"Thank you."

"I play, too," the boy said. "I think I've heard you before. Didn't you win a competition?"

Antal smiled and would have said yes; but the boy suddenly backed away, for the Soviet lieutenant had pushed forward.

"This was the very good thing," the officer said in his stilted German. "Not since I leave Kyiv did I hear something good like this. But why did these persons cry with the last song?"

Antal cast a glance toward the battered street. Wasn't it obvious why people were crying? *"Diese ist eine sehr schwere Zeit,"* was all he could say. *This is a very hard time.*

"And the song is of this? This hard time?"

"Yes."

The man raised his thick eyebrows. "Your country went with the German fascists, very bad and evil what your country did, this is why all is hard now. You see? But never mind, thank you for this very good music." He tipped his hat and left.

A middle-aged woman tapped Antal's shoulder. "Very, very nice," she said. "And I'd like to say hello to Hanák Márta. Except she was introduced as Záborsky today. Do you know where she is?"

"I'm sorry," he said carefully. "I don't know."

"All right. I've missed seeing her family at church lately. Thank you."

The woman walked away, and the man with the steno book approached him.

"My name is Faludi Lajos," he said, "and Mr. Boros invited me to come hear you. I'm from Radio Budapest. I think our listeners would enjoy your group's music, so I wonder if you'd consider playing on the air? Probably in June."

"Oh." Taken aback, Antal straightened up. "Just a minute." He craned his neck and still couldn't see Márta, but he beckoned adamantly to Sándor, Katalin and Miklós. When they had gathered, Mr. Faludi repeated the request, and they looked at each other in surprise.

"Of course," Katalin said.

"What about your cellist?" Mr. Faludi asked.

As Antal wondered what to say, Sándor broke in: "She's not always available."

"Should we look for a date when she can make it?" the man asked.

"I'm not sure," Antal said. Who knew what her parents would be saying by that time? "The rest of us will do it, and we'll include her if we can."

Mr. Faludi asked for Antal's telephone number and wrote it on his notepad. "We'll arrange the details later, including how to pay you," he said. "Plan on mostly the same set of songs. Better skip *malenki robot*, though. Let's include the Gypsy pieces."

Miklós crossed his arms, nodded.

"And definitely that last piece about Pest," Mr. Faludi added. "Now. Let's take your photo. For advertising. Or should we do it later to get the cellist in the picture?"

"No," Antal said. "Let's do it now."

They stood for the photo, instruments in hand, outside in front of the shop sign and the broken window. Mr. Faludi wrote down their names, handed Antal his business card, and said he'd be in touch. After he'd gone,

Sándor said he couldn't believe they were going to be on the radio, and Miklós said he couldn't believe they were going to be paid.

Katalin bounced on her toes. "Well, I'm going to believe it!" She threw her arms around each of them, and Miklós grinned.

Antal walked back inside. Most people had left. From behind the shop counter, Mr. Boros said, "Wonderful performance, Antal. And I hear you've been working on the Dvořák romanza."

"Do you know where Márta is?"

"In the back practice room."

Antal found her there, sitting backward on the piano bench, slumped as though waiting out an air raid.

"Is the Russian officer gone?" she asked.

"Ukrainian. Yes, he's gone."

"And what about the others? Have they left?"

"Most of them. Márta, there was a woman who wanted to talk to you—"

"Is she gone?"

"Yes."

"Good. I saw her. I didn't want to snub her, but she would have asked about my father."

He sat down with her, took her hand and told her about the radio job. She gasped. "The radio?"

"Absolutely."

"Antal, that's incredible! *You* are incredible." Her eyes danced. "Do you know what I was thinking while you were playing today? I thought, 'What a dazzling violinist, and I'm in love with him, and his kisses are as dazzling as his music.'"

He laughed.

"Play the Dvořák on the radio," she said.

"But the man asked for the group."

"So the group will play songs together, and then you play the romanza after that. You should do it. We all know you're the best musician in the group."

"The piece isn't ready."

"Then get it ready."

He raised his eyebrows. The girl he loved had told him to perform music he loved, and who knew when he'd have another chance? "All right. For you."

TWO DAYS LATER GERMANY SURRENDERED. CHURCHILL himself announced it. Antal and his family and the whole nation poured into the streets, dancing and laughing, shouting, hugging neighbors, hugging strangers. The war was over. For this one moment, let them all forget they were on the losing side.

CHAPTER FORTY-TWO

The Embers Suite

February 12, 2007

NOT THAT FEBRUARY WAS EVER WARM, but Varga had more difficulty with the cold this year. Indoors he wore long underwear, heavy cardigans and often his wool jacket. In past years, this had been enough—well, except during the war. But in past years his heart wasn't so sluggish. Today as he worked at tidying the apartment, he paced himself, sitting down to rest if his fool heart complained—which naturally it did. After all, he was seventy-nine today.

In a few days Kristóf would move in. It irritated Varga that the family had agreed on this before anyone asked his opinion. He wasn't sure how much time Kristóf would actually spend here, even less sure who might come home with him. There would have to be a discussion of the rules. If circumstances were different, neither of them would have stood for this.

Varga looked over the furniture arrangement in the living room, where Kristóf would open the fold-out sofa bed every night. Kristóf would need a bureau of sorts for his clothes. Maybe at first he could put up with using a few bookshelves.

With a rag, Varga began dusting the shelves and the things on them: books, the CD player and scores of CDs, an Italian plate, a painted Polish bowl. Except for the newer CDs, all these things had been here since before

Ildi died. It was she that had arranged their household for forty-one years. Things were so slipshod now without her, and so empty.

From the bookcase he lifted the old framed photo of himself and Ildi and ran the dust cloth over it. This was his favorite picture of her, and not a bad one of himself—in their early fifties, Ildi sitting on this piano bench, and he standing beside her with his violin. They had just played part of a Brahms sonata for friends, and someone commented on the romanticism of the piece: "Things couldn't get much more romantic than that." Someone else shouted, "Oh, yes, they could!" He and Ildi laughed, and a photo was snapped. Varga had had the picture enlarged and framed after she died.

He set the picture on the shelf again and felt a twinge in his upper back. Easing down onto the piano bench, he looked up again at Ildi's picture, the strong-boned contours of her face, the auburn tinges in her hair before cancer ravaged her.

Before the cancer she did so many things. The communist government had not allowed her to go to music academy, so she'd worked in a warehouse but gave herself to music anyway—teaching piano to the children of friends, accompanying small choirs and ensembles. In her last years, when more churches had re-opened, she played organ in a small parish. Occasionally Varga went with her to listen, especially if she'd prepared music by Bach. He'd seldom attended Mass in the years before then, and he only attended a few times after she died. He should have gone more often, out of gratitude to her priest if nothing else.

Varga rubbed his back where it had hurt a moment ago. To his relief, the twinge had faded.

He remembered Ildi's priest because the man had brought the Eucharist to her after her cancer left her bedridden. The priest was a thoughtful man and kind to them both. Near the end, when Varga was alone with Ildi and broke down at her bedside, she urged him to call the priest: "Not for me this time, Antal, but for you." He didn't. But she told him in her tired voice that week after week, first in the church and now here in their home, the priest's words and the Eucharist had pointed her to something beyond her own fear. "It's made a difference," she half-whispered. "I want that for you. Tell me you'll go to Mass."

"I'll right," he said. "I will."

Three or four times he went. There under the crucifix with its dying Christ, his grief was not out of place. The burden of loneliness lifted, if only for a moment.

Varga shifted on the piano bench. On the piano lay a stack of music, and he picked up the score on top. It was his *Embers Suite*, written in 1958 when he was thirty and Ildi was twenty-nine. Varga thumbed through it now, seeing again the pages lined out for two violins, a cello, a piano and a flute. Over the years he'd told so few people that the instrumentation recalled his violin and Kolompár Miklós's, Hanák Márta's cello and his cousin Sándor's piano, with the flute representing Katalin's clear soprano voice. When he wrote this in 1958, he and Katalin hadn't seen Sándor or Márta or Miklós in thirteen years. Katalin urged him to write something in memory of the quintet, and the suite grew from the group's old music. It ended harshly, for he couldn't imagine bringing it to a beautiful close. Katalin understood.

There was much he didn't explain to Ildi at first, but she had her own understanding of it. The war had been lost, the 1956 revolution had been lost, and their baby daughter had been lost. The drastic ending fit. He didn't tell her, not then, what else had been lost.

Last August, when Lisa arrived with both the suite and the quintet's original songs, she guessed that her grandparents had brought the earlier songs to America with them. She had no idea, though, how her grandparents got the later suite. But Varga knew. He himself had sent it.

IN THE SUMMER OF 1958 WHEN HE WAS THIRTY, it was a year and a half after the bloody chaos of the '56 revolution and less than two months after the revolution's hapless leader, Nagy Imre, was executed. When people tried to interpret the ending of Varga's suite, they guessed the final drum shot meant the catch of Nagy's noose. Varga let them think so.

Ildi came closer to the truth. She was sure the harsh end meant the death of their daughter, Zsuzsanna, at the revolution's terrible height. She hinted gently, worriedly, that maybe it also meant his own black fall into melancholy. At the time he wrote it, his remaining children were young: Gabriella was four, and Zoltán, Zsuzsanna's twin, was a year and a half. They were oblivious to the suite but lived with the melancholy, and Varga hated himself for it.

Only his parents and Katalin really understood the suite's ending. Circumspect, they did not ask him to talk about it. But Katalin said she wished Sándor could hear the suite or at least read the music.

"Is there any way to send it to him?" she asked.

Varga had no address to write to either Sándor or Márta. All he had to go on was the memory of an old message his parents had received from Márta's father in 1946. It seemed to have been surreptitiously conveyed from a friend to a colleague to a correspondent to another colleague to another friend, and it said that the Hanáks had made it to Chicago, and so had Sándor. So Varga had waited, hoping that if news of Sándor and the Hanáks had arrived once, maybe more messages would arrive. None did. He tried to believe this was for the best, considering the risk between Hungary and America, but he felt he had lost them twice.

With the suite written, however, he thought about Katalin's question. Through careful inquiries he found the name and address of a Hungarian Catholic parish in Chicago. When a concert clarinetist he trusted received permission to travel to Helsinki, Varga asked him to mail a package while there. He wrapped the *Embers* manuscript in brown paper and wrote a note for the Chicago priest, whose name he did not know.

Father,
I hope you have met my cousin and can give him this music. His name is Varga Sándor. I realize this is a common name. He is a little taller than average with dark brown hair, and he is musically gifted. He would be thirty-one years old.

Varga wanted to ask the priest about Márta and her family, too, but the Hanáks weren't Catholic. What were the chances that the priest would even know them? And how safe was it to put the name of Hanák Viktor in a letter to America, even if it were sent from Finland? He was risking enough just by looking for Sándor.

With the music manuscript he enclosed another note.

Kedves Sándor!
I don't know if you are still in Illinois Chicago, so I hope this will reach you. I wrote this music remembering the quintet, especially you and Márta. Some

of its threads came from you and from her. Do you know where she is, how she is? So often I think about you and about her.

This suite ends painfully. I think you will understand.

Time has passed. I teach at the music academy and play in the national orchestra. I got married in 1951 to Brauer Ildikó, a talented pianist. I don't think you ever knew her. Ildi and I have children—Gabriella came along in '53 and little Zoli in '56. Zoli had a twin sister who died of illness during the 1956 fighting. It was very hard. It still is.

Sándor, for the love of God, write me back if you possibly can. Send it in care of the music academy.

Five months later a reply arrived, quietly handed to him by the dean while Varga was leafing through music in the academy's library. The woman who brought it to the dean, Varga later found out, worked at the U.S. embassy.

Kedves Antal!
It was so good to hear from you. Thank you for writing to S. We have never stopped missing you.

He reread the opening, momentarily confused. Then his pulse quickened and he knew, without skipping to the signature, that this letter was from Márta. The "S" was Sándor, his name abbreviated because of censors. Her letter went on:

Your suite is beautiful. And heartbreaking. We played through it on piano, and I wept at the end. I couldn't help it. I suppose that if there is a public performance of the suite, you will be criticized. People won't understand, and if you need to change the ending for others, do. But S and I understand. Part of me will always grieve over what happened.

It was so painful for all of us. And now I find out that later you lost a little daughter. Jaj, this is such sad news.

Perhaps by now you have guessed this: I married S. He sends his greetings. S works as a longshoreman, but we hope that in time he will have other opportunities. We have a daughter named Ann. We recently managed to buy an old piano, and music consoles him (and me) when the hard memories flood back.

Antal, though it's been thirteen years, I still think of you and remember what you bore. May God bless you.

Szeretettel,
Márta

That night after his children were in bed, Antal sat down on the sofa and reread the letter, straining to hear Márta's voice, trying to picture their faces. Ildi joined him and asked what was wrong. He beckoned to her and she sat with him, leaning close.

"That suite I wrote," he said as he handed her the letter. "These are the people behind it."

She read it, and he told her about everything—all that had frozen during the winter of the siege, and the music that was their fire against the ice, and the guns, and the terrible losses. Ildi had endured the siege, too, and much of his story she already knew. But tonight in broken tones he told her about the girl he had loved first, and why she was gone, and why Sándor was gone. He gave Ildi the *Embers* score, and though it wasn't new to her she played through it again to the final crippling. At the end, she wept, like Márta had done. He joined her on the piano bench.

"Why didn't you tell me this sooner?" she asked.

"I didn't want you to have to carry it."

She laid her head on his chest. "Oh, Antal."

He took her in his arms, and in case she felt she was in second place, he whispered, "You're the woman I've loved with my life."

For everyone's safety, they burned the letter. It had included no return address, so he could not have replied even if he decided to risk it. She told him his suite should be performed. He didn't have to explain the ending, she said.

"This isn't the time to perform it," he said. "Not now."

"But someday," she answered.

He put the suite away until 1989, when communism was too weak to carry on and Nagy Imre was re-buried with state honors. Varga performed the suite at the academy, with Halmos on piano and other faculty friends on violin, cello and flute. The ending frustrated the musicians, but Halmos asked them to please trust the composer. At the performance, when

Halmos welcomed the audience, he said that at the end the lights would be turned out and everyone would leave in silence.

"Like a Tenebrae service on Good Friday," Ildi said afterwards, and Varga nodded.

Five years later in 1994, he received one more letter from Márta, sent to the academy. He read it standing in the small practice room he used for teaching, and when he reached the line that said Sándor had died, he leaned against the closed door and put his face in his hands. Her note said she was moving to a small apartment, but she did not include the new address, and he could not write her back. He never heard from her again—except, perhaps in some way, when Lisa appeared in the opera house foyer.

Sitting on the piano bench tired and old, Varga turned to the last page of this manuscript that Lisa had brought from her grandmother's attic. There was the ending of the suite, with its rampage of dissonance and its crash. The only public anger he had ever allowed himself, he'd told Kristóf. After the furious ending Márta had written her anguished words, *Oh, Antal, Sándor, why did it all have to end like this?*

Varga's back hurt with the weight of the war years and their violence, the communist years of looking over his shoulder, all these years with a secret he didn't want, and years of no word from America, years that his baby daughter should have grown into happy womanhood, years that Zoltán and Gabriella should have had happier parents, years that Kristóf should have had a happier life.

He rubbed his upper back behind his bowing arm.

Oh, Antal, Sándor, why did it all have to end like this?

Varga pulled a pen out of his breast pocket, and over the last page of the manuscript—top to bottom, through Violin I, Violin II, Flute, Cello and Piano—he drew one huge X.

CHAPTER FORTY-THREE

Shadows

May 20, 1945

MAY CAME AS A RELIEF. THOUGH ANTAL WAS STILL HUNGRY, at least he wasn't cold; and though the war had been bad, unspeakably so, at least it was over. Márta's father was still gone and her little sister was still thin, but—well, everyone was thin.

The quintet would play on the radio in a month. Antal tried to pull the group together twice a week to rehearse. On his own he practiced an hour each morning and two hours in the afternoon or evening, mostly on the Dvořák romanza, sometimes in the basement. Often Miklós was there, but certainly not always. Last week Miklós had left for three days and no one knew where he was. When he returned, he said he'd looked for an uncle of his and didn't find him.

It was now three weeks into May, a Sunday afternoon. In the back practice room at the music shop, Antal stood playing his violin. Beside him at the upright, Mr. Boros played a piano accompaniment, pulsing the last chords. Antal concentrated gentle pressure on the bow, holding the high final note to the soft close.

Mr. Boros took his hands off the keys. Antal lowered the bow.

"This is really smoothing out," Mr. Boros said. "Your sixteenth notes a few measures back are cleaner than last week, and your expression on that final note was near perfect. You'll have this ready for the radio concert. I've told Faludi to allow time for it."

"And you're sure you can be there that night to accompany?"

"Barring *malenki robot*, yes." Mr. Boros stood and closed the accompaniment score. "Listen, I need to tell you about something that happened."

Antal set his bow on the music stand. "What is it?"

"You know that photo that Faludi took," Mr. Boros said. "He gave me a copy, and I posted it out front, with a notice about your radio date."

"I didn't see it."

"No. Because someone stole the photo." Mr. Boros leaned against the piano, regarding him seriously. "I wasn't here yesterday. My niece was filling in. She said a young Gypsy came in, quite agitated, apparently. He was looking for the Gypsy in your group. Miklós. He'd seen the picture and recognized him."

"Oh, my God, where is the fellow? I have to tell Miklós."

"I don't know. And my niece couldn't tell him where Miklós was, didn't even know if you all would want us to pass that information on."

Antal shook his head. Damn it, after all the wandering and searching Miklós had done.

"He lives in our basement," Antal said. "If that Gypsy comes back, give him our address. And tell your niece that. And anybody else that works here. Please."

He rushed home and found Miklós in the courtyard, picking up spilled trash. Antal ran to him across the broken pavement and told him what Mr. Boros had said.

Miklós stared, eyes frantic, and dropped the trash bucket. "Who was it? What did he look like?"

"He was young. That's all I know."

"Nothing else?" Miklós pleaded.

"No. Who might it be?"

Miklós held up one palm. "Wait." He ran to the basement door, threw it open, and disappeared inside. A few moments later he returned and thrust a photograph into Antal's hands.

It was creased almost beyond clarity. Miklós must have carried this in his rucksack for months. The photo showed four people, one of them Miklós with a violin in rest position under his arm. To his left stood two men, one perhaps a little older than Miklós and the other middle-aged. At Miklós's right stood a girl in a kerchief and a coin necklace.

"My father and my brother Joska," Miklós said. "Joska plays cimbalom. And the girl is Timea. We gave her that necklace, my father and me. I have two other brothers and two sisters, but no picture of them."

Miklós pointed at the image of his brother. "Maybe it was him who was looking for me. Maybe another brother. Maybe a cousin, maybe a musician, I don't know." He swore with a moan. "How long this will go on, searching for blown dust?"

"But whoever it was, at least he's alive, right?"

Miklós picked up the trash bucket and turned away.

That evening after supper Antal knocked on Márta's door. After a few minutes it opened a hand's breadth and Sarolta peeked out. "Antal. We're having some trouble with Anni. Maybe you shouldn't come in. Just a minute."

She called to Márta, leaving the door ajar. An ill stench drifted out. Márta stepped out through the door and shut it behind her. Gray shadows ringed her eyes, and tendrils of hair had worked loose from her braid.

"Anni's sick again," she said. "We were up most of the night with her. She says her stomach hurts, and everything she eats goes straight through her."

"*Jaj*, no." Antal knew what his father would ask. "Have you been boiling the water?"

"Yes. But—wait. Yesterday my mother went to see someone in Buda, and she took Anni along. Buda's only had their pipes working for a week or so."

"But your mother isn't sick, is she?"

"No. But Anni's famous for finding trouble." Márta's voice carried exasperation and fear. "Maybe she wandered into the bathroom, helped herself to the sink, who knows."

Antal touched Márta's messy hair, wanting to reassure both of them that this was all normal enough. Nobody had made it through these months without some misery in the gut. But Anni hadn't been strong since the siege.

"I'll tell my father," he said.

Papa came with Antal to the Hanáks' apartment and brought his medical bag. Antal, Márta and Sarolta watched from across the room as Mrs. Hanák held Anni on her lap and Papa examined her.

"With the diarrhea, has she been passing blood?" Papa asked Mrs. Hanák.

"No."

Papa put a thermometer into Anni's mouth and listened with his stethoscope to her chest and back. He felt for her pulse at her throat and checked the thermometer.

"Yes, she has a fever." Papa looked directly at Mrs. Hanák. "Livia, her skin is dry, and I think she's becoming dehydrated. She needs water."

"We've been trying," Mrs. Hanák said.

"I know. She can't retain it. She needs salt and sugar in the water in order to absorb it."

Sarolta asked, "Why?" Mrs. Hanák said forlornly, "Sugar?" and Antal's hopes plummeted. His father might as well have asked for diamonds.

"We have a little bit of salt," Márta said, "but no sugar."

"We'll have to find some," Papa said. "This may be dysentery. It's hard on children, and it may be especially hard on Anni because she was weakened by typhus over the winter."

Antal felt Márta grip his arm, saw Sarolta looking worriedly from face to face. Mrs. Hanák squeezed her eyes shut as though holding back tears. On her lap, Anni squirmed.

"The good thing is that there's no bleeding," Papa said. He gave instructions to the family: they were to sponge Anni off with tepid water to keep her cool, check her stools for blood, and somehow, give her sugar water with salt.

Anni groaned. "I don't want water with salt in it."

"But you need it, little star," Mrs. Hanák said. She turned anxious eyes to Papa. "Do you have any sugar?"

"Not much. Antal, go get whatever we have in the kitchen, and then ask the neighbors."

The command was sharp, and Antal headed for the door. Mrs. Hanák called after him, "If the neighbors ask who it's for, remember to say Záborsky, not Hanák."

"Yes," he shouted over his shoulder.

His mother was shaken by the news. She gave him what little sugar she had, which filled only the bottom of a cup, and she handed him the salt cellar. Antal, his grandfather, Katalin, and Sándor divided up the task of asking the neighbors, and they each took a floor of the building. Antal went to the ground floor. Magda *néni* gave him the six cubes in her sugar bowl and said she was sorry she didn't have more. Most people said they had none, and Antal didn't know whether to believe them. When he and the others had finished the rounds, they had collected less than a cupful.

He took it to the Hanáks' apartment. Anni had fallen asleep on the sofa. At the stove, Antal watched as Papa coached Márta and Sarolta through boiling the water and dissolving the right proportions of salt and sugar in it. At this rate, they would run out of sugar quickly. They brought a cup of the sugared water to Mrs. Hanák. She awakened Anni, helped her sit up, and lifted the cup to her lips.

Anni tasted it and shook her head. "I don't like it."

"But you need it. Come on now."

The tension in Mrs. Hanák's voice was unmistakable. Márta and Sarolta watched nervously. Complaining, Anni took intermittent sips until half the water was gone. Then she pushed the cup away and clamped her mouth shut.

"All right, that's a start," Papa said. "Give her some more in a little while."

Anni wriggled, groaned, bent over.

"What's wrong?" Mrs. Hanák asked her.

Anni coughed. "I don't—" She gagged, and vomited into her mother's lap.

Mrs. Hanák gasped. "Oh, no. No. Oh, Anni."

She carried Anni back to the small bathroom. Márta and Sarolta began wiping the floor with towels. Antal and his father stepped out into the courtyard to give Mrs. Hanák and Anni privacy as they changed their clothes. It had grown dark. Soon Mrs. Hanák opened the door and told them she would try giving Anni more sugar water in a little while.

"All right," Papa said. "The vomiting isn't so unusual at first. Try not to be discouraged. Call me if you need me."

Papa left. Antal stayed another hour and a half, rinsing towels, boiling water and mixing the sugar-salt solution. Mrs. Hanák tried twice more to make Anni drink. The first time, Anni vomited again. The second time, she sat on Márta's lap and took one scant sip, then pushed the rest away.

Márta turned to her mother. "She doesn't want anymore, Anyu. And I'm afraid if I force it on her, she'll just throw up again and lose it all."

Mrs. Hanák nodded mutely. She walked over to them, placed her hand on Anni's head and closed her eyes. Sarolta stepped close. Mrs. Hanák began whispering. They were praying. Antal crossed himself, not knowing what else to do.

When he plodded upstairs for the night, Sándor met him at the door. Everyone else had gone to bed. "Is Anni any better?" Sándor asked.

"No." Antal told him what he'd seen tonight.

"And how is Márta?" Sándor asked.

"Getting more worried all the time."

Sándor grimaced as if every word stung.

EARLY THE NEXT MORNING ANTAL WENT downstairs with his father and talked to Mrs. Hanák at the door. Little had changed during the night. Anni had drunk some sugar water, vomiting most of it but not all. She was still feverish but had not passed blood, and she was now asleep.

Mrs. Hanák, wearing an old kerchief, looked as though she hadn't slept all night. "Should I take Anni to the hospital?"

"There isn't much the hospital could do for her that you aren't already doing," Papa said.

"But what about that thing they sometimes do, putting a tube into her vein—"

"Hydrating her intravenously. I wish we had the equipment for it. But we don't." Papa sighed in that weary way of his when he had to tell people no. "There's hardly any medicine. Hardly any available beds. Honestly, I think being in the hospital would just scare her."

Mrs. Hanák brushed her eye with the back of her hand. "I don't want her scared."

Márta appeared in the doorway with her mother and looked sadly at Antal. He murmured good morning to her.

"Do you have clean sheets?" Papa asked them.

"Yes," Márta said. "Magda *néni* brought some over a few minutes ago. And rags."

"And what about sugar?" Papa asked. "Do you have any left?"

Mrs. Hanák suddenly seeming tired to the point of confusion. She barely knew. Márta said they needed more. They talked about canvassing more neighbors, talked about the black market but didn't know where to go.

Mrs. Hanák looked at Papa. "László, should I try to get word to Viktor? It's hard reaching him. I'd have to leave messages with other people."

"Do it. He needs to know."

She drew in a shaking breath, and Márta clutched her mother's hand.

"And if somebody could please go tell my friend Messik Júlia," Mrs. Hanák said. "She doesn't have a working telephone."

"I'll go," Antal said.

"You'll be late for school," Papa said.

"For God's sake, who cares?" Antal cried.

Papa waved his hand. "Go."

Antal hurried to Mrs. Messik's apartment and brought her back with him. The woman immediately sat down next to Anni on the sofa bed. She stroked the child's hair in concern and told Mrs. Hanák to try to rest.

Antal looked around for Márta but didn't see her. Sarolta came over to him, still in her bathrobe. "Márta left a few minutes ago," she said, "with your cousin."

"What?"

"Yes, he came to ask about Anni, and we told him we needed more sugar. And we all thought the only people who would have it are the Soviets. So Anyu taught Márta and Sándor some Russian words and gave them some brandy to trade, and they went out to get some sugar."

"From the Russians."

"We didn't know what else to do." Sarolta blinked and her voice grew unsteady. "People say that the Russians like children. They can be nice if they feel sorry for you and they're not drunk. Sándor wanted to find that officer you met."

Antal's head had begun to hurt. The apartment smelled like a loo and Anni was whimpering and Sarolta was trying not to cry. Márta and Sándor were out bargaining with the enemy, and who knew whether Márta would be raped or Sándor dragged off for *malenki robot*. Who knew if they'd find sugar and if Anni would hold it down. He had to stay and see.

But Mrs. Hanák called out wearily, "Thank you, Antal, you may go on to school now." Clearly, the woman wanted to rest, as Mrs. Messik had told her to. So he left for school, hating his own helplessness, hating it that Sándor was with Márta and he was not.

HE ARRIVED AN HOUR LATE TO CLASSES. Sándor, it turned out, was three hours late. Antal saw him in the school courtyard during the lunch break and grabbed his arm. "What happened? Did you have any luck?"

"I'm not sure."

"What do you mean, you're not sure? You either bought some sugar or you didn't."

Sándor pushed Antal's hand off his arm. "We went home empty-handed. But we found that lieutenant, and he said he'd bring some sugar."

"*Jézus Mária*, do you believe him?"

"I don't know. But I'll tell you something. Poor Márta was falling apart, crying, telling him over and over in German how sick her sister was, '*sehr, sehr krank*,' and I think if he doesn't get her some sugar like he said he would, then he's an absolute shit. By the way, if you've ever wondered what the fellow's job is with the army, I think he's a sapper. He seemed to be leading a crew that was repairing pavement. For the sake of their vehicles, I suppose."

"And he didn't pull you onto the project."

Sándor shrugged. "Maybe he felt sorry for me, too."

At the end of school Antal rushed home, not bothering to wait for Sándor. When he reached his own block, he saw the officer walking toward the apartment house carrying a field satchel.

"*Herr leutnant!*" Antal shouted.

Kholodenko turned. "Ah, *violine Freund*." The man opened his satchel. "Today I see your friend girl and your brother—"

"Cousin."

"Ah. They ask for this, for the sick sister." He handed Antal a paper packet about the size of a cup.

"Yes, thank you. Thank you!"

Kholodenko bowed slightly. "May the sister make well. *Auf wiedersehen*."

Antal went to Márta's door and gave her the sugar. She leaned on his shoulder and told him, "We called my father. He's trying to get here."

Through the afternoon and into the evening, Antal went back and forth between his apartment and Márta's. Katalin and Sándor kept asking about Anni. So did Miklós. Papa was working the late shift at the hospital.

At twilight Antal headed for the Hanáks' apartment again. Márta met him in the courtyard. "My father got here half an hour ago," she said very quietly. "Right now he's on the telephone with your father."

Antal reached for her hand. It pained him to see her like this, so rumpled and worn.

"We tried to give Anni the sugar water again," she said, "had to spoon it into her mouth, but after a while she wouldn't even open her mouth anymore. Her muscles hurt, but aspirin doesn't stay in her, either." It was a moment before Márta could go on. "When Anni wouldn't drink, my mother broke down. She had to leave the room because she didn't want to upset Anni. But—Antal, I'm scared." Her breath was rough as she tried not to cry.

"I want to help you," he said.

"There isn't anything you can do—wait, no. Get your violin. Anni might like that."

When he brought the violin, Anni was resting but awake on the untidy sofa-bed. Mr. Hanák sat on the bed beside her and caressed his daughter's cheek. He greeted Antal with a silent nod, his face gray with stubble and anguish. Sarolta and Mrs. Hanák sat at the table.

Antal and Márta pulled up chairs near Anni. Under her blanket she seemed to be wearing one of her father's undershirts as a nightgown. Antal tuned his violin while Márta opened a hymnal. Anni's eyes moved, watching them.

"Anni," Márta said softly, "would you like Antal to play his violin for you?"

Very slightly, she nodded.

Márta flipped the hymnal pages and then held the book open in front of Antal, saying, "She likes this one." Antal began to play. It was a simple melody unfamiliar to him. His eyes caught a few of the words as he played, and he realized it was a children's hymn. Every time he glanced at Anni, her gaze was on him. He played the melody three times, and at the end Márta asked her if she'd like another song.

Her lips moved. *Igen. Yes.*

Márta turned more pages and showed Antal two hymns side by side. "Play both."

They were psalms set to music. As he played, he looked steadily at the notes, barely hearing his own music, trying not to see Anni's sunken eyes and the family's stricken faces. Halfway through the second song Mrs. Hanák began singing shakily. One by one the others joined in, their voices giving out on high notes or long ones. Anni listened, turning her eyes as each new voice entered. When the music stopped, she closed her eyes. A moment later she whimpered, squirming weakly.

"She's tired," Mr. Hanák said. "I think we should stop."

Antal told the exhausted child he'd play more music for her tomorrow if she wanted. He left the apartment, knowing he had to let the Hanáks get whatever sleep they could. Márta stepped outside with him. He held her, told her he loved her, said he'd come back in the morning. It had never been harder to leave her.

IN THE MIDDLE OF THE NIGHT, THE TELEPHONE RANG. Antal rolled over and heard his father answer it. Straining to listen, Antal picked up the words *blood* and *intestine*. He hurried down the bunk ladder and into the main room just as his father hung up.

"Is it Anni?" Antal asked.

"Yes."

"Is she worse?"

"Yes. I'm going down there. You stay here."

"But—"

"Stay here," Papa ordered.

Antal sat in the living room in his bathrobe instead of going back to bed. Sándor wandered out and asked, "Want me to wait up with you?" Antal said no.

At five o'clock Papa walked in the door again. Behind him plodded Márta. Motioning for Antal to stay where he was, she joined him on the sofa.

"I'll let you two talk," Papa said. "I'm going to bed."

The sound of his footsteps died out and the bedroom door closed. Márta twisted a messy lock of hair. "She's gone."

Antal caught his breath and felt his eyes filling.

"She started passing blood," Márta said. "And she was all confused and didn't know who we were. Your father gave her a pain shot and helped us try to take care of her. I was the one sitting closest to her when her breathing stopped. And I told the others."

Márta looked at him, traced her finger over the damp hollow below his eye. Then she threw her arms around his neck and wept.

THAT EVENING HE STOOD ON THE FRONT BALCONY with Sándor. On the street below, near the rubble heap that was slowly dwindling, a child shouted. Márta would never hear her little sister's shout again.

"It's terrible, Sándor."

"Yes." Sándor wiped his eyes. "Márta will be sad for a long time."

"I guess you would know."

Sándor nodded, and they watched the daylight fade.

IT WAS TUESDAY BEFORE SUNRISE WHEN ANNI DIED, and the burial was to take place on Friday. Each day after school Antal went walking with Márta, getting her out of her joyless apartment. On Thursday they went only as far as the Opera House, a short walk, and sat on the front steps. Across Andrássy Avenue, half-burned but still living trees had thrust out new leaves, showing green in front of the smoke-blackened buildings.

Márta told him Anni's burial service the next morning would have to be very small. Mostly just their family, and not even relatives. Márta's grandparents were dead, her father's one sister lived in the States, and her mother had no brothers or sisters. Antal's family could come, and Mrs. Messik and the Hanáks' pastor, but that was all. The event had to be private because her father was still trying to stay out of the public eye.

"He doesn't even live in Debrecen anymore," Márta said. "He's been on the move—I don't know where—because the communist insiders in Debrecen know about his connections in Britain. And America."

"How long can your parents go on like this?" Antal asked, too tired to keep the exasperation out of his voice. "Márta, don't you get tired of everything being so hidden?"

"I hate it! We're cut off from almost everybody. Even from our father, with him living apart from us—and look what happened while he was gone!"

She buried her face in her hands and her words went on, muffled and choked: "Anni only died two days ago. She got sick less than a week ago. It feels like years. And before that there was my father going away. And before that, my mother was—you know what I told you, about what that soldier did to her. And before *that*, our old apartment burned down. Weren't things hard enough? But now Anni's gone, too."

He touched her shoulder, felt the broken way she leaned against him as she asked, "Is this all there is, just one terrible thing after another?"

"No. No." He cupped her chin in his hand, desperate for some kind of hope to give her. "Remember the song we wrote? 'The light shines, and the darkness has not overcome it.'"

"My sister's light was overcome."

He could say no more, and she clasped his hand so hard it hurt.

ABOUT AN HOUR AFTER ANTAL GOT HOME, he received a phone call. "Antal? Horváth Ferenc here."

"Mr. Horváth!" Antal clutched the telephone. Oh, God, at last. Something good. His violin teacher was back. He hadn't fled the country, hadn't been taken away for *malenki robot*, hadn't died.

"I'm home," Mr. Horváth said. "My house is in terrible condition, but here I am. So I've been calling my students. Very glad to hear your voice, by the way. And my friend Boros György tells me you're working on the romanza."

"Yes."

"And doing well with it, he says. And what in the world is all this about a quintet? And a radio engagement?"

Facing the bullet-pocked window frames, Antal told him how it had come about.

"I'm just very impressed, Antal," Mr. Horváth said. "Look at all you got done while the city was under fire. And now you're preparing for a radio show."

"Mr. Horváth." Antal coughed, tried to pull strength into his spent body and voice. "I'm not sure. About the radio show."

"Ah?"

"Remember Hanák Márta?"

"Of course."

"Her little sister died. Day before yesterday."

"Oh, Jesus, I didn't know."

"Márta's in our group. I don't want to make her play. I don't want to make *me* play."

"Oh, Lord."

Antal could not go on. Mr. Horváth was quiet a long time, then said, "You don't have to do it, and neither does she. But here's something to think about. When things are at their worst, it's often best to do what you would have done under normal circumstances. If you can. I'd certainly like to hear you play the romanza, like to help you get it ready if you want."

Antal said, "Maybe," and he could get no further.

THE NEXT MORNING ANTAL AND HIS FAMILY WALKED through Kerepesi Cemetery, under damaged trees and over grass churned by recent digging. They joined the Hanáks, their pastor and his wife, and Mrs. Messik at a short open grave. Nearby, a small coffin rested on the clumped sod. Antal stood beside Sándor, who had not spoken at all on the walk here.

The pastor, in his heavy glasses and clerical collar, began to speak. He said he remembered baptizing Anni. Steadying his voice, he talked about her love for her family, her delight in stories and songs, and before her illness, her exuberant energy. He looked at the Hanáks and said God shows compassion to those who grieve.

And maybe that was true, but Antal could only wish God had spared them the grief in the first place. He glanced around. There were tears—Katalin sniffling, Mother biting her lip, Sarolta sobbing into her desolate father's shirt. Sándor stood with his hands shoved into his pockets, the toe of his shoe kicking the grass. In that horrid wooden box lay a little girl who should have been shouting and running. The coffin was lowered and Márta pressed her hands to her face. Mrs. Hanák bent over the hole, almost stumbling. Mr. Hanák helped her stand. He wiped tears from under his glasses and pitched the first shovelful of dirt into the grave.

After the final prayer, the pastor approached Antal and his family and explained that the Hanáks would stay here until they felt ready to leave. After that, they would go to Mrs. Messik's house for a meal. By this Antal understood that he was not to wait.

"Can't I talk to Márta?" he asked.

"Of course. All of you, go ahead."

Antal crossed the grass to Márta and put his arms around her but could not find words. She seemed to understand. "I love you," she whispered.

The others were waiting their turn. Antal stepped away as his grandfather and parents gave their condolences to Márta and Sarolta and talked with their parents. Katalin gave Márta a long hug.

Sándor stepped up to Márta. He set his hand on her shoulder and said something Antal didn't hear. Márta wiped her face and nodded, eyes on the ground. When she raised them, Sándor said something more. She listened, answered, wiped her eyes, and he replied. Whatever had been said, grief broke across Sándor's face like a sudden storm. He reached to her and embraced her. Hard.

Antal strode over the grass. Planting himself beside them, he pulled on Sándor's arm. When Sándor ignored him, Antal pushed. "Time to go. Come on."

Tearful, Sándor pulled back, and Márta looked at both of them in sorrow.

CHAPTER FORTY-FOUR

Ash Wednesday

February 18, 2007

IT WAS SIX A.M. ON A SUNDAY, a few days after Valentine's Day, which Lisa had not celebrated. She sat at her kitchen table with her laptop. On Skype, Kristóf in a heavy gray pullover adjusted his screen, revealing half a dozen people at old computers. It was three in the afternoon there.

"*Mi újság?*" he asked her.

Ah, yes, she'd told him about her Hungarian language CDs. She sifted through her memory for *Mi újság*. He'd asked what was new.

"*Semmi,*" she said. "I mean, *nincs semmi érdekes.*" *Nothing interesting.*

He smiled. "How can I believe this? With you, always something is interesting. You find secret music, you come to Pest and find cousins, you make an old man talk who doesn't want to talk, you are willing even to talk of impossible questions, so I think you are very much braver than other people I know."

She laughed a little. "I never thought of it that way. I hope you're right."

Her gaze flickered to the dark world outside the kitchen window, where dawn, when it happened, would barely made a difference. She'd never liked February, especially now. It was a year ago yesterday that Jake moved out.

"I want to hear about this *fiú* of yours," she told Kristóf. She had learned the word just this week—*fiú*, son, boy.

"Yes, already I saw him twice." Kristóf's expression clouded. "Five years, I didn't know, and now all sudden everything is changed."

He told her the story—hesitating, stopping to think, correcting himself, sometimes looking around and moving closer to the computer to lower his voice—about this boy who had come about through a summer affair, and about the woman who didn't tell him, and about how he shouldn't have ignored her calls. The child was beautiful and friendly and could sing solfege and was excited to see Ópa's piano and violin. He was a Varga.

"And I hate this," Kristóf told Lisa, "the way Blanka his mother says, 'You have a son. Now sign these papers so you don't have him anymore.'" Kristóf looked down, his voice dispirited. "She says her husband should be Misha's father, says already Misha loves him, and probably it's true. But I don't want Misha just gone, out of my life and that's the end."

"I understand," Lisa said, because her son *was* gone. "Kristóf, I don't know what Misha needs, but you need time with your son."

Across the screen, he looked at her bleakly.

"When my son was born," she said, "I had five minutes with him before he died. Five minutes. That's all. I have almost no memories of Alexander, except for him tumbling inside me." She paused to strengthen her voice. "While I was in the hospital, I heard about another woman there whose baby died after two days. People say that would be harder. Maybe. But I was jealous. I would have given anything for two days with my son."

Kristóf nodded. "*Jaj*, Lisa."

"Even if you do have to say goodbye to Misha, I'll hope they'll let you see him now and then. Not just for you, but for him."

"That's right. Absolute right." Kristóf's face set. "I said that to Blanka. I won't be a parent that walks away and doesn't care. Like my mother."

"But your mother came back, right? Isn't that what you said? And she wants you to forgive her?"

"Yes." He scowled. "She left when I was fourteen. Off to Germany, finds a new man. After fifteen years she comes back, 'Oh, forgive me,' and does this make things right?"

"Nothing would make it right." Lisa didn't think that was what forgiveness was for, she thought it was for finding some semblance of peace, but what did she really know? "Maybe your mother is just hoping to make things less awful."

"If she wants things less awful, she can say, 'I am sorry.' Then I could say 'All right' or 'Thank you.' Or nothing. But she says 'Will you forgive me,' and now it's my problem. If I say no, then this is all my guilt. If your mother did this, what would you do?"

It was the question that he'd asked in his email. "I don't think my mother would ask for forgiveness," Lisa told him, "because she doesn't think what she does is wrong. She's just being herself, she thinks. Doing what she wants, saying what she wants to. Giving her opinion whether it's wanted or not. Being 'up front,' she would say."

"Does she know you don't like it?"

"How could she miss it, that I don't like it?"

"*Na*, that is very easy, to miss something. All that a person has to do is, just not want to see it. Lately I find out, too many times, I am world's expert for this. All right, you say your mum wouldn't ask you to forgive." Over Skype, his eyes probed Lisa's. "But your husband. He trespassed you and he left you. If he came and said, 'Forgive me,' would you take him back?"

"I can't. He's married to someone else now. He has a baby."

"So you don't have to forgive him?"

"Well."

Lisa looked away into the living room, to the lamp table covered with Valentine cards from the school children but not from Jake, to the television she no longer watched with Jake, and to the coffee table where she'd thrown the divorce papers when they first arrived.

"I'm Catholic," she said. "Things are over with Jake, but I still have to forgive him."

Kristóf seemed genuinely confused. "If you can't take him back, then what is forgiving?"

"I can't punish him." She wasn't prepared for how hard this was to say. "I have to live with the mess he made. It's no good to pay him back. Or bad-mouth him. Or back-stab him."

"And this is difficult, yes?"

"How could it not be? I have to let go of loving him, and do it without hating him."

Kristóf considered this. "I think hating makes it easier."

A bare gray glimmer of dawn now showed at the window. Hate Jake? Maybe she'd loved him too long to hate him. Maybe she felt sorry for him.

The way things turned out in their life together, he didn't know what to do; he thought he'd married a happy woman.

"Maybe I'll hate him for you," Kristóf said.

"But he isn't hateful." It hurt saying it. "He's weak."

"A weak asshole, and he treated you like shit. Lisa, I think you are . . ." Kristóf groped for words. "You are very patient, very—I don't know what to say. You are like my grandfather. If a thing is not good to say, he does not say it. If a thing is not good to do, he does not do it. There is English word for this, but I forget—"

"Restrained? Self-controlled?"

"Yes. Sometimes I think you are like a nun. This is not a joke, what I am saying. And I respect you. But what do you do with your fire?"

"My fire?"

She searched his face. No, he wasn't joking, wasn't sneering, only gazing back at her in puzzlement.

"I . . . I don't know," she faltered.

ON WEDNESDAY LISA RECEIVED ANOTHER EMAIL from Kristóf. She read it on her classroom computer at the end of the school day.

Szia, Lisa—

Maybe my words to you on Sunday were too strong, and if that is true, then I'm sorry. Please keep whatever is good and forget the rest.

With all the bad stuff (you see how I use American slang?) I forgot to tell you the good news. My father has a new lady friend and I met her. I am not used to women blowing kisses to my father! She seems kind, has good sense, and I hope maybe she makes him happy.

Also I moved in with Ópa. My father and my aunt say this is best for him, not to be alone. Maybe Ópa agrees, maybe not, but they're right. I work day shifts lately, and I see how tired he is in the evenings. When he tries to wash the dishes or other such work, I don't let him. It's difficult for me, knowing that we try to keep Ópa well, but how long will that work?

It seems he is getting ready to be gone. I heard him talk on the phone to my Aunt Gabriella, said he would leave his violin to her daughter. He told me I would have his flat. I told him to go take his medicine and lie down so he can keep the flat. I don't like this.

Tonight he went to Ash Wednesday church, and maybe this is part of the same thing, the getting ready, because in the past he didn't go to church hardly ever. His friend Halmos went with him there. I would have taken him, to keep him safe on the way, but no, he said Halmos offered. And that is strange, because I don't think Halmos goes to church either, not usually. Then Ópa came home with the little cross of ashes on his forehead, and it looked so humble and sad, and I had to turn away so he would not see my face distressed.

Okay, I will try to quit saying "Poor us." But do you see what happens because you're the understanding person? Write back to me when you can.

Lisa tried to absorb it: Antal *bácsi* weakening, Kristóf upset and wanting his son. She wrote him back.

Kristóf, I wish I could say something that would make things easier. There is no easy way. But I'm glad that you've moved in with your grandfather. I think he needs you more than you know.

THAT NIGHT SHE ATTENDED ASH WEDNESDAY MASS. Lisa prayed for Kristóf, that he might have peace, and forgive his mother, and in some way keep his son. She prayed for Antal Varga's strength. But she felt inadequate praying. It had been that way ever since her baby's death. With her thumb she rubbed her wrist over the tattoo that was a remembrance of him.

At the front of the candle-lit sanctuary, Father Doyle stood with a bowl of Lenten ashes. He said this was a night for remembering our mortality, for searching our hearts. He urged the worshippers to consider their Lenten sacrifice. Lisa considered hers. Give up lattes? Nail polish? Television? Her life had already become so bare.

I don't want less, I want more. I want my fire back.

People had begun to file forward for the imposition of ashes. She stepped into line in the center aisle behind the father of one of her students.

"Repent, and believe in the gospel," Father Doyle was quietly repeating.

Those who had received the ashes left the sanctuary in silence. The line moved forward, one penitent at a time, until the man ahead of her stepped aside and Lisa stood before the priest. Father Doyle traced the oil-mixed ashes onto her forehead, down, over, in the sign of the cross.

"Repent, and believe in the Gospel," he said.

She was about to step aside, but it was as if the cross on her brow throbbed, and the one on her wrist pulsed, and her feet stayed planted.

"I *have* repented," she whispered back. "And I *do* believe."

"I know." Father Doyle clasped her hand in his sooty one and looked at her, concerned. "Lisa. 'Blessed are the poor in spirit, for theirs is the kingdom of heaven.'"

Lisa crossed herself. "Yes."

As she was leaving the sanctuary, the stations of the cross on her left and the pews on her right, her belly tightened in the first of this month's premenstrual stabs. She stopped. Setting her hand on the back of the last pew, she waited for the cramp to subside.

Lisa closed her eyes and was still. The pain ebbed out. In the quiet that followed, she heard—no, not really heard—a voice—no, not really a voice, but words within her, as plain and sure as if they'd been shouted: *Be ready to go.*

Lisa gripped the back of the pew. Her mind told her she was crazy, but her heart told her she wasn't. Go? Go where? Surely she wasn't called to the kind of getting ready that Kristóf's grandfather was doing? She didn't think so. She wasn't afraid, for the voice—or whatever it was—was kind. There was nothing more, only the sounds of the believers' footsteps as they left the church. Startled and alert, Lisa followed them out and went to her car.

She drove down to a parking lot on Commencement Bay. In the world beyond the windshield, lights shone on the ships and on the hills across the water. Was this still her world? She had come here to attend college and, God forgive her, to escape her mother. She'd stayed because of the job at St. Brendan's; then, feeling permanent, she'd stayed because of Jake. Now nothing held her here except St. Brendan's, and how strong a bond was that?

Lisa pushed her hair back from her forehead, and her fingers touched the smeared ashes. Yes, it was Ash Wednesday, Lent. Maybe she should give something up; but what she really wanted to get rid of was the constant feeling of being alone. It was funny, though; the feeling wasn't quite as bad right now, not after that strange, soft voice—or impulse, or whatever it was.

Go where? She turned the key in the ignition. For now, she would go home. For now, that would have to be enough.

PART FIVE

Romanza

CHAPTER FORTY-FIVE

The Poor in Spirit

March 1, 2007

LISA HAD A JOURNAL, A SMALL BOOK with an embossed cover, that some appreciative parents had given her several Christmases ago. She hadn't written in it often, but lately she'd been leaving it on her table to remind herself to use it. In the last week she'd made two entries.

2-23-07
"Blessed are the poor in spirit, for theirs is the kingdom of heaven." Father Doyle said this to me at Ash Wednesday Mass. It's in the Bible, Matthew 5:3.

2-25-07
A week ago when I was Skyping with Kristóf, he asked me what I do with my fire. The question won't go away.

No, it had not gone away. The question re-surfaced at odd moments, puzzling her while she was showering, driving, trying to sleep, trying to work. When she tried to write about it in her journal, she drew a disheartening blank.

It was now the first of March, a Thursday, five in the afternoon. As Lisa was about to head home from school, a new email message came in on her classroom computer.

From: Jacob Fischer   Subject: Stuff for you

Her throat went dry. She'd not heard from Jake since the divorce last June.

Hey, Lisa, turns out one of the boxes I took when I moved out had some of your stuff in it. There are some letters that look to be written in Hungarian, and also a Hungarian Bible with your grandma's name in it. If you want, I could drop them off tomorrow after school. Where? Your apartment? The school office? Your classroom?

Lisa touched the keys to reply. It was stupid that her hands were trembling.

I'd rather not have those things left in the school office. Bring them to my classroom. The outside door should be open. I usually stay until 4:30 or so. Does that work?

She sent the email off and left for home in a blur.

THEY HAD LASTED EIGHT YEARS TOGETHER.

When she married Jake, he'd wanted her with him for a lifetime. During her cyclical pain, he did more than his share of the household work. When the medical bills piled up, he took on extra tutoring and coaching and said they'd manage. After the first miscarriage, he told her not to blame herself, not to worry, they'd try again. After the second one, he fell silent when Lisa voiced fears that things would keep going wrong. After the third, he said he didn't want to be a jerk but everything would sure be easier if she could bounce back faster.

With Alexander's death, Jake said it felt like this season of mourning had already gone on for a couple of years and he didn't think he could take much more. But the season of mourning went on. Two months after Alexander died, Grandma Márta was dying. Lisa flew back to Chicago to say an agonized goodbye to her. Jake stayed home.

When Lisa returned, something had changed: where before there was desperation, now there was only distance. November, December, January he was away evenings—meetings with other teachers, he said, meetings with parents of problem students, grading to do, and other paperwork. No, it wouldn't work too well to bring it home. He'd just do it in his classroom. But when Lisa called him on those evenings, he usually didn't answer, and she hung up bitter.

One windy evening a year ago they sat opposite each other at the kitchen table in their brick house. She wrote lesson plans; he corrected math papers. They had barely spoken.

He pulled off his glasses and set them aside. "I have to tell you something."

His flat words sent dread coursing through her. "You've been gone a lot," she said.

He looked beyond her. Moments passed. "I've been seeing someone."

She sat, hands cold, face taut. "Why?"

"I don't know what to say, Lisa." Wind shook the kitchen window. "It just happened."

Lisa clenched her pen. "Things don't just happen. People do them."

"All right." He nodded. "Yes."

"And—" Her voice rose. "How long has this been going on?"

"Since you went to Chicago."

They were supposed to grow old together. They had promised. That was the deal.

"So." Lisa tried to push the panic out of her voice. "You had a fling and you'll end it."

Lines deepened at the corners of his mouth. He was thirty-three and looked forty-three tonight. "Well, but she's pregnant."

Lisa stood, strode to the counter, yanked a paper towel off the roll, and pressed it to the tears she felt forming. "Pregnant," she repeated, her back to Jake.

"Yes."

"And as we know, these things don't always work out." The words tasted like poison in her mouth. "How far along is she?"

"I'm not sure. The baby's due in October. There haven't been any problems."

Lisa whirled to face him. "No problems there. Big problems here."

"I know." Jake had put his glasses back on, and his eyes looked—what? Ashamed? "I should marry her. She doesn't want an abortion. And I don't, either."

"So this 'just happened,' you said, and now you're going to marry her. Jake, is this what you want?"

He was still, but finally nodded.

"After all we've been through together?"

He looked away. "Yes."

She knew: what they'd been through together was pain. He was sick of hurting. So was she. Lisa gazed around the kitchen, the refrigerator they'd bought together, the table where they'd shared countless meals, the stove where in happier days Jake cooked and she hugged him from behind until he turned to kiss her.

"We're talking about a divorce, then," she said.

"Yes."

Lisa drew a low breath. "So who is it? The woman who's pregnant."

"Amanda Reichert."

Oh. The phys ed teacher at Jake's school. Lisa had met her and thought her annoyingly loud. At one time Jake had thought so, too.

A million arguments, a million questions all rose in her, but they would all end in the same bare certainty: he was leaving.

Lisa wandered to the bedroom and closed the door. She sat down on the bed, numb yet throbbing, shocked yet not really surprised, wishing Jake would leave, wishing he would beg for forgiveness and stay, wishing all this were some horrible nightmare and at any moment she would awaken. After a long time, Jake came in to pack up some of his clothes. She left the room.

That night he left the house. He came back a few days later for more of his things, but when he did, she made herself scarce. They never really said goodbye, and Lisa never told him that she still loved him. Some things were unspeakable.

She stuck to the facts when she had to tell others. Their reactions weren't easy to take. Her mother told her she didn't need that kind of a man; it was too bad, but she could handle life on her own. Her brother, emailing from Africa, said only, "Sorry to hear it, sis, but try to let it go."

Lisa's married friends didn't know what to say; their husbands still liked Jake.

When she told her boss, Francie listened kindly and let her cry, but in the end, since they were both Catholics, Francie said, "Find it in your heart to forgive him, Lisa."

Maybe Lisa could have done that, if she could walk on water.

Re: Stuff for you
Okay, I'll bring the stuff to your classroom. See you tomorrow.
Jake

AT THE END OF SCHOOL THE next day, Lisa combed her hair and refreshed her lipstick. It was a small point of pride that she was looking better than when Jake left. He might as well see that. About four-thirty she heard steps in the hall and he appeared in her classroom doorway. "Hi."

"Hi, Jake."

He hadn't really changed. Same extra few pounds, black-framed glasses, coaching jacket. But as she approached him, she saw a new heaviness about his eyes. Maybe he looked a little older, maybe just tired.

She beckoned him in. He handed her a rather ragged Bible and a set of letters bound with a rubber band. "I didn't read the letters."

It took her a moment to realize he was trying to joke. "Oh, right, Hungarian," she said and set the Bible and letters on the marimba table.

What were they supposed to say to each other now? She could thank him and be done with it; but after what they'd once had together, it seemed so depressing to say nothing more.

"Are classes going all right?" she asked.

"Well, what can I say, it's middle school." He wouldn't quite look at her. "And how about you? How was your Christmas concert?"

"Fine. The choir sang a piece that my Hungarian relatives wrote."

"Yeah?" Jake turned to her now, eyebrows raised. He was one of the few people that would know what this meant to her.

"Yeah." She pulled up the grit to ask, "How is your baby? Strong?"

"Yeah, he is." Jake looked away again. "Yeah."

Lisa swallowed. "And your wife?"

"Oh, you know Amanda."

No, actually she didn't really know Amanda. But Jake didn't elaborate. His eyes roamed the classroom. "I see they finally installed carpeting," he said.

"Yeah."

"You've always been a good music teacher."

He seemed unready to leave, and sad in some way, or maybe guilty, or maybe lonely, and she hadn't counted on how it would tear at her to see his eyes sagging like this. If he really was unhappy—

No, it wasn't her job to read him anymore, it was that phys ed teacher's job, and this was getting worse by the minute, standing here unable to speak.

"Thank you for bringing these things," she said.

"Sure."

They stood simply facing each other until Jake said, "Well, see you."

"Yeah."

Lisa listened to his footsteps departing all the way down the linoleum hallway. The outside door banged open and shut. Maybe she would never see Jake again, this man who had known every inch of her body and most of her heart, who had given her eight years and the beginnings of children. Everything went wrong. Everything was aborted.

As Lisa ate a ham sandwich for dinner that night, she looked through the old letters Jake had given her. There were about twenty of them, some from as far back as the 1950s. Grandma Márta had written all of them to her sister, Sarolta, Lisa's great-aunt. Lisa turned through the letters slowly, wishing she could read Hungarian, trying to remember Aunt Sarolta. She'd been a pediatrician in Syracuse, married late in life, bore no children of her own but had two step-children. She had died before Márta by several years. It was probably Sarolta's step-daughter who had given the letters back to Márta.

Lisa perused the letters again, looking for Hungarian words she recognized. There weren't many. But she saw *Anyu*, which meant Mom and must have referred to Lisa's great-grandmother Hanák, whom Lisa had never met. The name Ann often came up, as did Sándor. Sometimes Grandma Márta seemed to abbreviate it as S, and sometimes she called him Alex, as Americans had done.

On the earliest letter, dated 1948, Lisa saw the name Antal. She tried to read the sentences around the name but could not. If only Kristóf were here.

She set the letters aside and picked up the Hungarian Bible Jake had brought. Inside the front cover she saw the name Hanák Márta. Her grandmother must have had the Bible from before she was married and kept it all her life. Lisa thumbed the pages, looking for the kind of records that families sometimes kept in Bibles. There were none, but on some pages she saw handwritten notes. These were in Hungarian and she couldn't read them.

Lisa reached for her journal, which was lying on the table. She opened it to the most recent page, checking again what Father Doyle had said to her, noting the Biblical chapter and verse. How would it read in Hungarian? She turned to St. Matthew's gospel in Grandma's Bible.

Szent Máté 5:3—Boldogok a lelki szegények: mert övék a mennyeknek országa. Matthew 5:3—"Blessed are the poor in spirit, for theirs is the kingdom of heaven."

A margin note in Grandma's faded handwriting said, *Sándornek és nekem.* After these weeks with the language book, Lisa knew what it meant. *For Sándor and me.* When had her grandmother written that? Was it when she and Grandpa Sándor left Hungary? Or with some later grief? Lisa had once heard her say she'd wanted more children. Was it a sorrow to her that no more came? Or perhaps Grandma's daughter, Ann, was the sorrow.

Blessed are the poor in spirit. An unbearable blessing.

Lisa skimmed through old entries in her own journal, stopping at what she'd written two weeks before her baby died. *Jake and I have decided to name the baby Alexander, after Grandpa Sándor. It means "defender, protector."*

So many hopes abandoned: children, marriage, Alexander, Jake.

She flipped the pages forward again to her recent entry about her talk with Kristóf. Trying to answer his questions, she'd come up blank. How do you forgive a man for abandoning you? What if before abandoning you he gave up hope, and what if he gave up hope because he couldn't find any in you? What did it mean to forgive a man for being no stronger than you are?

She picked up a pen. In the journal she would have written an answer if she had one. But instead her hand wrote, *Kristóf asked me what I do with my fire. And now I wonder, what fire? Is anything left? The fire of joy? Of love? Even of anger?*

Her questions flared now. Her hand bore down on the pen as she wrote the first one to her dead father.

Dad: When Ann left you, she took Paul and me, and you didn't come for us. We asked for you. We waited. Soon, someday soon, you said. And then you drove drunk and someday never came. Didn't life mean more to you than that? Didn't we mean more?

The next question, to her brother.

Paul: Living in Africa doesn't mean dropping off of the planet. What would it take for you to answer my emails now and then? Doesn't it mean anything to you that your sister still cares? That you even have a sister?

Next, she scribbled questions to her mother.

Ann, at least you didn't give up the way Dad did. You were tough. But did being tough have to make you so hard?
Why couldn't you see the pain Grandma and Grandpa bore?
Why did you sneer at their faith? At my faith?
When I was a child, why couldn't I just be a child?
When I was a teenager, why couldn't you see—as Grandpa saw—that I wasn't ready for adulthood yet? Why did he have to protect me? Why didn't you? Why couldn't you have made a few sacrifices for me? Like

Lisa clenched the pen, clenched her teeth.

—Like keeping naked men out of our house?
—Like coming out here even once for one of my concerts?
—Like being warmer to my husband, instead of just predicting the end?
—Like visiting me when my baby died? Yes, I know I didn't invite you. But you're assertive. If ever there was a time to just get on the plane anyway, that was it.

Lisa rested her forehead on the heel of her hand. After a long stillness she turned to a new page and wrote her husband's name. The list of both their offenses could go on and on.

Jake, was this the best we could do? Were we so short on grace? Couldn't you have waited with me? I would have found my way out of the darkness if you were there. I would have grabbed your hand and we would have found our way out together.

Kristóf said you're an asshole and you treated me like shit. But I didn't marry an asshole. I didn't marry a man who treats people like shit, and I had absolutely no intention of __being__ shit.

I know you have your own story of what happened. I'm sure that you've told your new wife how you just couldn't take it anymore, living with such a weepy wife. But I wonder if she ever worries about you turning your back on her if life gets sad. BECAUSE YOU CAN'T HANDLE SADNESS.

I don't want to handle it, either. But I have no choice.

I told Kristóf that you're not an asshole, just weak. But maybe there's no real difference. The end result was the same.

Her hand hurt as she kept writing.

Blessed are the poor in spirit, for theirs is the kingdom of heaven, Jesus said.

Blessed are the bummed out and depressed and broken-hearted, because maybe you don't give the kingdom of heaven a moment's thought until you've been disappointed over and over, fighting off pain, crying in the hospital, keeping your son's ashes on a shelf, wondering where your husband is, trying to make do without him, wondering where God is, but it simply is not an option to make do without God because that would be like throwing away your own soul.

Lisa slammed the journal shut and went to her electronic keyboard. She turned the volume down low, since her neighbors didn't deserve her ire, and began knocking out the worst, most pathetic blues runs she'd ever played. Then from her stack of music she fished out a Bartók piece and played it because it was Hungarian and it was as dissonant as her life. Her fingers slipped. So what. At the end she grabbed her folder of the Varga family music.

She propped up the music to the song she'd adapted for her choir, and as she played, she sang. "The light shines in the darkness, and the darkness has not overcome it." She kept going, singing whatever came to her, changing the melody and rhythm if need be. "An ugly war did not overcome it. And Grandpa lost his family, and that didn't quench the light, either. And my absentee brother and my dead father and my cynical mother have not overcome it. And my defective body has not, and Jake didn't take the light with him when he left." She pounded the keys. "And I'm alone and the light is NOT GONE."

She picked up Antal Varga's violin music called "Song to Our Enemies." The first page jarred her attention as never before. It mourned like her life did. Lisa got out her cello because the piece demanded the smoothness of a bow. She played, adjusting the octave as she went along. Long notes alternated with arched slurs in a lament so simple, so human it could be sung. It could almost be wept. She played the first half of the page over and over, and the cello's voice sang of the poor in spirit. Lisa played through the lines once more, then let the bow lead out as it willed. Her left-hand fingers flew over the neck. The notes spilled, clashed, coursed, cascaded.

They circled and drew to a close. But when they ended, the song to enemies had changed. The notes shone light into darkness.

A FEW DAYS LATER LISA EMAILED KRISTÓF.

You asked me what I do with my fire. I'm not sure what to say, except that when I played "Song to Our Enemies" again the other night, it was burning up.

I saw new things in the music, and I took some liberties. I hope your grandfather won't mind. In the first half-page, the melody is simple and straightforward and begging to be sung. I want my eighth-grade choir to sing it. If it's all right with your grandfather, I'd use some words from the Bible, "Blessed are the poor in spirit, for theirs is the kingdom of heaven."

Also, while I was playing around with the music, a string of notes came to me and kind of grew. The string connects that portion of the song to the main theme of "The Light Shines," which I'd like to use as a closing reference, a hint,

so to speak. I've attached a PDF of that musical line, to be played by cello as kind of a cadenza. Could you show it to your grandfather? And if he doesn't want me to do this to his music, then I won't.
Thanks, Kristóf.

Oh, and one more thing. Just thought I'd tell you I called a store that buys up old jewelry, and I'm going to sell my wedding ring.

Within hours a reply from Kristóf arrived.

Lisa, I will print the PDF and give it to Ópa.
Also, I am glad you will sell your ring. I hope you do not still love that man, because he does not deserve it and I wish you would be free.

Lisa read his terse message and then could not put it out of her mind. Kristóf didn't understand. Jake was not just "that man," and she couldn't just turn off love like turning off the television. She couldn't just get over a marriage like getting over a cold.

But *free*, Kristóf had said. He wanted her to be free. The word itself sounded so unburdened she found herself opening her hands, imagining it. *Free.* She wanted it, too.

CHAPTER FORTY-SIX

Blind Valley

May 25, 1945

AFTER THE FUNERAL, LATE IN THE AFTERNOON, Antal's mother asked him to go see if Katalin was in the basement. She'd left half an hour ago to get wood for the cook stove and hadn't returned. Antal went downstairs and found her sitting on a bench, face flushed with tears, a bucket of wood at her feet. Miklós sat across from her, and he turned to Antal and glowered.

Antal picked up the bucket. "I seem to be interrupting something. Go upstairs, Katalin."

"Why?"

"Upstairs. Now."

She followed him out of the basement. In the courtyard he pulled her aside. "What was that all about?" he demanded.

"Maybe I'd like to ask you the same question! Is it a crime to talk to Miklós?"

"It's a terrible idea to go cry with him."

She glared, wiping her eyes with her sleeve. "I saw a little girl buried today. And Miklós told me about his wife and baby that died. *Jézus Mária*, who wouldn't cry?"

"Katalin, how blunt do I have to be? You can cry all you want, but not there, not with him, in what amounts to his bedroom."

Katalin huffed. "There's nothing like that going on. Quit being awful."

"Tears are too personal," he insisted. "Too—you know—intimate."

That was it. Tears were intimate. And this morning he'd seen Sándor crying with Márta.

He'd barely spoken to Sándor all day. That night as Antal studied alone in the bedroom, Sándor walked in and pushed the door shut. He leaned on the armoire, arms crossed, and regarded Antal silently.

Antal closed his chemistry book. "What do you want?"

"What do you think I want? An explanation of why you shoved me at the cemetery."

"What did you say to Márta?"

"What's that to do with anything?"

"What did you say to her?" Antal repeated.

"I told her I know what it's like to say a permanent goodbye. Like she had to do."

"And then what?"

"What do you mean, and then what?"

"What did you say after that? You were going on and on."

"I was *not* going on and on," Sándor said, "I was just talking to her."

Antal waited.

"Look, I said the kind of thing that people say to each other when they go through shit like this," Sándor said. "I told her there are days, maybe weeks, when you think you're doing better, and then all of a sudden you're a pile of wreckage again. And I told her to remember that some people care."

"She already knows that. And what else did you tell her?"

Sándor spread his hands in exasperation. "My God, what's this interrogation for? Márta and I are friends, and what's wrong with that? What's wrong with *you*?"

"What's wrong is that you ended up wrapping yourself around her like a—"

"Shut up."

"Like a snake," Antal spat out. "And back off."

"I'll back off when *she* tells me to back off."

Sándor slammed out of the room, and a moment later the apartment door banged.

Three hours later Sándor hadn't come home, though it was after curfew, after the family had grown worried and phoned neighbors, including the Hanáks, and after Antal had gone to bed and lain awake remembering Sándor's other goddamned risks, like his horsemeat run, and like dashing out carelessly to find firewood for the Hanáks, then ending up on *malenki robot*. What was he going to do next? Get himself shot? Was that why he was still gone?

Half an hour later, Sándor finally walked in.

"Sándor, damn it, where were you?"

"Who cares."

THE NEXT NIGHT ANTAL WENT TO THE BASEMENT to get away from Sándor. He sat with Miklós and listened to him play. The music was a melancholic folk tune with Turkish-sounding intervals. As Miklós went on, he embellished it, inverting a phrase or adding arpeggios.

"Improvisation," Antal said when he'd finished.

"Sure. I always thought the song was too boring, too sad, but hell, who's happy anymore? So I'm fucking around with the melody. Making things up, like you and your cousin do." Miklós set the bow and violin on a pile of clothes and stretched out supine on the bench.

"You know what we could do?" he asked, staring upward. "A street concert. Set out a basket. Or a hat. People don't have money, so maybe they drop in cigarettes or something."

"Where would we do it?"

"I don't know. Out front, maybe. Your sister thinks it's a good idea. Says it'd be good practice for the radio show."

Antal couldn't imagine Márta wanting to do it, and right now he didn't want to do anything that involved Sándor. "I don't know," he said.

"*Na*, you're tired because you were with a dying child. That steals the spirit. And anyway, you have everybody's problems."

Antal looked away and only repeated, "I don't know."

ANTAL HAD BEEN SPENDING AS MUCH TIME AS HE COULD with Márta. It seemed her parents kept her home more than ever, and he certainly wished they'd ease up. On Sunday evening he went to visit her in her apartment. The Hanáks were clearly worn out, so he said an early good night to Márta. As he stepped out into the courtyard, Sándor approached.

"What are you doing?" Antal asked.

"I'm going to talk to Mr. Hanák. For a paper I'm writing. He said I could."

"They're exhausted. Leave them alone."

"He said to come by." Sándor pushed past him.

"Sándor! Give them some peace, for God's sake."

But Sándor was already knocking on the door, and Sarolta opened it.

Half an hour later, as Antal packed his school satchel for the next day, Sándor came home. "Hanák is being very, very cautious," he said, as though in defeat.

"What else did you expect?"

"I hoped he'd be a little more forthright with someone that's on his side."

"Do you think he's forthright with anybody?" Antal asked. He headed for the kitchen, not waiting for Sándor's answer.

HE AND MÁRTA HAD LONGED FOR TIME ALONE, and finally a few nights later they found it. Miklós was gone again, so after supper they went to the basement and sat together on his bench bed. She told him in a half-whisper that her father had left that morning.

"I guess he thinks he has to," she said. In the light of the hanging bulb, Márta's face looked gaunt and faded. "Did you know Sándor came to talk with Apa about the book he wrote?"

Antal sighed in annoyance. "That's what he was asking about?"

"Yes. Apa had thought he just wanted to know what it's like being a journalist, but then Sándor asked about that book."

"Wait, do you mean the book he's writing now, or a different one?"

"One he wrote several years ago. I haven't read it, but it's something about what Stalin did in Ukraine. Which was awful, but the world didn't really know. The book was published in Britain. In English. There were some Hungarians who read it, but not many. So with the way things are going now, my parents were hoping the book had been forgotten here."

"But Sándor knew about it," Antal said.

"Yes. It really set my parents on edge, finding out that Sándor knew. If a high school student knows, then the Communist Party must know, too. My mother is scared."

Troubled, Antal pulled Márta closer on the bench. The communists would say the book was reactionary, incendiary, full of capitalist propaganda from its British publisher. Antal had heard about Hungarian merchants being interrogated for importing goods from Britain or France. The interrogations probably started under Hitler, but they hadn't ended with him.

"And your father is writing another book, isn't he?" Antal asked.

"Yes. I thought Apa was helping a sick friend in Debrecen finish a book. And that was true, but now Apa's told me it's more his book than Mr. Vajda's. It's in English and it tells about recent things, like Stalin's treatment of Poland, and—"

She broke off, because the door at the top of the stairs had opened. A neighbor woman trotted down the stairs with a coal bucket. Antal called hello and tried to sound natural and cheery, but neither he nor Márta said anything more until the neighbor left.

Márta leaned close to him and spoke quietly. "It's risky, what my father's writing. So his name won't be on the book. Only Mr. Vajda's, because he has cancer and he'll be dead by the time the book's published. Apa will still be trying to make a living." Her voice hardened. "And trying to stay out of prison."

"Márta. Oh, no."

"He's in Debrecen again to help Mr. Vajda's wife make arrangements with the publisher."

"The British publisher."

She nodded. "But he won't stay in Debrecen long. He'll keep moving around."

"Your sister just died, and your family's been through one disaster after another, and now this?"

"I asked him to please move back. Move *here*. He said we'll be together again, but he won't say where."

She clung to him, her arms gradually loosening not in peace but in weariness. He touched the shadows under her eyes.

"You're tired," he said.

"It's been hard to sleep. I hear my parents whispering and crying. Sometimes my father gets up and writes. Sarolta climbs in bed with me in the middle of the night. She's scared. And I lie there remembering Anni's last days. Even the good memories I can't bear. Yesterday I was setting the table and I just fell apart. Her chair is so *empty*."

Antal stroked her hair, wishing he could steer her through this black, blind valley, but where was the way out?

"Stay with me, Antal," she said. "Don't stop loving me."

"No! How could I stop?"

"But I don't even feel like myself anymore. Sándor said that's the way grief is, and he said that when you're in grief, other people run out of patience. They'll be understanding at first, then they'll want the old Márta back. But what if the old Márta is gone?"

"No." He held her tightly. "You're still you."

He told himself, furiously adamant, that nothing would steal her spirit. No. The old Márta was not gone.

CHAPTER FORTY-SEVEN

What Good Men Do

March 2, 2007

T HE NIGHT AT HÁROM PÁVA HAD BEEN VERY BUSY. Kristóf left the restaurant at eleven o'clock and walked to Ópa's apartment, which was now his own home as well, carrying a plastic canister of chicken soup. Lately he had taken to buying the restaurant's leftover soup because of the way Ópa's appetite had dropped off. Some days, soup was all he would eat.

Opening the apartment door, he was dismayed to find the lights still on and Ópa at the table in his bathrobe. He should have been in bed a long time ago, but here he was, pencil in hand. Pages of handwritten music lay on the table under the extra lighting of the piano lamp.

"What are you doing up?" Kristóf asked.

"I couldn't sleep."

Kristóf looked down at the music. It was the *Embers Suite*, plus the music Lisa had sent in a PDF.

"Interesting what Lisa has done," Ópa said. "A connecting thread that moves from the enemies song to the light shining song. Oh, I called your father tonight."

Kristóf put the soup in the refrigerator. "I suppose he was out with his girlfriend."

"No, Erzsi was helping her daughter with something, Zoltán said. Which was just as well. I wanted to talk to him alone. I told him to marry Erzsi."

"God, Ópa, isn't that his business?"

"She's a good woman. He wants to marry her. But you know what he's like, doubtful, can't believe he could really have what he wants, has to think things over for half an eternity." Ópa smirked with a hint of triumph. "So I turned up the heat. I told him I want to see him get married. If he acts fast, I can be there. If he dithers, maybe not."

"If the goal is to be around to see him married, you'd better sleep more. Go to bed."

"Yes, yes, but just a minute. There's something else." Ópa pushed the music into a haphazard stack. "Your great-uncle Péter is coming tomorrow for a visit. Kristóf, I hope you don't mind. I took the liberty of telling him about your situation with Misha."

"Why?"

"Because Péter used to be in the position of that man Endre. I trust Péter's judgment, trust him to keep things confidential."

Kristóf thought about it as he showered, washing away the smell of the restaurant's cooking oil. Benedek Péter had been married to Ópa's sister, Katalin, until she died two years ago. Kristóf remembered Péter as a strong man, perhaps because of all his years of farming. The family story was that when Katalin married him, both had been hit hard by the communist state. Péter's land had been seized as collective property. Katalin had a small daughter, Mari, whose father had disappeared during a Party purge. If Kristóf remembered right, the father went to prison but not for long, and he never returned to Katalin. Péter married her and raised Mari, along with their son János who was born a little later. Everyone in the family knew that János had been the easier child.

Kristóf soaped and rinsed his hair, his thoughts turning to Misha. Uncle Péter would probably ask questions about him tomorrow, and there was so much Kristóf didn't know. The acknowledgment hurt. He didn't want to be like Mari's shitty birth father, a stranger.

UNCLE PÉTER ARRIVED THE NEXT MORNING as Kristóf made coffee. They sat down with Ópa at the table. Uncle Péter looked a little thinner and sadder since Aunt Katalin died, but otherwise he hadn't changed much, his curly hair gray but still ample, his eyes still probing and alert behind his glasses.

"Katalin was only eighteen when she got pregnant," he explained, for Ópa had asked him to tell Kristóf the story. "She wasn't married. The father was a music student named Róbert. A communist on the wrong side of a Party fight. And all of a sudden, he was taken away."

"Yes," Ópa said. "Like so many people back then."

Péter continued his story, saying Róbert didn't know Katalin was pregnant when he was taken. When Péter met her, it had been almost two years since she'd last seen Róbert. By then her daughter, Mari, was a year old.

"Then she got word where Róbert was," Péter said, "and she asked me to take her to see him. So I did."

"Did you meet him?" Kristóf asked.

"No. I only saw him across a cow pasture." Péter grew quiet, holding his cup. "Apparently he'd gone through hell with the secret police. And when Katalin showed him Mari, he just broke down. But that was all. He could have married Kati, but no, she never saw him again. And that was the only time Mari saw her father. She was tiny and has no memory of it."

"*Jaj*," Kristóf said. "Did you hate him?"

"At first, yes. When you love a woman, naturally you hate the man that's hurt her."

Kristóf stirred his coffee. Maybe that was how Endre felt about him. Seeing that Peter's cup was almost empty, Kristóf went for the coffee pot and refilled it. "When did Mari find out she had a different father from you?" he asked Péter.

"There was no way to keep it from her." Péter lifted his hand in a gesture of futility. "Everybody in the village knew. Sometimes the village children teased her about it, threw it in her face. It was hard on her. On all of us."

It was harder still during Mari's teenage years, Péter went on to say. Like most of her friends, she fought over every family rule and constraint, and Péter bore the brunt of her anger.

"Then one night, more of the same, only worse," Péter said. "She threw it in *my* face that I wasn't her real father. At that point, we'd had months of arguing. I'll tell you, I was tired of it. And I said to her, 'That's right, Mari, your real father is nowhere to be found.'"

Ópa nodded; he seemed to know this story.

"So I told her I was the fake father," Péter went on, "the one that bought her food and clothes and put a roof over her head. I was the fake father that had seen her through measles, the one that loved to hear her sing, the one that *knew* her." Péter's hand thudded onto the table. "And yes, I was the fake father locking the door and looking her boyfriends over, because if things went bad, I was the fake father whose heart would break."

Péter looked directly at Kristóf. "So you see, I feel for this man Endre. And I feel for you. Your grandfather tells me this hasn't been easy."

"Endre and Blanka don't understand how difficult."

"They want to make things easier for their family. I know and I understand. But I don't think there's any easy way. Misha is connected to you, whether they want that or not."

"I want it and they don't. Did Mari ever ask what her father was like?"

"Yes. Kati tried to tell her, good and bad. Said he was talented, smart, handsome. She gave Mari the one little photo she had of him, told Mari her eyes were like his." Péter ran a hand through his gray hair. "But Kati also told her that Róbert carried terrible memories from the war. He was scared and angry. It was hard for Mari to hear that, but she needed to."

"Yes," Ópa agreed.

"And did she ever wish she could see him?" Kristóf asked.

"She said she did. So Katalin and I decided that if he ever showed up, we would let her visit with him—with us right there. But of course he never came." Péter rested his forehead in his hand as though it hurt. "And then we found out he'd died, long before."

"What happened?" Kristóf asked.

"I think Mari was about sixteen when we found out," Péter said. "A musician in Pest told Katalin. Róbert had been dead about ten years by then, killed in the '56 revolution. So Katalin and I sat Mari down and told her. Kati handled it kindly, said he was brave, said he died as a freedom fighter."

"And how did Mari take it?"

"She cried. Then she reached for my hand."

"*Your* hand," Kristóf said.

"Yes," Péter answered thoughtfully. "At that point, I really was her only father."

As Ópa and Péter sat in silence, Kristóf asked the question that had tugged at him throughout this story. "Do you think it was best that Mari didn't know Róbert?"

"At the time, I thought so. But later, when Mari was a young woman, she said, 'I didn't even matter enough for him to come say hello.' So Kati and I wished he'd visited."

"That's exactly it!" Kristóf heard himself shouting. "That's why I don't want to sign those papers."

"I know," Péter said. "But if you do sign off, at least they can tell Misha you insisted on meeting him, and I hope they'll tell him you're a good man."

"They don't believe it. I'm not even sure I do."

Péter gestured toward Ópa. "Your grandfather does."

Ópa touched Kristóf's sleeve and said, "That's right, Krisz."

Sitting here between the two old men, Kristóf felt the weight of their concern and his. He had a son and an ill grandfather. Whether he was a good man or not, he had to act like one.

At Három Páva that night a pretty, red-haired customer sat down in Kristóf's section and asked for a glass of Tokaj. He brought it to her and she ordered strudel. She smiled and said, "I've met you before. I was here a year ago. Remember me? My name is Luca."

She looked vaguely familiar. "Ah, of course."

"We had a drink together after you finished work," she said with another smile.

Chances were very good there'd been more involved than just a drink. If he wanted the same tonight—and she certainly looked inviting—he could tell her when his shift would end. That would probably do the trick. If he wanted. He told her, a little uneasily, that he'd be back with her strudel.

He went to the pastry cabinet in the kitchen, and as pans sizzled and dishes clattered, he took out the strudel. The last time he'd taken a woman to bed was in October, with his head stitched up. That was, what, four months ago? When had he ever gone four months? It was with the married woman from Linz, the one who'd started crying, and he'd not forgotten that night's guilty misery. He would like to forget it. Maybe tonight with the redhead.

He cut a generous portion of strudel and slipped it onto a plate.

But how to make it work? Obviously he couldn't bring the woman to Ópa's apartment. He supposed he could ask where she was staying. Or he could pay for a seedy room somewhere.

Both of which options ignored the question of whether someone who needed to be a good man would fuck around with a customer when he was supposed to look after his grandfather.

The busboy had just walked into the kitchen. Kristóf shouted to him. "Karcsi!" He handed the boy the plate of strudel. "Take this to the woman at table nine."

Karcsi looked up at him. "Is something wrong?"

"Just go! Hurry!"

HE WENT STRAIGHT HOME AFTER WORK AND FOUND ÓPA at the table with the music again.

"What's going on?" Kristóf asked. "Don't you believe in sleep anymore? Ash Wednesday, and then last night with the music, and now tonight."

"I couldn't sleep. I wasn't comfortable."

"Didn't your doctor give you pills for that?"

"Pills can't do everything." Ópa turned over a page and set it aside. "And maybe I just want to get this done."

Kristóf joined him at the table and looked at the page that lay face-up. Ópa had penciled in some words, the handwriting so cramped that all Kristóf could read was the name Sándor.

"All right, Ópa," Kristóf said, knowing his tone was irritable, but for God's sake he had passed up sex tonight. "When are you going to tell Lisa and me what's behind this? This Sándor is her grandfather, right? And he wrote some of this music, and then you put it together, but the ending is like—" He made a gagging noise and a throat-slitting gesture. "What's that about?"

"I'm repairing the ending."

"Were you pissed off at somebody? At the world? The communists? At Sándor? Why did he leave, anyway? Nobody's ever told Lisa why."

"I know that."

"So, Márta's father was a journalist, right? And the communists were after him?"

Ópa rubbed his tired eyes, nodded slowly.

"And that's why Márta's family left?"

"Yes."

"Did Sándor leave with them? Was he married to her then?"

"Not then. As for whether he left with them, probably. Yes. I suppose he did."

"Mmm." Kristóf stretched back in his chair. Maybe asking wasn't polite, but if he went on being polite, he'd never find anything out. "Seems like you knew Márta pretty well?"

Ópa sighed and eventually said, "Yes."

"Ópa—maybe this is none of my business—but, were you in love with her?"

Ópa shifted on his chair, his eyes turned away. "Yes."

"Then that must have been really shitty, right? The girl you loved was gone, and your cousin was gone—and he was your friend, wasn't he? And there you were, alone? Is that what the crap ending of the suite is about?"

"Not all of it."

"There was more?"

"Of course there was more. When there's been a whole war and an occupation, then one boy's loneliness is nothing."

But as Ópa turned to him, the pain in his eyes was everything.

Chapter Forty-Eight

On the Street

June 9, 1945

IT WAS JUNE NOW, THE SUN HIGH, THE DAYS LONG. Often in the evening light, with sleeves rolled up and collar open, Antal practiced violin on his apartment balcony overlooking Dessewffy Street. At first it felt more public than he liked; but really, if he could practice in a crowded basement, he could do it here; and if he was going to play on the radio, he'd better get used to going public. As he played on the balcony, people below would glance up and wave, often shouting thanks. Sometimes Márta stood with him, occasionally offering suggestions: "Try a crescendo on that line," or "Maybe less vibrato there." It relieved him to hear strength in her voice.

The radio concert was only two weeks away, the end of school, three. Antal practiced far more than he studied. But Sándor studied late and constantly, preparing for the exit examinations he would take. He had applied to Eötvös University, and if academic standing was the only thing that mattered, he had a very good chance of getting in.

But Antal wasn't sure what mattered now, or how much could be built from ashes.

MID-JUNE ON A SUNDAY AFTERNOON THE QUINTET MET in the basement to rehearse. Sarolta joined them; she'd stuck close to Márta since Anni's death. Before the group pulled out their instruments, Antal opened a notebook, hoping to schedule more rehearsals for the radio show. In the meantime, he told them, the neighborhood was organizing a goods exchange for next Saturday, and Miklós and Katalin had suggested doing a street concert there.

"It'll be a good warm-up for the radio show," Katalin told the group, "and we could set out a basket."

"I don't think my mother will let me," Márta said.

Sarolta sighed, "As usual."

"I understand," Antal said, very tired of this. He turned to Sándor. "You?"

Sándor leveled his gaze back at him. "It's close to the end of school. I have exams."

"Are you saying no, then?"

"I'm saying I don't know."

"That's a stupid excuse, Sándor," Katalin said. "You're just angry at Antal."

"Katalin, stop," Antal told her. "Sándor, suit yourself. But look, I came here to rehearse, and I'm going to rehearse. And I hope I'm not the only one."

Sándor tuned his guitar and the group practiced half-heartedly.

SATURDAY DURING THE GOODS EXCHANGE WAS SUNNY, the torn-up street dusty and crowded. Antal, Sándor, Miklós and Katalin performed on the sidewalk in front of their apartment house, their donations basket slowly filling with cigarettes, screws, and other odds and ends. They stood on crates to be seen and heard above the crowd. Along the curb and in front of buildings, blankets lay covered with clutter: old chairs, a tablecloth, rope, ashtrays, a Tyrolean hat, a sofa cushion without the sofa, lampshades without lamps, and countless unmatched plates. Neighbors and strangers sorted among the wares and bartered. Across the street, Lieutenant Kholodenko stood watching, listening to the music, maybe doing surveillance. The group, minus Márta, had played for most of an hour, using the pieces that had become their stand-bys. Katalin and Sándor half-sang, half-shouted to be heard. The sun beat down.

Antal signaled the others for a fifteen-minute break. Miklós and Katalin wandered off to look at the dwindling wares. Sándor set aside his guitar and sat down on his crate with a textbook. Antal stepped a few meters away into the shade of a building.

From out of the crowd, a thin figure limped forward, his shirt dangling like rags on a scarecrow, a faded yarmulke lopsided on his close-shorn hair. The man looked like he might be forty, might be a hundred. He approached, and Antal tried to smile.

Faint stubble showed red-brown on the man's sunken cheeks. "You play violin very well," he said.

"Thank you."

This emaciated person had to have stepped off one of those trains returning from the work battalions and concentration camps. Thank God the man had survived. Surely the last thing he wanted was questions, but Antal blurted out, "Please, do you know Weisz Jenö?"

"Weisz?"

"Yes. Eighteen years old, black hair, a violinist."

"I've heard of him."

"Do you know, is he all right?"

"I don't know, but I think the likelihood of him being all right has never been lower."

Appalled, Antal watched him hobble away, knowing the man spoke the truth.

Antal made his way back toward their crates. Sándor had set aside the textbook and now strummed his guitar. A boy that Antal recognized as a classmate of Sándor's stood next to him, laughing as Sándor sang. A loose circle of onlookers had gathered, among them a fellow in a shabby canvas cap and a red star armband.

"Oh, oh, oh, oh, oh, *malenki robot*," Sándor sang.

Antal rushed to him and grabbed his sleeve. Sándor scowled and stopped.

"Looks like something's come up," Sándor said to the gathering.

Sándor's classmate turned to Antal. "What's wrong?"

"Come on, it's funny," a girl in the crowd said. "No harm done."

Catching Sándor's eye, Antal shook his head. Sándor raised his eyebrows. Antal shook his head again.

"Well, that's it," Sándor said aloud. "Sorry, folks."

When his friend and the others had left, Sándor asked Antal, "Why not?"

"You can't sing that here," Antal hissed. "Didn't you see our Soviet officer over there?"

Sándor looked toward Kholodenko across the street. "He can't hear me."

"There's somebody else, too."

Antal looked around, but the fellow with the communist armband was gone. Climbing onto his crate, Antal looked out over the street but didn't see him. Across the way a peasant woman had arrived with a wheelbarrow of strawberries and a crowd had formed around her, Katalin and Miklós with them.

"Katalin!" Antal shouted. "Miklós! Five minutes."

He scrambled down and picked up his violin.

"Hello," an accented voice called out. Kholodenko approached, tipping his service cap. "Yes, good," he said to Antal in his awkward German. "Always I like it, what you play."

Antal thanked him nervously. Had he heard Sándor singing?

"Tell me," Kholodenko said. "Your nice girl that plays the big instrument. Her sister was sick, and I brought the sugar. Tell me, the sister is better? I hope this?"

"*Nein*," Antal said and dredged up the German words for *She died*. "*Sie starb*."

"*Starb*." The lieutenant's face grew serious. "A child. This is very bad, a child dies. I leave you. You play more music."

The officer retreated through the crowd as Miklós and Katalin arrived. Miklós went to his violin. Katalin showed Antal a red stain on her hand. "We had strawberries, and they were so good."

A voice from behind them spoke. "You like berries? Here. Have some of mine."

They turned. The fellow with the red star armband stepped close. He reached for Katalin's hand, put three strawberries into it, and winked. Katalin pulled back.

Antal looked him in the face, saw his cleft chin and pale eyes. He seemed somehow familiar. "My sister and I thank you," Antal said curtly.

The fellow smirked at him and turned back to Katalin. "Pretty sweet singer," he said.

Suddenly Antal realized where he'd seen him before: the tram, the day Horthy tried to surrender. The fellow had leered at Márta and pushed a woman around and given Antal a sprained finger. He'd been an Arrow Crosser then; he was a communist now. Antal clasped Katalin around the shoulder. The fellow backed up.

Antal signaled to Miklós, who was supposed to start the next set, and to Sándor, who was supposed to announce it. They jumped onto their crates. Sándor cupped his hands around his mouth and shouted, "Everybody find a partner! Time to dance! Look here in front, we have two neighbors ready to go—Mr. Balázs and his fine wife! Here come some others, too. Off we go!"

Miklós lifted his bow and thrashed out a rollicking *csárdás*. The dancers stomped. More joined in. Others whooped and clapped. Even the lieutenant danced, hopping and bumping into the black-haired girl he had chosen. She laughed in confusion. Antal could barely remember how to dance a *csárdás*, but he grabbed Katalin and began twirling with her so that the shithead with the armband wouldn't—

"Miki!" someone screamed. "Miki!"

Instantly Miklós halted. The dancing stopped. A dark, tattered stranger pushed through the crowd.

"Joska!" Miklós cried. He thrust the violin at Antal and ran to the newcomer. The two threw their arms around each other. The crowd backed up.

Miklós and this Joska stood head-to-head. Antal could see Miklós speaking, Joska answering, but could not hear what they said. Miklós spoke again, shaking Joska's shoulders. Joska nodded and said something in reply. Miklós's eyes squeezed shut. He let out a soul-stabbing wail, fell on Joska's shoulder and wept.

Antal faced the crowd and lifted his hands. "We're done for the day."

Those who had gathered to listen and dance now drifted away, some looking back at Miklós in sad pity. Antal waited with Katalin and Sándor. Miklós spoke again to his companion, wiping his eyes, then beckoned to them.

"This is my brother," Miklós said. "It's as I thought. My family is all dead except Joska."

Antal swallowed hard. *Sweet Christ, no.*

Katalin said, "Oh, Miklós."

"Lord," Sándor said. He turned to Joska. "Miklós has been living in our basement. We were hoping for better news. Oh, God, we're sorry."

As Miklós stared down at the broken cobbles, Joska told them, "I came back from the army and I tried to find our family. They were all taken away, our whole settlement, taken to some camp. Everybody died except one of our neighbors. I found her in a pub in Vác. She told me what happened."

"And Miklós's wife and baby?" Katalin asked.

"The baby was a boy. Born in the camp. He died. So did his mother."

Katalin touched Miklós's hand and started to cry. Miklós hugged her. For one brief moment he buried his face in her hair, then broke away. Glancing at each of them, he hoarsely said, "Goodbye."

Side by side, Miklós and his brother walked away.

Antal looked down at the old loaner violin in his hand, ran back and stuffed it in its case. "Miklós!" he shouted. "Wait!"

He tore out after the two Gypsies. Reaching them, he handed the violin to Miklós. "You'll need it."

THAT EVENING ANTAL TOLD MÁRTA WHAT HAD HAPPENED. Afterward he went to the basement and swept and tidied Miklós's space. He left the blankets spread neatly on the bench, just in case Miklós returned. But Antal knew he wouldn't. He sat down on Miklós's bench and stared off toward the shabby door in a wave of loneliness.

CHAPTER FORTY-NINE

Lost Voices

March 4, 2007

VARGA SAT AT HIS KITCHEN TABLE WITH HALMOS, who'd been paging through the Bomb Shelter Quintet music, the *Embers Suite*, and the new musical suggestions that Lisa had sent. From the CD player drifted the strains of Dvořák's *Romanza in F Minor*. Varga's hand moved with the 6/8 rhythm.

"Could you turn that off?" Halmos asked. "So I can hear this." He pointed at the sheet music.

Varga clicked off the player, chiding himself. Of course he should have done that sooner. Halmos couldn't be expected to hear one piece in his mind while another grabbed his ear.

"This is interesting, Varga," Halmos called out as Varga made his way back to the table. "I knew your suite had something to do with music you wrote during the war, but I'd never seen the original pieces. I feel as if I'm reading your autobiography."

"Heavens. I hadn't intended something quite so personal."

"But the music is effective."

"Except the ending to the suite. You've said loud and clear it doesn't work. I've come to agree, now that I don't have much longer to repair it."

A pained look crossed Halmos's face. "Does Kristóf know this? About you not having much longer?"

"He knows what he sees. I don't say much about it beyond that." Varga pointed to the music, returning to the subject at hand.

Soberly Halmos studied the page of lines that Lisa had composed. Most of these bits consisted only of four to eight measures, but one contained thirty-two. They drew on the patterns and themes in "Song to Our Enemies" and "The Light Shines." Guesses, she'd called what she'd written. Attempts. Possibilities to insert into those pieces.

"This niece of yours," Halmos said, "or cousin, or whatever—she's a good collaborator." He peered closely at a Bomb Shelter Quintet page with lyrics written in. "'The darkness has not overcome,'" he read aloud.

"It seemed hard to believe that during the war," Varga said. "But we kept singing it. I suppose sometimes we say we believe something, in the hopes that we actually will believe it."

"I'm not sure that's wrong."

"Neither am I," Varga said, for they had both done that when their wives were dying. They'd bought CDs of sacred music and helped their wives attend Mass, and they'd said this was good. Wanting to believe, hoping to believe—maybe it was the reason Varga had gone to the Ash Wednesday service this year.

Halmos turned over more Bomb Shelter Quintet sheets. "So, these songs, 'Pest, Along the Danube' and 'A Good Mother.' I hear strains of them in your suite, but it's a light touch. Looks like you used these melodies as a starting point and spun off from there?"

"Yes. My cousin Sándor wrote those. I didn't borrow heavily from them. The melodies are good but really nothing unusual. Sandor was better at writing lyrics than music. When we performed his songs, I think it was the words that captivated people."

Halmos came to the old quintet piece that had once been called "Song to Our Enemies." "This one is excellent," he said. "Hard to believe you wrote it as a teenager. But it doesn't seem to have been finished. Not really. And at the bottom I see a note that says, 'Ask Márta.'"

"Yes." Varga felt that troubling tightness in his chest, and he pulled in a slow breath. "That's the one you said had a cacophonous ending. I couldn't find an ending that I liked, and Hanák Márta was going to help me with it, but then one thing after another got in the way, and then everything broke apart, and she was gone, and the Gypsy was gone, and my cousin was gone.

They were gone, and—" He coughed, waited. "I couldn't hear their voices anymore."

Over the next several days, whenever Kristóf was at work, Varga spread out the music and studied it. Sometimes on piano, sometimes on violin, he played portions of it and tried inserting Lisa's short arpeggio patterns. They slipped into and out of "Pest, Along the Danube," wove between the verses of "A Good Mother." Just as Sándor's guitar used to do. In the songs' melodies he heard Sándor's voice. Quietly with the piano, Varga sang Sándor's songs.

Long after he left the piano, Sándor's voice returned to him again and again, singing, shouting, speaking. Sándor called to him from across the schoolyard—"Antal! Wait up!" Sándor shouted from the piano bench—"Anybody happen to have a functional *F* key?" Sándor complained sarcastically in the shaking basement—"Well, let's see, one more shell blast and we'll have filled today's quota." Forlorn and quiet, Sándor spoke of his brother and parents, his tone edged with a grief that Varga would later understand all too well.

Alone, Varga sat down on the piano bench and opened the *Embers Suite* to the last page. There would be no crowning finish for this suite. But if only the poor thing could end in peace.

CHAPTER FIFTY

Trust

March 6, 2007

KRISTÓF DROPPED BY THE INTERNET CAFÉ almost every day now to see if Lisa had written, often writing to her even if she hadn't. This morning she had. He read the text of her message.

That's great that your grandfather is interested in those music sound bites I wrote. Honestly, I felt a little embarrassed about sending the music. I mainly sent it to let him know that his work had inspired me, and to let YOU know that YOUR glaring question ("What do you do with your fire?") inspired me, too. (Americans call that kind of inspiration a kick in the butt.) Please thank your grandfather for letting me put lyrics to his "Song to Our Enemies." I've been working on that when I can.

Kristóf, I'm glad you talked with your uncle about Misha. I get the feeling you're moving toward signing off, for Misha's sake. How hard. If Endre adopts him, I wish there were some way you could keep seeing him. Could you give him piano lessons?

Lisa went on to say that a Hungarian man in Seattle was arranging one of her grandfather's songs for his choir. At the end of her note she used a Hungarian closing, phrased correctly but misspelled. She probably didn't have the necessary diacritical marks on her keyboard. He wrote her back.

This is a good idea, piano lessons. Probably they don't have a piano, but let me think.

I may change my job. Two years I have worked at the restaurant, and that's enough. But I don't know, should I change my job, should I wait, because will Ópa need more help? Always this is the question now.

There is news, my father will get married on this Friday! So I'll have a stepmother. Ópa and I will go to Pécs for their very small wedding.

I have to go to work now, please write to me soon again.

His phone rang as he walked to work. It was Blanka. "When are you going to sign those papers?" she asked. "Kristóf, can't we stop dragging this out?"

"I can't talk, I'm on my way to work." He covered his ear, trying to block out the traffic noise. "Do you have a piano?"

"A piano? No. Why?"

"Misha wants to learn how to play."

"Is that what he told you?"

"It's what I could see."

"You're probably right, but could you please take care of that paperwork?"

"We'll see. I'll talk to you later."

HE WORKED BOTH THE LUNCH AND DINNER SHIFTS that day, and when he came home at night he found his grandfather asleep, fully dressed and in his glasses, on the sofa. Ópa startled awake as Kristóf entered the living room. "Sorry, what time is it?"

"It's ten-thirty, Ópa."

"Damn. Three hours ago I was working at the piano and thought I'd take a break, and now look what happened. But how was work? What was tonight's special?"

"Perch."

Ópa rose and sat sleepily on the piano bench. Kristóf set his wallet and keys on the bookcase which was now his dresser, and he pulled open the sofa to make up his bed.

"Lisa had an idea," he said. "What if I give Misha piano lessons? It would be a way to keep on seeing him. At least for a while. Well, then Blanka called—'Sign off, sign off,' and I asked her if they have a piano. And they don't. But I thought about it, and I want to *give* Misha an electric keyboard. If they'll let me teach him how to play it."

"Can you afford it?"

"I'll put it on my credit card."

"Let me buy it. Halmos can help us find one." Ópa sighed. "It may be the only gift I can ever give my great-grandson."

THAT FRIDAY IN THE EARLY AFTERNOON, Kristóf sat with his grandfather and a small gathering of others in a courtroom of the Pécs city hall. In front stood his father in a suit and Erzsi in a light green dress. Softly overcast light from the window fell on them as hand in hand they faced a magistrate, answering questions: Yes. Yes. Yes. Ópa nodded approval. Kristóf watched and listened as his father turned to Erzsi and promised to love her and care for her as long as they lived. She promised the same back to him, and in a tremulous voice said, "I love you, Zoltán." Apa took her in his arms and kissed her.

"Good," Ópa whispered.

Applause spread through the room. Vati laughed, lifted Erzsi off her feet, and cried, "*Hurrá!*" Kristóf clapped in bewilderment. When had he last seen his father joyful?

As the ceremony broke up, Kristóf and Ópa could not linger. They handed Erzsi the gift they had brought, which was a bottle of champagne and a card that contained a check. As she talked with Ópa for a moment, Kristóf congratulated his father. "It seems good," he said.

"It is. And this time I really believe that in years to come, it still will be good." Vati lowered his voice. "How's your grandfather doing? He seems tired."

"That's why we're heading right back."

"Erzsi and I are going on a short honeymoon. To Lake Balaton. But call me if you need to. Please." He clasped Kristóf's shoulder. "See you at Easter, unless you need me before then."

THE RIDE HOME WOULD TAKE TWO AND A HALF HOURS. As their train clacked northward, Kristóf sat beside Ópa, the facing seats empty across from them. He said little, in case Ópa wanted to sleep. But Ópa watched out the window as the fields and the windbreak shrubbery passed.

"I'm happy for Zoltán," Ópa said. Lately he'd been doing this, saying "Zoltán" instead of "your father," or "Ildi" instead of "your grandmother."

"You set this up today," Kristóf said, teasing. "You pushed him."

"I pushed him to do what he already wanted to do. I'd like to push you to get married, too, but I don't think the result would be the same."

"I'm not looking for a wife."

"Nevertheless, since I'm taking more liberties these days, I'm going to point something out. You've wasted time with women who were not much more to you than puppets."

"You've pointed that out before, Ópa."

"But listen. You've finally found a woman you trust. Lisa."

Kristóf sat quiet in the rocking of the train. Although the family ties were several generations loose and he knew it, he said, "She and I are cousins."

"Third cousins. Like the queen of England and her Prince Philip."

"Ah." Somehow he was glad to hear this; but still there were these other facts. "Lisa probably needs an American. A non-smoker. Someone who's religious and not—" He groped for the right description, and all he could think of was, "Profane."

"All right, Kristóf, but you could do worse—far worse—than to consider this. She'd be good for you. However, I insist that you be good for her, too."

Kristóf looked out the window, where the sun was lowering over fallow fields to the west. Yes, Lisa was a good woman, and in recent Skype calls he'd thought she was pretty, even lovely. Every day he looked for her emails. When anything happened with Ópa or Misha, he had to tell her. When anything happened with Lisa, he had to know. It was true he trusted her.

The person he didn't trust was himself. Kristóf watched the sunlight fade, hating the doubt, unable to shrug it off.

CHAPTER FIFTY-ONE

Not Yes, Not No, Not Yet

March 11, 2007

TWO DAYS LATER VARGA SAT AT HIS TABLE with the telephone to his ear. He and Kristóf had decided that he should be the one to make this call. Kristóf, having already finished the early shift at the restaurant, stood leaning against the kitchen counter, arms crossed. Varga coughed and went on explaining to Blanka why they wanted to buy Misha a keyboard.

"The boy obviously has aptitude and enthusiasm," Varga told her. "A keyboard won't take up much room in your apartment. And we got lucky. We found one that won't cost much." This was not precisely true; the thing was not cheap, but it had seemed best to downplay the gift. "So we'd like to get it for him."

"I don't know," Blanka said. "I should talk to Endre."

Despite all likelihood, Varga had hoped she would say yes *without* talking to Endre.

"We can't teach him to play it," Blanka added, "and we can't afford lessons."

"Kristóf would be happy to teach him."

Across the kitchen, Kristóf nodded vehemently. Blanka was silent.

"At least Kristóf could get him started," Varga said. "Or of course you could find someone else."

Kristóf frowned and shook his head.

"Why do you want to do this?" Blanka asked.

How much of the truth could she take? Varga measured his words. "Because no matter what happens, in some way Misha is one of us."

Kristóf mouthed, "Yes."

"This is very nice of you," Blanka said, "but if this is to make us stop the legal process, then I have to say no."

"I understand that. It's just a gift for Misha."

"You understand, but does Kristóf?"

"Yes," Varga said, though maybe Kristóf didn't.

"I don't know," Blanka said. "I'll have to call you back."

Varga hung up and told Kristóf. Neither of them expected she would call back, but in fact the phone rang two hours later. Blanka said, "I talked with Endre, and Misha overheard us, and then he begged and begged. So I guess the answer is yes. About the keyboard. I'm not sure about the lessons."

"Well, very good, then." Varga signaled to Kristóf, smiled, pointed to a bottle of red wine on the counter. They would celebrate. "Thank you, Blanka. Kristóf will be in touch with you."

As Kristóf whooped and poured the wine, Varga called Halmos and told him to make the purchase.

Coughing kept him awake that night. About one o'clock he went to the living room for the suite music, tiptoeing around Kristóf on the sofa bed. Back in his bedroom, Varga sat at the small desk and wrote notes for revision.

Part 1, Moderato con moto (Light Shines in the Darkness)

More flute in the opening section (like the light, like Katalin's voice). A few upper register piano trills, bottom of p. 2. End section: Bass heavier; shorten the flute line, and DON'T RESOLVE. Move to three loud, disso-nant piano chords (bombing), then a limping rhythm to transition→

Part 2, Larghetto (Stille Nacht, Csendes Éj)—

He coughed as that winter came back to him: hungry days and cold nights in the basement; Miklós appearing, ragged but alive; horsemeat; Mr. Lukács disappearing; Hoff Dietrich lying dead in the bomb hole.

Varga gripped his pencil and wrote.

The Christmas hymn doesn't have to be so recognizable. Just hint at it, don't sing the whole damned song. Insert some of Miklós's old syncopations and violin slides for a moment of joy, and for God's sake lift the tragedy a little.

He repositioned the music under the desk lamp so he could read it better.

Part 3, Allegretto (Pest, Along the Danube)

He'd based this part on Sándor's piece, but only loosely. Since Lisa had noticed the similarities, Varga guessed she must have compared the music closely. Maybe she'd noticed that the ending measures were an ornamented version of Márta's cello line. He made a note.

Work in some of Lisa's arpeggios, echoing Sándor's guitar.

Varga rubbed the small of his back.

Part 4, Andantino (A Good Mother)

He read through this section three times, unsatisfied. Back in 1945 it had been a good song in Sándor's voice. But this 1958 arrangement of his own seemed bare.

It *was* bare. He saw that now. Writing it into the 1958 suite, he hadn't let it take hold. The song was about mothers and their children, and that was too much like fathers and their children, and 1958 was too close to 1956 and losing Zsuzsanna.

Varga pressed his hand to his chest. The little girl's death had plunged him into such darkness he had barely seen her twin brother, either. Even now his memories of Zoltán's early life were a blur of sorrow. Was that what he had given his son? Had it planted Zoltán's decades of melancholia? And would the melancholia rear up again and attack Zoltán's new happiness?

Lighten the bass chords, Varga wrote. *Movement in bridge section.*

He paused.

Talk to Zoltán.

He turned the page.

Part 5, Andante (inspired by Dvořák's Romanza)

Dvořák had lost children, too. Three of them in quick succession, and how did he manage to go on?

Varga read through Part 5 of his own suite. He'd written all of it at age thirty, none at seventeen. Its arches and sweeps were mature whisperings of Dvořák. That was enough. He would make no changes to Part 5.

And as for Part 6, based on his old song to enemies . . . Varga looked at his bedside clock: three-fifteen, no more of this tonight. He set the music aside, took some aspirin, and eventually slept. In the morning he spread the suite manuscript, Lisa's fragments, and the Bomb Shelter Quintet pages on the piano's music rest. With his violin and a pencil close at hand, he began work on the sections he'd notated the night before—but Part 6, not yet.

ON THURSDAY, TWO DAYS LATER, HALMOS brought the keyboard he'd procured for them. He came in the afternoon before Kristóf left for the dinner shift. Varga and Halmos watched as Kristóf opened the large flat box and set up the new contraption in the living room. They took turns trying it out.

"A pretty good imitation piano," Varga said.

Kristóf played the opening bars of Mozart's "*Rondo alla turca*" while pressing different buttons. "Not just an imitation piano. You want trumpets? Flutes? Drums? Here they are."

Halmos chuckled. "Your five-year-old boy can have his own parade."

Before Halmos left that day, Varga told him he'd been reworking the suite. "But not the ending yet," he confessed as they stood at the door together. "I'll get to it."

"Very good. I'll call you tomorrow."

Yes, Halmos would call. He'd been checking in daily. It made Varga feel mortal, but he thanked Halmos.

CLIMBING OUT OF BED THE NEXT MORNING, Varga's knee buckled. He fell against the nightstand, bruising his thigh. He would have hurt himself worse if he'd fallen to the floor. Kristóf ran in and helped him hobble to the bathroom.

"Enough of this!" Kristóf scolded. "You don't get up by yourself, you yell for me. Understand?"

"Yes, yes."

Saturday morning over breakfast Kristóf told him he'd taken a leave of absence from work. "Starting Wednesday," he said as he twiddled his spoon in his muesli.

On the table beside him lay a book, a beginning piano primer that Ildi had used for teaching. Kristóf tapped the book and said, "I'm going down to Kőbanya this morning to take the keyboard to Misha. I'll give him a lesson if they'll let me."

"I hope they do."

Kristóf had been gone a couple of hours when Varga, hungry for daylight around him, put on his coat and stepped out onto the small front balcony. Across in the opera house, a tenor was practicing. There was a breeze but no biting wind. Was spring coming? It seemed so long since he had walked the streets. He sat down in a chair Kristóf had set out here.

A door rattled. Kristóf joined him on the balcony and lit a cigarette, positioning himself so the breeze would carry the smoke away.

"Erzsi was right," Kristóf said. "Blanka's pregnant. It's obvious. I set up the keyboard in their living room. Endre helped a little, and Blanka was there. But Misha, good God, he couldn't stand still, he was going out of his mind, he was so excited. We did the first lesson in the book. He caught on really fast."

"I'm not surprised."

"Misha wanted you there. He asked why you didn't come. I said you weren't well."

"Ah." The thought was bittersweet, and Varga wished he'd been there.

"Endre stayed there in the room with us while I was teaching Misha," Kristóf said. "It felt awkward being watched. Ópa, I'm so sick of their distrust."

Kristóf squinted into the distance, the smoke rising from his cigarette. "So after the lesson was over and Misha was running around everywhere, I took Endre aside, and I said, 'Look, I'm not trying to take your place. When I talk to Misha, I call you his father.' And I tried to say reassuring things. But he said this is hard on Blanka and him and he should just pay me for the keyboard and find a different teacher, and la la la, and then he said—oh, what a surprise—that it would be better for everybody if I'd just sign off."

Kristóf smashed the cigarette butt on the balcony railing and hurled it onto the street below. "So I said—and I promise you, Ópa, I didn't scream this at him—I said, 'It would be much easier for me to sign off if it didn't mean never seeing him again.' And then, maybe I was crazy but I went into this long story about Uncle Péter, and about how Péter needed to have Mari accept him as her father—of course! I know that!—but also Mari wanted her birth father to actually care. And Endre just stared at me, like it had never occurred to him that I would ever matter at all in Misha's life, or like I was out of my mind, or like he just wanted me to shut up, or—I don't know—"

"Good for you."

"What?"

"Go on."

"All right, so I said to Endre, 'I swear to God I won't tell Misha who I am, but please let me teach him.' And Endre didn't say no. He didn't say yes, but he didn't say no, and for now, that's all I have."

Varga crossed his arms against the breeze. "Are you going to sign?" he asked gently. "When?"

"Ópa." Kristóf looked at him, his face desolate. "This is all like horrible shit. I don't want to lose you and Misha at the same time."

"Ah. I understand losses."

But Varga could barely get the words out; and if ever he had wanted to cut a bargain with death, it was now.

CHAPTER FIFTY-TWO

The Choices We Don't Have

June 19, 1945

A FEW DAYS AFTER MIKLÓS LEFT, ANTAL PRACTICED the Dvořák romanza with Mr. Boros accompanying and Mr. Horváth coaching. Antal wanted to play this piece in the radio concert, which was only four days away. They rehearsed in the back practice room of the music shop, Mr. Boros at the piano. Mr. Horváth sat or paced with the musical score, moving his right hand in rhythm. For an hour and a half Antal worked with them on phrasing, precision, and balance, and this felt like a banquet after months of famine.

"You've done a marvelous job with the piece," Mr. Horváth told him. "This is bound to become one of my favorite teacher stories, a student of mine learning Dvořák in a bomb shelter. Tell me, how do you like the piece by now?"

"By now? I love it."

Mr. Horváth smiled as though in triumph. "What do you love about it?"

Antal tightened his bow, thinking. "Its warmth."

At the piano, Mr. Boros nodded.

"Good," Mr. Horváth said. "Play it again, start to finish, with warmth. Heat, even."

Antal played it again, its ardor radiating, and Mr. Horváth nodded vehemently, coaxing with his hands, kindling the flames until they danced, softening the music to end in a final glow.

"Yes, yes," Mr. Horváth said. "Now what about your group? Do they have the other pieces ready for this radio program?"

Antal told both the men about losing Miklós. Mr. Boros was relieved to hear that Miklós's brother had found him. Mr. Horváth, when he understood the situation, was glad as well. Antal went on to tell them that Katalin would sing in the radio show. Márta planned to play her cello that night despite the hardship in her family.

Mr. Boros closed the piano score. "And Sándor?"

Antal hesitated. It had been hard and very frustrating to get Sándor to show up for rehearsals. Had to study, Sándor said. Tired, he said.

I guess we'll see what Sándor wants to do," Antal told them.

Returning home, Antal stepped into the building foyer and found Márta sitting on the steps—and Sándor beside her. Antal swore under his breath. So Sándor didn't have time for rehearsals, but he had time to chat up Márta.

Sándor stood and walked up the stairs. "Goodbye," he called over his shoulder.

"Goodbye, Sándor," Márta called back. Carrying a book, she crossed the foyer and hugged Antal.

"He follows you around like a lost puppy," Antal griped.

"No, he doesn't. He was returning a book he borrowed from my mother."

"Then let him take it to her."

"Antal, stop it. How do you think this makes me feel, you being suspicious every time your cousin talks to me?"

"I'm not suspicious of you, I'm suspicious of *him*."

"Well, I don't like it."

With a slight nod she gestured toward the front door, and he knew to follow her out. When they'd walked up the street out of earshot of anyone else, she said, "My father arrived two hours ago. From Debrecen, or wherever he was."

"How long will he be here?"

"I don't know. I asked him that. He said he'd try to tell me later in the week, and then he and my mother glanced at each other."

"What's going on?" Antal asked.

"Do you think I know? Do I ever know?"

He wished she knew.

LATE THAT NIGHT ANTAL SAT IN HIS LIVING ROOM and tried to list the music for the radio concert. He wrote "Romanza" then paused, stuck. Which of the group's pieces could he count on at this point? Everything that Miklós had played was out. Everything that included Márta had to have a back-up plan. She'd said she could come, her mother had agreed to it last week, but now her father was here, and when did both parents ever give Márta an unqualified yes anymore? At least he knew for sure that Katalin would be there. He could ask her to sing some extra solos if need be, and either he or Mr. Boros could accompany her.

Then there was Sándor, and who knew what he was planning? It would make sense to go ask him. If he wanted Sándor to come. If. He looked over at Sándor studying at the dining table. Antal headed off to bed without speaking to him.

BUT THE NEXT DAY HE COULD NO LONGER PUT IT OFF. Antal went into the bedroom where Sándor was studying at the desk. Sándor looked over his shoulder and eyed him quizzically. Antal shut the door. "I want to talk with you."

"Well, finally." Sándor turned in his chair to face him. "I had begun to think I was invisible."

"I need to know if you want to be in the radio concert. If you don't, I'll adjust the music."

"Who's going? Katalin? Márta?"

"Both of them."

"Márta's going. That's a surprise. Then do you want me there? That would be an even bigger surprise."

"And what does that mean?"

"That day after Anni's funeral, you pretty much told me to fuck off." Sándor picked up his pen, set it down again with a thud. "So I've stayed out of your way. And contrary to what you think, I haven't been flirting with your girlfriend. Whom I have thought of as a friend, just as I've thought of Katalin as a friend, and even Miklós, for God's sake, before he left. And just as I've thought of *you* as a friend, my best friend, since before we could even tie our shoes. So yes, I would like to come, *if* we're friends." Sándor's eyes flared. "But if I'm *persona non grata,* then no thank you."

Antal sat down on the lower bunk and looked hard at him. "We need you."

"Well, I have two things to say about that. The first is that a minute ago you didn't need me. You said you'd adjust the music, 'No problem, Sándor. We'll be just fine.' And the second is that I'm not talking about whether you need me there. I'm asking if you *want* me there."

"You're my cousin."

"I'm all too aware of that."

"Things would be bad if we weren't doing this together."

"Things are already bad."

Antal heard himself shouting. "All right, then, what do *you* want?"

"That's beside the point. I can't have what I want." Sándor fixed his gaze on him. "So what I'd like instead is for you to acknowledge that for years we didn't hold anything back from each other—not until now, which is one of the absolutely shitty things about *now.* Everything we've been through, we've been through together. And like it or not, we're part of each other's strength. Or weakness."

Antal nodded.

"So do you want me to come?" Sándor asked.

There Sándor sat, wearing one of the shirts they shared, in front of the desk they had to share, in this apartment, this life they shared. Antal looked around this room that Sándor had moved into but never really settled into. What if that bomb that crushed his home and killed his mother hadn't stopped there? What if it had killed Sándor, too? What if nothing were left, none of Sándor's heart nor creativity nor fight? What if Sándor were not just sad or angry but *gone?*

Sándor shrugged. "Well?"

Antal tried to find words. "There's as much of you in the music as me. I don't think I should do the concert without you."

"I guess we do things together, like it or not."

"So you'll come?"

"I'll come." Sándor twiddled his pen. "I don't want to do 'Pest, Along the Danube.'"

"But I thought you liked it. The audience always does."

"It wears me out. I can't get through two teary songs, and I'd rather do 'A Good Mother.' Anyway, I think it's time to quit using 'Pest, Along the Danube' as a closing for 'Song to Our Enemies.' Your piece should stand on its own. Wasn't Márta going to help you write a good ending?"

"Every time we meant to work on it, things stood in the way."

"Things like her father's risks. And her mother's worries. And her sister's death."

The words were so blunt as to sound sarcastic, but Sándor's face was only sad.

"Maybe Márta and I can work on the piece Saturday morning," Antal said. "If you don't want to do 'Pest, Along the Danube,' then don't."

Antal left the room. At least for now, there was a plan. At least on Saturday night they would be strong or weak together. After that, he didn't know.

HE CHECKED WITH MÁRTA, AND SHE SAID SHE REALLY WOULD be there for the radio performance. She also would help him figure out a good ending to "Song to Our Enemies." She'd come to his apartment at eight-thirty Saturday morning.

But by nine o'clock Saturday she hadn't arrived. Antal went downstairs with his violin and knocked on her door. There was no answer. Confused, he listened for any sound within, but heard nothing. He knocked again and heard a shuffling. Finally the door opened a little and Márta peered out, her eyes shadowed and her hair uncombed.

"Oh, I'm sorry," she said. "I overslept. Come in."

He stepped inside. Márta stood in her nightgown with a shawl over her shoulders, the gown draping softly around her hips.

"Where are the others?" he asked.

"They went to spend the morning with our pastor and his wife."

He looked at her questioningly. They weren't hiding?

"They wanted me to come with them," she said. "But I told them you and I had plans and I refused to cancel. They left early, and then I fell back asleep, because I was so tired." As though making a bitter confession, she added, "I was up late arguing with my parents, and then I hardly slept at all. Antal, I have to tell you something."

"What's wrong?"

"Everything." She was not joking. "Let me go get dressed."

"Don't." He touched her slender neck and wanted to kiss it. "Please."

She cocked her head. Did this confuse her? Didn't she know how gracefully the thin nightgown skimmed her body? How lovely her legs were? How her shawl begged to be lifted?

"You're beautiful," he said. "Please. Stay like this."

Her eyes softened. "I'll clean up a little, at least."

She moved to the small bathroom. He set his violin case on the floor and wasn't sure where to sit. The sofa bed had been opened out and slept in. Maybe he should make the bed and close it, but he stood as if paralyzed. When Márta returned, she had brushed her hair. He caressed her face, cool from washing. "What's the matter?" he asked.

She went to the unmade bed and propped the pillows against the sofa back. They sat together, leaning on the pillows, legs stretched out. He waited for her to speak.

"What's the matter?" he repeated.

"You can't tell anyone."

"I've always kept your secrets. You know that."

She gripped his hand. "We're leaving Hungary."

"No." He pulled back and stared at her. "No."

She nodded, more a tremor than a movement. "Tomorrow. Early."

"That can't be." His pulse raced. "This was your father's decision, wasn't it? It's a terrible decision, this is your home, he can't just—"

"It was mostly my mother who wanted it."

Antal sank back against the pillow. Her mother. Of course. Her terrified mother.

"We're going to America," she said. "I don't know where. My parents won't tell me until we're out of Hungary."

"Oh, my God." America. If it were somewhere in Austria, somewhere in Czechoslovakia, even somewhere in wrecked Italy or Poland or Germany, maybe he could find a way to go to her—but America. "No," he groaned.

"Last night they told Sarolta and me," she said. "Sarolta accepted it. She hates being shut inside this apartment and says she'd rather be free on the other side of the world than locked up here. But I—" Márta's voice cut. She sucked breath in. "I was furious. I've never sworn at my parents before, but I did last night. I don't want to leave you. I can't."

He pulled her tightly close and she cried in his arms. His head hot and his throat aching, he asked her why—why this? Why America? Why now? Why?!—and in broken phrases, flung out or whispered or choked, she tried to explain. Her father had finished writing the book with his sick friend. They'd sent it off to the British publisher, and her mother didn't think they'd been secret enough. He'd also wired articles to London and to Washington—articles detailing the Soviet Union's rapes, ransacking, deportations, and war crimes.

"Because he can't keep quiet about wrong," Márta said. "That's the way he is. And if he doesn't shut up—who knows, maybe it's already too late—he'll end up in prison. And that's why my mother demanded to leave. She says she's already lost a daughter and can't lose her husband, too."

"If he's being watched," Antal asked miserably, "how will you leave?"

"I'm not sure, I was confused, too upset when they told me. But tonight we go to somebody's house, and in the morning before dawn there will be some delivery lorry that we have to get in—oh, I don't know how it all will happen, my parents were so secretive. I don't even know which way we're going. Austria then a refugee camp, I think, but I don't know."

"Then I have to come to the delivery lorry. I have to say goodbye."

"No, my parents say it isn't safe for you."

"I don't care."

"But they care." Her voice broke. "And so do I."

He closed his eyes and held her. *Tomorrow. Gone. No.*

"I have to be with you tonight," he said. "If this is your last night here, then I won't do the concert. I'll stay with you."

"I told my parents I'm going to play in the concert." Márta sat up, looking at him, and her shawl slid off one shoulder. "And I'm going to listen to you play the romanza. I told them if they didn't like that, then they'd better remember that it was you who came looking for me in the winter, and you who told everybody my name was Záborsky, and you who played music for Anni when she was *dying*—"

Márta coughed, struggled with her voice. "I told them that I'm going to walk out that front door with you, and if they don't want me going out, then they can blockade the door. And that will make a scene. And attract more attention than they want."

He touched her anguished face.

She said, "But we can't tell Katalin or Sándor about any of this. We have to act like everything is just fine."

"That's impossible."

"I know."

He pressed her close, wanting to take her, run with her, push away every threat and keep her. Oh, God, if he could only keep her. She lifted her head and kissed him hard.

He stroked the contours of her back, feeling her body tighten and loosen with his touch. The shawl fell away from her sleeveless nightgown. He caressed the perfect curve of her neck and her shoulder, let the loose lacing at her neckline come undone, found the wondrous, white rise and fall of her breasts. Longing burned in him. She whispered that she loved him.

"You overwhelm me," he whispered back.

He kissed her hungrily, heard her moan. They eased down together and did not stop. Beauty and torment caught them up. All was stripped away in a blur of tears and heat, and he was lost in her.

Afterward she lay in his arms, her hair and tears falling on his chest.

"Márta, if we should have held back, I'm sorry."

"It's not that."

"Did it hurt?"

"It will hurt when I remember this moment, and you're not with me."

"Don't go to America. Stay here. Tell them you won't go." Desperation surged in him. "Move in with us. You can sleep in Katalin's room with her." He pushed on in reckless agony. "And when we're old enough, I will marry you."

Márta gasped.

"Do you want that?" he asked.

Against his shoulder, her head moved, nodding yes. "I'd begun to let myself hope for it. Life with you."

He rose on one elbow to look at her. "Please. Don't go."

She reached up and touched his hair. "My family will be back soon. We have to get dressed. For right now, I have permission to go with you tonight and play at the concert. That's all I have."

"It's not enough."

"No." She pressed her damp cheek to his shoulder. "Practice today and get ready to do a beautiful performance tonight. Music is your future." Her voice choked. "And I'm not."

CHAPTER FIFTY-THREE

Minor Victories

March 18, 2007

EXCEPT FOR A FEW BASIC DISHES, such as the stew she'd made for Varga last August, Lisa didn't really know how to cook; Jake had always done it. Since the split-up, she'd come to hate her steady diet of canned soup, ham sandwiches, and Safeway chicken. So this Sunday afternoon she'd opened a cookbook she bought in Hungary and painstakingly followed the recipe for goulash—no, *gulyás*. It was a soup, not a stew like the American version. Stirring it, she smiled in satisfaction. The concoction contained enough onions to choke a horse, enough paprika to turn her insides red, and it smelled delicious. This was victory.

In fact, it was the third victory of the weekend. The first was yesterday's haircut, an actual, good cut that worked with the light curl in her hair instead of fighting against it. This morning it had taken her a mere five minutes to deal with her hair, and it looked good. Lisa lifted the pan of *gulyás* off the stove and fingered her hair, which was still soft, still nice.

The second victory happened a couple hours ago at the Hungarian-American meeting, playing cello while Kálmán Barcza's choir performed her grandfather's song. She'd have to tell Kristóf about it.

And now a bowl of *gulyás* on the table. She dug in. The soup was bold and hearty, warm on her tongue, with a fragrance like her grandparents' kitchen. How long had she been hungry and hadn't even known it?

After a second bowl, she pulled her laptop close and wrote to Kristóf.

Thanks for your note. Please let your dear grandfather know I'm thinking of him. And I hope your dad will be very happy in his new marriage.

Wow, you gave a keyboard and a music lesson to Misha! I know you're concerned about how this will all turn out, but that was a great thing to do. So was the way you talked to Endre about it. You said what was right and true, and I can only hope he respects you for it.

I have to tell you two things. First, I made gulyás! I just ate a lot of it, with more left over for tomorrow.

The other thing is that I went to a Hungarian gathering for that holiday you have in March. (Sorry, I get your battles mixed up.) I played cello while a small choir sang my grandfather's song about Pest. In Hungarian, of course. There was one part when just the men sang, and I almost felt I was hearing Grandpa Sándor's voice. On a repeated line (which I think means something like "I love you, Pest") people joined in singing, and some of the old ones had tears in their eyes. Afterward a man told me the song was a gift they needed.

Lisa lifted her hands from the laptop and looked out the kitchen window into the night, remembering the moment. The man was a member of the choir. When she left the meeting, he offered to carry her cello for her. He was probably about forty and had a nice smile. When she thanked him but said she could manage, he held the door for her, thanked her earnestly for the music, said he hoped she would come again and think about joining the choir. She had a strong hunch he was, um, interested, but she'd hurried to the door.

She went on typing.

When your grandfather finishes revising the Embers Suite, could you send me the new version?

Her phone rang. She reached across the table and picked it up. It was her mother.

"I've been reading that book you sent me," Ann said. "About the siege of Budapest. At first I was bored. Page after page of which army was where on what day."

"I skipped a lot of that," Lisa admitted.

"But today I read the section about what happened to ordinary citizens," Ann said. "Oh, my God. Lisa, did Grandma and Grandpa ever say anything to you about this? I mean, do you think maybe your grandma was raped? Or did Grandpa get a gun pointed at him?"

"I don't know." Lisa heard herself speaking gently, as with bad news. "I think I told you, a bomb fell on Grandpa's apartment house. His mother was killed. But Grandpa didn't tell me that. I found out about it from the relatives in Hungary."

"And what else have these relatives told you?"

"Grandpa Sándor and Antal *bácsi* lived in their basement for weeks, hardly any food or water." Lisa rose, paced the living room as she tried to recall what else Kristóf had told her. "They buried a German soldier in their courtyard. And also, Grandma Márta's little sister got really sick, and it was sometime in there that she died. But there's a lot I don't know."

"I wish I'd understood this a long time ago," Ann said. "I wish they'd told us."

"Maybe it was too hard to talk about." She told Ann about Grandpa's song mourning the destruction of Pest, and how the Hungarians in Seattle today had understood, and they mourned with him. Out the window the first star of evening blinked in the lonely dark.

Long after Lisa hung up, Ann's troubled tone lingered with her. The words that she herself had written in her journal came back to her, a question flung out in anger—*Ann, why couldn't you see the pain Grandpa and Grandma bore?* But could Ann really be blamed for not seeing what they had kept hidden?

Later Lisa returned to her email and told Kristóf about her mother's phone call.

And I'm reminded, Kristóf, of the questions you've asked about forgiving a hard mother. I've never known what to say. But just this, if my mother will make peace with Grandpa Sándor's memory, I'll find it easier to make peace with her.

Lisa could have said much more, but it would take all night to write it, and even then it would only be half-said. She wished Kristóf were here, or she were there.

She signed off by saying *I miss you.*

CHAPTER FIFTY-FOUR

The Fire Beneath

June 23, 1945

THEY HAD TUNED THEIR INSTRUMENTS. THEY'D tried out the microphones. Katalin had done vocal warm-ups a few minutes ago in the women's toilet room. Now they waited for eight o'clock, when they'd go on the air.

Antal sat with Márta, Katalin, Sándor and Mr. Boros at the side of a large studio room for musical groups and radio dramas. A ceiling-hung microphone dangled above a grand piano. A second microphone on a stand had been placed near the piano, and not far off stood a third one on a boom. Mr. Faludi bustled between the microphones and technical workers, his bald head shining under the ceiling lights. Through a window across the studio, a man with headphones sat surrounded by turntables and by metal boxes with reels and dials.

Antal glanced at his watch. Eight more minutes. Beside him, Márta stretched her fingers. She had not managed a real smile all evening. Seven more minutes. On Antal's left, Sándor rose, wandered to the piano, and straightened his music. Returning, he asked Antal and Márta, "What about 'Song to Our Enemies?' Did you write a new ending for it?"

It was the ending they'd meant to write in Márta's flat this morning. "We're skipping the piece," Antal said, and Márta looked away.

Nervously Antal fingered his watch. He hadn't worn it since the siege because of all the robberies. But tonight, or tomorrow morning, or whenever the goodbye couldn't be put off any longer, he would give it to Márta. God willing, it could buy her some food or safety, or bribe someone to turn a blind eye.

"Antal," Márta whispered, "I don't know if I can get through this concert."

He spoke low. "The music is all written out. If you lose your place, just improvise. If you have to stop, act as if it's in the music to stop. If you have trouble, I'll try to cover."

A technician beckoned them to the microphones. He led them through a final sound check, signaling back and forth to the man behind the glass. At exactly eight o'clock, a sign lit up. ON THE AIR. The man behind the window pointed, and Mr. Faludi spoke into a microphone: "Welcome to Danube Voices! Tonight we have with us a remarkable set of teenagers who began their musical partnership—imagine this!—in a bomb shelter. Varga Antal, Varga Sándor, Varga Katalin and Záborsky Márta are here to regale us with their delightful combination of folk, classical, and original pieces. They'll lead off with 'Erdő, Erdő, Erdő.' Ladies and gentlemen, the Bomb Shelter Quintet! Eh—quartet."

Antal glanced at the others, mouthed a two-measure count, and yanked the bow. The song bounded forward. Katalin sang joyously into the microphone as though she'd been created for the airwaves. Sándor, on piano, played some new trills and flourishes. Antal could have done that on violin but didn't. Márta was playing with her gazed fixed on the sheet music, so on edge tonight that he dare not confuse her.

He went on to play "Miklós's Fiddle," the Gypsy-style ditty he'd written. He wished Miklós himself were here. Katalin beat a hand drum. Márta pulled a steady bass pattern. By the end, she had not faltered. He turned to her and whispered, "Good job."

He signaled to Mr. Boros. Barely trusting his voice, Antal stepped to the microphone and said, "Shostakovich's second waltz, accompanied on piano by Boros György."

It almost felt out of place, doing Shostakovich in the warmth of summer. He'd played it in the chill of their damaged apartment after the siege, remembering Sándor's dead brother and mother. He'd repeated it on the winter street, his hands stiff with cold, when the Soviet lieutenant Kholodenko asked for something Russian.

Kholodenko, who had brought sugar for Anni. Anni, who had died. Antal's left little finger slipped. *Concentrate! Focus!*

Avoiding looking at Márta, Antal played on and finally finished the piece. He stepped back. Mr. Boros rose, and Sándor and Katalin sat down on the piano bench. Neither of them announced the upcoming song, "A Good Mother"; Sándor had said the song was hard enough to get through without blathering about it, too.

"A kind, good woman was with me at the start," Sándor sang, the piano notes a backdrop to the memory of his mother. Antal sensed Sándor's tension in the song. Sándor played only the basic chords, leaving out the extra touches he usually put in. Beside him Katalin sang along softly. Antal had heard them talking about this on the way to the studio: she would take over if Sándor choked.

He did choke. "And I believe, yes—" His voice gave out.

"I believe," Katalin sang on without him, "that the love of a good woman never dies."

She finished the song without Sándor. At the end he nodded, played the closing chords, and dropped his hands into his lap.

Mr. Faludi stepped up to a microphone for the scheduled break. "Isn't this marvelous?" he asked the radio audience. "If you're just now tuning in with us, this is the fabulous Bomb Shelter Quartet. Can you believe they're only teenagers? They've played in a music shop owned by Boros György and at a flea market out in front of their home on Dessewffy Street."

Antal grimaced. Who had told Mr. Faludi that? Katalin? Mr. Boros? Did the whole city have to know where they lived? He glanced at Márta's stricken face.

"That's just the kind of musicians these young people are," Mr. Faludi went on. "Happy to play, no matter where. And now a word from our sponsors. Stay tuned."

Antal sat down and reviewed his notes for the second half of the performance. He wouldn't have to play on the next piece. Katalin would sing and Sándor accompany—and Márta, too, she'd told him yesterday. She'd arranged a cello part from the piano score, and they'd meant to go over it this morning. But nothing this morning had gone as they'd intended, nothing at all.

The break ended, and the others began Mozart's "*Ave Verum Corpus*." The purity of Katalin's voice hovered over the piano's current. At a pause in the singing, the piano died away and the cello's tones arose. Márta played an echo of the melody but turned it, changed it. Was she improvising, like he'd told her to do if she choked? But she hadn't choked. He sat forward as the cello strings quivered and sang. Márta's music was warm and good and softly alive. It was intimate.

Intimate and warm and good, just like *her*.

His head sank into his hands as sorrow slammed. *No. America. No.*

Katalin sang again, and Sándor played again, and the music ended. Somehow Antal stood, picked up his violin, went to his spot next to Márta. He turned the page on his music stand.

"Are you all right?" Márta whispered.

"I'm doing the best I can."

Katalin spoke into the microphone. "Antal wrote this next one, with some help from the rest of us, especially Márta. Of all our music, I love this piece the most. 'The Light Shines.'"

Antal touched the bow to the string. It was a mercy that he'd played this piece so many times before. Habit kept his hands moving as if his heart were here. Márta played steadily, her head bent and her hair partially hiding her face. It was what she'd been doing for months: hiding herself, trying to stay steady through loss after loss.

Steady. They kept playing. *Steady.*

Tomorrow and for the rest of her life, he couldn't be there to steady her—but maybe he never had—maybe he'd only made things harder—like he did today, taking her under the coverlet, where her secrets throbbed and bled. Light? How could Katalin keep singing about light when darkness was about to close in? And when the sun rose again, the sun that had lost the game, Márta would be gone.

Somehow his hands kept moving. So did Márta's, until Katalin sang the last phrase and Sándor touched the ending note. Somehow Márta rose from her cello, and Sándor from the piano, and Mr. Boros took his place on the bench. It was time for the romanza. Márta touched his sleeve and whispered that it would be beautiful.

He told himself not to look at her as he played. It would break his concentration, if not everything within him. Antal stretched his shoulders, loosened his knees and nodded to Mr. Boros. During the piano's long opening, Antal breathed the music in, letting its rhythm become his own pulse. He raised the violin.

Márta and Mr. Boros and Mr. Horváth had all told him he knew the music; they'd said it was in him. He had to believe it. He was too tired to chase through his memory if the music escaped him, too flattened to fake it. He drew the bow for the opening note. The violin lifted its voice. His hands followed the patterns he'd demanded of them over hours and days and weeks and months. The minor-key romanza flowed out in understated beauty. He yielded to the flow. The music was all he had.

No, it was more than what he had. It sang above his weary grief. He played on, through the tender long notes, through the spiraling sixteenth notes. *Halfway finished. Three-quarters.* The key changed, lifted from minor to major. He pushed on, though his left hand hurt. Warmth surged in strength and brilliance. From somewhere deeper than his own despair, light and music flamed.

At the end, a shining hush. He was vaguely aware of all in the studio remaining still. He lowered his violin, his bow, his head.

The concert was over. Katalin hugged him and Sándor clapped him on the shoulder. Mr. Boros shook his hand, said he was impressed. The station crew congratulated him and all the group, said they were headed for great things. Mr. Faludi circulated, paying the group members each three American dollars. Antal stuffed the green-and-gray bills in his pocket, thanked the man in a daze, and looked around for Márta.

Mr. Faludi said something else, but Antal barely heard it. He spotted Márta subtly gesturing to him, pitching her head toward the studio door. He followed her into the empty hallway. Her eyes were reddened and her face flushed.

"I've always thought the romanza was a gentle piece," she said. "But tonight I felt *you* in it—and your passion—and I fell apart listening. Sándor and Kati thought I was crying because of Anni and I had to let them think that."

"They still don't know what's going on tonight, do they?"

"No."

"Márta, stay here. I mean it. Refuse to go."

She gripped his hand. "My parents can't lose another daughter. Sarolta can't lose another sister. They need me."

"*I* need you. Stay—"

But the pain in her eyes told him to stop.

"I wish I could undo the hurt to you," she said, and waited through a tight breath. "We have to leave soon. Or you'll miss curfew getting home."

"I don't care about curfew. Wherever you're staying tonight, I'm sleeping on the floor. I'm not saying goodbye until you're gone."

"Then I'll sleep on the floor beside you," she said.

"Come on, then."

He put his arm around her, desperate for one more plan, anything but America.

CHAPTER FIFTY-FIVE

Our Trespasses

March 19, 2007

THESE DAYS WHEN THE PHONE RANG IN VARGA'S APARTMENT, it was usually Kristóf who answered it. This made sense, since it took Varga so long to reach the phone. What bothered him, though, was that his family and Halmos invariably asked Kristóf how Varga was doing before they asked Varga himself.

"I don't need you telling everybody whether or not I took a nap today," Varga told Kristóf as they ate supper, which was soup again. "You're not my nanny."

"True. You'd better eat some more so I don't have to tattle on you to Aunt Gabriella. I think I should take you to the doctor. Or Mr. Halmos could. He's offered to drive you."

Varga saw no point in extra doctor visits; the reasonable options had been used up. "The hospital scheduled me for a whole blitz of medical tests after Easter," he said. "That's soon enough."

"All right, then. But for God's sake, take it easy."

Varga tried to make more headway with his French bean soup, which once upon a time he had liked. He did not tell Kristóf that he was already taking it easier than he wanted to, pacing himself so he could be strong at Easter, three weeks away. Zoltán and Erzsi, Gabriella and Bálint and their girls would all gather here, just as they had at Christmas.

Though he hoped Kristóf hadn't noticed it, Varga felt himself losing mental ground. He sensed that if he needed things said, he'd better say them soon. That night he phoned Gabriella and she immediately asked if he was all right.

"I'm all right," he said. "I just wanted to make sure you are, too."

"Why wouldn't I be?"

"No reason. It's just that you're my beautiful daughter, so I have to know."

Her voice softened: "I'm fine."

"Good. I love you, little heart."

Two nights later, while Kristóf watched television in the living room, Varga again sat down with the kitchen phone. He hesitated long. Should he be pestering Zoltán about this? Was there really any point after all these years?

Maybe there was. He rang Zoltán's number. After they'd chatted a few minutes and his son assured him that the honeymoon was great and married life was good, Varga said, "Zoli, there's something I need to say, and please, just humor me by listening." He rested his head in his hand, gathered his breath. "You know, you were only a baby when your twin sister died."

"I know."

"And, well, when you and Zsuzsanna were born, the birth was hard for your mother. Twins are hard—" Varga shifted on his chair and coughed.

"Apa?"

"I'm sorry. If this doesn't matter to you, then after tonight you can forget it, but for years I've wondered if I should say something about it."

"Well, then, what is it?"

"Yes, well, your mother was a little weak, couldn't nurse two babies, but you didn't like having a bottle. So at night Ildi nursed you, and I fed your sister, and—I don't really know how to explain it, but Zsuzsanna became very attached to me. If I was in the room, she didn't want anyone else to hold her. It seemed she chose me. It was as if you were Ildi's baby and Zsuzsanna was mine. And then Zsuzsanna died."

Varga coughed again. This was getting harder and harder. "And everything went dark for me. The early years of your life, I lived with that shadow. And so did you."

In his living room the television chattered, but no sound came through the phone.

"Zoli, are you there?"

"Are you saying you blame yourself for my depression?" Zoltán asked.

"I don't know. But I wonder. And regret."

"I didn't blame you."

"No, you were a child. You didn't know to blame me. But maybe things could have been different."

"How can we guess at things like that? Apa, I don't know how you faced losing a child." Zoltán's voice had strained to the point of shaking. "If I lost Kristóf, oh my God."

"Zoli, are you all right?"

"Of course I'm not all right! Because this is not the kind of thing you would have said to me if you were in fine blooming health. Damn it, Apa, don't blame yourself, because I don't think you failed me, and if you did, you more than made up for it with my son. In this whole world, who's done more to steady Krisz than you have? Nobody."

"Well. Thank you." Varga stood unsteadily.

"And forget waiting until Easter, I'm going to come see you this Sunday."

"You don't have to, but that's nice. My regards to your bride. Good night, son."

AFTER KRISTÓF WAS ASLEEP ON THE SOFA, Varga sat in his bathrobe with the old Bomb Shelter Quintet pages and the *Embers Suite* score spread over his bedroom desk. He'd go to bed soon, because he couldn't become a flat wreck for Easter. But he'd just look over the last few pages of the suite. *Part 6, Adagietto ma accelerando con fuoco:* This was the hardest section, the one that began as a lament and then pushed and drove *con fuoco*, with fire, until it exploded. Varga rubbed his sore neck.

Maybe he'd take a look at the first version of this. He flipped through the Bomb Shelter Quintet music until he found the original piece dated *1945 február.* At age seventeen he didn't know how to complete it. "Song to Our Enemies," he had called it back then.

But which enemies had he meant? The Germans, with their edicts and flame-throwers; they were enemies. But what about that German buried in the courtyard? Was he an enemy? Or just a scared boy who wanted to go home?

And the drunken, riotous Soviets? Yes, they were enemies, too—except that Ukrainian lieutenant, Kholodenko. *Jésus Mária.*

Varga looked again at the suite score, turned slowly to the last page where in 1958 he had tried to finish the story. Beneath the huge X he'd recently drawn, the score called for the final drum crash. Lower on the page, like a memorial inscription, stood the words Márta had written later: *Oh, Antal, Sándor, why did it all have to end like this?* He knew why it ended like that back then, knew who he'd once thought the last enemy was.

But if an enemy's granddaughter crosses the ocean, carrying music, holding out peace, what then? He tried to breathe deeply but gasped instead.

THE NEXT MORNING WHILE KRISTÓF SHOWERED, Varga called Halmos. "I've almost finished correcting the suite," he said. "All that's left is the very ending. The drum crash is out."

Halmos whistled softly. "Good, then."

"Halmos, eh, you offered to drive if I needed—"

"Of course."

Varga summoned the words. The time had come. "I've decided to talk to Ildi's priest."

"Right. I'll drive him to your place. And I'll invite Kristóf out."

FRIDAY AFTERNOON VARGA LAY ON THE SOFA, dressed except for shoes, with a blanket over him. This was all he'd asked Kristóf for, a little more warmth, and half a pain pill. He had declined the other half in order to stay alert. Father Barnabás sat in the armchair with a book in his lap. The man had aged since Varga last saw him, his hair sparser, the folds at his eyes heavier.

"I always remember Ildikó fondly," the priest said.

"You helped her. She wanted me to come to your church more. I was remiss—" Varga grimaced. He'd been hurting all day. "But now you've come to me. Thank you."

The priest moved his chair close. "Are there things you'd like to say? Ask? Pray for?"

At a loss for how to talk to God or His men, Varga measured his words between breaths. "I have a daughter. Gabriella. She is strong like her mother was. And I don't worry about Gabriella and her husband and her girls. But my son, Zoltán, he takes pills for depression." Varga shifted his shoulders. "Zoltán just remarried and is happy. If you pray, please, pray for his happiness to last."

"Of course. I remember your wife talking about him."

"And his son, Kristóf. He lives here with me and turns thirty next week." Varga paused, rested, decided to be frank. "Kristóf's sad and angry and promiscuous. But he's loyal, very loyal, very devoted to the few of us that he trusts. He doesn't let many people into his heart, but I'm one of them. And when I'm gone . . ."

"It will be hard for him."

"Yes."

"We'll pray for him, then."

"Thank you."

"And for you?" Father Barnabás asked. "What would help?"

"Strength." Varga breathed as deeply as he could. "But I've used up what I was given."

"Ah. And are you afraid?"

"More sad than afraid, I think. I've had too many goodbyes already."

"Brother Antal." The priest's voice was kind. "Can you trust that this isn't the end? Christ gives us that."

"I hope you're right."

"Is there anything you want to confess?"

Varga couldn't remember all seven deadly sins; but whatever they were, he wasn't above them. "My human weakness," he said. "Not just body, but—" He coughed. "Sometimes I think maybe people needed me more than I believed, and it grieves me."

The man reached out and touched Varga's arm. "Do you need to ask anyone's forgiveness?"

"I already asked Zoltán. He was more gracious to me than I am to myself. If there are others, I don't know who, but I'm sorry I didn't pay attention."

"If it's any consolation, Ildikó knew you really loved her."

Varga turned his head and looked gratefully at the man. "It is a consolation."

"One more question," Father Barnabás said. "Our Lord taught us to pray, 'Forgive us our trespasses as we forgive those who trespass against us.' Is there anyone you need to forgive?"

It became clear now. "Yes," Varga said. "But he isn't alive anymore."

"It's still important."

It wasn't only important, it was urgent. "Please, could you help me sit up?"

The Father slipped his arm behind Varga's back, gently helped him turn, and adjusted the pillows so Varga sat resting against the sofa's arm.

"Tell me," Father Barnabás said.

"It was my cousin. He didn't mean for it to be this way, he didn't know."

The priest murmured something Varga had heard before, maybe in the Easter Mass, something about forgiving those who didn't know what they were doing.

"It was my cousin," Varga repeated. His silence broken, the words poured out in a torrent. "Sándor. He left Hungary. Before he left, we were best friends. Then something terrible happened. It was after the siege. I was seventeen and he was eighteen. We were both in love with the same girl. And on an awful night there was a horrible scuffle—I'm sorry—"

"Go on," Father Barnabás said.

Part Six

Song to Our Enemies

CHAPTER FIFTY-SIX

Crash

June 23, 1945

CLUTCHING THE HANDLE OF HIS VIOLIN CASE, Antal rode home from the radio station in the aisle of the streetcar, which was finally up and running after the siege. In front of him and behind him, Katalin and Márta held onto the ceiling-hung loops, while Sándor stood behind Márta with her cello. Outside the tram windows the midsummer sun had set and the sky glowed pink.

Antal mentally rehearsed the next steps. They'd get off at the stop nearest the apartment. He and Márta would hand off the violin and cello to Katalin and Sándor. Márta couldn't take the cello to America, and when Katalin and Sándor crossed the ring boulevard to walk home with it, they wouldn't know they were taking it with them for good.

The tram wheezed. Antal replayed the ruse he'd given to Sándor and Katalin: he'd told them Márta was going to spend the night with some family friends nearby, and he would walk her there. He'd said that if things got too late he'd spend the night, too.

The goodbye with Katalin and Sándor would have to be quick. And then he and Márta would head east to one of those streets over there. Márta had the address in her pocket.

The tram passed the Oktagon, then Aradi Street. Antal looked over his shoulder at Márta and Sándor. "Next stop," he said, although they knew it as well as he did.

Sándor repositioned the cello, anchoring it against the tram's rattle and sway. "Back there a minute ago," he said, indicating the window with his thumb, "I could swear I saw that Soviet officer, what's his name, Kholodenko."

"Ah, the *leytenant!*" Katalin half-shouted over the din. Lately it seemed to amuse her to use the Russian words they were all picking up.

The brakes screeched. The tram trembled to a stop and the doors opened. Antal glanced at Márta, seeing the day's weight in her eyes. Following the queue of passengers, they stepped off one by one. The breeze smelled of untended trash.

They gathered on the debris-littered sidewalk, pedestrians walking around them. Antal said, more heartily than he felt, "So, Kati, here's the violin. Sándor, if you could take Márta's cello home—thanks—"

"Márta, is this really all right, you going out?" Katalin asked. "It seems like you never—"

"It's fine." Márta squeezed out a smile. "So I guess we'll get going."

"See you tomorrow, then."

As Katalin hugged her, Antal saw the pain in Márta's eyes over this last goodbye.

Katalin headed for the curb with the violin. "Come on, Sándor," she called.

Sándor held the cello with one hand and put the other arm around Márta. "Goodbye, girl. Nice, nice playing tonight."

A tear spilled onto Márta's cheek. Antal shook his head in alarm. She couldn't cry. Sándor pulled back and looked at her. "What's the matter?"

"I'm sorry. I'm tired and everything else." She wiped her eye. "You know."

"Right, remembering your sister," Sándor said. "I understand."

Antal beckoned to Márta. "Come on."

Behind them something clattered. Antal turned. A shop door banged open with a roar of raucous laughter. A window broke as a bottle flew out. Antal jumped back. Out the open door burst a knot of soldiers in fatigues—laughing, whooping in Russian, bumping into each other. One of them pointed and yelled, "*Devushka!*"

Wasn't that the Russian word for girl? Two soldiers headed for Katalin. "Antal!" she screamed.

He rushed to his sister, shouting behind him, "Márta, Sándor, look out!"

People scattered up and down the sidewalk and ran across the street. Antal grabbed Katalin's arm and the violin and tried to break away, but the two soldiers blocked their path. Others, maybe a dozen, bunched near him. He was surrounded. Antal craned his neck, trying to see Márta and Sándor. He could only spot the back of Sándor's cap.

"Eh, *gyönyörű lány!*" a soldier cat-called.

Antal tightened his grip on Katalin and whirled around, looking for whichever drunkard had called his sister gorgeous.

In the fading light he faced the two nearest. A tall blond and a thick darker fellow stood leering at Katalin. Antal thrust his arm in front of her. The dark oaf took a last swig from a bottle and dropped it. It shattered at their feet. The blond smirked at Antal and pulled a knife from his pocket. Antal backed up. Katalin's clutched his arm.

And oh God, where were Sándor and Márta?

"Márta! Sándor!" he yelled, his voice drowning in the chaos around him.

The blond soldier held the knife at Antal's chest and pointed at the violin. "Give," he ordered in Hungarian.

Antal's throat tightened. His held the violin behind his back and shook his head.

"Give," the soldier repeated.

"Katalin, reach into my pocket," Antal said quietly. "Give him the American money."

Katalin fished out the dollars and the dark fellow snatched them. The blond pointed at the violin again.

"No!" Katalin said. "*Nyet!*" She thrust her own dollars at them. "Now go away!"

The men pulled up Antal's sleeve and demanded the watch. Damn it, he'd meant to give it to Márta. He unstrapped it and handed it over. The dark soldier then pointed at Antal's shoes. Katalin clutched Antal's arm. How long could this go on?

"Stand behind me and take the violin," he whispered to Katalin.

She slipped behind him. After he released the violin into her hands, he untied his shoes and kicked them to the dark soldier.

"That's all!" he shouted. Oh, what was the Russian word? "*Vsyo!*"

Antal turned carefully, avoiding broken glass on the ground, looking for Márta and Sándor. But more of the Russian gang stood in the way, moving the other direction, shouting. Were they threatening Márta? Pushing her around?

Holy Christ, Sándor, don't let anything happen!

He turned back. The blond soldier twiddled the knife and circled him. The man grinned lazily at Katalin.

Antal shook his head. "You don't want her, she's diseased!"

The man shrugged, clearly not understanding.

Antal insisted in German, "*Krank!*"

But he'd run out of tricks. The soldiers only snorted. Trying not to panic, Antal looked at Katalin, saw her face go hard, saw her open her mouth.

"Kholodenko!" she screamed. "Kholodenko *leytenant!*"

The two soldiers glanced at each other, uttered rushed words. The dark one berated Katalin in Russian. The blond snapped the blade closed and dropped the knife into his pocket. He gripped Antal by the shoulders and shoved. Antal stumbled backward. The violin was jarred from him. He thrust down his left hand, trying to grasp the case, but he fell full force on the little finger. Pain shot through him. He clutched his hand, feeling a lump of bone where it shouldn't be. In the gathering darkness he heard more than saw the Russians fleeing.

"Pick up the violin," he told Katalin through gritted teeth.

"Antal, are you all right?"

"Get the violin!"

She grabbed it up. "Those thugs ran away. Can you stand?"

"Yes." He pulled himself to his feet and looked around. The gang of drunks had mostly moved off; the street was almost empty. "Where's Márta?"

"And Sándor." Fear edged into Katalin's voice. "I haven't seen them since before that fellow pulled the knife."

"We have to find them."

He hurried to where he'd last seen Márta. Katalin followed. Cobbles and debris pressed into the soles of his stocking feet. A streetlamp glowed dim, giving him barely enough light to skirt broken glass and spilled wine.

"Where would they have gone?" she asked.

He tried to think, but his hand throbbed and his breath heaved and it was only five minutes ago that a knife had been pointed at him.

"Maybe a side street," Katalin said.

He headed for the cross-street just behind them, Szondi. "Márta! Sándor!"

Katalin lagged behind, frantically taking up the cry. "Sándor? Márta?"

No one was about. Curfew, he remembered. Antal looked up at the apartments above them. A woman peered out and shut her window against their calls.

Somewhere to the east, a gun blasted. Antal ran east.

"Antal, stop!"

Katalin caught up, carrying the violin, and grasped his sleeve. "Don't go that way. Please. I want to go home. Maybe Sándor and Márta went home."

He couldn't tell her that Márta would never go back to the place they called home. And now it broke in on him anew that he did not know where Márta was going. The address was in her pocket. Izabella Street, was it? Or Rózsa? Those streets turned off of this one, but he didn't know to go right or left, or how far. He didn't even know whether Márta would still go there if Sándor were along. Sándor wasn't supposed to know.

"Give me the violin," he told Katalin. "Let's go farther up this street."

"No," she pleaded. "I heard a gun."

Sweating, his hand pulsing pain, Antal knew he had to get his sister home. Months ago he had made that promise to his father. Still he wandered, dragging Katalin with him. At cross-streets they called out Márta's name and Sándor's, and waited, and listened. But the only replies came from people opening their windows, leaning out, telling them to get off the street, and didn't they know it was past curfew?

"We *do* know," Katalin miserably shouted back to a woman. "We can't find our friend and our cousin."

"They're inside somewhere, if they aren't idiots." The woman slammed her window shut.

Little traffic was out, only a few horse-drawn cabs. But at a corner he looked down the cross-street and saw a police car slowly patrolling. Antal ordered Katalin to back up, and they waited in the shadows until the car passed.

FINALLY REACHING THEIR APARTMENT HOUSE, Antal ran to Márta's flat. With his good hand he pounded on the door. No one answered. Against all hope he shouted her name, waited. There was still no answer. He trudged upstairs with Katalin to their own apartment and opened the door.

"We listened to your radio show," Mother shouted. "It was fabulous! Mr. Horváth called to say congratulations."

Antal strode into the living room with Katalin. "Is Sándor here?"

His parents and grandfather sat on the stained upholstery, their faces suddenly serious. "He isn't with you?" Papa asked.

"No."

Grandpapa asked, "What happened?" and Mother asked, "Antal, where are your shoes?"

Antal told Katalin to explain it to them and dragged himself off to the kitchen. He heated water to soak his hand, overhearing Katalin talk about the drunks and the knife and Antal's hurt hand and Antal's shoes being taken but not the violin. Katalin broke down when she said they couldn't find Sándor and Márta.

Papa came into the kitchen and helped him wrap a hot damp towel around his hand. "I'm going to call for a cab," he said, his words clipped with worry. "You and I and Katalin will drive around and look for them. Your mother and grandfather will stay here in case Sándor comes back. I'll lend you some shoes."

For an hour and a half they rode the cab through streets, up and down, back and forth between their apartment and as far east as City Park. The horses' hooves clopped, the seat jostled, and Antal's hand throbbed. He stared out the window, his heart screaming at Sándor for getting lost and taking Márta down some dark street. Nothing, but nothing, had gone as it should have. He was supposed to have slept on the floor of that house and held Márta back. He was supposed to have gone on loving her. He had tried to tell her that this morning after they made love. Turning away from the searing memory, he searched anew through the dark.

IT WAS ALMOST MIDNIGHT WHEN THEY returned home. At the dining table a police officer sat with a clipboard, Grandpapa and Mother waiting anxiously across from him. Antal, Katalin and Papa sat down with them.

"This is my husband László," Mother told the policeman, subdued. "And my son Antal and daughter Katalin."

The middle-aged policeman scratched his mustache and greeted them soberly. He introduced himself as Officer Kenez.

"What's going on?" Papa asked him.

"You didn't find your nephew?" Officer Kenez asked.

"No."

"Do you have any guess where he might be?"

"No."

Mother said to the man, "Tell them what you told us. Please."

"Of course." Kenez looked at Papa, then turned to Antal and Katalin. "I understand you two were held up at knife point tonight."

"Yes," Antal said. "By some drunk Russians."

Kenez checked the notes on his clipboard. "And when that happened, you were separated from your cousin—let me see, Varga Sándor—and from a girl that was with you. Záborsky Márta."

"That's right." Antal didn't like Márta's name coming up, but at least the man had been told Záborsky, not Hanák.

"And where was this?" the policeman asked.

Katalin told him. The man wrote. "And were there other 'drunks,' as you say?"

"Yes. Maybe fifteen or so, some with bottles." Antal rubbed his hand. "Maybe they found somebody's wine cellar, I don't know. Most of them came between us and Sándor and Márta. That's how we got separated from them."

"Were Sándor and the girl threatened, too?" the officer asked.

"Maybe, probably," Katalin said. "We couldn't find them afterward. They must have run. I heard Márta shout for Antal."

Antal winced. Márta had called to him. She needed him and he wasn't there.

Kenez asked Katalin, "How did you get away from the drunks?"

"I called the name of a Soviet lieutenant that we know," she said. "Sándor saw him from the tram window. I don't know if the man heard me. But when I called to a Russian lieutenant, it scared the soldiers, and they ran."

Antal set his sore hand in his lap. Katalin was rubbing her eyes, Mother chewing her lip, Grandpapa watching the officer, Papa telling the man, "We have to find my nephew," and Kenez staring down at his notes.

"And that lieutenant," Kenez said. "What is his name?"

"Kholodenko," Antal said.

The policeman turned the pen in his fingers. "Kholodenko is dead."

Katalin gasped.

"No!" Antal shouted.

Papa leaned forward, his eyes on the man. "What are you telling us?"

Mother set her hand on Papa's. "László," she murmured, "this is what he was saying before you arrived. It's very hard."

Antal stared at the officer. Kholodenko was dead. Sándor was gone. Márta was gone. With infuriating slowness the officer read over his notes yet again and turned, grim-faced, to Katalin. "Did your cousin or the girl have a cello?"

"Yes. It's Márta's."

"A cello was found not far from where you say the trouble happened. We have it at the station. Where should we take—"

"Here," Antal interrupted. "Her family lives here. Downstairs."

"I don't care about a cello," Papa insisted. "Tell us what happened to my nephew."

"And to Márta," Antal pleaded.

"All right." Kenez set down his pen. "Earlier tonight, about dusk, we got a call that a gun had gone off over on Szondi. Near Izabella."

Antal's chest tightened.

"I went over there with another officer to investigate," Kenez continued. "We went to the home of the man who had called. He showed us, out the window, the direction the noise had come from. So my partner and I walked down the street. Some people were gathered, very upset, in front of a half-demolished building, and they said a man had been shot. So we walked onto the lot, and it was true. We found a body. It was the lieutenant named Kholodenko. Pavel."

Across the table, Papa sat in bleak horror.

"What—" Antal forced his voice to steady. "What's this to do with Sándor?"

"Someone said he shot the lieutenant."

"No," Papa argued, furious. "That's impossible. Sándor doesn't have a gun, and he doesn't know how to use one."

"And he has nothing against Kholodenko!" Antal added.

Katalin shook her head and began to cry.

"Explain it to us," Grandpapa told the officer, voice taut. "This is all very confusing, and László is right. Sándor would not have done this."

"All right. A woman in that bunch of people said she'd heard the yelling. She said it sounded like a girl was being threatened. Maybe some of those same soldiers were doing it. The woman said she heard men yelling in Russian, said it sounded like the girl tried to use some Russian words, too. Trying to make them leave her alone, probably, but it was obvious the girl was Hungarian."

Antal knew. It was Márta. "Please, is the girl all right?"

"We don't know what happened to her. The woman said she heard a male voice yelling at the harassers. In Hungarian, it sounded like, but the woman didn't catch what he said. Then there were angry voices back and forth, and a gun went off."

"Why is Sándor being blamed for this?" Papa demanded.

"Because someone said they saw him running away."

"How could anyone see anything? It was night."

"There was a street light."

Papa stood up. "We know no one in that neighborhood. No one there knows Sándor. Who could possibly have reported this?"

The officer held up his hand. "It was a young man who reported. Hungarian. He said that the person he saw running away was the guitar player with a band on Dessewffy Street."

Sick heat coursed through Antal. Katalin's hand flew to her mouth. Papa sank back into his chair.

"So I asked him, where on Dessewffy," Kenez said. "He told me this block. When I arrived, I asked the neighbors where the guitar player was, and that's why I'm here. I'm sorry."

Antal's head pounded. "Just because Sándor was running away doesn't mean he shot anybody. There was a gang of drunk Russians. Who wouldn't run away?"

The man's eyes sagged. "I'm sorry." He pursed his lips as though making a decision, and said to Papa, "I'd like to speak to you alone, if I may."

"Please do."

The officer collected his notes. He and Papa went to Katalin's bedroom and shut the door. Antal waited with the others as the mantel clock ticked off the minutes, five, ten, twenty. At last the men came out and the officer said a somber goodbye. Papa saw him to the door. Returning to the table, he said, "Antal, go downstairs and see if the Hanáks are here."

Antal couldn't tell them the Hanáks had had absolutely no intention of being in their apartment tonight. He went down, hoping that by some miracle they would be there, desperately wishing that by some upending of the universe Sándor would be there, too. But the apartment was dark, and no one answered his knock. He went back and sat down with his family again, shaking his head.

"Listen, all of you," Papa said. The furrows of his face showed deep and gray. "I'll tell you what Kenez said, but he took it upon himself to speak to me privately as a man, not as a representative of the law. He doesn't want to be quoted on any of this."

"We understand," Grandpapa said. "Go on."

"Kenez said he doesn't trust the witness who reported on the guitar player running away. This isn't Kenez's first encounter with him. The fellow used to be a member of the Arrow Cross. Now he's sworn allegiance to the Communist Party to keep from getting hanged."

"And he's been here?" Antal asked. "Listening to our group?"

"It seems so."

"Then I know who it is," Antal said. "The first time my little finger was smashed up, he did it. He was on the tram throwing his weight around. Wearing a green shirt and an Arrow Cross armband. Now he walks around with a red star armband. I've seen him here."

Grandpapa asked, "What does this mean for Sándor?"

"The policeman didn't know," Papa said. "But here's what he thinks probably happened. This group of drunks surrounded Sándor and Márta. Who knows, but maybe that fellow who accused Sándor was among them. The officer guesses that Sándor was trying to keep the drunks away from Márta, and Lieutenant Kholodenko caught wind of a fight—"

"Yes, I yelled his name," Katalin said.

"Maybe other people did, too," Papa continued. "Maybe Sándor and Márta did. Maybe one of the drunks pointed the gun at *them*, who knows, maybe Sándor tried to wrest it away. However it happened, Kholodenko came running, and somebody fired the gun. Maybe not meaning to hit the

lieutenant. But whoever did it will pay dearly for killing an officer, and . . ."
Papa shut his eyes.

"And what?" Antal asked.

"And since that Arrow Cross dolt wants to get in good with the Russians, maybe that's why he pointed the finger at Sándor. They'll want to blame a Hungarian rather than a Soviet."

Katalin cried, "But that's not right!"

"No," Grandpapa said. "Lord, no."

Mother put her face in her hands and her shoulders began to shake.

Antal sat up with Grandpapa most of the night, distractedly turning pages in one music book after another. Across the room in its case, the violin leaned against the wall. It alone had come through the evening unscathed. He opened the music to Brahms' second violin sonata, which he'd always assumed he would study someday. But maybe he wouldn't. Assumptions, plans, dreams: they broke, like the left little finger that you needed. They burned, like the gunshot your cousin got blamed for. They vanished, like the girl you loved in the morning and couldn't find in the night.

THE NEXT DAY, SUNDAY, PAPA IMMOBILIZED ANTAL'S LEFT HAND with tight swaddling and threatened a cast if Antal refused to give the hand a rest. On Monday Antal's parents told him and Katalin to stay home from school, for several days if necessary. No one wanted to answer questions about Sándor. Antal also found himself fending off questions about Márta. For now, it was easy enough with the neighbors, much harder with his family. His father had been making phone calls to Officer Kenez. There was no news.

In the bedroom, around the apartment, Sándor's things were everywhere. Antal left them alone. He tried to remember what Sándor had taken with him to the radio station. Maybe only his sheet music. Or maybe his journal as well. It wasn't on the desk where he had left it.

By Thursday Antal still had not returned to school. That afternoon, unable to play violin, he lay on his bunk reading. His mother peered through the door.

"There's someone here to talk to us," she said. "A Mrs. Messik."

Antal slid from the bunk and rushed to the living room. There the Hanáks' friend sat on the sofa next to Katalin. She greeted him with a tired smile. He sat down on the piano bench while his mother and grandfather pulled up chairs.

"You have word of Sándor?" Grandpapa asked.

"He's safe," Mrs. Messik said. "He's out of the country."

Though the others stared in confusion, Antal nodded.

"The Hanáks had plans to leave the country early Sunday morning," Mrs. Messik explained. "On Saturday night they stayed with some friends across the ring boulevard from here. The hostess, Mrs. Cseh, came to see me on Sunday. She told me about what had happened the night before. The terrible story."

"Awful," Katalin interjected.

"Sándor protected Márta," Mrs. Messik said. "The two of them managed to get to the Csehs' home. So now the Hanáks are protecting Sándor. They left the country early Sunday, and he went with them. When I heard about all this, I wanted to come right over here and tell you, but they asked me to wait until they truly were out." Mrs. Messik handed a paper to Mother. "This morning I received a telegram from Livia. Here it is."

They passed the message around. Antal was last to see it.

SAFE IN SALZBURG WITH VARGA RELATIVE -STOP- TELL HIS FAMILY

Safe. And gone. Antal's fist closed around the telegram.

"Salzburg?" Grandpapa asked.

"Code. It's really Vienna. But—" Mrs. Messik tapped her lips with her finger. "You have to keep this confidential. They leave soon, probably for a refugee camp, perhaps in Bavaria. They don't know for how long. After that, America, they hope."

"America," Grandpapa uttered, and Mother and Katalin sat in silent misery.

"Sándor is safe," Mrs. Messik repeated gently, "though it may not be safe for him to write to you, if he's a wanted man here."

Antal could no longer hold back. "Did Sándor do it? Did he pull the trigger?"

"I don't know, Antal. Mrs. Cseh said Sándor himself was very upset and wouldn't speak of what happened. And all Márta would say was that he protected her."

Antal went to the kitchen to take an aspirin. As he was swallowing it, Mrs. Messik came in. She opened her handbag and gave him a folded paper. "Mrs. Cseh brought me this. For you. Márta only had a minute to write, but here it is." She quietly left the kitchen.

Antal shook the note open.

Oh, Antal, what a hard ending this is. I love you, and I could have loved you the rest of my life. I will never forget you.

Antal stumbled, blind with anguish, to the bedroom. He leaned against the bunkbed post, re-reading Márta's note, longing to hold her, knowing that he could have loved her through the years just as she loved him, worried that maybe—maybe—she was pregnant, desolate that he couldn't go to her, wrapped in a fear and sorrow heavier than any he'd ever known.

Lifting his eyes, he saw Sándor's guitar in the corner. The one friend who would have understood, back before the world crumbled, was gone. Sándor would not return. It wasn't safe. Even if it were, Sándor would not return. Antal knew it. Sándor would do what he himself would have done: he would follow Márta.

CHAPTER FIFTY-SEVEN

Return to the Light

March 23, 2007

"**A**ND WHEN EVERYTHING WAS OVER,**"** VARGA told Father Barnabás, "Sándor was gone, and Márta was gone."

"Your closest confidantes," the priest observed.

"Yes."

"You must have felt very alone."

Varga inclined his head. It was a relief to be understood.

After a silence, Father Barnabás asked, "And did you feel betrayed?"

"It wasn't their fault."

"That's true, but you said you needed to forgive Sándor. What was his offense?"

"Really, he didn't do anything wrong."

"You say that as a mature, charitable man. But you were a seventeen-year-old boy then, and that's the person who was hurt."

Varga sat in stillness and waited while that boy within him said *yes*.

The priest bent forward, and below his clerical collar a silver cross shifted. "Your life changed that night," he said. "Although Márta didn't mean to, she gave you loneliness. And Sándor didn't mean to, but he gave you anger, yes?"

Varga blinked as faded images of Márta and Sándor rose before him. "Yes."

"And you had no communication with either of them after that?"

"Over all the years I heard from Márta only twice, Sándor not at all." Varga glanced down at his wrinkled hands, and something occurred to him. "Except that their granddaughter came last summer. And found me."

With as few words as possible, conserving his breath, Varga told him about Lisa's visit, and the music, and her questions, and her correspondence with Kristóf.

"Antal, my brother," the priest said, "the arrival of their granddaughter was a gift. Can you consider that perhaps that terrible night was not the end of the story?"

Varga considered, and breathed in deeply, and felt stronger. "It wasn't the end."

"Is there anything else you'd like to tell me?"

Varga looked around the room at all the pieces of his life here: his violin in its case, the piano, the photo of Ildi, even the basket of Kristóf's laundry in the corner. This was all a gift, too. Anything else to tell the priest? Only a question.

"The granddaughter, Lisa, has been asking for the story," he said. "Because her grandparents didn't tell it. And I didn't want to tell her, either, because the story is hard. And because telling her means telling Kristóf, because he would have to translate it for her. But he's been asking, too. They both want to know. Do you think I should tell them?"

"Are they strong?"

Varga weighed it, thought of Lisa's kindness to Kristóf, of Kristóf's yearning to know his son. "I think they are. They're sad, too, but stronger than I knew."

"Then maybe you ought to tell them. Sometimes truth is hard, but not as hard as silence. And perhaps this story is being redeemed."

Varga felt soreness in his body, clouded weariness in his mind, but he said, "Redeemed. Let me see. Long ago I wrote a suite based on the music we wrote, Sándor and Márta and I. And the suite ended badly. On purpose. Because our story ended so badly. But then Lisa came with her questions, and I re-opened the music." He winced and rubbed his chest. "I'm almost finished revising it. And now I remember that Lisa sent a possible ending for it. I'll look at that."

"And will your family hear the new version?"

"I think . . ." Varga breathed. "Halmos wants to gather some musician friends . . . to play it for my family. When they come at Easter."

"And this new ending, will it tell them your heart is at peace?"

"I hope it tells them I want their hearts to be at peace."

"God give you strength for this task, then. Would you like to receive the Eucharist now?"

"Yes. Please."

The priest opened his book and said some sacred words that Varga didn't quite catch. He prayed with his hand over Varga's head. Then he opened a box he'd brought. He spoke of the body and blood of Christ, broken and poured out for us, and served Varga the sacrament. Varga felt the wafer on his tongue and tasted peace.

As FATHER BARNABÁS PACKED UP THE CASE AGAIN, Kristóf and Halmos arrived. Halmos drove the priest back to the rectory, then returned. Feeling a little stronger, Varga sat down with Halmos at the piano as Kristóf cooked dinner.

"Let's see if we can finish this thing," Varga said. "Take a look at what Lisa sent."

Halmos sorted through the music, found the sheet Lisa had notated, and set it on the piano's music stand. Varga adjusted his glasses and read it. She'd copied out the first half-page of "Song to Our Enemies," the old 1945 version he'd never finished. Beneath the staves she had written some English lyrics he couldn't read. Now he recalled she'd asked permission to use a saying from the Bible so her students could sing it. The song was certainly short. Maybe she intended to add some variations.

Wait, no, the music went on. After the lyrics stopped, Lisa had written "cello." That must be the English for *cselló*. There followed four lines of what looked like a cello solo cadenza.

"Let me try this out," Varga said, and Halmos brought him his violin.

Adjusting the octave, he began playing Lisa's cadenza, picturing her sitting with the cello, her strong fingers moving and her face intent—like her grandmother. Varga felt Lisa's music in his own hands on the violin strings. The cadenza pulsed like the lifeblood that had coursed through Sándor and Márta and now flowed on in Lisa. His own breath and spirit moved in the music, not burdened by sad feebleness, but vigorous like Kristóf and joyful like Misha.

When the music ended, it was just beginning, for it hinted the opening notes of "The Light Shines."

"Good Lord," Halmos exclaimed. "That's it."

"It's like what you thought I should do," Varga said. "Go back and connect the opening."

Halmos helped him write the connecting revisions into the suite. Just before the crossed-out drum crash, they notated a *ritardando* in the music, then added Lisa's cello cadenza.

"Wait a minute," Varga said. "It's Lisa's music. Should we be inserting it into mine?"

"I have a feeling she'd be honored. We'll add her name to the manuscript."

"All right, then. On we go."

Where the cadenza ended, Varga instructed Halmos to write the old, unadorned theme of "The Light Shines," with the first violin on the melody, lower register. Halmos nodded, and they worked through bringing in flute, then second violin, piano and finally cello again.

"Some legato eighth notes," Varga said, "and some movement in the bass. Harmonically, let's keep it simple. After all that this piece and I have been through."

Halmos made suggestions. Varga agreed to them all. He was tired and he trusted Halmos.

"And at the end," Halmos said, "maybe we'll have the violins and flute drop out."

Varga lifted his pencil and ended the piece on piano and cello, three soft chords.

As Halmos played the last few measures, Kristóf came in and stood next to the piano, a wine glass in his hand. "Don't you two ever want to eat? The food was ready a long time ago."

Varga looked up. "Krisz, the suite is finished."

Kristóf raised his glass and grinned.

THAT NIGHT VARGA WOKE AT ONE IN THE MORNING, and after lying awake for too long, he rose and went to his bedroom desk. He took out paper and a pen and with some strain pulled the desk lamp close. Unsure how well he could speak the 1945 story to Kristóf, he began writing it out, working slowly because his hand tended to tremble. He told Kristóf about the radio concert and the drunken soldiers, about Kholodenko's death and how they never knew for sure whether it was Sándor who pulled the trigger.

If he did, I have no doubt he was trying to protect Márta. Then they were gone, Márta and her family and Sándor, and the loss was terrible. I hope you will understand I didn't want to explain all this to Lisa, especially since her own grandparents had not told her. But you know her better than I do, and if you think it best to tell her

His hand hurt, and sitting up had become painful. Well, he would finish this tomorrow. He turned the letter face down and carefully made his way back to bed.

IN THE MORNING KRISTÓF HELPED HIM RISE AND WALK to the bathroom, then helped him back to bed. Varga needed more rest but didn't want to lie down, so Kristóf propped pillows and helped him sit up. He brought coffee and set it on the nightstand.

"I cooled it a little for you, Ópa. Do you want anything else?"

Varga didn't know what to say. *This damned muddle-headedness.*

"Music?" Kristóf asked.

"Yes."

"What would you like?"

"Maybe—let's see—that Dvořák piece I used to play with Ildi."

"I don't remember you playing Dvořák with Óma."

Varga's vision blurred. Where were his glasses? And what was Kristóf doing? Or was it Zoltán? Something with the CD player. The *New World Symphony* started playing.

Zoltán—or whoever it was—moved the coffee cup closer to him. "Anything else?"

"No, no, you may go. Thanks."

"Call me if you need me."

Varga sat listening to the music. He looked at the cup on the nightstand. He didn't really want the coffee, but maybe he'd drink some because it was nice of Zoltán to bring it. Or was it Sándor? Varga reached for the cup—

Dropped it—oh, no—

It crashed to the floor— what a mess—he tried to reach it—

His shoulder slammed on something—the floor—and someone was running—

"Ópa!"

Varga's arms hurt and his chest hurt and his back and his neck, and someone was grasping him. He tried to speak but could not.

"ÓPA, I'M HERE, HOLD ON."

Kristóf hoisted his grandfather onto the bed. God, how limp he was.

"Ópa!"

There was only silence.

Kristóf pressed Ópa's neck but—oh, Christ, no—couldn't feel a pulse. He put his fingers under Ópa's nostrils and felt no breath. Kristóf ripped back the pajama shirt and laid his ear against Ópa's chest. God damn that music, he couldn't hear! He listened again, harder, and frantically began chest compressions. The minutes passed. No. *Jaj, nem.* No.

Kristóf kicked aside the broken cup shards on the floor. He sank down on the edge of the bed and sat vigil with his grandfather, his hand on Ópa's motionless chest. *Jaj, nem.*

CHAPTER FIFTY-EIGHT

Go

March 25, 2007

LISA HAD JUST FINISHED DRESSING FOR CHURCH when her phone rang. She grabbed it off her nightstand. "Hello?"

A lag; then, "Lisa. Kristóf here."

"Kristóf?" He had never telephoned before, only called on Skype. "Are you all right?"

The connection crackled.

"My grandfather died," he said. "Yesterday in the morning."

"Oh, no." She sat down on the bed. "Oh, Kristóf."

His words came haltingly as he told her he'd brought Ópa his morning coffee, helped him sit up, and left the bedroom to make breakfast. "But then I hear the cup breaking on the floor. I run back, Ópa's heart is stopped, his breath is stopped." Kristóf said something in Hungarian, then, "Our family, we thought we had more time. We said Easter, my father, my aunt, everyone would come for Easter, even Ópa said Easter. But then Friday, here comes his friend Halmos bringing a priest. And I wanted to scream, 'No! This is not the end!' But it was."

Lisa swallowed down the tight ache that rose in her throat. The room was dim, the world dark, Antal Varga dead. "Is anyone there with you?" she asked.

"My father. Soon as I called him yesterday, he came on the first train. He sat by Ópa's side, then he called the—oh, what is the word—ah, graveyard. Tomorrow his wife will come, and later my aunt from Switzerland and her family."

"When is the funeral?"

"Wednesday. Just the family at the grave. But first of April is a concert of his suite. At the music academy, a public remembering of him. His friend Halmos leads this."

"The suite," she said. "I wish I could be there."

"Oh, God, I wish this, too. It isn't just his music, it's your music, and your grandparents' music, and—" Kristóf's voice cut, came back in rough. "And I just wish you are here. All is so fucked up. My grandfather, he made the difference between things good or things bad. And this apartment, it's my *lakas* now, my house, home, but without him, it's just, I don't know the English words, all is blank, do you understand?"

Yes, she understood. Her old house had been so horridly blank after Jake left, and now this apartment was nothing but walls and a smoke alarm. "I know what you mean."

"And other things," Kristóf went on. "Misha's mother still is telling me, 'Sign the papers, sign the papers.' Also I go to a work interview this week. I wrote the paperworks for a Lufthansa job, and I thought I would wait a long time, but already they called me. So I have to present myself and act like I am the person they need, happy and smart and calm, and that is ridiculous, completely a joke—"

"You *are* smart."

"I'm not so sure." The phone reception clouded. When it cleared, Kristóf was talking about what to do with his grandfather's things. "It's terrible. My father, he came, he helped, he was holding himself so strong, then he—eh—he broke down just folding Ópa's glasses. This is the way it is."

It was the way of grief. "Yes."

"Lisa," Kristóf went on, "also I found something Ópa wrote for me, and for you, too. It's about your grandparents, when they left."

Lisa wiped her tear-damp cheek with her thumb. After all this time, an answer?

"I'll try to translate it for you," he said, "but it might take a long time, and—" The connection blurred and hissed. "Damned telephone. I wish you are here."

"I wish it, too," she said.

"I really wish you are here, very much I wish."

"You do?"

"Oh, God, yes."

Be ready to go.

"Listen. Kristóf." She hesitated, wiped her cheek again. "Maybe I could come."

"What?"

"Maybe it would work. The first week of April is my school's spring break. And I have a little money from selling my wedding ring." She took an anchoring breath. "Maybe I could come for the concert. And then stay that week. If you want. If it would help."

"Yes. Yes. Please."

By dinnertime that evening, Lisa had arranged with the principal to take the day after spring break off. She'd lined up a substitute and ordered her flight tickets. She began making a packing list: a dress for the concert, her plan book for writing lessons on the flight home, her Hungarian phrasebook, her journal, Advil.

Pen in hand, she thought of the little metal box in her bedroom closet. The time had come. Surrendering, she wrote, *Alexander's ashes.*

EARLY ON THE MORNING OF SUNDAY, APRIL 1, Lisa wearily found her way to the Ferihegy Airport baggage claim and pulled her suitcase off the carousel.

"Lisa!" a familiar voice shouted. "Lisa!"

She turned. "Kristóf!"

Amid the crowd, he hugged her, his touch sad. "It's good you came."

That afternoon, after she'd managed a couple hours of sleep, she and Kristóf walked up Andrássy Avenue to what was called the old music academy. A few blocks from the main academy, it hosted some student events, and Kristóf said that the small recital hall here was the best venue that had been available today on short notice. Lisa climbed the stairs with him and they entered the hall. It was a serviceable space, but plain: a scratched wood floor, audience chairs with green cushions, a stage backed by green sound panels, and on the upper wall behind it, an old sepia scene of gods and goddesses in the clouds. On stage, four chairs had been placed near a grand piano. At the side of the room a table was set with coffee and tea.

Lisa sat in the front row with Kristóf and with family members she'd met on the way in: his father and new stepmother, and an aunt named Gabriella and her family. Zoltán and Erzsi didn't speak much English, and Lisa wished she knew more Hungarian. Today Kristóf's translations seemed rough and incomplete.

The hall filled, and soon every seat was occupied and people stood at the back. Kristóf told Lisa that the audience members were his grandfather's colleagues, former students, neighbors, and friends, and probably a few strangers who just wanted to hear the music. The audience grew quiet as the musicians walked onstage. Two violinists, a cellist and a flute player took their places. A man with thin white hair stood beside the piano and turned to the audience.

Kristóf leaned close to Lisa. "My grandfather's friend. Halmos."

Mr. Halmos began to speak. Among his Hungarian words, Lisa heard the name *Varga Antal* and a few sentences later *Varga Sándor* and *Hanák Márta*, and then *Denman Lisa*. She turned to Kristóf in surprise. He smiled and nodded. Halmos continued speaking. Lisa recognized *háború*, the word for war. He said a little more, choked up, stopped, then quickly finished. After a bow, he sat down at the piano.

The piano began with three soft bass chords. One by one the other instruments entered. The melody lifted; harmonies opened.

In the swells and reaches, in the pulse of pain and longing, Lisa discerned echoes of the old Varga music. It drew her, swept her in. *The light shines in the darkness. The darkness has not overcome it.* Lisa closed her eyes to see past the darkness. *Csendes éj, stille nacht, silent night. Heavenly peace.* Yes, peace. If only. *May God spare you further pain. May it never, no, no, never, be this way for you again.* No, no, never. Please, never. *The love of a good mother never dies.* Oh, how Lisa knew it. She would love Alexander the rest of her life.

The violins led into a tender melody Varga had spun from the Dvořák romanza. It was unbearable beauty. The music flowed on, now singing the song to enemies. The flute stopped. The piano faded. The violins hushed. But the cello pushed forward, flooding the hall with—what? Her cadenza?

Kristóf whispered, "You wrote this part, yes?"

She nodded. Yes, she'd written it the night Kristóf asked what she did with her fire. It was the ember that burst into flame, and now it leapt bright. It circled, wrapping the final notes of the cadenza into glowing chords.

But that chord series: it wasn't hers. She leaned forward, spellbound. Varga must have written that part, the last music of his life. In the darkness of loss, the light shone. Lisa blinked back tears.

The musicians did not bow but left the stage quietly. The audience held silence until the Varga family rose, Lisa with them, and went into the hallway. Mr. Halmos joined them there. Kristóf's Aunt Gabriella gathered the family around. Wiping her eyes, she asked Halmos a question in Hungarian; he answered, and there was a discussion among the family. Lisa heard her name and saw them glance at her.

Kristóf told her, "Halmos explained to them about the part you wrote, how it helped Ópa make a new ending."

Gabriella smiled at her. "Thank you, Lisa," she pronounced in careful English. "What you did, this was right, this was good."

MANY WHO HAD ATTENDED THE CONCERT CAME to the refreshments table and spoke with Kristóf and his family, and he introduced Lisa to some of them. A priest named Father Barnabás knew enough English to tell her he had respected Antal Varga and his wife. Kristóf's great-uncle Péter, who spoke no English, clasped her hand warmly and smiled. Most of the older people didn't stay long. As they began to depart, Lisa waited while Kristóf helped walk them down the stairs.

She lost track of him for a while but then spotted him several feet away. A woman about fifty, with hair so black it had to be dyed, spoke intently to him. The woman pulled a tissue from her purse, dried her eyes, and went on talking. Lisa watched Kristóf's troubled face as he shook his head, nodded, shrugged. The woman hugged him and he patted her back awkwardly. Maybe this was his mother.

Jet-lagged in mind and body, Lisa helped herself to another cup of coffee. Nearby, an attractive woman slightly younger than herself stirred sugar into a cup. Their eyes met.

"You are with Kristóf?" the woman asked.

"I'm a distant cousin of his."

The pretty woman cocked her head, perhaps not understanding the English words.

"You know the Varga family?" Lisa asked, speaking slower.

"My name is Zsófi. My boyfriend, name is Feri, he is there." She tipped a finger toward a guy whose back was turned. "Feri is Kristóf's friend. Once I was with Kristóf, his girlfriend, but not still."

"Ah."

"He had many girlfriends, maybe still he has many girlfriends, foreign women, always changing, I don't know. I hope he is okay. With his grandfather he was very . . ." She put her hands together, indicating closeness.

"Yes, I know."

Lisa reached for a napkin and excused herself. She went and sat with Erzsi, who was a comforting presence even though they couldn't converse. Not far off Kristóf stood, strikingly handsome in a gray jacket, talking with Mr. Halmos. Many girlfriends, always changing, the woman named Zsófi had said. This weighed on Lisa and she hoped it was an exaggeration. But maybe that other woman, Misha's mother, would have said the same thing.

BY SUPPERTIME AUNT GABRIELLA AND HER FAMILY had left for the airport, and Zoltán and Erzsi had left for the train station. Kristóf heated up something called *lecsó* that Erzsi had made the day before, a kind of ratatouille with sausage in it. Lisa sliced bread and set it on the table. She'd changed into her jeans after the concert, wishing she could put on her pajamas, reminding herself she was in a man's apartment and she'd better not. Uneasily she remembered what the woman named Zsófi had said today.

Kristóf set out glasses and a bottle of red wine. "It's Kékfrankos," he said. "One of Ópa's favorites." He poured it, his eyes narrowing as he watched the glasses fill, and something in that look reminded Lisa of the woman who'd hugged him.

"Was that your mother you were talking with?" she asked as they sat down for supper. "The black-haired lady?"

"Yes. My father told her Ópa died, so she came."

"Were you glad she came?"

"I don't know. I was glad she honored Ópa. God knows he deserved that."

"I'm sure she came mostly for you."

Kristóf lifted his glass. "To Ópa's memory," he said quietly.

"To his memory."

Lisa raised her glass and clinked his. She tasted the wine and the *lecsó*, liking both, wishing she had a better appetite.

"My mother wants to see me before she leaves," he said. "I meet her on Wednesday."

"I hope that's good?"

"We will see."

"Kristóf, I know it was terrible that she took off and left, but at least she apologized. I wish my husband would apologize to me. But I doubt that he ever will."

He looked soberly at her. "Ah."

When he had finished eating and she hadn't, he asked, "You have what you need for tonight? The bedroom is comfortable, I hope?"

"Yes. Thanks." She laid down her fork. This wouldn't be easy. "Um, I need to ask you—I mean, I think it's okay for us to be direct with each other, right?"

He raised his eyebrows, surprised, perhaps confused. "Okay."

"At the academy today, I talked with someone named Zsófi."

"Yeah?"

Lisa dropped her gaze. "One time on Skype we talked, you and I, about our past . . . our past lives, and—I mean, we both got an early start with sex, I don't know how else to say it. But I'm not casual about it now." She blushed but looked at him, saw him looking back at her seriously. "Do you understand?"

"Yeah."

"Okay. But this Zsófi, she said you go from woman to woman."

He fingered his glass stem. The refrigerator whirred. Somewhere a motorcycle roared.

"I wish I could tell you this isn't true," he said. "What she said is not so true as it used to be, but also not a lie. This is not something I am proud about."

"Well." Having waded in this far, she pushed on. "It makes me feel strange about staying in your apartment."

"No. Lisa. No. Don't feel strange." He seemed even more embarrassed that she was, if that was possible. "When you tell someone something that you don't say to others, what's the word for it?"

"Do you mean, confiding in someone?"

"Yes. In the world I confided in two people, you and Ópa, and now Ópa is gone."

Lisa nodded, knowing. "I used to confide in my grandparents," she said. "And they're gone. And I confided in Jake, and he's gone, too. Now you're the friend who listens."

His brown eyes gazed anxiously at her. "I don't want, ever, that we don't trust each other."

"Neither do I." She blinked, not wanting to cry. "Oh, crap, Kristóf. You've had things so hard, and I'm a jet-lagged wreck."

Gently, cautiously, he patted her hand. "Go to bed whenever you want to. Don't worry, I won't come with you."

She laughed—it felt good to laugh—and took a swallow of wine.

Chapter Fifty-Nine

With Lisa

April 2, 2007

K RISTÓF NEEDED TO MOVE MORE PERMANENTLY into this apartment that was supposed to be his now, and the next morning Lisa helped him with it. She boxed up Ópa's clothes and shoes, which he'd dreaded doing. After she emptied the closet and dresser, he hung up and put away his own clothes. Then, bracing himself, he went into the bathroom and threw out Ópa's old razor, toothbrush, pill bottles, and the muscle salve he'd used after long violin sessions. The salve smelled like Ópa, and Kristóf was hit with a fresh onslaught of grief.

Lisa helped him crate up Ópa's books as well. Kristóf replaced them with his own language texts from university, German novels he'd read for classes, a few English and French novels he intended to read for practice, books on hiking the Alps and touring Italy cheap, his old dreams. It had been so long since he'd dreamed.

Lisa sat cross-legged on the Turkish carpet, sorting through music books and manuscripts on the bottom shelf. "Here's a bunch of your grandfather's compositions," she said.

"Yeah, for Aunt Gabriella. She forgot to take them."

Lisa held up one of the music sheets. "This one has your name on it."

"I know. He wrote that when I was born."

Kristóf ended up sitting beside her on the carpet. He stretched out his legs and told her his early memories: running up Ópa's stairs, hearing his violin, singing solfege with him for jelly bears. He told Lisa about doing jelly-bear solfege again last month with Misha. She listened, her hair catching light from the window.

They worked through the day. Whenever Kristóf turned his head or heard footsteps or walked into a room, in a forgetful split-second he would expect to see Ópa. Then with a slam he'd remember. He said something about it to Lisa, and she seemed to understand.

That night after dinner, she taught him a board game she'd brought in her suitcase. It was something named after an old Beatles song and involved building little train routes across an American map. At some point, they started laughing.

One of Ópa's CDs played in the background. "What's the music?" Kristóf asked, testing her the way Ópa used to test him.

"Copland," she said. "*Appalachian Spring*."

"Right." He went and changed the CD to Hungarian alternative rock. "Now what's playing?" he asked as he returned to the table.

She laughed. "I haven't the faintest idea."

"Quimby."

"Oh, of course. How could I forget a band I've never heard of."

"Well, you're in Hungary so you have to remember it now."

"Will do." She gestured to the game board. "Now sit back down so I can beat you."

He sat down. What a mercy that she was here. If she weren't, he might be out getting drunk. He couldn't tell her how badly she was needed.

THE NEXT MORNING KRISTÓF DRESSED IN HIS ONE SUIT, put on a necktie, and reported to the main Lufthansa desk at the airport. A woman about his mother's age, Frau Zimmer, escorted him into an office with posters of Venice, Copenhagen, and Neuschwanstein on the walls. He had already taken written language tests for German, French, and English. In spite of the mistakes he'd been making in conversations with Lisa, Frau Zimmer said he'd tested well. She told him she'd conduct the interview in German because they needed attendants for flights to Germany.

Frau Zimmer looked over his resume and began with what he'd

expected, asking why he wanted to be a flight attendant for Lufthansa. He gave her the answers he'd prepared: at the restaurant he'd become good at customer service, and Lufthansa was a strong company, no doubt a good employer. He didn't tell her he would have preferred working for Malév, the Hungarian airline, if he were sure it wouldn't fold.

She smiled and thanked him. "And of course in this kind of work you'll often be away from home, away from family. Is that a problem?"

He shook his head and stated the new reality: "I live alone."

Frau Zimmer checked something off on her paperwork. "All right. Let's talk about stress on the job. Sometimes passengers get angry. How would you deal with that?"

He considered. In the restaurant, if he needed to, he'd thrown out louts and drunks. Here, he had no recourse. "In the airport or on a plane," he said, "people are probably tired and worried. I think the main thing in dealing with them is to stay calm."

But people like Zsófi, Blanka, and his mother wouldn't say he was calm. They'd borne the brunt of his temper. Kristóf glanced at the Copenhagen poster, trying to formulate a truthful comment. "My grand-father was a professional musician. He couldn't afford to be nervous, and he sometimes said that if he acted calm, he would feel calmer. A good example, I think."

She agreed. When she asked if he'd ever dealt with an emergency, he told her he'd performed the Heimlich maneuver on a customer. Twice he'd helped customers who'd fainted. Once when he was filling in for the manager, he'd dealt with a burst pipe and the kitchen flooding. After a pause, Kristóf told her he'd called an ambulance when his grandfather had a heart attack.

Frau Zimmer thanked him and looked over her notes. "So, Herr Varga, what would you consider to be your main strength, coming to Lufthansa?"

Strength? He should have prepared an answer for such an obvious question. There was his language training, but she already knew about that. What came to mind again was his grandfather. Well, and Halmos, and Uncle Péter, and the elderly friends at Ópa's concert.

"I suppose," he said, "I've learned to look out for old people. I watch and make sure they can get in and out of their seats, and manage stairs, and carry things. Not that all older people need help, they're strong in their own way, and I don't underestimate them—" He broke off, not at all sure if this was what the woman wanted.

But she looked at him thoughtfully. "I've never heard an applicant say that before. That's helpful. Very helpful." She made a note. "And what do you consider your main weakness?"

Weakness. Ugh. Zsófi had tried to tell him, and he was no longer blind to it: he'd been alone, refusing to trust, guarding his loyalties as though the faintest tremor could shatter them.

He told her the truth. "I'm not at my best on my own. I want to be part of a good crew."

"We have excellent crews. I'm glad you want to work with others." She smiled. "I'd like you to come in for a second interview next week."

He shook the woman's hand. He'd tell Lisa.

Riding the bus home, he calculated he had five days remaining with her. Sunday night she'd fly out. That meant that on Monday this city would be flat-out blank.

The bus churned along Üllői Street. Kristóf pulled out his phone and called Halmos, who had connections. "I was just wondering," Kristóf said, "is there some place, some school, that needs an English-speaking music teacher?"

"You mean Lisa?" Halmos asked.

"Yes."

"And does Lisa want this? A job here?"

Chagrined, Kristóf leaned against the window and said he didn't know but he hoped so.

"Let me think about it," Halmos said. "Your grandfather would have hoped so, too."

WHEN KRISTÓF TOLD LISA THAT LUFTHANSA wanted a second interview, she shouted, "Yes!" and slapped his palm with her own.

That night she opened her Hungarian language book, and he helped her with a chapter using family words: son, *fiú*; daughter, *lány*; child, *gyermek*. They practiced the words, but the talk shifted to English. It turned to Misha. Then it shifted again to Lisa's miscarriages and especially the child she'd thought would live, the one she'd named and, for a few minutes, held.

"Both of us," she said, "we're parents, and we're not."

"Other people don't understand, I think."

"No."

He thought of his mother, whom he'd see the next day, who was also a parent and also not. Kristóf reached for Lisa's hand, because she understood what other people didn't, and because she was with him when other people weren't, and because in this hard, soiled world, there was still something about her that was soft and untarnished. When he touched her hand, she clasped his, and for a long time neither of them let go.

In the morning, Halmos called and said the American international school would need a music teacher next fall. He offered to drive Lisa there and give her a tour.

Kristóf yelled, "Lisa! Want to see the international school's music classes?"

"Okay," she yelled back from the bedroom.

So far, so good.

KRISTÓF WAS AWARE, AS HE SAT in Művész Coffee House with his mother, that he'd never replied to her plea for forgiveness. The morning overcast showed through the arched window behind her. He stirred his espresso.

"Thank you for coming to Ópa's memorial," he said. "The concert."

"When Zoltán told me, I had to come. I always thought so well of your grandfather." She picked at her walnut *bejgli* roll. "And I wanted to see you. I'm glad you said yes."

Kristóf nodded. He'd learned what it was like to want to see a son and hear *no*.

"How are you, Kristóf?"

"I miss Ópa."

"I've been concerned for you, losing him. He always was strong in your life." She hesitated. "Even when your father and I weren't."

Nothing would be easy if his mother kept going in this vein. "I'm all right," he said. "My cousin Lisa is here from America."

"That helps for now."

"Yes."

"Maybe you could visit your father more often. His new wife seems, eh, nice. Right?"

"She is."

Was this a new generosity in her, to give credit to another woman who'd stepped in? Sad traces of her old beauty showed in her brown eyes.

"Or you could come to Stuttgart," she said.

Travel to Stuttgart could be worked out if he got the job with Lufthansa, but he wasn't ready to raise her hopes. "For now I'm just trying to settle into the apartment," he said.

"Oh." She set aside her plate with the half-eaten pastry. "About a month ago your grandfather wrote to me, urged me not to stop trying to see you. He said you'd been going through something difficult."

The difficult thing, Kristóf knew, was Misha.

"Your grandfather didn't say what it was," she said. "But he told me you understand more about how people can handle things badly and lose out, and then later want what they'd lost. That's me, Kristof."

"I understand," he murmured, because now he did.

"For a long time," she said, "I was distressed over my mistakes because I loved you and I missed you and I wanted you back. That's still hard. But lately what's hardest is when I think of what it must have been like for you when I left. Feeling like your mother didn't care." She lowered her eyes, dark with mascara and regret. "Feeling abandoned. Is there any way for me to undo that?"

"I think you're trying to undo it now," he said. Maybe in some way, so was he.

"I'm glad I heard your grandfather's suite again," she said. "The ending used to be so abrupt, so harsh. But he rewrote it, made it kinder, I guess. I wish I could do that with us."

He took a swallow of coffee, remembering what Lisa had said about her husband never apologizing. "At least you said you were sorry," he ventured. "You've tried." He couldn't look at his mother. "And I haven't."

"Some things take a long time."

"A long time, yes."

"Try to get some rest," she said. "Oh, and I almost forgot. I brought you a little something for your birthday."

Birthday. He kept forgetting. On the day he buried his grandfather, he turned thirty.

She reached into her big handbag and handed him a beribboned wine bottle. "A nice Spätburgunder for you."

At Christmas, she'd given him a too-small pullover. This German wine was a less personal gift, but at least it fit him. He'd share it with Lisa.

"*Finom*," he said. *Delicious*. "Thank you."

Kristóf paid the bill. He hadn't told her about Misha, not yet. Maybe the time would come. She hugged him and he kissed her cheek, which felt less firm than it used to. Her goodbye sounded melancholic. Probably so did his. He walked the short distance home, not certain he could call things good, but they were less bad, and something within him had eased.

As KRISTÓF PUNCHED IN THE CODE of the apartment house's street door, someone called out, "*Úr!* Varga *úr!*" He turned. It was one of the Gypsies that sometimes hung around next door, the one that sometimes talked to Ópa. The man approached and pulled off his red cap. "Kissing your hand," he said, "please, I haven't seen Antal *bácsi*. Did something happen?"

Kristóf clutched the door handle and settled his voice. "He died. His heart."

The man's face fell. "*Á, nem.* I'm sorry, *jaj.* We liked him."

"So did I," Kristóf said, and he excused himself before this got harder.

Entering the apartment, he saw that Lisa had not returned from her time with Halmos. He went out on the front balcony and smoked. If Lufthansa hired him, he'd have to quit this habit or be miserable during long flights; but for now, the cigarette helped unwind his nerves.

"Kristóf!"

Lisa waved to him from the street below. He threw aside the stub and ran down.

"Guess what?" she said. "This is so crazy! At that school, they offered me a job."

"Smart school!"

She told him about it as they walked up the stairs. Mr. Halmos introduced her to the American woman who taught elementary and middle school music. Lisa talked shop with the teacher, saw the music room and equipment, and sat in on a fifth-grade class. After that, Mr. Halmos introduced her to the principal.

"The principal asked lots of questions," Lisa said as they stepped through the apartment door. "Then I found out that the music teacher is leaving. And now that I add things up, I think Mr. Halmos took me there because they need to hire somebody."

"I hope you said yes."

She pulled off her coat. "I said I'd think about it, but wouldn't it be nuts, all of a sudden, to move across the world?"

"Your grandparents did it."

"Yeah, but—"

"Not 'Yeah-but.' You should come."

She laughed; but turning and looking at him, she suddenly stopped. "You're serious."

"Absolute serious."

She seemed a little flustered as she hung up her coat. God, how he wanted her to take that job, but he kept his mouth shut about it and set out lunch: cheese, bread, and Spätburgunder.

"My mother gave me the wine," he said as they sat down.

"How was it, seeing her?"

He tried to tell her about the conversation, the small, hesitant steps, the maybes. "She was sad, and I was sad, but not angry, at least there was this."

"Maybe it was the forgiveness she'd asked for?"

"I don't know." They sliced cheese, broke bread, poured wine.

"And you?" he asked. "With your mother? And your husband, you said you had to forgive him, too. But if you hate him, that makes sense to me."

She was quiet, bread in hand. "That time you and I talked on Skype, you said I was like a nun. Remember? You asked me what I did with my fire, and I didn't know how to answer."

He nodded, remembering her stricken bewilderment.

"Kristóf, I don't want to be a nun," she said now.

She sipped her Spätburger, and she was beautiful, the deep red of the wine at her lips, and her hair curling softly around her face. He didn't want her to be a nun, either.

"Afterward," she said, "I thought a lot about your question. I got out my journal and wrote letters to the people I was mad at. Not letters to send. Just letters to dump the crap onto paper instead of it tearing me up inside."

Kristóf waited, distressed that his question had upset her so.

"And after that," she said, "I wrote the new part to your ópa's suite. So I guess your question was what I needed."

"Then I'm glad I asked you."

"I brought the journal with me." She paused, fiddling with a bread crust. "Would you, do you think, would you like to read the letters?"

"Yes."

She brought out a small book from the bedroom and laid it open before him. "This page and the next few," she said, and left the room.

He read, hearing her voice through the angry sorrow. In her slanted American cursive, she had written *why* to a father who promised he'd come, and then didn't, and then died; *why* to a distant brother who never wrote to her; and *why* to a tough mother who became hardened. But the deepest *why* went to her husband, and in the letter to Jake, Kristóf saw his own name: *I told Kristóf that you're not an asshole, just weak. But maybe there's no real difference.*

Kristóf read on into a paragraph addressed to no one; it was Lisa's own cry.

Blessed are the poor in spirit, for theirs is the kingdom of heaven, Jesus said. Blessed are the bummed out and depressed and broken-hearted, because maybe you don't give the kingdom of heaven a moment's thought until you've been disappointed over and over, fighting off pain, crying in the hospital, keeping your son's ashes on a shelf, wondering where your husband is, trying to make do without him, wondering where God is, but it simply is not an option to make do without God because that would be like throwing away your own soul.

Kristóf reread the pages. *Depressed. Broken-hearted. Disappointed. Fighting off pain.* "*Jézus Mária,*" he murmured.

He closed the journal and went to the living room, where Lisa stood at the windows, her arms drawn in like a shy child.

"Lisa. You were so alone."

She eased closer to him. He took her into his arms, aware of her warmth and womanliness, aware that in these lonely months he had looked for her messages and awaited the Skype calls, knowing how in these days together he'd been longing to hold her, and he'd been afraid to.

He kept his touch gentle, chaste. "You're not alone," he said, and he wanted to tell her if she would just stay here, neither of them would be alone. But he did not know how much he could say; so he only spoke her name again and let her rest against him, her head on his shoulder.

LISA HAD SAID SHE WANTED TO GO SOMEWHERE with a view of the city, so the next day he took her on the walk up Gellért Hill. At the summit citadel, they stood by the low stone wall and looked out over the river cutting between Buda and Pest, between the castle and the Parliament house. They watched the barges, and she asked him what he was going to do about Misha.

The wind stirred and he clutched his jacket around him. "For so long I didn't want to think about it, said to hell with Blanka's questions, I would just take care of Ópa and look at the papers later. Now I have no excuses."

He told her what he'd known all along and what Uncle Péter had confirmed. "Misha needs to know I cared, I tried." The next words came hard. "And he needs the father that already he loves. I can't take care of him like Endre, and I am a stubborn asshole if I don't admit this. But I'm afraid, if I sign the papers, then Blanka will say, 'Good, now I have what I want,' and no more piano lessons, and I won't see him again ever."

"I don't want that for you, Kristóf. It's so hard to lose a child."

They began walking down the hill. On a path through the trees she said, "There's no way to make it easy, giving him up. But maybe—I don't know—here's something to think about. In America, when a mother gives up her baby for adoption, sometimes she writes the child a letter. Then it's kept with the adoption papers. Maybe if you wrote Misha a letter, he could read it when he comes of age."

"Why would Blanka give him the letter?"

"She wouldn't now. But maybe later. He'll probably ask about you."

The whole conversation had pained him, and he said little more. But farther down the hill when they reached the portico of St. Gellért, they took a selfie photo with the city stretching behind them, and maybe it was a memento of a decision made. He knew what he had to do.

KRISTÓF WROTE TO MISHA THAT NIGHT while Lisa read in the living room. She'd told him she'd stay up as long as it took him to write it. He kept Misha's kindergarten photo on the table and looked at it often. But Misha would be different when and if he ever read this letter. Kristóf tried to picture him tall and strong, playing rugby, jumping onto the Metro with friends, walking with a pretty girl. Kristóf wrote painstakingly, crossing out words, lines, paragraphs, rewriting until at ten-thirty he called it the best he could do.

Dear Misha,

I don't know how old you are as you read this letter, but tonight as I write it, you are almost six years old. At this point, I sometimes see you, but I don't know how long that will continue. I am your first piano teacher. I am also your biological father.

He went on to tell Misha how he'd found out belatedly that he had a son, and how he wished he'd known at age twenty-four what really mattered, and how much it meant to him that he'd met Misha.

Your grandfather and great-grandfather also met you. None of us wanted to let go. I had no idea how hard it would be to give you up. I'm sorry that I wasn't there to love you from the beginning. But I love you now.

I hope I can keep on teaching you piano. You have musical sense, and your great-grandparents Varga Antal and Ildikó gave you that. I hope I can keep seeing you. Even if that isn't possible, I'll make sure your mother's attorney always has my address and phone number. Please call me, find me. No matter what happens, I hope you will always be strong and happy. I will never forget you.

Your first father,
Varga Kristóf

Kristóf read the letter once more and called to Lisa. When she stood beside him, he signed the release form.

Lisa touched the letter, which of course she couldn't read. "Do you want to tell me what it says?"

A few words at a time, he translated it for her, sometimes stopping to calm his voice. At the end, spent, he folded his arms on the table and laid down his head. On his shoulder she placed her hand, and he grasped it tight. He had lost Ópa, he was about to lose Misha, and oh God but he wanted to keep this woman.

THE NEXT DAY WAS GOOD FRIDAY, A HOLIDAY. Kristóf and Lisa rode the

Metro to Kőbanya, the working-class district to the southeast where Misha lived. Kristóf carried the letter and the legal form in his jacket pocket. On the way, he told Lisa that Blanka had called to postpone Misha's piano lesson—for Monday, she said. "But I asked her if I could please come talk to her today. And give her the signed papers. So of course she said yes."

They left the Metro and walked four blocks to Misha's concrete communist-era apartment house. As they turned down the fifth-floor corridor, Misha pumped toward them on a scooter, wearing a cowboy hat.

"Kristóf *bácsi!* I learned the music you gave me, and you know what else? I remembered how to play the happy birthday song, like you showed me before." He flung a hand toward Lisa. "But who's this?"

"This is Lisa. She came all the way from cowboy country in America to hear you play 'Happy Birthday.' She speaks English. Can you say hi?" Kristóf said it again, giving Misha the pronunciation. "*Háj.*"

Misha laughed. "*Háj.*"

Lisa smiled. "Hi, Misha. *Szia.*"

The door opened. Blanka stood with her hand on the knob, her round belly prominent under a red sweatshirt. "Kristóf, I didn't know you were going to bring someone."

Hurriedly he introduced them. "Lisa wanted to meet Misha," he told Blanka in Hungarian. "Please. She doesn't speak much Hungarian, and if you're worrying that she'll tell people, don't."

"Tell people what?" Misha asked.

Kristóf shook his head. He had started this badly.

Lisa leaned close. "Tell Misha I want to hear him play piano. Then you can talk to Blanka."

Thank God Lisa could think fast. They stepped in the door, and Kristóf pointed Misha toward the keyboard. "Play for Lisa."

Blanka led Kristóf into the kitchen, where Endre cleared breakfast dishes from the table.

"Good morning," Endre said soberly.

They sat down together as the one-finger melody of the birthday song sounded from the living room. Hands sweating, Kristóf laid the form in front of them and pointed to his signature.

Endre looked up. "Thank you. I know this wasn't easy."

The birthday song repeated again and again. As Misha plunked out the melody, sometimes off rhythm, Lisa was filling in bass chords. Kristóf pulled out the sealed envelope with Misha's name on it and placed it on the table.

"What's this?" Blanka asked.

"Lisa told me that in America when mothers have to give a child up, they sometimes write a letter. For the child to read someday." He told Blanka, as he'd already told Endre, that Uncle Péter had said an adopted child needed to know that his biological father cared. "And I do care." Kristóf coughed, set his voice. "I'm relinquishing him. As you asked me to. But I have to ask you in return, when he wants to know, when he comes of age, tell him who I am. And let him read this. Please don't lose it."

Lips pressed together, Blanka blinked. Endre touched her shoulder. In the living room Misha was now carefully playing his assignment.

"I still want to teach him," Kristóf said. "I'll keep my mouth shut about who I am."

Blanka nodded. "Kristóf, thank you."

"We have to leave in a few minutes to visit his grandparents," Endre said. "But come back on Monday."

Kristóf had told the Lufthansa woman that it was possible to act calmer than you actually felt. He went to the living room to say goodbye. He wanted to hold Misha close, but it wasn't what a piano teacher would do. A handshake was the way his grandmother used to end every lesson. Kristóf clasped Misha's hand, no emotional display. He'd be back Monday.

"Good music, cowboy," he said. "I'll see you soon."

Misha faced him seriously. "Anyuka told me that Antal *bácsi* died."

"Yes."

"That's sad."

"I know." Just for an instant Kristóf hugged his son around the shoulders. "Goodbye," he said hoarsely.

On the Metro home, Lisa said he had done what he could, he had done right. Kristóf told himself he would see Misha in three days. At least there was Monday.

"It must hurt," Lisa said.

"It kills me."

She nodded. She knew.

WHEN THEY REACHED HOME AND WALKED through the building foyer, Lisa said, "You were going to tell me about something your grandfather wrote to you."

"Tomorrow. I'll read it tonight again, then tell you. It might be hard to translate."

It would also be hard to tell her.

Chapter Sixty

Easter

April 7, 2007

WITH HER LEGS PULLED UP UNDER HER, Lisa sat tightly at one end of the sofa, her thumb fidgeting on the handle of her coffee cup. Strains echoing the Dvořák romanza drifted from a CD of last Sunday's *Embers Suite* performance. It was a gray Saturday morning, and Kristóf sat near the lamp at the other end of the sofa, the light catching his hands and a letter from his grandfather. He had already translated most of it for her. It told of the old music group, and the siege, and the pressure on Grandma Márta's family. Some of the story Lisa had known or surmised, but its shadows now lengthened and deepened in the words Antal Varga wrote the night before he died.

Kristóf's forehead wrinkled as he perused the letter again. "Lisa, there's something more, maybe you don't know. Ópa loved your grandmother, your Márta."

The CD music crescendoed. Lisa's hands tightened around the coffee cup. "But did she love him back?"

"I'm not sure, I think so. He tried to keep her away from all what would hurt her, the dangers, the soldiers. But that was not possible always."

"No. Everything was so difficult, so brutal."

"He says the hardest was when Márta's little sister got sick and died."

Lisa nodded. The little grave in Kerepesi Cemetery.

"Ópa tried to . . . eh, tried to bear Márta's grief with her, but he says that maybe he didn't know how. But Sándor knew. His family was dead, so he knew." Kristóf turned to her with a look of troubled sympathy. "Ópa would see Márta and Sándor talking together, crying together, and he felt like these two people very close to him had a world that he was no part of it. He was sad. And jealous."

Lisa tried to take it in, this triangle of love and pain.

"And then he found out Márta had to leave forever," Kristóf said, "and Ópa was—oh, damn, what's the English—he was beside himself." Kristóf set aside the paper, as though he'd read this part of the story so many times he'd absorbed it. "And that night before Márta leaves, such chaos! Ópa and his sister and Sándor and Márta, they're attacked by a drunken mob, and a gun goes off. And a Soviet officer is dead."

Lisa's hand shook. Carefully she set her cup on the coffee table.

Kristóf looked at her closely, his dark eyes anxious. "Ópa says, the way the police wrote the report, Sándor had the gun."

Lisa's head swam hot. "Oh, no."

"But Ópa says, maybe it's not true. He knows for sure Sándor didn't own a gun. Also Ópa said that the witness was . . . *na* . . ." Kristóf picked up his English-Hungarian dictionary from the coffee table and searched for the word he needed. "Unreliable," he said at last.

It couldn't be. Lisa drew her knees up to her chest and laid her head on them. She closed her eyes against the vision of a scared young man with a gun, protecting the girl his cousin loved, maybe the girl that he himself loved silently.

From the CD player, a violin sang the opening lament of "Song to Our Enemies."

"Kristóf? Our grandfathers were cousins. And friends. Did they become enemies?"

"I don't know. But Ópa said when you came, when you made friends with us, you mended what was torn."

She lifted her head. "What did he mean?"

"I'm not sure what *he* meant. But for me, well, things would be like shit, like ashes, if you weren't here."

"I'm here and things *are* ashes."

"Not like they would have been." His voice was dead earnest, almost fierce. "Not for me."

Overwhelmed, Lisa looked at him. The window lamp light grazed his cheek, his jaw, his neck. All these months she'd seen him on Skype, a handsome but flattened image, like a model's photo in a magazine. But here he was, live and real, and if she just moved closer—

She dropped her gaze. "I have one more thing for you to translate."

Lisa went into the bedroom and returned with a letter that had been in the packet from Jake. She handed it to Kristóf and sat down beside him. "My grandmother wrote this to her sister Sarolta," she said. "It's dated 1948. I think that's the year my grandparents got married. The letter mentions your grandfather's name."

Kristóf took the yellowed letter and read it silently. A rumbling engine on the street below clashed with the song to enemies.

"This tells about why your grandmother married Sándor," he said.

"Okay." She bit her lip.

"All right, Márta says, 'Sándor loved me before we left Hungary, but I didn't pay attention. I loved Antal.'" Kristóf paused. "Then she says, eh, 'Sándor protected me on the terrible night before we left.' And she says she hates that memory, Sándor pulling a gun away from a drunkard, and the gun fires, and then the Soviet officer is dead."

"Kristóf. Stop." Lisa pulled in her breath. "So he did have the gun?"

Slowly Kristóf nodded.

"And then what?" Lisa asked.

"And then Márta says, 'I love Sándor because he loves me, and he always did.'" Kristóf laid the letter down.

Lisa bent her head, remembering her grandparents' strained silences. Did they wake at night hearing the gun? Seeing the man fall dead? Panting as though in terrified flight? Did they grieve over goodbyes they hadn't said? Did America ever really become their home, or was it just a hideout? And Antal Varga, did he grieve for them or curse them?

"They went through so much, and we didn't even know," Lisa said.

Kristóf put his arm around her. She leaned into his side, needing his warmth.

"This has hurt you," he said.

"If I had known—oh, Kristóf, if my family had known, if we had just understood."

He smoothed a lock of her hair. "Would it help? Really? This is hard knowledge. Maybe they didn't want to put that on your family. Like Ópa didn't want to put it on us."

She closed her eyes. From the CD player she heard the song to enemies—no, not to enemies this time, but to hurt lovers, to estranged and lonely cousins, to torn families.

"I can only hope it's true," she told Kristóf, "what your grandfather said. So much was torn, and I hope I helped to mend it."

"You did."

He reached both arms around her. She raised her face—maybe he would kiss her—

But he said, "You leave tomorrow night."

"Yes."

He looked away. "I don't want you to go."

Quiet in his arms, she didn't want to go, either.

LATE THAT NIGHT LISA WALKED WITH Kristóf by the Danube. A tragic line of bronze shoes stretched along the embankment as a memorial to the Jews that had been shot here during the siege—men's ankle boots, women's pumps, some containing notes or flowers people had left. A votive candle glowed on the pavement with a new pair of canvas baby shoes beside it. Lisa stopped. She would have bought shoes like that for Alexander if he had lived.

"Kristóf, tomorrow can we go to the cemetery?"

"Yes, good, I wanted to show you the grave."

He waited as though he sensed there was more. It was time to tell him. "I brought my little boy's ashes to scatter," she said.

"*Jaj*, Lisa. Of course."

They walked on, the Margit Bridge ahead of them, the clouded night overhead. Lights on the bridge reflected in the rippling water.

"I'll miss being here," she said, and then ventured, "I'll miss you."

Their pace slowed. He stopped and faced her. "Please work at the international school. And live here."

"I'd be lost here," she said. "I don't think like a European. I don't speak Hungarian."

"But I'd help you learn."

Three tipsy students passed them, laughing noisily. Kristóf scowled. "*Részegek*," he muttered and tugged on her hand. They walked farther north, onto the bridge and then down the slope into the park on Margit Island.

The park was quiet, with only couples remaining or small clusters of friends. Near the darkened zoo, Lisa and Kristóf sat down on a bench. Peacocks squawked in the distance. A streetlamp touched light to Kristóf's hair.

"I know this is not a small thing," he said, "you coming to a place where everything is different. But I wish you would stay." He looked away for a moment, turned back to her earnestly. "You make me more hopeful."

"You've been good for me, too."

She laid her hand over his as the truth of this sank in. Their messages back and forth about the music had kept her composing. His emails had eased her terrible loneliness. And then there were his questions over Skype. "You made me think, even helped me *feel* again," she told him. "I don't know, Kristóf, but I think maybe you kept my soul alive."

A little tentatively he hugged her, and she leaned against his shoulder. All week she'd taken comfort in his voice and his hesitant touches. She'd drawn courage as she watched him on his arduous path—saying goodbye to his grandfather, letting go of Misha, opening the door to his mother, and preparing to change jobs. How much could a person face all at once? But he'd done it.

She turned to look at him. "You've been very strong," she said.

"Because you were here with me. That made the difference." His eyes pleaded. "I hate thinking of you gone. Please say yes to that school, and come back."

Torn, she pulled her gaze away from him. "I don't know, Kristóf. What do I have here? You're the only person I really know."

And when it came to that, how well did she actually know him? She hadn't forgotten what the woman named Zsófi had said: Kristóf, many women, always changing. The remembrance stung.

"The life I know is back home," she said.

"Yes, but are you happy in that life?"

Barely moving, she shook her head. Whether or not she knew him, he knew her. The breeze rustled and the trees swayed darkly, and for a long time they were quiet.

"Lisa," he finally said. "If you stay, or if you don't, I ought to tell you . . ." He spoke humbly, as though confessing. "I love you."

She caught her breath, grasped his hand.

"My grandfather told me that you and I are third cousins," he said. "Like the Brit queen and her husband. I think he wanted me to marry you."

Her hand went still on his. "Do you want that?"

"A year ago, I would say no. No marriage. But you came here and nothing is the same."

"No, nothing."

She turned to him in wonder. He lifted her chin and looked at her as though asking. She nodded. His kiss, gentle and careful, skimmed her lips and left her aching for more.

"Are you afraid?" he asked.

She swallowed and nodded.

"Please trust me," he said.

It all came down to this. "I want to," she answered. The trees rustled in the wind.

"I haven't been with a woman since last fall," Kristóf said. "I don't want to go back to the way I was. I took care of my grandfather, and I met my son, and I came to know you, and everything changed." He spoke haltingly. "It had to change. The old way was no good."

Though she had not meant to cry, she broke down, leaning on him and spilling tears onto his jacket, because of all they had lost and mourned, and because anger had scorched them both, and forgiveness cost so much. Kristóf held her. "I don't want us apart, alone," he said.

"Neither do I."

He brushed away a tear from her cheek. "I love you, and I love what's deep in you. I'm loyal to you. Don't be afraid, I won't leave you."

Somewhere inside her, she knew this was true. But—

"Kristóf. Do you understand, I can't have children?"

"I have Misha."

"But maybe not."

"I know. I still want you."

His eyes held anxious hope. She put her arms around him, and he kissed her so softly she barely felt it. She almost let go, but suddenly could not bear to. *You gave me back my fire.* She clutched him and kissed him with all the ardor and longing within her, the deep rapture that not even grief and fear could snuff out.

"Let's not be afraid," she whispered.

"Lisa," Kristóf whispered back, astonished. He kissed her with a passion as strong as life itself, and a smoldering ember of joy became a blaze.

THE NEXT DAY, EASTER, THEY WENT TO THE CEMETERY. The breeze blew chilly as they walked among the old stone monuments and the trees showing the faint green cast of early spring. Following the way that Antal Varga had once showed her, Lisa took Kristóf to the small marker of her grandmother's sister, Anni Hanák.

It began raining lightly. She pulled the little metal box out of her handbag and opened the lid. Once more she touched these few remaining ashes, the last traces of her son's tiny body, and showed them to Kristóf. He nodded and stroked her hand.

Lisa crossed herself. She emptied the cinders into her palm, lifted her hand and opened it. "The peace of Christ," she whispered.

The ashes took flight, swirling with the wind and the rain. Lisa felt Kristóf's arm around her shoulder. She leaned close, knowing she had anchored herself here. This city was the place of her heart, the place of her son, the place where grief and beauty intermingled in the man she loved.

Taking Kristóf's hand, she followed him to the fresh grave where Antal Varga's body had been buried atop his wife's. Soil lay unsettled around the recently lifted family marker. The new inscription had not yet been added to it.

On his phone Kristóf opened an email from Gabriella and showed it to her. "This is what it will say."

VARGA JOZSEF LÁSZLÓ ANTAL
1928 FEBRUÁR 12 – 2007 MÁRCIUS 25
ZENE, ERŐ, FÉNY

"What do the words mean?" Lisa asked.
"Music, strength, light."
"It's what he gave us."

They stood quietly. Tonight she would begin the long trip back to the place that only last week she'd called home. In the coming weeks Kálmán Barcza's choir would sing Grandpa Sándor's song "A Good Mother," and maybe she would go to listen. Maybe she could bear it now. She would lead her students in singing "Song to Our Enemies," the music now healed and reconciled. On the last day of school, she would hug the students goodbye. Then she would pack up her classroom and apartment. Kristóf would wait for her, and she would return.

The rain stopped. A streak of sun broke though the overcast, brightening the Easter sky. Kristóf beckoned to her and they left the cemetery, walking under the trees of spring.

CHAPTER SIXTY-ONE

Gifts

May 26, 2019

KRISTÓF SAT TOWARD THE REAR OF THE RECITAL HALL where his grandfather's suite had been performed twelve years before. It was almost summer, the room over-warm on this Sunday afternoon. He fanned himself briefly with the program bulletin that he and his wife had been passing back and forth, *Gimnazium Graduation Recital of Lengyel Mykhaylo*. At the grand piano on stage, Misha was finishing a Schubert impromptu, the second-to-last piece on the program.

"Kristóf," Lisa whispered, "*Szép van.*" This is beautiful.

Igen, bámulatos," he whispered back. *Yes, amazing.*

He glanced around at the audience. The room had filled with adults who were probably musicians and Misha's teachers, and with young people who were probably his friends. Up in front sat Blanka, Endre, and their daughter. Halmos István, now very old, listened from his wheelchair in the side aisle. It was he who over the years had kept Kristóf informed of Misha's recitals. Kristóf himself had taught Misha piano for three years, but the boy progressed so rapidly that Kristóf reluctantly sought a professional teacher. Halmos recommended his daughter, a respected music professor. So Kristóf had gone from seeing Misha weekly to seeing him once every six to twelve months, when Halmos told him

Misha had a recital or, later, a solo with a youth symphony. Sometimes after these performances Kristóf was able to speak with Misha; usually, though, Misha didn't have time for more than a few words, and Blanka or Endre hovered nearby.

The Schubert piece ended. Misha rose and bowed. He'd grown tall, and with secret satisfaction Kristóf recognized the Varga brow line on his son's face. Today Misha wore a dark blue jacket similar to Kristóf's uniform for his managerial work at the airport.

"Thank you all for coming," Misha said. His strong voice carried well as he told the audience that next year he would attend the music academy.

"I'm especially grateful to my teacher, Halmos Julianna," he continued. "And to my parents, Lengyel Endre and Blanka, for all their help, even when I was a pain to put up with." The audience laughed. Misha gestured toward Halmos in his wheelchair. "And Halmos *úr* has been terrific, and he told me some people helped pay my expenses when I traveled to competitions. If that was any of you, thank you."

Kristóf glanced at Lisa. They'd done that. She smiled. He put his arm around her, touching her hair, which had darkened a little but still delighted him.

"And for my last piece," Misha said, "here's Chopin's *Prelude in E Minor.* My favorite."

Kristóf watched his son's fluid movements over the keys, listened to the music's poetry. His grandmother used to play Chopin. Ópa had taken such affectionate pleasure in it. Kristóf wished his grandfather could have heard this, and at the end he especially wished Ópa could have heard the audience cheer.

After Misha's last bow, Kristóf and Lisa went out to the hallway. They chatted with Halmos and with some of Lisa's musical acquaintances, but Kristóf kept glancing at his son. Misha stood a few meters away surrounded by well-wishers and his family. It would be a long wait to talk with him, so Kristóf trotted down the stairs and made a phone call.

As he hung up, a young male voice called, "Kristóf *bácsi!*" He turned. Misha dashed down the stairs, jacketless now and his shirt sleeves rolled up.

Kristóf hurried toward him. "Misha! Beautiful performance—"

"Oh, my God, I have to talk to you."

They stood together at the bottom of the stairs. Misha glanced back up as though making sure they were alone, then turned back to Kristóf, his Varga brow creasing. "My parents told me."

Kristóf had waited twelve years for this moment, not knowing if it would ever come. Now it had, and he struggled to speak. "So you know," he said.

"Yes." Misha's eyebrows lifted. "And it was good news."

Relief flooded Kristóf as he faced this son of his, now so close to manhood—broad shoulders, dark sideburns, a deepening voice, steady brown eyes.

"How long have you known?" Kristóf asked.

"I've known for a long time that my dad adopted me, and that was all I knew. But back when I was, oh, maybe fourteen, somebody at a family reunion let it slip that you and my mum had dated." Misha gestured toward Kristóf's face, then his own. "And we look a bit alike, and I thought, 'What if Kristóf *bácsi*'s my birth dad? What if it's my old piano teacher?' And you know, I started hoping that it was."

Kristóf smiled, speechless.

"But my parents never seemed to want to talk about it," Misha said, "not until last month when I turned eighteen. Then they gave me your letter." Misha spread his hands as though at a loss. "That letter was so *nice*, I don't even know what to say, except—I'm glad."

"Thank God," Kristóf sighed, and could only add, "I'm proud of you."

"Now I know why you kept coming to my recitals," Misha said. "And I remember a little bit about my lessons with you. Wasn't there some funny game with candy bears?"

Kristóf laughed. "Yes, my grandfather's game."

Suddenly Misha was full of questions. Wasn't the grandfather a violinist? And were there other musicians in the family? What kind of work did Kristóf do? Was he married? Oh, yes, now Misha remembered seeing his wife at other recitals.

Misha blurted out, "Do I have any brothers or sisters from you?"

"No," Kristóf answered.

But he hoped someday he could explain to Misha that though Lisa was not able to have children, their life together was not childless. The little neighbor girls came over to bake American cookies with Lisa and learn English words. Kristóf went with Lisa to her students' swim meets, football matches, and bar mitzvahs. Living with Lisa meant welcoming children.

Kristóf glanced up the stairs and saw Lisa at the top. He beckoned insistently. She rushed down, and he introduced her to Misha.

"Lisa," Kristóf said. "Misha knows."

"Oh." She looked hopefully at Misha. When he smiled, she grasped his hands. "We've always wanted this, to be with you and have you know."

"So I guess you're in my family, too," Misha said to her.

"Yes." She nodded vigorously. "Yes!"

Lisa still spoke Hungarian with an accent, and Misha asked her, "Are you British?"

"American."

He grinned. "Crazy. Everybody I know wants to go *to* America, not leave it."

"Lisa and I did things backward," Kristóf said.

"What brought you here?" Misha asked Lisa.

"Music. Have you ever heard of the *Embers Suite*?"

"Sure. A friend of mine played flute in a performance of it."

"Hungarian groups in America perform it, too," Lisa said. "Seattle, Cleveland, New Brunswick. Chicago. Kristóf's grandfather wrote it. It's our family's music."

"Incredible." Misha's eyes softened thoughtfully. "So if it's your family's music, I guess it's mine, too."

"Absolutely," Kristóf said. "Come over sometime, and we'll show you the original manuscripts."

Walking home with Lisa along Andrássy Avenue, Kristóf glanced over his shoulder toward the Oktogon, a place where Ópa had said Arrow Cross men were once hanged on lampposts. It was now a place of Burger King and Samsung. But down nearby side streets, Kristóf knew, some of the window frames were still pockmarked by siege bullets. Ópa had said those damned reminders always kept him checking up on his family. Kristóf understood such vigilance now: during his years as a flight attendant, he'd replaced the apartment locks for Lisa's safety and called her twice a day when he had to be gone. She teased him about being like his grandfather and hers. Protectiveness was a Varga trait.

They turned onto Hájos Street, talking about how well Misha had played, and how for his next recital they would invite Kristóf's father and Erzsi, and how good it would be when Misha came over for dinner a week from now. They turned again onto Lázár Street, taking the familiar route behind the opera house to their apartment building.

"Lisa *néni!* Kristóf *bácsi!*"

They looked up. Their six-year-old neighbor leaned out her window. "Guess what! My grandpapa is going to buy me a bicycle!"

"*Szuper*, Hanni!" Lisa called back.

"Nice grandpapa!" Kristóf shouted.

Gifts. That was what grandpapas did. Kristóf punched the key code to open the street door of this home that Ópa had given him. He entered the foyer with Lisa, whom he'd always felt was Ópa's gift to him as well.

She slipped her hand into his as they climbed the stairs to the apartment. "Can Misha be my son, too?" she asked.

"He's *ours.*"

They reached the apartment. Kristóf turned the key in the lock. Thankful beyond words, he followed his wife in.

Connie Hampton Connally holds a BA in English from the University of Washington and an MFA from Antioch University. She has taught high school English and elementary music, worked as an editor, led workshops at writers' conferences, and written both fiction and non-fiction. Her debut novel, *The Songs We Hide*, was published by Coffeetown Press in 2018. *Fire Music* is Ms. Connally's second novel.

Ms. Connally has played guitar most of her life. She especially loves folk and classical music for its beautiful evocation of joy, sorrow, longing and transcendence. Her experiences with music influenced her novels *Fire Music* and *The Songs We Hide*, which deal with artistry amid hardship.

Ms. Connally lives in Tacoma, Washington with her husband. The Connallys travel frequently to visit their three adult sons and their families. Ms. Connally is currently writing a novel set in Andean Peru, where her second son lives.

Find her on the web at conniehamptonconnally.com.

Printed in the USA
CPSIA information can be obtained
at www.ICGtesting.com
CBHW03204502062A
9359CB00003B/6